H THE AMMER

PRINTED IN CANADA
NOVEL CONCEPT BOOKS
© 2008

THE HAMMER

The Hammer
Copyright © 2008 Vance Neudorf

Published by Novel Concept Books
Box 2744, Three Hills, Alberta, Canada, T0M 2N0

Cover photography by Jim Potter
        www.jimpotterphotography.com
Illustrations by Delynne Lorentzen

Canadian Cataloguing in Publication Data
Neudorf, Vance 1961
The Hammer
ISBN - 978-0-9783740-0-6

Novel Concept Books
Box 2744
Three Hills, Alberta, Canada,T0M 2N0
Email - thehammer@novelconceptbooks.com

Printed in Canada
        2nd Edition Printed January 2008 - 2000 copies

NOVEL CONCEPT BOOKS
good reads and good deeds

A primary goal in writing this novel is to financially support education around the world. $5.00 from the sale of each book sold on the internet and $2.50 from each bookstore sale goes to support a school or library. You can find out more at www.novelconceptbooks.com.

If you know of a school, library or charity that would like to use this book as a fundraiser, please direct them to www.novelconceptbooks.

DEDICATION

This book is dedicated to my family.

To my daughter Alyssa. Every Christmas, birthday and special event for years on end she would ask for a few more chapters of "The Hammer." Without her constant encouragement this book would never have come into being.

To my son Jaron for critiquing the draft and suggesting a myriad of ways to improve the storyline. Without his input a lot of creative bits would have never come into existence.

To my eldest daughter Charissa for reading and rereading the manuscript and finding better ways to improve the flow of the story (while her husband Phil watched the grandkids).

To my wife Sherri for putting up with a year of concentrated effort in getting this book ready for print. Its wonderful to be married to someone who believes in me.

To my mother for asking me so many times if I knew what I was doing that I had to make sure that I did.

APPRECIATION

I have been blessed by the skilled editors and reviewers who help me polish my writing. Working with these wonderful people was truly one of the most enjoyable parts of writing this story. To Kaye Dacus, Gwen Ellis, Kathy Ide, Eileen Key, Jeanne Leach, Susan Lohrer, Pat Massey, Camy Tang and Marjorie Vawter. My heartfelt thanks for sharing your artistic wisdom with me.

Thank you to all the family and friends who kept reading drafts and suggesting changes. I enjoyed finding ways to creatively bring those ideas to life in the story.

To the Circle of Six: Hunter, Harold, James, Phil and Ron.

Special thanks to the people at www.entrouragearts.com for their training on creating the maps with Google Sketchup. Check my website for more information.

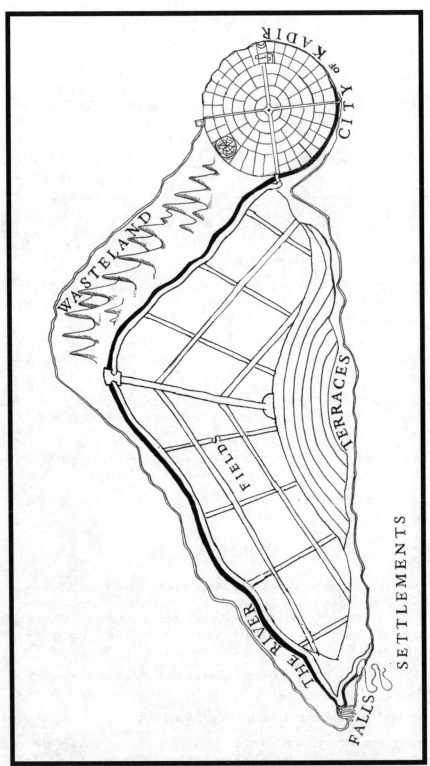

PROLOGUE

The baby curled his tiny hand around Jokten's finger and grinned up at him. The old man tried to return the smile but the pain in his heart stifled every other emotion.

He had no choice. He must leave his son behind in this strange world with its wide-open spaces and searing heat.

The baby's smile faded, replaced by a trembling cry. Jokten fumbled inside his cloak at the pouch tied at his waist. He pulled out a small stone hammer, and laid it on the infant's chest. The baby's slender hands wrapped around the smooth handle, and his cries eased. The child fell into a peaceful sleep.

Jokten wished he could be that calm. The idea of returning to his home without his son and without the hammer was tying him in knots. At first, the plan had seemed so sensible. Now he found himself fighting the urge to take the child and retreat through the open door, closing it forever behind him. He pushed the idea aside. That path could only lead to disaster for both worlds.

The baby stirred and Jokten rocked him gently in his arms. Turning his infant son over to a people he had observed only from a distance did not bother him, for he had met their leader. He was a man of honor; the

THE HAMMER

hammer assured him of that. He touched the black stone, nodding to himself as a soft blue glow from the handle lit the face of the sleeping boy. The hammer must remain here with his son. He would need its guidance once he was old enough to return home as the rightful heir to the throne.

Jokten scanned the horizon of the vast plain that stretched westward to a shadowed ridge of hills already shedding their gray mists. The leader had agreed to meet him here before the sun was in the sky. Perhaps his settlement was not close by. Jokten had not yet figured out how they were able to move their settlement of pointed homes about on the vast plain. Perhaps they used the large beasts with four legs to drag them. He had seen the leader ride on top of one of these creatures and knew it could move rapidly. Surely, if the man were coming, the animal would already have brought him to their meeting place.

But he had not come, and Jokten could not stay in the open under the naked heat of the great light.

Gently he extracted the hammer from the infant's grasp. The first harsh rays of a new day glinted off the polished stone and bit at his face. His plan had failed. Disappointment mixed with a sense of relief as he hugged the child to his chest and stepped back into the circle of rocks behind him.

As he turned toward the open door, he heard the drum of distant hoof beats.

Part I

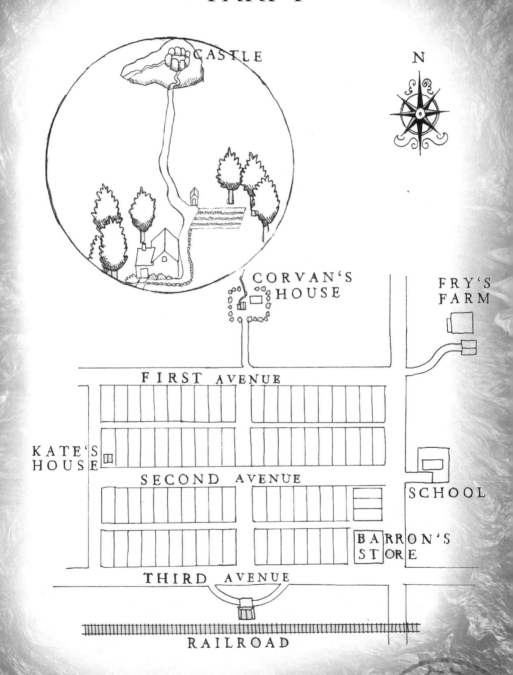

CASTLE

N

CORVAN'S
HOUSE

FRY'S
FARM

FIRST AVENUE

KATE'S
HOUSE

SECOND AVENUE

SCHOOL

BARRON'S
STORE

THIRD AVENUE

RAILROAD

THE HAMMER

CHAPTER ONE

Corvan pressed himself against the damp stone wall of the tunnel and peered into the gloom. The foul smell of the beast lingered in the air. It was somewhere ahead in the darkness, waiting for him to betray his location.

The shadows shifted. A hulking shape swayed from side to side at the far end of the passage. Had it seen him?

Too afraid to breathe, he slid back around the corner and out of sight. The way out had to be nearby. The creature must be guarding it. He inched forward in the murky light to where a jagged fracture broke the cavern floor. Was this it? Musky fear filled his mouth as he searched the darkness. Yes, there it was. A translucent green rope dangled over the void, just out of reach.

The rustle of scales on rock set his heart pounding. A glance over his shoulder revealed an enormous black shape sweeping up the passage, red eyes piercing the shadows.

Corvan leaped off the edge, caught the rope, and climbed. A roar filled his ears as the creature's fetid breath rolled past him, propelling him upward even quicker toward the rock shelf above. This time he would make it.

His breath came in ragged gasps as his sweaty hands slipped on the rope. He heaved himself up higher, but the rope stretched and dropped him back toward the open jaws.

His stomach jumped into his throat at the sensation of falling. He gripped the rope even tighter but it squirted out like jelly between his fingers. A scream erupted from his lungs as he dropped into the darkness.

Corvan jerked awake, gasping as if he'd been trapped underwater. Cold sweat trickled past his ear. He hated that nightmare. Not only for the way it always left him sleepless and frightened, but also because he had an overwhelming sense that it was much more than just a bad dream.

THE HAMMER

He swung his shaking legs out of bed. Should he tell his parents about it? He shook his head. He would turn fifteen in just over a week. He couldn't be running down to their room like a frightened child.

But he *was* afraid.

Walking to his window, he sat on the wide ledge and leaned against the wall. A cool breeze, fresh with the scent of approaching rain, raised goose bumps on his skin.

Like it or not, by this time next week he would be considered an adult member of their family. He wasn't totally sure what this meant, but judging from the conversations his parents were having, it was significant. It would change his life. That could be why the dream was coming more often. Maybe it wouldn't go away until he quit running and climbed down the rope to face the dark fear. A shiver crawled up his spine. He pulled his knees up, wrapped his scrawny arms around them and looked out the window.

The sun, rising over the trees, caught the silver leaves of the aspens dancing in its hazy light.

Beyond the trees, the gentle wind stirred his family's crop of wheat into waves that swept out to run ashore along a massive mound of granite. The rounded sides of the rock climbed thirty feet above the golden lake of grain in an unbroken curve until it reached "the castle," Corvan's name for the ring of boulders crowning the summit. From his window, the circle of stones looked like the beginnings of another Stonehenge or the ruins of an ancient island citadel. He could almost see the warriors fighting in the shadows flowing around its defenses.

The whistle of the kettle boiling in the kitchen broke the spell. Corvan sighed. Imagination was much more fun than the real world. He would almost prefer going back to bed to face the dark monster than getting dressed for another day of school. At least with the nightmares, he would eventually wake up and the fear would fade. In real life, at least for the past year, his fears clung to him like burrs on his socks.

"Corvan!"

He jumped away from the window to find his mother standing in the doorway, her long blonde hair squashed up against the unusually short door frame.

"I should have known you'd be daydreaming. Didn't you hear me call you down to breakfast?"

"I was sleeping."

She looked at him sideways. "I heard you holler."

Corvan shrugged. "I must have been dreaming." He walked around the bed and pulled on his patched jeans.

She squinted at him. "No doubt you were." She stepped through the doorway and straightened to her full height. "I met Mrs. Thompson at the store yesterday."

Corvan's heart dropped at the mention of his teacher. What had he done wrong now?

"She says you've been coming in late since the beginning of school. I told her you must be dawdling on the way, for you certainly leave here in plenty of time."

Corvan slowly tugged his T-shirt over his head, not wanting her to see the guilt written across his face. The truth was, he wanted to be late for school—for the whole year if possible. His head poked out just as the horn of their truck honked in the driveway.

His mother turned to the door. "We'll talk about this later. Your father has been called to a meeting at the mine. We aren't sure what it's all about." The horn honked again. "I'm going along with him to sell my cider at the farmer's market. Your breakfast is on the cupboard." She shot a warning look his way. "Be on time today, and make sure you concentrate on your schoolwork."

She ducked back through the door and hurried down the stairs. Corvan listened for the sound of the truck pulling down the long lane out to the main road. As soon as he was certain his parents were gone, he grabbed a couple of mismatched socks from the pile behind his door, then sat on the top stair and pulled them on. His parents seemed to think he would enjoy school more if he tried harder. But he couldn't focus on schoolwork when there was so much going on outdoors. Who decided that a schoolroom should have so many big windows? It would be much easier to learn in a dark box.

The kitchen was still warm with the heat from the woodstove, the steam rising lazily from the kettle's dented spout. A pot of oatmeal sat on the cupboard. Corvan poked at the sticky lumps. He didn't usually mind oatmeal, but for the last few months there had been no brown sugar and very little milk.

He looked through the open door of the pantry. It sure would be nice to put something sweet on top. His stomach rumbled, and he stepped inside the tiny room to check the nearly vacant shelves. Only one tin was heavy enough to warrant investigation. He popped the lid off. White sugar! His mother rarely bought it. He tipped up the tin and let a trail of white crystals cascade over his porridge.

At the table, the smile left his face as a sense of guilt settled over him. Mother was probably saving the sugar to make a treat for the family. Of course! It was for his birthday cake. Oh, well, it was too late now. He stuck the sugar-encrusted spoon into his mouth . . . and spewed it over the table. Salt! No wonder there was so much left.

As he scraped the salty porridge into the dying embers of the woodstove, his lunch pail beckoned to him from the far end of the cupboard. There wouldn't be much inside, but there were always two sandwiches. He could eat half of one for breakfast.

A dog barked in the lane. Corvan grabbed his lunch pail and ran to the front door, but there was no one there, just a mangy stray slinking through the trees.

THE HAMMER

Every morning since the start of grade seven, when Kate and her mom had moved back to town, she had picked him up for school. But last week she had informed him she wouldn't walk to school with him anymore. She wouldn't say why. Kate could be so secretive and stubborn at times. It had made for a hard week. Kate hadn't even shown up at school the last two days, and he felt lost without his one and only friend around.

The morning breeze had died away, and a soft brown dust hung over the tree-lined driveway. A large hawk dominated the weathered fence post at their gate, its dark eyes following Corvan's every move, just like the bullies at school. He hated feeling like they were just waiting for him to make a mistake so they could swoop down and pick him off.

Plucking a stone from the road, he whipped it at the post to scare the hawk off but missed, simply rustling the grass. The hawk blinked its disdain, rose up into the air, and soared out over their field. Corvan ran a dusty hand over his crew-cut hair as he trudged toward town and the school. If only he could fly above the world and go wherever he wanted.

Avoiding the busier streets, he made his way up a back alley. The school was just across the main road so he crossed quickly, ducked under the barbed wire, and followed the well-worn path through the underbrush. The sound of playing children grew louder as he poked his head around a clump of saskatoon bushes.

Their one-room schoolhouse had seen better days. It was new when his father attended. Now its faded red paint hung from the rough boards in brittle strips. Most of the windows on this side were cracked; one had been boarded over last spring when a rock aimed at Corvan's head had shattered it.

Corvan scanned the playground. Bill Fry, the hand behind that rock and the sole reason for his coming late each day, was nowhere in sight. Corvan breathed a sigh of relief. The bully's frequent truancy was one of the few things that made school days bearable. Whenever Bill showed up, Corvan could count on being harassed all day.

A muffled sneeze rattled the bush beside him. Corvan bent down and discovered a small boy huddled under the canopy of leaves. Tommy Cobb had just started grade three, although he hardly looked big enough to be in school at all.

"Hi, Tommy. Are you playing hide and go seek?"

The boy shook his head. "Waitin' for the bell to ring," he whispered.

Corvan swallowed. He remembered doing the same thing in grade three. He frowned. He was still doing it.

"Hey, Tommy, how about I push you on the swings." The boy's face brightened. "One good thing about being short is that I can give great under ducks."

Tommy jumped out from under the bush. "Thanks, Corvan. I'll race ya."

The younger boy took off like a shot, sprinting through the gate of the schoolyard toward the swings. Corvan sauntered after him.

Kate sat alone against the broken-down fence that surrounded the playground. Her bangs were flopped over her eyes, and he didn't think she saw him until she jerked a thumb toward the boys' outhouse. Bill must be inside. Corvan stopped short just outside the gate. If he could make it to the school door, he would be safe—at least until lunch.

"Come on, Corvan." Tommy clambered into the worn swing seat and wriggled in anticipation. Corvan took a deep breath and walked toward the swings. Kate was watching and he didn't want her to think he was a chicken. He glanced at the outhouse; hopefully Bill was constipated.

The outhouse door sprang open and Bill stepped into the light, looping the strap of his coveralls over his broad shoulder. He surveyed the playground like a wolf looking for the weakest member of the herd. His eyes locked on Corvan. A cruel grin spread over his face.

Corvan knew he could easily outrun the heavyset boy but there was no point. Once Bill had decided you were his target, he would pursue you until he had you in his grasp. It only made him meaner when you tried to get away.

Corvan glanced at Kate. She was biting her lower lip and looking hard in the other direction. He didn't expect her to fight Bill for him, but her presence usually curbed Bill's bullying instincts. All the boys kept their distance from Kate's lightning fists. Her thin frame hid a feisty fighter who could blacken an eye and get away before a larger opponent could pin her down.

Not to be deprived of his prey, Bill lumbered over to Corvan. "If it ain't the Great Chief Skinny Britches. It's good to see you on time for once. I got a few things to tell ya."

"I'm all ears," Corvan replied, attempting to disarm Bill with a wide grin.

"I can see that." Bill flicked the lobes of Corvan's ears until he winced in pain. "The way these things stick out, you look like Dumbo the elephant."

Corvan tried to pull away but Bill stepped on his toes, pinning him to the ground and forcing him to look into the boy's broad chest.

Kate spoke from behind Bill. "Why don't you pick on someone your own size?" Bill pushed himself away to face her.

"Didn't ya notice, Kate? There is no one my size in our school." He laughed and looked back down at Corvan. "Maybe Corvan's dad could fight me." He spread out his hands out in pretend shock. "Oh, yeah, I forgot. Corvan's dad is a shrimpy chicken." He took a measured step back from Kate. "And you don't even have a dad."

T The Hammer

Kate squinted through her bangs for a long moment, her jaw tense as she chewed the inside of her cheek. Her eyes flickered over to Corvan. She shook her head and walked away.

Bill watched her leave, then turned his attention back to Corvan. "My dad says your kind don't belong in our school. We don't want you around here anymore."

Corvan looked at the ground. This was not the first time someone had talked this way to him.

Bill flicked his ears again. "Are you listening to me?"

The bell rang and children scampered past to beat one another into the small building. Tommy Cobb walked by with his head down.

Bill slapped an open hand the size of a baseball glove on Corvan's head and shoved him to the ground. "Best find yourself another school, Stumpy, 'cause you ain't gonna enjoy this one as long as I'm around."

Looking past Bill's legs, Corvan saw Kate watching them, her fists tightly clenched. She took a step in their direction, then turned back and walked into the school.

A plume of dust exploded in Corvan's eyes. "And don't go lookin' for Kate to save you. My dad's been talking with people. Kate's mom ain't gonna let her help you no more." The bell fell silent. Bill kicked another spray of dirt at him. Corvan heard Bill's footsteps fade toward the building.

Corvan sat on the ground, allowing his eyes to water. That was why Kate wasn't coming around anymore. Gritty tears slid down his cheeks, clearing his eyes. Great. Now the other kids would think he'd been crying.

Jerking to his feet, he slapped the dust off himself. This must be what the skinny boy in his comic book ads felt like. The ads promised that in just six weeks he would be strong enough to defeat the bullies. He looked to the school and fiercely shook his head. It was time to use his fifty-cent piece and order that body building book from Charles Atlas. Somebody had to stand up to Bill Fry.

The door to the school stood slightly ajar. He glanced back to the gate, where freedom beckoned. This would be a good day to skip school. Then again, with his mother and teacher comparing notes, it might not be the best idea. His shoulders drooped as he walked up to the building and slipped through the door.

Mrs. Thompson stood at the chalkboard, the words "Oral Report" printed neatly over her head. He eased the heavy door closed.

"Corvan's here, ma'am." Bill Fry's voice broke the silence like the brash call of a raven.

Mrs. Thompson did not turn around. "You're late again, Corvan. You will stay after school to write lines."

Bill sneered at him, but one row over, Corvan saw sympathy in Kate's eyes. He gave her a quick smile as he headed toward the back of the room.

Mrs. Thompson's voice pulled him up short. "Since you're already standing, Corvan, you will be the first to give your oral report."

When had she assigned an oral report? His empty stomach clenched. He must have been daydreaming again. His fingers twisted the worn hem of his T-shirt. He jammed his hands deep into his pockets. The other students still joked about how he would twist the buttons off his shirts whenever he was nervous.

He vaguely remembered something about a report on the summer holiday. Corvan racked his brain for a topic as he dragged himself to the front of the class. It had been a boring summer. The weather had been hot and dry, and his father had stayed in the cellar most days. There was no money for gas to take a vacation.

But . . . something *had* happened, something he hadn't even told Kate yet. He reached Mrs. Thompson's desk and turned to face the class.

"My oral report is on the large green lizard that lives near the big rock in our field. I tracked it all summer. It's about this high." He held a hand up past his waist. "It has dark blue markings around its chest and face. It walks upright on its hind legs and—"

Mrs. Thompson's ruler smacked her open hand. "Corvan, the assignment was an oral report about your summer vacation, not another of your tall tales." She shook her head. "You know as well as I do, there are no three-foot-high, green-and-blue dinosaur-like lizards around here. This is 1952, not the Mesozoic era."

Corvan's mind wandered while she continued rambling. So maybe it wasn't quite three feet high. But could the lizard have been a dinosaur? Their town was near one of the largest deposits of dinosaur bones in the world. What if an egg had risen to the surface, was warmed by the sun, and somehow hatched? That could happen, couldn't it? Maybe there were more eggs out—

"Corvan!" Mrs. Thompson's voice pierced his mental fog. "How many times do I need to tell you to sit down?"

Coming to his senses, he looked out at rows of laughing classmates. His face burned as he walked past the younger children to the back of the class. True to form, Bill Fry stuck out a huge foot, and Corvan tripped over it, stumbling against his own desk and scattering his pencils across the back of the room.

Easing himself into the seat, he opened his desk and hunched down to hide behind the lid. At a touch on his shoulder, he looked up. Kate leaned over from the next row, one of his pencils in her hand. But her smile had been replaced with a disapproving frown. He closed his desk and took the pencil, unwinding the narrow piece of paper wrapped around it.

T THE HAMMER

We need to talk. Meet me at the rock after supper.

Corvan barely had time to read the message before it disappeared into Bill Fry's grimy hand.

"Bill, what are you up to now?" A weary Mrs. Thompson walked up the aisle.

Bill grinned at Corvan, then turned around. "Sorry, ma'am, but Corvan's writin' notes in class." He held the strip of foolscap up to the teacher.

As she took the paper from Bill, Corvan slouched further into his chair.

Sure enough, Mrs. Thompson recognized the handwriting and turned to Kate. "Miss Poley, you will stay after school and write one hundred times on the blackboard, 'I will not pass notes in school.'"

"I can't, Mrs. Thompson," Kate pleaded. "I have to clean the house and make supper before my mom gets home."

Mrs. Thompson nodded and her posture softened.

Bill Fry twisted his wide frame around to face Kate and mouthed a few words behind the teacher's back. He often directed insults at Kate, but Corvan knew they cut her afresh each time. Kate's eyes blazed and Mrs. Thompson's back stiffened.

"Then you will eat lunch with the small children and write your lines then."

Corvan's heart sank. Kate never ate lunch with anyone, as she never brought any food. He always made sure the second sandwich his mother put in his lunch pail found its way into Kate's hand.

Pink crept up Kate's cheeks. She pushed her thin shoulders back.

A look of satisfaction covered Bill's face. "Her mom probably spent the lunch money at the bingo hall," he snickered.

Mrs. Thompson whirled around and broke her ruler over Bill's head. Kate was halfway up the aisle before the pieces hit the floor.

"Kate!" Mrs. Thompson's voice brought the girl up short near the classroom door. "You do not have permission to leave class." Her tone softened. "Please take your seat. We can talk about this later in private."

Kate's lower lip quivered as she pulled her brown hair even farther over her eyes. She had cried only once in front of Corvan. He knew there was no way she would ever let the class see her cry.

Kate took a step forward and put her hand on the doorknob. "I don't need permission to leave, because I'm never coming back." In a flash, she was gone, leaving the students sitting in stunned silence.

Corvan ground his teeth. He hated Bill. What right did he have to make fun of Kate's home life? It wasn't like his was any better. If only Corvan had the strength of one of his comic book heroes, he'd make Bill pay for all the misery he caused. But he was no hero. He hadn't even stood up for Kate and taken the blame for the note.

He slumped in his seat. Once again, he had given in to his fears. Bill was right; he was a chicken, a runt, a pathetic excuse for a human being.

A dark cloud hung over Corvan the rest of the day. Fortunately, Bill left at lunch, complaining of a headache. To avoid taunts about his "green lizard friend," Corvan ate by himself in a corner of the weed-choked baseball diamond.

After lunch, Mrs. Thompson announced that she would be gone the following day so there would be no school. The black cloud lifted.

As soon as classes were over, Corvan worked on writing his assigned lines with fervor, not wanting to waste precious moments of freedom. By the time he was finished his fingers were cramped into a claw from scratching with the chalk for over an hour. Before he could leave, Mrs. Thompson called him to her desk.

"Corvan, I have been your teacher since you were in grade three. Soon you will be in your last years of school. It's time you stopped daydreaming and exaggerating."

"I'm sorry, Mrs. Thompson. I promise—"

"Ahht!" Her finger waggled in the air. "I don't want to hear another promise that you have no intention of keeping." She picked up a vase of daisies from her desk. "What would happen if I dropped this on the floor?"

He looked at the vase, momentarily distracted by thoughts of gravity and whether a force field could suspend it in midair. Mrs. Thompson cleared her throat and he forced himself to concentrate on the delicate vase. "It would break?" he replied tentatively.

"Exactly," she said. "And there is only one way to break a bad habit—you must make the choice to drop it. Keep holding on and it will never go away." She placed the vase back on her desk and spoke softly. "I know some of the other boys pick on you. I will do my best to see that it stops. But you add fuel to the fire when you tell the class an outlandish story about a giant lizard." She leaned toward him and gently squeezed his shoulder. "Integrity is a basic building block of a successful life. Think of your father, Corvan, and try to follow his example."

Corvan nodded but couldn't look her in the eyes. He turned and dragged his feet out the door.

On the walk home, the image of a shattered vase turned over in his mind. He really did want to be like his dad, whose reputation for integrity had earned him the title Honest Tom. But instead he found himself continually making excuses and telling lies.

He wasn't even sure it paid to be honest. People took advantage of his father's honesty and then bragged about it behind his dad's back. Because of his darker skin they called him Tonto, referring to the Lone Ranger's Apache sidekick. They also loved to make jokes about his height, for he was the shortest man in town, possibly even the county.

To his dismay, Corvan had inherited his father's darker skin tone and stature. A good ten inches shorter than any of the other kids in his grade, his small size gave others all the ammunition they needed to make his life miserable. Corvan had tried to win their respect through telling fantastic stories, but that had only earned him a reputation as a liar.

He savagely kicked a stone on the gravel road. No doubt everyone believed that his description of the lizard was just another lie.

But it wasn't. He'd seen it clearly three times this summer.

He stopped at the top of their lane. There was only one thing to do. He was going to catch that lizard and prove them all wrong.

Chapter Two

Corvan rounded the bend in the path that led home and saw his parents' rusty pickup parked in front, slouched on its broken springs. Great. Now his parents would want to know why he was late. There was nothing worse than getting in trouble at school and then again at home when his parents found out. If he got grounded tonight he wouldn't get a chance to search for the lizard and he would also miss meeting Kate at the rock. Maybe he could sneak around to the back porch, climb the maple tree to his room and pretend he had been napping.

The screen door banged open as his mother stomped out. Here was living proof that opposites attract, for unlike his father she was very tall, and no matter how much time she spent outdoors, her skin remained pale.

"About time you got home," she snapped. "You can help me carry the cider jars back to the panty. I only sold three." She opened the tailgate and slung a crate full of jars at him with an ease that denied its weight. Carrying the load, Corvan barely managed to stumble onto the porch and through the front door. If he had his mother's strength, he could knock Bill Fry clean across the river.

Entering the kitchen, he found his father staring out at the field. A pair of sunglasses stuck out from his hand, as if he were signaling out the truck window to make a left turn. His deeply lined eyes scanned the bright horizon with the look of a man who detested sunshine.

As Corvan scraped the crate across the table, his father turned and looked at him blankly.

Corvan dropped into a chair. "Are they going to reopen the mine?" His father looked past him without saying a word. "If you get your job back you wouldn't need your sunglasses down in the mine." His father didn't catch the joke; he just nodded, put the sunglasses on and trudged out the back door.

⊤ THE HAMMER

Corvan wanted to grab his father's shirt and ask him what was going on, but he knew it was no use. His father had become increasingly reclusive the past year. He really missed his job at the mine, and farming was not his thing. He couldn't stand being out in the hot sun—it seemed to wear him down even though he covered most of his skin and wore a wide hat.

Corvan watched the hunched figure walk through the field. He missed the days when his dad came home in the evening and read the paper or played games with him after supper. Now his dad spent most of his days down in the cellar, tinkering with his metalwork projects. He was glad his father didn't get drunk like Bill Fry's dad, but withdrawing to the cellar didn't seem like a great way to deal with problems either. If his mother pushed too hard for a response, an argument inevitably ensued. Corvan hated those.

Mother entered and hefted two loaded crates onto the kitchen table. She stared at her husband, as he walked out past the rock, and shook her head. "I've no time to make supper tonight. Grab yourself some jerky and a piece of bread. I'll dig you up some carrots before I start weeding the garden."

His mother's response to problems was to spend time in her garden. Corvan didn't mind; he liked eating the fruit of her labors, and her obsession with gardening usually meant he would be left alone to pursue his own interests.

After stuffing three long strips of dried meat from the stoneware crock into his pocket, he sauntered outside, where he found his mother on her knees in the middle of her huge garden, the dilapidated scarecrow watching over her in mute concern. Picking up the bunch of carrots that lay on the lawn near the water pump, he began working the long iron handle.

The pump squeaked as he washed the dirt off the carrots and Mother stretched her back. He avoided eye contact, hoping she wasn't going to ask him to help. He needed to be at the rock to meet Kate. Besides, the last thing he wanted was another lecture on how to do better at school.

The water ebbed to a dribble and his mother went back to her weeding. He crept from the yard and headed out to the rock.

The mound of granite was the only outcropping of its size this side of the mountains. Some folks had suggested the town buy it and declare it a monument like Ayers Rock in Australia, but his father declined the offer. Corvan was glad. He didn't want strangers crawling all over his special place.

It was a steep climb up the south side of the rock, but Corvan knew every foothold like the stairs to his bedroom. Reaching the top, he leaned back against the wall of rocks, like a king surveying his domain.

Their home was one of two farms that adjoined the main streets of their small town. The other belonged to Mr. Fry. Corvan's home was north of town at the end of a long tree-lined lane that pushed the house far out into a sea of grain. His father liked being separated from the town and always kept his gate closed and locked.

Corvan couldn't see why he bothered. There were no sheds full of machinery and no barn. Their property didn't even have any grain bins. People joked that they just grew big rocks on their farm.

Their yard was bounded by twin rows of trees, one line of tall aspens and another thick screen of spruce. In the center of this living wall of green was their home—the Guard Tower, as his grandfather had named it. It was a fitting name, for it was a small square structure, two stories high, with a pointed roof and it was the only home in town made of thick stone blocks. It had been built long before the surrounding area was settled. A history professor from the college in the city wanted to see it but his dad wouldn't let him past the front gate.

The rest of the houses were clustered along three wide gravel roads that ran parallel to the railway tracks. All in all his town had one grain elevator, one corner gas station, two vacant lots, and seventy-five houses of various types and sizes. The total population was 257 residents. Most of them worked in the city of Fenwood, fifteen miles past the railway crossing. Corvan didn't like the city. It made him feel even smaller and less important.

He crunched a carrot. He really should be helping his mother in the garden instead of imagining himself as the king of the world, but Kate needed to talk and he hoped it would set things right between them. He eased the feelings of guilt by walking around the outside of the castle.

Out to the east he caught a flash of light from the attic window of Bill Fry's house. At times he wondered if the bully went up there at sunset with a mirror just to irritate him from a distance. Ignoring the flickers of light dancing around him, he stepped around the castle to face north. He loved this view of their field. He was glad they were on the edge of town, where he could see for miles.

His father, a tiny figure in the distance, disappeared into the tangle of brush-filled coulees that marked the edge of their property. Beyond, the land dropped steeply down to the river. His father was likely going out to the caves where the Indians used to take shelter and paint on the rocks. Corvan had been there only twice; he didn't like thinking about how horribly all those people had died.

Corvan continued around to the west side of the rock, where he would be able to see Kate coming. Just over the poplar trees, he could see the roof of the ramshackle house Kate and her mother were renting. The slope was gentler here, and a shallow depression in the rock made a comfortable resting spot. It might also be a good place to keep an eye out for the elusive reptile.

THE HAMMER

The rock beneath him radiated its stored heat into his body. He closed his eyes to block out the setting sun.

The next thing he knew the bell on the back porch was ringing. He had dozed off and the sun had gone down behind a thin band of clouds on the horizon, bronzing the scenery around him.

Kate had not come. Maybe her mother had come home in a bad mood and refused to let her leave. He knew he shouldn't ignore the bell, but checking on Kate would take only a minute. He decided to take a walk up the street and see if she was in her yard or on the front porch.

As he passed through his backyard, Mother called him into the house. With a disappointed glance toward Kate's place, he entered the kitchen to find a bowl with a few strawberries waiting for him at the table. Mother was sweeping the floor.

"There's not many left and they're not the sweetest but I thought you might enjoy them."

"Thanks, Mom, do you—." He was about to ask for a bit of sugar when the salt incident burned in his mind.

"Do I what?"

"Have any idea what's bugging Dad?" He dropped his head. Where did that question come from? His mother had enough things to worry about.

She pulled up a chair and lifted his chin so he met her eyes. "We haven't wanted to burden you with adult worries. But I guess that's a moot issue with your fifteenth birthday just around the corner. You will soon be an adult member of this family."

"Are we going to lose our home?"

His mother's shoulders sagged. "We'll lose everything if your dad doesn't get called back to the mine. This crop will only pay off what we owe the bank this year, never mind our debt from the past."

"Is that because Old Man Fry has been talking to the bank?" He couldn't hide the bitterness in his voice.

Mother shook her head. "You shouldn't refer to Mr. Fry that way."

"But why is he always trying to make trouble for our family?"

She looked out the screen door. "Your father says Mr. Fry still holds a grudge against your grandfather." She turned back to him. "But I don't think he's behind the letters from the bank."

Corvan nodded, the knot of fear driving away the taste of the berries. "Didn't Dad get called back to work at the meeting today?"

His mother stood, a deep frown on her face. "The mine owners called the meeting, but not enough people heard about it in time. They postponed it indefinitely.

So we don't know what's going on. Some people in town think the mine is in deep financial trouble." She picked up his empty bowl from the table and sunk it into the sink full of soapy water. "But don't let all this frighten you. We've been through tough times before; we'll make it through this one too."

She patted his back as he passed her to climb up to his room. She was right about one thing: no matter how difficult life might get, he knew their family would stick together.

Corvan lay in bed a long time, thinking about how he could catch the lizard this weekend so he could prove he'd told the truth. He dozed briefly, but when the dark caves of his nightmare started closing in, he shook off the sleep and sat up in bed. A full moon was pouring its ghostly light onto the large oak chest in the corner of his room. In the moonlight it reminded him of one of those stone coffins, with its extra thick lid that hung out over the sides, like the sarcophagus that King Arthur was buried in.

He thought about reading and looked over at his bookshelf, where a ragtag collection of adventure stories and comic books were piled haphazardly on top. The shelves held a variety of bird nests, plant samples, animal bones, and an extensive rock collection.

The books were his doorway to worlds where adventure lived on, a doorway he entered often and with great ease. When it was too late to read, he would lie in bed and make up his own stories until sleep finally took over.

He flopped onto his back and stared at the ceiling. When he was younger, the other kids at school used to like hearing him tell stories; now they just called him a liar. That stupid oral report on the lizard hadn't helped any. He groaned as he thought about the mocking laughter.

Corvan sat up and leaned against the headboard, looking out the window at the moonlit rock. How could he catch the elusive creature? The three times he had caught sight of it, the lizard had simply vanished into the evening shadows. Maybe that was the answer. Unlike normal lizards, this one did not like the heat of the day and did its hunting at night. It could be out there right now. He looked out at the rock. Nothing moved except the shadows of the clouds. He knew he should try to sleep some more, but a midnight hunt for the mysterious reptile in the familiar safety of the castle sounded much more attractive than facing dreams of caves and monsters. Besides, there was no school tomorrow; he could sleep in.

Pulling on his jeans and faded T-shirt, Corvan crept down the stairs, through the kitchen, and out the back. The screen door usually squeaked like a trapped mouse, but Corvan had learned to press down firmly on the latch to avoid waking his parents.

THE HAMMER

Swirls of dust rose between his toes as he moved past the outhouse and onto the worn path leading to the rock. A coyote barked at a moon ringed by dark clouds. Perhaps the lizard would be out in the cool air. If not, he could catch some frogs or a turtle to put in his empty aquarium. His mother still called it his washbasin, but she had long since quit putting towels and soap next to it, afraid of what might jump out at her.

Approaching the rock, Corvan left the path and circled around beside the tall stalks of grain. He needed to be downwind to avoid alerting the creature if it were out. His heart beat faster. He had never seen it up close. What if it was dangerous?

Finding the stair-like channel cut into the west side of the rock, Corvan dropped to all fours and crawled forward up the slope. The lone coyote barked again, closer this time. Corvan flattened himself against the cool stone. He could handle one coyote but had no wish to run into a pack alone in the dark. He listened intently but there was no answering call. Instead he heard the scuffling of leathery paws heading directly toward him.

CHAPTER THREE

Corvan caught his breath as a shadow detached itself from the protection of the castle rocks and shot toward him. The lizard! It was running toward him on its hind legs. Its eyes, glinting in the moonlight, scanned the path before it.

He had nothing to catch it in. How could he have been so stupid? Very close now, the lizard ran alongside the worn channel leading down to Corvan's hiding place. It was almost upon him when it abruptly veered to the right and disappeared down into the field.

Corvan waited. Had it seen him? If not, it might come back the same way. This time he'd be ready. Slipping out of his T-shirt, he tied the neck shut with the sleeves. It didn't look big enough to catch the large reptile. What if it had claws and ripped it to shreds? What if it ripped him to shreds? He thought of running for home. But this was his chance to prove he was not a liar. He flattened himself into the smooth channel and waited.

The minutes crawled by as the dark shadows of clouds moved across the rock and launched out into the sea of grain like an armada of pirate ships sailing away in the night. A brilliant flash illuminated the open prairie. Thunder rumbled overhead. In the deep silence that followed, Corvan heard a sharp hiss.

He whirled to find the bright eyes of the lizard watching him intently from the rise over his head. It dropped a small bundle and moved slowly toward him, its gaze fixed on his. Corvan opened his mouth to yell, but nothing came out.

The lizard was so close he could see the intricate blue markings on its chest and a black collar around its neck. He hadn't noticed that before. Was it someone's pet?

In a moment, it would be close enough to strike. The lizard scraped its sharp claws across the rock, hissing and clicking in angry tones.

It paused, then lifted its nose to sniff the air. Out of the darkness, a lone coyote sprang over the castle rocks behind the lizard's back and rushed toward it. Corvan shouted a warning, and the reptile twisted about and evaded the attack. The coyote skidded to a halt just in front of Corvan, whirled about, and stalked its prey back toward the circle. It sprang. The lizard rolled to one side, its front claws raking the lean face. As the wounded coyote yelped and stopped to wipe a paw over its torn nose, the lizard made two quick bounds and disappeared within the circle of rocks. The coyote shook its head and leaped after it.

Corvan listened to the growls and snarls from inside the castle. If the coyote killed the lizard and dragged it away he could never prove he wasn't lying. In desperation, he darted through a gap in the rocks, waving his arms over his head and yelling at the coyote, now digging furiously in the loose dirt. It turned and crouched, snarling and weaving its head from side to side. Bubbles of saliva dripped from its black lips. Rabies!

Corvan stepped back. Resisting the urge to run, he waved his hands over his head to make himself appear larger. The angry growl gave way to a whimper. Rabid animals were more aggressive. Something was making it sick. Fear shone in its eyes. It stumbled away and disappeared in a flash of lightning. A blast of thunder rolled across the darkening prairie.

Drops of warm rain fell on Corvan's bare torso as he walked back to where he'd dropped his shirt. His hands were shaking as he reached for it. Lightning crackled, illuminating a small sheaf of wheat on the ground. Picking it up he discovered that the dozen or so short stalks had been neatly tied with a leather thong.

"Animals can't tie knots," he told himself. He walked back up to the rocks and set the strange bundle down so he could untie his sleeves and tug his shirt over his head. A spatter of rain fell on his upturned face. Dark clouds boiled in the sky above. The rain would be good for the crops, but this storm could turn into hail, maybe even a tornado. It was time to get back to the house.

He reached for the strange bundle of wheat. It was gone. Across the castle, a shadow disappeared beside the large boulder. The lizard had returned for its prize.

The wind came in strong gusts, and the temperature was dropping. A blast of rain whipped past him. He made a dash for the old fort he and Kate had built on the north side of the castle.

The rain fell harder as Corvan ducked inside. The tattered tarp leaked badly. He squinted out the door at the light bulb on his back porch. He was about to make a run for it when the clouds burst and sheets of freezing rain obscured his view.

Backing away from the door, he found a dry corner and hunkered down to watch. A storm this hard never lasted long.

The rain pounding on the roof of the fort began to mix with the intermittent patter of small hailstones. The walls swayed with the gales of wind, and water whipped into the open doorway. Huddled in the corner, Corvan watched the water run in muddy rivulets toward a pool forming next to the boulder in the center of the ring. The large stone that had once been a part of the circle of castle rocks, standing in the gap that now faced his house. As the water deepened and spread around the dirt piled up against the large rock, a column of bubbles shot into the air. When they stopped, the strange sheaf of wheat bobbed to the surface and swirled slowly around.

Corvan stumbled out of the fort and splashed to the edge of the pool. Crouching, he blinked against the driving rain and stared into the swirling water. The bundle of wheat came closer. More large bubbles broke the surface. The water gurgled and a whirlpool formed, like a bathtub drain, spinning around and sucking the sheaf of wheat away from his grasp.

Reaching out to where the funnel disappeared, Corvan gingerly pushed his hand in the hole, finding only rushing water. He waded in closer, but the chilly water pulled the muscles of his legs into excruciating knots.

He sprinted back to the fort and yanked on one of the longer boards. It came loose, along with the tarp, dousing him with frigid water as the fort collapsed in on itself. Shivering, he struggled free of the soggy canvas and staggered back to the pool, dragging the plank behind him.

With the board over the pool like a narrow bridge, he crawled across it until he was directly over the swirling drain. He extended his arm deeper into the hole. His hand slid between two smooth slabs of rock and then jammed against something wedged between them. He wrapped his numb fingers around a smooth rock with oddly angular sides. It would make a great addition to his collection.

He pulled but the rock was wedged tight. His fingers were numb with cold yet the rock felt strangely warm. He gave it another sharp tug.

The plank snapped in two, plunging him into the muddy water. His hand, still grasping the smooth stone, plunged into the hole, wedging his shoulder in the crack and trapping his face beneath the swirling water. He tugged and yanked, pushing with his free hand against the muddy bottom. His lungs screamed for air. He pushed with all his strength. The mud filled around his trapped arm and the water rose higher. Suddenly his shoulder slipped free through the mud and he stumbled from the pool, gasping and choking.

Corvan's body shook, and the entire mound of rock shuddered with him. A rumble of thunder seemed to echo in the stone below his feet. In the silence that followed, the swirling vortex vanished, and the water rose slowly around his legs. Lightning arced across the sky. Corvan turned and raced for home. Thunder crashed as he tore open the screen door. The low rumbles thrust him up the stairs and into his room, where he stood by his bed, dripping, and staring through the gray curtain of rain at the rock mound.

The numbness in his arm gave way to intense pain. Under the coating of sticky mud, he still clutched the thing from the hole. Heat filled his hand. The muck between his fingers steamed and prickled as if tiny spiders were crawling between them.

A cry pushed past his lips. He flung the thing into the corner of the room. It bounced off the wall and landed in the wastebasket with a dull clank.

His mother burst into the room. "What's going on in here?"

Corvan lifted his good arm and pointed out the window.

"You were out there? At this hour of the night? In the storm? What were you thinking? And look at all the mud." Shaking her head and muttering about that stupid rock she went to the kitchen and brought up some warm water for his washbasin.

She paused before leaving his room, a disapproving look on her face. "Make sure you're completely clean before you get into that bed. You'll be lucky if you don't catch your death of cold." She left, briskly closing the door behind her.

While Corvan washed his bruised arm, his eyes remained fixed on the corner of the room, where a thick trail of mud snaked down the wall and into his garbage can. He noticed a large dent in the rim that hadn't been there before. He pulled it over to his bed for a closer look.

His spine tingled with the realization that he'd almost drowned to retrieve whatever lay below the crumpled papers. In the panic of being under the water, his mind must have played tricks on him. He'd probably just picked up some old bone. Moving the papers aside, he peered into the wastebasket.

The mud that had coated the object now formed a halo of dry gray crumbs. This was no dog bone.

Chapter Four

The small hammer at the bottom of the trash can was so black it seemed to absorb the light around it. Its angular head was supported by a handle that looked too short for it to have any practical use.

Corvan sat perfectly still on the edge of his bed. Over the drum of the rain on the roof he could hear a powerful hum. Sliding to the floor, he pulled the wastebasket closer. A low noise emanating from the hammer was amplified by the tin walls of the can. He leaned closer. The sound intensified and the pitch dropped.

He inched a sweaty hand toward the hammer. The volume grew incrementally as his hand came closer. Closing his eyes, he touched the handle. The sound stopped.

Corvan opened his eyes. He moved his hand away and a low, powerful hum throbbed in his ears. He touched the shaft with a finger, and the hum stopped. Wrapping his hand around the smooth shaft, he lifted the hammer out.

It felt so lightweight and beautifully balanced, he could hardly believe it was in his hand. How could something so light have made such a deep dent in his garbage can?

He felt his hand tingle again but this time he was not afraid. A strange sense of power filled him.

He smoothed out a spot on the bed and lay the hammer down. Against the yellow and white triangles of his bedspread, the object looked even darker than before, like a velvety black hole cut into the cloth. It sank into the mattress as if it would tear the fabric with its weight.

Corvan knelt on the floor to examine the hammer more closely. It was all one piece, with no seams to mark the transition from handle to head. The head had seven distinct sides—a heptagon. Mrs. Thompson would be proud that he remembered the name of the unusual geometric shape.

THE HAMMER

He traced a finger over the handle. It was so smooth, he couldn't even tell that his fingers were touching it.

Picking it up, he examined it carefully. He could see no identifying marks. Perhaps his magnifying glass would reveal something.

Standing, Corvan stepped past the window toward his shelf, and the hammer pulled on his hand, turning his body like a magnet around to the north. The sense of power grew, coursing through him in dizzying waves.

A voice quietly stated, "It needs to go back." It was his own voice.

The hammer tugged again on his outstretched arm. Fear overwhelmed his muddled thoughts. He wanted to hurl the hammer through the window screen. His head swam. His vision swirled. In a haze, he stumbled past his washstand and fell facedown onto his bed.

As his pulse slowed, the nausea eased and Corvan rolled onto his back. He slowly opened his eyes then clamped them shut. The room still felt like it was crawling around him. Was he dreaming all this? He was so tired he could hardly think. He slowly exhaled and let the exhaustion take over.

The smell of bacon pulled Corvan from his sleep. Over the hum of the rain on the metal roof, he could hear his father washing up on the back porch. He was singing. He hadn't heard Father sing for over a year. He had forgotten how much his father loved dark rainy days.

His father sang in what he called the Old Language. As the song floated up over the porch roof and into Corvan's room, it filled the morning air with images of ancient battles and long-lost civilizations. Even after Father came back into the house, the refrain continued to cycle through Corvan's mind like the chant of prisoners in chains going to captivity in a far-off land. With each clank and shuffle of their feet, he heard it:

Makroum av isdray,

Makroum iv lon,

Makroum av intee,

Pire od som.

It was a sad song, yet the words seemed to contain some hope for the future—as if it were a prayer.

A soft, throbbing hum gave him a start. It was only a hummingbird passing his window, but it brought back the fear from the previous night. He sat up and looked around his room, then felt under his blankets and pillow. There was no hammer there. Was his imagination becoming that powerful? Maybe he had caught a fever out in the rain.

"Corvan," Mother called from the foot of the stairs, "food's getting cold."

He pulled on his clothes and reached for the door. He felt hot and dizzy. He turned to his washstand to splash water on his face.

The sight of the hammer lying there in the shallow water did not frighten him. It was a relief to know that it really existed. He must've dropped it as he stumbled back to bed.

Placing his hands on either side of the basin, he leaned closer. It was so smooth it seemed to float above the water. He lightly stroked the handle.

"Corvan!"

He whirled around to face his mother.

"Why didn't you answer? I was worried that you might be sick!" She came closer. "Are you sick? You don't look that well."

"I'm fine. Just a bit tired." The last thing he wanted was for his mother to keep him inside on a Friday with no school.

"I would imagine you are a bit tired. Now wash those filthy hands. You obviously didn't wash up like I told you, before going to bed."

Corvan dipped his fingers in the water, keeping the washbasin screened from view. Wiping his hands on his jeans, he moved to follow his mother downstairs, shutting the door firmly behind him.

Father waited at the table, a mug of steaming coffee in his hands. He looked at Corvan with a teasing smile. "You sure are getting hard of hearing these days. Must come from being outside in a thunderstorm."

"That makes two of you." Mother commented as she brought a plate of pancakes to the table.

His father patted her arm as she sat down. "It's impossible to stay inside on a wonderful night like that. I might even enjoy farming if I could do it in the dark."

Father passed the pancakes to Corvan. "Do you remember running past me last night by the outhouse?"

Corvan's heart beat faster, but he tried to look nonchalant. "I didn't see you."

"I was right by the path when you came bolting by." Father's brow furrowed. "You looked like you'd been wrestling some poor creature out of a mud hole. What did you find this time?"

Corvan's mind raced. What should he say? Would they take the hammer away from him? He bought some time by filling his mouth with bacon and passing the plate of scrambled eggs to his mother.

"I didn't find anything. I just needed to get the mud off my hands." His heart sank, and the bacon lost its flavor. He'd done it again. He'd lied to his parents. Why did lies roll so easily off his lips? His stomach churned, and he forced himself to swallow the bacon, replacing it quickly with a forkful of eggs. He was sure his father knew he'd lied. He could feel his eyes looking through him.

It seemed like forever before his father spoke again. This time he talked to Corvan's mother, suggesting they go into the city and pick up a few things. Corvan continued to shovel in food. He'd lost his appetite, but the only way to get out of his father's presence was to finish eating as quickly as possible.

"Would you like to come along to the city?" his father asked. "Maybe you could pick out something for your birthday. Just over a week to go until your big day. Or perhaps you'd rather stay here and try to find the one that got away."

Corvan met his father's eyes. The love and trust in them made his misery unbearable. He wanted to blurt out, *I lied to you, I'm sorry!* Instead, he looked away.

"Well, you're welcome to come if you wish." His father said. "But if you stay here, remember to stay out of the cellar. It's not your birthday yet."

When his parents began to discuss the trip to the city and what they could afford to pick up, Corvan took the opportunity to mumble a quick "Thanks, Mom," grab his rain jacket off a peg, and exit out the back door.

The rain had tapered off into a light mist. Gray skies mirrored his feelings as he passed under the dripping trees and skirted the mud puddles on the path to climb the rock.

He found the castle ring half full of water, with boards and bubbles of tarp scattered over the surface. The water must be draining down into the rock.

Corvan walked inside the ring. The screen door creaked and he saw his father appear in the back porch. He crouched down. Why was his dad so interested in everything that happened out at the rock? He wouldn't have to lie to him if he wasn't so nosey.

"Corvan," he called out, "we're getting ready to go. Are you coming?"

He was sure his father knew where he was, but he stayed low and remained perfectly still.

A few minutes later, he heard their old truck clunking down the lane.

As the sound of the truck faded, Corvan returned to the house. Making his way into the living room, he flopped down on the old brown couch and closed his eyes. The silence gathered around, squeezing against his head. He felt odd, as if he were light enough to float up to the ceiling. Pulling himself from the couch, he looked out the front window.

He needed to find Kate and tell her what had happened. Maybe she could help make some sense of it. He pushed off the couch and climbed up to his room.

He stood a long while at the washbasin, admiring the hammer's cold beauty. Why should he share it with Kate? It belonged to him. He was old enough to manage this on his own. If he had to lie to keep the hammer a secret, then so be it. He leaned closer. "You belong to me now. No one can take you away. That's the only truth that matters to me."

As his fingers touched the handle as hot blue shaft of electric light erupted from the end of the hammer. It twisted up his arm toward his face, the crackling shafts blinding him and then slamming him against the wall. The room plunged into darkness.

A swarm of wasps buzzed about his head. Corvan flailed his arm to get rid of them. Their noise filled his ears. He pushed his eyes open and realized there were no wasps. The sound came from his washstand, where a column of steam rose from the basin.

Corvan struggled to pull himself onto the bed, his right arm hanging limply at his side. The hammer had tried to kill him. But why now? Why not last night? Grasping the bedpost, he stood up and looked into the basin.

The water was gone. The sides of the basin were scorched black and dreadfully warped. Flakes of enamel had fallen off its twisted sides creating a speckled ring on the washstand. Sinking down on his bed, Corvan massaged his aching arm.

Was the hammer reacting because he'd left it in the water? No, it was underwater when he found it. Maybe he touched it in the wrong spot. But it was the same spot he'd touched last night.

Maybe it was responding to how mad he was. If the hammer felt threatened by Corvan's anger, it might have been defending itself.

The only way to know for sure would be to change his feelings and approach the hammer again.

But how could he change? He was mad at his father, but he didn't really know why. He thought it over. He was actually more angry with himself for lying to his dad again.

Corvan thought of Mrs. Thompson's lesson with the vase. He had to do something to break his habit of lying. But if he admitted that he'd lied, would his father forgive him or get mad? "It doesn't matter," he murmured. "I have to at least tell him I'm sorry." The words lifted a weight off his shoulders, and the pain in his arm eased.

Corvan moved in front of the basin. The thought of the searing blue light pulled him back into fear but as his hand hovered over the handle, he could feel it drawing him closer.

Shutting his eyes, he gently closed his hand around the shaft. He felt a tingling sensation, and then only the warmth of the stone. Carrying the hammer back to his bed, Corvan lay back and held it against his chest. His heart beat against his hands, and for a moment, it seemed the hammer pulsed in return. Peace wrapped itself around him like a warm blanket and he began to dream.

This time, as he wandered through the caves, he felt at home in the darkness. The monster was gone; his fears had dissipated. Ahead he saw a softly lit opening cut into the cavern wall. It was a window, complete with a screen, just like the one in his room. Was it the one in his room? Was he still dreaming?

A shadow fell across the rusty metal mesh. A razor-thin claw thrust in at the top and tore its way down to the bottom.

CHAPTER FIVE

The bang of the screen door jolted Corvan awake. He blinked and looked at his window. There was no jagged slit. It had just been another bad dream.

Voices floated up from the kitchen. Mother and Father had returned, and judging from the light coming in his window, the day was almost gone. He rolled over and the handle of the hammer jabbed into his ribs. Grunting, he pulled it out and examined it. He considered showing it to his father but decided to leave it under his pillow for the time being.

"Where were you?" his mother asked as he entered the tiny kitchen. "I thought you wanted to go into town with us."

"I need to talk to Dad."

"What about?"

"Nothing. I just need—"

"If it's nothing, it can wait until you fill the wood box."

"I'll do it later."

"Do you know how many times I've heard that?"

Corvan nodded. "I know. I'm sorry. I really will do it as soon as I talk with Dad."

Mother stopped what she was doing and just looked at him a moment. She nodded. "He's working on the truck."

Corvan bolted out of the kitchen.

He found his father leaning under the hood of the truck, looking at the dipstick. "Hasn't lost a drop since the last oil change. I think the old girl will still be going when you take her over." He smiled at Corvan as he replaced the stick.

Corvan leaned on the fender. His father took the air filter apart and wiped the inside, seemingly oblivious to the tension his son was feeling.

"I lied to you." There, he'd said it.

"I know." Father straightened and looked at him, eyes full of pride. "Would you like to talk about it?"

Corvan nodded.

The dinner bell rang on the back porch.

Father pushed the hood shut. "After supper. I'll meet you out at the rock." Their eyes met briefly, then they walked in silence around to the back yard.

After supper was over Corvan filled the wood box while his father helped do the dishes. His dad nodded at him to go ahead without him. No doubt he wanted to talk to his mother about what was going on.

The long shadows of the aspen trees were creeping across the yard. A lone star shone in the darkening sky but the warmth of the day still clung to the autumn air. Leaving the yard behind, he approached the rock. It always looked so mysterious at twilight, as if it were the grave of some ancient warrior king waiting to arise and lead his people into battle. His father said the rock was a sacred place to a band of natives who once lived in the area. They believed the rock had the power to protect them from a hostile tribe that lived nearby, but in the end, they were betrayed and massacred.

Corvan climbed to the top and entered the gap in the rocks. He turned and looked back. His home was slightly elevated on a knob of rock and from the gap he could see directly across into his bedroom window. He wondered if his grandfather had broken off the rock so he could see into the circle from the house. He looked down at the telltale marks of a borehole. He doubted there was anyone else in town who understood that the twenty boulders in the circle were not separate rocks but had actually been cut out of the crown of the hill. His father knew but he had told Corvan it was a secret. He didn't want the people from the university poking around.

Corvan turned and stepped into the castle. The water had drained from the center of the rocks, leaving a soggy patch where he'd found the hammer. A crusty mass of tarp and broken boards lay drying in the mud. The firepit area still had a puddle in it. The campfire would have to be built out on the western slope.

Corvan walked through the circle and out the gap that faced the setting sun. There had never been a rock in this space. This one led to the path that dropped down the long incline. He kicked at the dirt and sand that had accumulated in the space. No wonder the water had risen so high. He needed to dig the debris out so the water could flow down the channel again.

He looked over the plains with apprehension. Something both beautiful and frightening hung in the air. Closing his eyes, he let the feelings sweep over him with the evening breeze.

His father's song rose strong and clear on the wind as he approached the rock. This time Corvan thought he understood a few words—something about truth and freedom.

Father carried something wrapped in an old blanket and an armful of firewood. He set them on the ground. "How about setting things up in the castle while I go get a bit more wood?"

"I think we might have enough if we use the broken boards from our fort. It got knocked flat in the storm." Corvan gestured toward the circle.

His father took a look. "I see what you mean. The fire pit is too wet. Let's build our fire on the west edge. I'll pick some of this up while you get the fire ready."

Corvan arranged the firewood his father brought up. As his dad came through the gap in the castle rocks with a few more boards, the last rays of the day captured a noble look on his face, like a wise sage about to embark on an important quest.

His father brought the boards over and retrieved a package of matches from his pocket. A moment later, flickering flames lit the craggy features of his face. The wood crackled and they sat looking into the flames for a long while before Father spoke.

"There is a lot of pain in this broken world, Son. Some people want to avoid it. But they don't realize that pain and love grow side by side. If you try to escape pain, you will miss the opportunity to love."

Corvan nodded. He knew about pain.

"I am proud of you for telling me about your lie. It shows me that you are beginning to understand what it takes to be a man of integrity."

Corvan's chest swelled with pride. He'd done something right for a change. Perhaps there was hope for him after all. Now he just needed to tell his dad about the mysterious black hammer. "I want to tell you about last night."

His father did not respond. He just leaned back and looked into the sky. "Can you imagine not seeing a single star in your lifetime? Never enjoying the vastness of a night sky or feeling the pull of a full moon?"

Corvan shook his head. Father continued, "There was a time when our people didn't see these things."

Our people? Grandfather only had one son and his mother didn't have any living relatives.

Father leaned forward. "I'm not sure where I should begin or how much I'm supposed to tell you." He paused, as though searching for the answers to his own questions.

Corvan had expected his dad to speak to him about lying or to question him about what he'd found. This didn't make any sense.

THE HAMMER

His father unwrapped the blanket from around a black wooden box. The firelight flickered across the polished surface as if it were on fire. Was this an early birthday present his parents had picked up in town? He glanced up to find his father studying him.

"Your grandfather left this with me. I made the case to keep it safe for you. I'm not as good with wood as he was."

"But you can make just about anything out of metal. Sometimes when I lay on the rock I feel you pounding on stuff in the cellar."

His father's eyes narrowed. "You can feel that out here?"

Corvan nodded.

"Then the cellar has to be connected to this hill. I thought so."

"I really felt it the night of the storm. Like you'd set off an explosion down there."

His father looked like a boy caught stealing apples, and a small proud smile crinkled the corners of his eyes. "I've been working on something. I'll show it to you after your birthday."

He glanced over at the castle rocks. "Your grandfather was supposed to be here on your birthday to tell you everything that you need to know. He didn't tell me very much about it." He looked up into the sky a long moment and a lone tear trickled down his cheek. "He was gone so often, and he and I never talked that much even when he was around."

Corvan shifted nervously. He had never seen his father cry.

"All he told me was that you would need this someday." He tapped a finger on the black case. "'He must have it,' he told me, 'when he is ready. For this one is the Cor-Van.'"

The way his father said his name, pausing in the middle and stressing the last syllable, made Corvan's skin prickle. He pulled his jacket tightly about him. The shadows grew blacker, and he leaned in toward the fire.

"It was he who named you," his father said softly. "Your mother had picked a different name, but he insisted on Corvan. If he was right, you will know soon, for your day is almost here."

He looked intently into Corvan's eyes as the shadows flickered about them. "Do you remember the story of this rock?"

"The native massacre?"

Father nodded. "The chief worked hard to instruct others in the old ways, but not all would follow. There are always those who want power over others. The old ways leave no room for that. In the end, the people were outnumbered and wiped out, except for one warrior."

"The one who built the castle, right?"

"Oh, no. That part of the legend is not true. The circle of rocks goes back much further than him or his tribe. It started eons ago, back with the lost people."

"Who?"

His father frowned. "I'm not sure what to tell you. I'm not completely sure what I believe myself." He stared beyond the fire at the castle, then turned back to look intently into Corvan's eyes. "One thing I do know is that your future is tied to that stone circle."

The banging of the screen door echoed off the rocks. His father shrugged. "I think we're being reminded that it's getting late. I promised your mother we wouldn't be long." He wrapped the wooden case back in the blanket. "I'll show you this another time. Definitely before your birthday. Your grandfather made me promise I would give it to you before your fifteenth year began. He said you would be old enough to choose between fear and duty by then." He stood. "You proved him right today."

Corvan knew he was telling him this to make him feel better but instead he found his stomach churning. The thought of becoming an adult held no attraction for him. The future held many more things to worry about. The only positive part about turning fifteen was being allowed to grow out his hair as a sign of his new adult status. He hoped that once he looked a little less like a child some of the teasing would go away.

They left the dying fire and returned to the house. On the porch, they stopped and looked back. The flickering embers and wisps of smoke gave the rock the appearance of a smoldering volcano teetering on the edge of a major eruption.

Inside the house, they paused at the foot of the stairs. Father put a hand on his shoulder. Corvan looked up into his eyes. They were full of sadness. His dad patted his back and entered his own bedroom.

Back upstairs, Corvan lay on his bed beside the hammer. Was it connected to the thing in the black box? If so, how did the hammer end up under the hill? He gently stroked the cool stone and a soft blue glow from the butt end of its handle sprang to life. He yanked his hand away. Was it going to shock him again? The light ebbed away, but as soon as he touched it the blue markings came back to life. He leaned in closer. The light came from an insignia, a ring within a ring, with strange figures between the two. He knew that design. The markings on the hammer were identical to those on the oak chest in the corner of his room.

Corvan threw back the covers, picked up the hammer, and swung his legs over the side of the bed just as the phone rang. The light in the stairwell went on and he heard his father pick up the phone. There was a short, muffled conversation, then

THE HAMMER

Father hung up. He heard his mother's voice, the scraping of chairs, and water being poured. They were settling in at the table for a talk.

The glow from the hammer filled Corvan's bedroom with waves of blue light, as if his room were suddenly underwater. Corvan pointed the hammer like a flashlight across his room to light up the front of the oak chest. The rings and the strange markings were larger on the chest and there was a hole in the center. A hole that looked about the same size as the handle of the hammer. Maybe his grandfather had made the stone hammer as a key.

Corvan let his feet touch down on the floorboards and froze as they groaned under his weight. There was no way he could make it to the chest without his parents hearing him. He listened carefully. There was a pause in their conversation and then the back screen door squeaked. Corvan quickly pulled himself back into bed and pushed the hammer under his pillow. One of them must be heading for the outhouse. He couldn't have them see his room full of blue light. He would have to wait for them to go to bed before checking out the chest.

Turning onto his back, he folded his hands across his stomach and stared up at the ceiling. There was lots to think about. He was happy that he and his father had a chance to talk but there were so many questions he needed to ask him. He tried to make mental note of everything he wanted to ask his father tomorrow, but found himself nodding off.

CHAPTER SIX

Daylight filled his room. Corvan rubbed the sleep from his eyes and rolled over.

He studied the oak chest across the room. Made for him by his grandfather, it was four feet wide and so heavy it had never been moved from the place where it rested. If his theory was correct, when he inserted the hammer's handle into the hole in the front of the chest, a secret compartment should open up inside.

Jumping out of bed, he opened the heavy lid and checked inside. Each of the sliding trays was filled with treasures he had collected over the years: bottle caps, agates, arrowheads—anything he could find at no cost.

Kneeling in front of the chest, he examined the design his grandfather had carved into the front panel. It looked identical to what he'd seen glowing on the end of the hammer's handle, only it was twice the size. In the middle of the design was a shallow hole the size of a half dollar. He knew this for a year ago, he'd pushed the fifty-cent piece he got for his birthday into the hole. It got stuck but seemed as good a place as any to save it, so he left it there.

He dove back under the covers and fished around for the hammer.

"You sure are sleeping in a lot these days."

Corvan poked his head out of the covers to see his mother at the door. She shook her head and frowned.

"You won't get a proper rest if you go to bed late and then sleep in."

Corvan pulled his head back under the covers like a shy turtle. Hopefully she would think he was too tired and let him be.

"Don't even think of going back to sleep. You need to eat and then clean up the rest of the dishes. Your father was called to another meeting at the mine, and I'll be baking bread and canning peas. You've got ten minutes." Her footsteps retreated down the stairs.

THE HAMMER

Corvan lay under the covers in the dim light. He hoped his father's meeting at the mine went well. Personally, he wouldn't like to work underground all day and only come up at night, but his dad thrived on it. He spent as much time underground as possible and was always reading about mines and caves. More than a few times Corvan had heard him say that the continental crust of the earth was more than twenty-five miles thick but most mines and caves were less than a mile deep. "There's a whole world below us waiting to be discovered." He would say. "We just need to find the door."

Corvan pushed in farther under the covers. His hand touched the smooth stone and the blue glow came to life. His grandfather must have made the hammer as a key to open the chest. Whatever was hidden inside must be his special fifteenth-birthday present.

Throwing the covers back, Corvan slipped to his knees. His hands trembled as he lifted the hammer toward the hole in the chest.

A loud thump almost made him drop it. His mother banged again on the kitchen ceiling with her broom handle.

Corvan groaned. If he didn't move fast she would come up to get him. He placed the hammer into one of the cubbyholes and covered it with his stamp collection. After quietly closing the lid he got dressed and moved silently down the stairs.

The scene in the kitchen caught him off guard. Mother stood at the sink, holding a dishcloth limply in her hand and staring into the backyard. She was singing his special song in a quiet, broken voice. Corvan stood watching, not knowing what to say.

He backed out of the kitchen and crept upstairs. What was going on? Everyone was acting so strange. After crouching at the top of the stairs for a few minutes, he heard Mother putting dishes away in the cupboards. Corvan bounded down the stairs, humming loudly. As he rounded the corner into the kitchen, the screen door banged shut behind his mother. The cupboard door hung open and a stack of plates sat on the counter.

His breakfast of two pancakes covered in raspberry jam sat on the table. He rolled one up and slurped up the jam that squeezed out of the center. He thought about telling his mother about the hammer. He shook his head. Not yet. First he needed to see what was hidden in the chest. He ate as quickly as he could and added his plate to the pile of dirty dishes by the sink.

He didn't mind washing dishes—the water was warm and as he worked, he could look out the window toward the rock and let his imagination run wild.

As he was drying the last plate, Mother came around the corner of the house to the back porch, a basket full of peas in her hands. A contented glow lit her eyes, and she smiled at him through the window. He hurried to the door and took the basket from her.

"Thanks for finishing the dishes." She patted his back as he set the basket on the table. "I'll be canning peas today, so I'll need the kitchen space."

Corvan detested shelling peas, but he should at least offer to help. "Is there anything I can do?"

Mother laughed. "Your father told me I should let you have a break from your chores since it's almost your birthday. You could spend the day out at that rock if you like."

"Why don't you like our rock?" The question came out before he could stop himself, and he winced.

She pulled a blue ceramic bowl from the cupboard and returned to the table. "Why would you say that?" Mother's fingers flew with practiced ease, the shelled peas rolling against one another inside the chipped bowl.

Corvan took a handful of pea pods and sat across from her. "I never see you come near it except on my birthday."

Mother's fingers slowed. "I don't like to think about what might happen out there."

Corvan didn't like the sound of that. He was about to ask what she meant but Mother continued.

"It's not the rock itself, Son. It's . . . it's so much more. I'm not sure what I'm supposed to say to you . . . or what I believe myself."

He hunched over the peas in his lap. "That's what Father said." Something was happening that both of his parents knew about. It made him mad that they wouldn't tell him what it was.

"Your father is trying to do what he thinks best for you." She stopped shelling and looked at him. "If what your grandfather told us is true, things will unfold in their own time. I don't understand how it could happen when the key piece is still missing."

Corvan thought about the hammer sitting in the chest upstairs. Was it the key piece?

He raised his head to find his mother studying him intently. "If it isn't true, or it's not the right time, why should we burden you with things that might never affect you?"

"Can't you at least tell me something that makes sense?"

Mother came around the table and held him close. "Don't be afraid. If the words are true, we will see you grow into a great leader."

Corvan frowned. A great leader? How could the shortest, skinniest, most picked-on kid in the school ever be a great leader?

Mother smiled at him. "Don't worry about it. I'm sure things will all come together in time. I'm just not ready to say good-bye to my only one."

Corvan's heart lifted. He liked it when she called him "my only one." It was a special name she used only when no one else was around.

She patted his head. "So are you going to shell peas all day or is there something else you want to do?"

"You'll finish the peas faster if I am not here to distract you with my questions."

Mother laughed as he headed for the stairs. "Well, don't say I didn't give you a choice."

As Corvan climbed the stairs, he heard the dull plunk of peas hitting the growing pile. As he reached the landing she began singing the song she used to sing when she tucked him into bed. It enveloped him with a deep sense of peace.

My precious one, the night has come,
My only one, the dark is at the door.
But there's no need to fear the night,
For the stars bring hope as the moon gives light.

And though the shadows grow and sway,
They'll never take my love away.
Look deep inside, my only one,
And there you'll find the truth.

My precious one, my only one,
You'll find that you are brave.

He climbed the stairs with the rising melody, his heart taking comfort in the familiar words.

Back in his room, Corvan retrieved the hammer from inside the chest and knelt on the floor. His mother's words had him worried. What if using the key was like Pandora's box and bad things would start to happen? For a moment he cradled the hammer in his hands. No, this was different. This key contained hope for the future, not evil. He could feel it. Holding his breath, he held the hammer like an oversized key, and slowly fed it into the hole.

A loud humming filled his ears, and excitement rose in his chest. The sweet smell of burning oak filled his nostrils as wisps of smoke curled into the air. Sparks shot out from around the butt of the handle.

The coin! He'd forgotten the half dollar. He yanked the handle out of the hole and stuck his finger inside. The scent of singed skin mixed with the aroma of burned wood. He yelled in pain, pulled his blistered fingertip from the hole and ran to the washbasin. The charred bowl was completely dry. Corvan's other fingers throbbed in sympathy. Bouncing up and down with pain, he searched the room for something cold. The smooth blackness of the hammer beckoned to him. He jumped back toward the chest and pressed his stinging finger against the black stone. Instantly the pain eased. He pushed more firmly and the pain melted away. Releasing his breath, Corvan pulled his hand back.

He examined it closely. It was a little red but there was no welt or blister. He looked in amazement at the hammer. One minute it seemed intent on killing him and the next it was healing his hand. How could his grandfather have made something this powerful?

Corvan turned his attention back to the chest. The wood around the hole was charred and cracked. The blackened coin still stuck inside. Opening the lid of the chest, he took out his grandfather's carving set. Choosing the smallest chisel, he pried gently on the coin.

The blackened circle of warped metal flicked out of the hole and skittered across the wood floor, tracing an erratic path toward the washstand. Corvan crawled after it as it wobbled to a halt and fell flat. He touched it gingerly and found it cool enough to pick up.

One side still showed a person's head, but the other now carried the imprint of the design on the bottom of the hammer's handle. Corvan slid the coin into his pocket and crept back to the chest. Holding his breath, he carefully inserted the handle again. He heard a whispering buzz, but it was only a bee at the window. He tried again, turning the head of the hammer as he held it in place. Nothing happened. He pushed harder, twisting it around in circles. Still no response.

That stupid coin had wrecked it. Now he would never know what the hammer was supposed to do. Standing, he let the heavy lid fall. As it banged down onto the chest a thin panel of wood on the top of the lid flew open on a hidden hinge, rose a few inches, and snapped back down into place.

Corvan stared for a moment, then stooped to grasp the front lip of the lid. He pulled gently. The entire lid rose from the chest. He let it drop again but nothing happened.

Falling to his knees, he fumbled to get the handle of the hammer back into the hole. A faint hum came from inside the chest. Holding his breath, he grasped the top edge. A thin panel separated and lifted away, revealing a bed of gray cloth. A secret compartment was built right into the lid. He smiled. His grandfather would have laughed at all times he had lifted that heavy lid to look for a secret compartment inside the chest.

Running his hand over its surface, he found odd shapes outlined beneath its supple folds.

He pulled the cloth. It stretched but didn't come free. Looking closely, Corvan discovered a small black button holding the corner of the cloth in place. Feeling along the edges, he found five more. He unbuttoned them all and slowly pulled the cloth toward him.

Each move of the cloth revealed a new artifact carefully fastened into the inner recess of the lid. A few of these were immediately recognizable, but others were of a strange design.

Corvan pulled the last of the cloth into his lap, where its warm folds conformed to the contours of his body. He drank in the beautiful arrangement of the objects. His grandfather must have spent a lot of time on this part of the chest. His eyes wandered over the different items. A coil of rope, a pair of soft shoes, and a book! Finally, he'd get some answers. He leaned over to examine it. Bound in thin metal covers, the book's top was etched with the hammer's insignia. He tried to pick it up, but like all the other items in the lid, it was held into its softly padded indentation with a set of black metal clips. His attempts to twist them to one side only resulted in a broken fingernail.

The chisel from the carving set would give him more leverage. Carefully, he slid it under a clip and pulled up. Nothing budged. He pulled harder. The chisel snapped, leaving a thin scratch across the cover of the book.

Whirling around, he grabbed the hammer and then spun back to the chest. "When all else fails, give it a smack." He rapped on one of the clips. Instantly all the clips around the book popped up and swiveled 180 degrees.

"Now that's cool." Corvan picked up the book and settled back against the end of his bed.

It was about five inches square and no thicker than his baby finger. But it was heavy for its size, as if he held a history of the entire world in his hands. Thick pages lay between the covers, but he couldn't open it.

Picking up the hammer, he placed the handle in the center of the insignia. Without a sound, the covers separated.

The pages were soft and flexible, more like cloth than paper. The first page contained only the original insignia and what looked to be a signature at the bottom. Corvan's hands trembled. He turned the first page and then another and another. The book was written in pictograph figures interspersed with small sketches of trees and simple figures of people.

As he fanned through the last pages, a yellowed paper fluttered to the floor. It was a folded section of a newspaper printed September 20, 1938. Inside was a scrap of lined notepaper written in English. The first words leaped from the page.

My dear grandson, Corvan . . .

CHAPTER SEVEN

The letter was written in a scrawling hand that slanted steeply across the page.

Here you are, not even a year old, and I must lay the burden of the ages on your small shoulders.

It would be good if you would stop your yammering so I can finish writing in peace. I could let you hold the hammer and you would be sleeping in no time, but if your mother caught me, it might be the last time I get to visit you.

Your mother has a great heart, but since I returned just before you were born and insisted upon your name, she has been a little wary of my ways. She knows I was angry with your father when he took covenant with someone outside our people, but I see now I was wrong. I studied the old songs and legends for a long time, but somehow I missed it. It is clear to me now. The Cor-Van has to be in both spheres; it is the only way you will be able to defeat the evil.

Corvan shuddered at that line. Why would his grandfather expect him to defeat evil? And what were the spheres he was talking about? He looked back to the page.

I have made a terrible mess of things. I should have stayed with your father after he married. I could have taught him everything he needed to pass on to you. But instead I let anger rule me. I hope I am not too late.

THE HAMMER

I did not believe the day would ever come when they could
function outside their sphere. I should have seen it coming. He will
never be content until He conquers everything.

I must return tomorrow if I am to stop them. I should not leave
you, but I must do something to put things right. When I complete
my task, I will return both to you. You are the Cor-Van. They must
come back to your hand.

I am looking forward to the times we will have together as you
grow. I will do a much better job of explaining this in person. I can
hardly wait to begin your training.

Keep both close by at all times. Learn to understand their
differences but remember that they must be used together.

Both? Corvan looked down at the hammer on the floor. That had to be one of
them but what was the other? Was it the book? How could he keep them close if he
didn't even know what they were? Maybe the rest of the letter would clear things up.

Do not trust any of the dark-eyed ones. Sooner or later, they
will betray you. And whatever you do, never mention the hammer
to anyone, not even those you think are with us.

Do not use your title until all is ready. Use only the name your
mother calls you.

Make sure that you take along . . .

The letter ended with an inch of space left on the sheet but the back side was
blank. Why had his grandfather folded the letter up in the newspaper without
finishing it?

A sense of helplessness overwhelmed Corvan. Something was about to happen
to him, and he was totally unprepared. His grandfather's letter was unclear, and it
didn't sound like his father would be much help.

In the stillness of his room, Corvan read the letter again. His grandfather's
writing was almost as messy as his own. He swallowed. He wished his grandfather
were here to explain things.

The hammer was obviously the key to everything, but beyond that, the letter
was nonsense. Shaking his head, he folded it back inside the newspaper and tucked it
into the book. Maybe something else in the chest would give him more clues. As he
pressed the book into its niche, the clips pivoted and snapped into place.

He turned his attention to the indentation that held the rope. In this light, the soft coils looked like a living green vine. Was this the rope from his dream? He pinched it. It felt almost soft enough to squish apart. He picked up the hammer to release the clips.

The sound of his mother's footsteps on the stairs threw him into a panic. He shut the secret compartment, jammed the hammer into his back pocket, and pushed the chisels under the bed.

His mother stepped inside the door and shut it behind her. "Kate is downstairs, and she's not happy. Did you promise to help her pick berries this morning?"

Corvan's face flushed. He had told Kate he would help her but that was before she had quit talking to him. How was he supposed to know she still expected him to show up? "She said something about the grain elevator at nine o'clock. What time is it?"

"Ten forty-five." Mother shook her head. "You have to keep your word, Corvan, or people won't trust you." She looked around his room. "What have you been doing up here anyway? What was all that banging?"

"Just looking at some stuff in my chest." He glanced down and saw the gray cloth lying in a pile at his feet. He tried nonchalantly pushing it under the bed with his foot.

"You need to get downstairs and make things right with Kate." She turned to leave and looked back at him. "By the way, kicking that quilt under your bed does not constitute cleaning your room. Fold it and put it back into the chest."

He nodded.

"Do it now so I know it's been taken care of."

Corvan rolled the cloth tightly in his arms. His mother stared at him, a frown on her face.

"It took me hours to sew those quilt pieces together."

Corvan looked from her face to the cloth. Was she joking? How could his mother mistake this gray cloth for his brightly colored winter quilt?

"Fold it neatly. And don't make Kate wait any longer, or you'll get an earful." She left the room.

Corvan waited until he heard her on the stairs, then pulled the hammer from his back pocket and unlocked the secret compartment. He rolled the cloth out over the tray, then hurried downstairs.

In the kitchen he found Kate sitting at the table, finishing off a piece of bread with raspberry jelly. Two full pails of berries sat on the table. Judging from the twigs and leaves stuck in her tangled hair, Kate must have worked pretty hard to get them. As Corvan entered, she gave him a withering look from behind her bangs.

"Sorry, Kate, I was—"

"Oh, don't give me any of your excuses. I know how much you hate picking berries. Trust me, it's not my favorite chore, either, but my mom needs these by tonight."

Kate's mother baked the best saskatoon berry pies for miles around and made some extra income by selling them to the café where she worked. Unfortunately, she usually lost it all playing bingo.

"I was going to come, Kate, honest." He did want to help her. She'd be in a lot of trouble if the berries weren't ready when her mom got home.

"I'll help you, Kate," his mother said, giving Corvan a disapproving look. "I'll mix up some pastry for you to take home."

Kate's face brightened. "Thanks. I'm sure my mom will really appreciate it."

"How many pies is she going to make, dear?"

"I think she said nine. They aren't selling as many now that summer vacation is over."

"I'll fix the pastry while you two clean the berries." She smiled at Kate as she passed her a clean pail.

Corvan followed Kate out to the back steps with the pails of berries. As he sat down beside her the sweet aroma of lilacs swirled about him. But the lilac bush in the yard bristled with brown seedpods, its flowers long faded and blown away. Kate tossed her head and a fresh wave passed by.

He leaned closer to her and sniffed. "You're not wearing perfume, are you?"

Kate bent over her pail of berries, and a pink blush touched her cheeks. "My dad sent it for my birthday."

Shoot. He had forgotten her birthday. Maybe that's why she refused to walk to school with him this week. He caught another whiff of her perfume. It reminded him of warm spring nights on the front porch swing, looking at the stars. "I lick likelacs. I mean, I lake laclicks." He stopped and took a deep breath. "It smells nice."

She looked sideways at him from the berries, a smile tugging at her lips. "Thanks, Corvan. I like lilacs too."

Now Corvan found his face getting warm. He wanted to say something clever and impress her but all he could think of was, "I found something out at the rock."

Kate rolled her eyes. "Don't tell me you were trying to catch that imaginary lizard."

"I have to prove—"

"The kids will laugh you out of town if you don't drop that story. I couldn't believe you used it for an oral report. That was your tallest tale yet. My mom even heard about it at the café. She said that . . ."

"What?"

"Nothing. My mom says goofy things sometimes."

Corvan fell silent as they sorted berries from the debris.

"So, what was it?" Kate looked at him.

"What was what?"

"The thing you found that you couldn't tear yourself away from to meet me on time."

Whatever you do, never mention the hammer to anyone, not even those you think are with us. "Nothing." Corvan shrugged. "It's no big deal."

"Fine, keep it to yourself. What do I care?"

They cleaned quietly for a while. "These are nice berries," Corvan said to break the heavy silence. "Where did you find them?"

A sly smile stole over Kate's face. "Fry's pond."

Corvan shook his head. Everyone knew that Bill's father did not allow people on his land. Two boys from school had tried fishing at his pond once, and he let them have it with a shotgun full of rock salt.

"You're not supposed to go on his property."

Kate's smile vanished. "The bushes aren't even on his land. His property stops at the edge of the pond."

"Yeah, but does his shotgun know the difference? It's not very smart to go there."

"Yeah, well, if someone showed up on time, I wouldn't have to take such 'stupid' chances."

There was nothing he could say. Corvan stood to shake the berries and twigs from his lap. He felt a sharp tug on his jeans, and he turned to find Kate holding the hammer, a dazed expression on her face.

"Give me that," Corvan whispered. "It might hurt you." He held out his hand, but Kate pulled the hammer close to her chest. She stared vacantly past him. Corvan knelt on the step. "Are you okay?"

Kate's eyes filled with tears.

"It's what I found at the rock. It belonged to my grandfather."

Kate looked at him as if seeing him for the first time. She nodded slowly and looked at the hammer. "Your grandfather must have been a great man."

"My dad told me he was descended from a mighty warrior."

"It feels more like something a king would own." She reluctantly released the hammer into his hand.

Corvan slipped the hammer back into his pocket and found Kate looking up at him through moist eyes.

THE HAMMER

"I'm sorry I quit walking to school with you." She wiped a sleeve over her face. "I get so mad when the boys start picking on you. I'm not afraid of them, but my mom said if I were in one more fight, she'd make us move away." She blinked back tears. "I don't know how to help you."

Corvan sat with a heavy sigh. "I don't know either. I hate being so short."

Kate put her hand on his shoulder but it didn't make him feel better. Even Kate was two inches taller than he was, and a lot tougher. "At least you're a boy—your dad probably wouldn't mind if you got in a fight once in a while."

Corvan wasn't so sure. "Maybe if your dad was around he wouldn't mind you fighting either."

She pulled away, and Corvan instantly regretted bringing up her father's absence.

Corvan picked through another handful of berries and they sat quietly, listening to the hum of the bees in the wild roses. "What happened when you held the hammer?"

Kate smiled faintly. "It's silly, but I felt better about myself . . . like it's okay that I get mad at the bullies. But it was scary, too, as if I was in charge of making things right. Like a judge or a . . . a queen."

Corvan nodded. The way she put it made sense. He had felt something similar.

As they finished cleaning the berries, Corvan's mother appeared on the porch, a cloth-covered bowl in her hands. "Here's the pastry, dear. You'd better get it home and put it in the fridge right away." She shot a glance at her son. "Corvan will carry it for you."

He stood to take the bowl and Mother shook her head at him. "Did you have to smear the berries all over your pants? As soon as you get back, throw them into the washing machine. You'd better hope they aren't permanently stained."

Kate poured the clean berries back into her pails, hiding an amused grin.

The afternoon sun filtered through the freshly washed leaves as the two of them reached the tree-lined alley beside Kate's house. As Corvan put the bowl down and opened the gate for her, a voice drawled from the shadows.

"Looks like you got yourself some real good berries there." Bill Fry emerged from behind a stout maple tree and sauntered over, a shotgun cradled haphazardly in the crook of his arm.

"My dad and me was out hunting prairie chickens by our pond this mornin' and seen someone in the bushes. Don't suppose you two would've been picking berries on our property?"

Kate shook her head.

Bill smiled crookedly. "I'll just check them berries and see for myself." He stuck a grubby hand into a pail and stuffed a handful into his mouth. "Sure taste like our berries." He grabbed more and added them to his already full mouth. "Shor 'nuff," he mumbled, a string of purple drool sliding down his chin. "Them is our berries."

Kate raised her eyes from the ground. "Bill, my mom needs these to make her pies. Let us go and I promise I'll bring you a fresh-baked pie tomorrow."

"Don't want to wait till tomorrow. I want my berries now." Bill pushed himself closer. "Besides, you can tell Corvan to pick you some more. He can get his three-foot lizard to pick the berries he cain't reach." He laughed as he grabbed the handle, spilling berries into the dirt as Kate tried to hang on.

Kate's mouth tightened. "Two pies, Bill. Just let me take the berries."

Corvan stared at the ground. It would not be good if Kate got mad and fought with Bill.

A breeze caught the open gate and it slapped against the hammer stuck in his back pocket. As Corvan's hand touched the smooth stone, everything around him instantly became clearer. He looked at Bill, and for the first time he was not afraid of him.

Bill twisted the pail's handle but Kate held on.

"Leave her alone, Bill."

The large boy jerked back in surprise. He stared at Corvan for a second, then the wicked smirk returned to his face. Pushing Kate aside, he moved to stand toe to toe with Corvan, his bulk blocking out the sunlight. "Did I say you could speak? Mind your own business, Stumpy."

Corvan tightened his grip on the hammer and looked into Bill's narrowed eyes. "When you bully Kate, it is my business. I'm telling you to leave her alone."

Bill blinked, then laughed. "And if I don't, what are you going to do about it?" He jabbed a thick finger at Corvan's chest.

"I'll do whatever it takes."

Bill's smirk vanished as he stepped away, then a sneer lifted at the corner of his mouth. "Oh, I remember; Stumpy's got hisself a girlfriend, got to show how brave he is. Well, short stuff, you can have her. She's white trash, just like her mother."

Kate whirled to face Bill, her cheeks and neck bright red. The boy moved back.

"Why do you have to be so mean?" she asked quietly.

Confusion flickered across Bill's face. His eyes narrowed, and he gestured with the barrel of his gun. "I'm goin' to be taking them berries, Kate Poley, so I suggest you hand 'em over."

The sun glinted off the barrel of Bill's gun. Fear tightened around Corvan's chest, but he stepped between Bill and Kate.

THE HAMMER

"Leave us alone or you'll be in a whole mess of trouble for pointing a gun at people."

Bill turned to look at Corvan. "Yeah? Who's gonna tell?"

Corvan steadily returned his gaze but didn't answer.

Bill hesitated and then turned back to Kate. "Aw, go ahead and keep your berries. Everyone knows your mom makes rotten pies anyway. I'd rather eat a cow pie than the soggy mess she cooks up." He walked out the gate and swaggered off down the road, hollering over his shoulder. "When you two get married, your kids will be so short, people will mistake them for gophers and shoot 'em." He gave a loud guffaw and continued on his way.

Corvan let out a sigh of relief and released his grip on the hammer. He turned to find Kate gazing at him with admiration. Embarrassed, he picked up the pastry bowl from the grass.

"I'll take that," Kate said.

Corvan straightened. Although he and Kate had been friends a long time, she'd never invited him inside her home. She put the berry pails down and reached for the heavy stoneware bowl. For a moment, her hands wrapped around his. Corvan gently pulled his hands out from under Kate's. The scent of lilacs filled the air as a summer breeze rippled between them, flicking a lock of hair across her eyes. He brushed the hair away and she smiled at him. "Thanks, Corvan. Thanks for standing up for me."

Stammering out a good-bye, Corvan stepped through the gate to hide the flush rising up his face. He turned the corner and kicked a pine cone, sending it flying into the ditch. Why was he so flustered? Over the years he had endured a lot of teasing about him and Kate, and he tried to ignore it. If he had a dime for all the times he had heard that stupid rhyme about them sitting in a tree and kissing, he would be rich. Kate on the other hand, always reacted and stated emphatically that she would never have a boyfriend. He thought about it as he walked along, draping one hand over the hammer in his back pocket. Truth was, he really wouldn't mind kissing Kate. Problem was, she might punch his lights out if he tried. Corvan smiled. Maybe someday he would give it a try anyway.

Back at home, Corvan stopped at the outhouse and then washed up on the porch, humming a tune he'd heard on the radio. The blue on his hands reminded him of his pants, and he peeled them off and dropped them into the tub of the washing machine. A pair of patched coveralls lay draped over the old stuffed chair. He pulled them on and stepped into the kitchen.

Mother turned to look at him. "Those fit you pretty well considering they belonged to your grandfather."

Corvan ran his hands over the faded cotton. "He was as short as me?"

"Shorter." She laughed. "Looks like you're expecting a flood."

He looked down. The pant legs rode high over his ankles.

A glass of water and a piece of bread waited at the table. He sat down. "You never told me how my grandfather died."

Mother dried her hands. "We don't really know for sure. He left without saying a word to anyone."

"So maybe he's still alive?"

"I don't think so. There's nothing in this world that could keep him from you. You're what he lived for. I never could figure out why he left the day before your first birthday. He was so looking forward to it."

As she turned to the stack of pots and pans by the sink, Corvan grabbed the slice of bread and slipped from the room.

Within seconds, he was sitting on his bed, unfolding the newspaper from around his grandfather's letter. Grandfather left the day before his first birthday. That would have been September 20, 1938. The same day as the newspaper clipping.

He scanned the front of the paper. There was a long article about terrible storm in Asia. The other side was all car advertisements except for one short article.

New Evidence Comes to Light

Representatives from the Industrial Power Company confirmed today that last Saturday's explosion, which resulted in the deaths of three miners, may have been intentional. The explosion took place during the boring of an experimental shaft.

At first the mine operators claimed that the machinery overheated, igniting dust raised by the drilling. Investigators now report that footprints were discovered around the test bore. They claim someone was trying to tamper with the evidence, although it is unclear how anyone could have reached the site before the shaft was cleared.

One member of the investigation team, who has asked not to be identified, says he saw a person retreating down the borehole. This claim has been rejected by the mine officials as there are no other levels below the test site.

The matter is now in the hands of the police who will be checking all leads on persons who may have had reason to stop the test bore.

The Hammer

Corvan recalled his father talking about the disaster of '37. Just days after the shaft was cleared, another massive explosion had collapsed the main shaft and forced the closure of the mine. IPC went bankrupt, leaving only the small Red Creek mine still in operation.

The thump of his mother's broomstick interrupted his thoughts. Stuffing the letter under his mattress, he returned to the kitchen, his mind whirling.

"Where did you disappear to? You need to run to the Barrons' and get some baking soda. Make sure you let Mrs. Barron know that your father was called back to work, and we'll pay our bill soon."

The Barrons owned the local gas station, and although it was long past closing time, they were always available to open the store and get something a neighbor needed. Corvan liked going to the store. Mrs. Barron often gave him a chocolate bar or licorice cigar that the mice had nibbled on. "Can't go selling that to my customers, can I?" she would say as she cut off the nibbled corner and handed him the treat.

Corvan wondered how one store could have so many mice. Given her size, it might have been that Mrs. Barron had been doing some of the nibbling herself.

It was a great evening for a trip to the store. The sun had disappeared over the horizon, painting the sky orange-pink above the low hills to the west. Corvan whistled as he walked down the center of the road. A few birds called in response. It was great to know that he and Kate were friends again. Things had finally started to look up for him.

By the time Corvan returned home, the taste of chocolate still lingering in his mouth, his father was sitting at the supper table. While they ate, Mother tried chatting about her day but Father didn't respond. Normally on a Saturday night, they'd sit at the table after supper and play games, but Mother said it was getting late so she'd do the dishes and let the men get washed up for bed.

Corvan went out to the washstand on the back porch. Looking back through the screen, he saw his father staring at his half-eaten supper.

"We've managed through hard times before," his mother said, "and we can make it again. If he's old enough for what your father suggested, he's old enough to understand that we'll have to celebrate his birthday another time." Corvan plunged his hands into the cool water. What were they talking about?

His father's voice responded in tones too low to catch. Then he left the table and vanished into the bedroom. Corvan washed up and returned to the kitchen, where his mother was scraping the plates.

"Maybe it's time we got a dog to eat the scraps," Corvan said as he finished wiping his hands on his shirt.

Mother shook the spatula at him. "This is not the time to get a dog. And how many times do I have to tell you to dry your hands on a towel? What good does it do to scrub your hands and then wipe them on a dirty shirt?"

"But this one's clean."

"It's not clean now that you've wiped your dirty hands on it, is it?"

Corvan realized this would be one of those circular arguments he could never win. "I'd better head to bed. Good night." He leaned forward to kiss his mother's cheek, but she pulled him close and gave him a tight hug. When she released him, he turned for the stairs.

"Now, don't stay up all night reading. If I see a light under your door after ten o'clock, I'm going to take your bulb away for a week."

Corvan smiled. She couldn't put a book down herself, often reading until all hours of the night.

Back in his room, Corvan undressed and settled into bed. He wanted to get the rope out of the chest, but he couldn't take the chance of being discovered. He would wait until he was sure his mother was in bed.

He lay back and stared at the cracks in the plaster above his bed. Over the years, he'd developed an entire constellation in the pattern of the cracks, and now he methodically rehearsed them in his mind.

Outside, the crickets were tuning up for their nighttime symphony. The screen door banged as his mother went out on the back porch to set their ancient wringer washer into action. Soon its rhythmic swish and bump drowned out the crickets. Corvan closed his eyes and let his breathing fall into sync with the familiar sound.

The dream returned, but this time he was the one pursuing someone through the damp tunnels. He would almost catch up to him but the person would disappear and call out to him. "Who? Who are you?" It sounded like Kate's voice.

Corvan awoke to the repetitive hooting of an owl on the maple tree outside his window. "Whoo-oo," he called back. It swept out across the yard on its nightly hunt.

A gentle breeze wafted the scent of rich earth and moist wheat into his room. The house was silent. This would be a good time to check out the rope. He picked his pants up off the floor and tiptoed to the chest. Kneeling down he searched through the pockets.

The hammer was gone.

The Hammer

CHAPTER EIGHT

Corvan felt frantically through the dirty clothes he had kicked under his bed. The hammer was not there. Where could it be? He was sure he had put it back in his pocket at Kate's house.

It came back in a flash. The hammer was in his dirty pants when he changed his clothes, and Mother was doing the wash when he fell asleep. If she'd tried to put the pants through the wringer, the hammer would make a real mess of things. Two years ago, he'd left some marbles in his pockets, jamming the rollers and ruining the gears.

His only hope was that Mother had gone to bed without wringing out the wash. Glancing out the window, he saw his pants swaying gently on the line. "Oh great," he muttered.

He made his way silently down the stairs but forgot about the third step and put his foot right in the middle. The stair let out its customary low groan. Corvan waited until his mother's snoring resumed, then crept silently out to the back porch.

The wringer washer grinned at him from its corner. It always reminded him of a robot from a science-fiction story, with its wringer head hanging over its squat body and the rollers looking like two rows of yellowed teeth in an oversized mouth. He inspected the rollers. Everything looked fine. Either his mother had found the hammer, or it was still down in the rinse water she always saved for her garden.

Rolling up his sleeve, he plunged his hand into the dingy water. He felt around the groove at the bottom of the round tub but only came up with a coin. The half dollar from the chest. Dropping it into his pocket, he looked through the screen door into the kitchen. If Mother had found the hammer, she would most likely have put it into the secret hiding place where she kept the family cash.

Holding the screen door down to avoid any squeaks, he went to the pantry and pressed on a knot in the wall. A small door popped open to reveal a shallow alcove. Grandfather had built the hiding spot for his mother, but Corvan found it one day while searching for the chocolate chips. This time it contained nothing: no chocolate, no cash, and no hammer. Corvan clicked the door shut. Where could she have put it? Unless . . . maybe it had slipped out of his pocket when he used the outhouse. He retreated through the kitchen and out to the backyard.

The path felt warm to his feet. The dust was coming back after the rain, and the moonlight illuminated his footprints from earlier that afternoon.

The wooden latch on the outhouse had been left open, the rough plank door hanging ajar on its leather hinges. Corvan pulled the door wide. The familiar rank odor wafted out as he crouched to search around the wooden platform and behind the stack of old newspapers. The hammer wasn't there. Puzzled, he pushed the door closed and latched it.

As Corvan retraced his steps, he glanced up the path that led to the rock. A set of tracks were outlined by the moonlight. He bent low. His father had trained him to track most animals known on the prairie, but this was something new. The mark in the center must be from a tail, but the tail was dragging in the front—the paw prints overlaid it. How could that be? Maybe the animal had killed something and was dragging it away. But there was no blood.

Corvan followed the tracks out to where they vanished on the rock. High overhead he heard pebbles rolling and clinking together. Crouching low, he climbed on all fours toward the crown of broken rock.

At first, Corvan saw only black shadows inside the castle. He heard something, though—rocks pushed around and the grunts and puffs of a small creature. Peering through the gap, Corvan caught sight of a shadowy figure near the solitary rock in the center.

Dirt and pebbles sprayed out as the animal dug a hole at the base of the lone boulder. The creature stood on its hind feet. The lizard!

Corvan watched in fascination as the reptile picked up two strips of cloth and wrapped them carefully around its front claws. In the soft light, it looked as if it were wearing mittens. Corvan stared, transfixed by this bizarre sight.

It stooped to drag something back toward the place where it was digging. The hole seemed too small for the large creature but as it stepped back its body appeared to flow into the gap, until only its cloth wrapped claws remained outside holding a dark object.

It was the hammer.

The claws suddendly disappeared into the hole leaving the hammer standing upright for a moment before it toppled to the ground.

Corvan couldn't let the reptile take his hammer into its den. He sprang forward and reached for it just as an explosion of dirt flew from the hole into his eyes. Blinded, he sat back, shaking his head. Dirt peppered his body and then stopped.

A guttural screech snapped his head up as a dark blur hit him squarely in the chest, knocking him onto his back. The lizard pounced on top of him, raking its cloth-bound claws across his face. It screeched in frustration. Corvan screamed back and knocked the creature off his chest and across the ring.

Rolling onto his knees, he tensed for another attack. The lizard was unwinding the cloth, its keen eyes burning with hatred. Corvan felt around on the ground for a weapon, but there were no rocks or sticks within reach.

The lizard leaped toward him, landing with its front claws outstretched, straddling the hammer.

The creature's eyes narrowed and it hissed at him, but it didn't move. Of course. For some reason it couldn't touch the hammer with bare claws. If Corvan could take the hammer away, he might be able to use it to keep the creature at bay.

Its lean body inched forward, staying between Corvan and the hammer. Claws scraped on the muddy tarp that had ripped off his fort. Corvan glanced down. If he could yank the tarp out from under its feet, he'd have a chance to grab the hammer.

The lizard hissed at him, pulling its thin lips back in a wicked grin and exposing its pointed teeth.

Corvan inched his hand toward the loose end of the large canvas sheet. The lizard's eyes darted down. Corvan yanked as hard as he could, pulling the lizard's feet from under it and tumbling it back past the hammer. In one motion, Corvan jumped forward, threw the dirty canvas over the creature, and scooped up the hammer. He retreated as a flurry of claws tore the old canvas to shreds.

The lizard emerged with eyes blazing. It took two quick steps toward him, but when it saw the hammer in his hand, it stopped.

Glaring through narrow slits, it snarled in a low, raspy voice, "You will never be the Cor-van. You could not survive the wrath of my master."

Corvan blinked. It could talk? Fear rose in his throat but he managed to choke it back and croak out, "Go away."

The lizard fell back as if it had been kicked, its eyes wide in fear. Corvan held the hammer higher and took a step forward.

The creature retreated, eyes flickering from one side to the other. Hissing, it gave him one last glance, then melted into the dark hole.

Corvan grabbed the biggest rock he could lift with one hand from the fire pit circle and dropped it over the hole. He stuffed the hammer into his pocket and piled on rocks until he couldn't lift any more. His sides heaved. He fell to his knees and retched. Shaking uncontrollably, he stumbled across the circle and collapsed against the rocks. Never in his life had he been so afraid. People like Bill Fry were mean, but this thing was so. . . evil. Who was its master? Was that why it wore a collar? Corvan shook his head. This couldn't be happening. How could an animal talk?

He pulled out the hammer. All these weird things had started since he found it. As he held it, he sensed a growing awareness of great danger. He was about to drop it when he sensed something else. The sensation of evil was greater than he could ever have imagined, but holding it back was something much more powerful, a force that flowed around and through him. The hammer was actually holding the evil at bay.

A shadow flickered past his feet.

Corvan ran for the gap in the castle wall. An owl swept overhead on silent wings, hunting for prey. He let out a long breath. Then the thought crossed his mind that gophers always had a second entrance to their holes. The lizard could be watching him even now. Or maybe it had gone to bring back more of its kind.

A cold sweat broke out on his forehead as he scanned the circle of rocks. The shadows around them could easily conceal the vicious creature. He backed out of the circle and bolted for home. As he ran, he felt certain he heard an entire pack of lizards bearing down on him from behind. With a final burst of speed, he reached the safety of the porch and turned to look back. The owl hooted, but everything was still. The pressure in his chest slowly eased.

Since the lizard had retrieved the hammer from the outhouse, it must know where he lived. If it came back with reinforcements, the only thing that could save his family would be the hammer.

Corvan looked out the porch door at the dark rock. It didn't make sense. Animals couldn't talk. And what about the cloth wrapped around its claws? Thankfully that wasn't a dream. He put his hand to his face. It felt sore, but at least there were no bloody scratches.

"I'm afraid," he whispered. It was a relief to admit it. It was all right to be afraid. Who wouldn't fear something like that?

He considered waking his parents to tell them what had happened, but quickly dismissed the thought. He had no scratches on him and, as his teacher pointed out, no one would believe a lizard like that lived in these parts. Maybe it had escaped from the city zoo. That would explain why it had a master. But the lizard was the one that said it had a master and animals couldn't talk. This was all too crazy.

Corvan moved into the shadows of the porch and sank into the moth-eaten armchair. Tonight he must keep guard over the house. Taking the hammer firmly in his right hand, he stretched his arm out on the armrest, like a king with his scepter on a royal throne. The hammer gave him a sense of authority, and he envisioned himself holding an entire legion of lizards at bay. He closed his eyes to rest for a moment.

A rooster crowed, and Corvan opened his eyes. The sun was just coming up, caressing the tops of the aspen trees. The long night was past and every muscle in his body ached. He hoped his Mother would let him sleep in. He crept up to his room and hid the hammer under his pillow. As he undressed, the blackened half dollar fell out of his pocket and rolled under the bed. Too tired to chase it, Corvan crawled under the sheets and fell asleep.

When he awoke, the sun was directly above the house. That was odd. His parents never let him sleep in this late. He listened to the buzz of flies at his window, but below him, the house remained silent.

"Mom," he called out, "what's for breakfast?" There was no answer. Worry crept into his soul and exploded into full panic. Had the lizard attacked while he slept? He slipped from his bed, pulled on his pants, and crept down the stairs, hammer held out before him.

The bed in his parents' room was not made, and a few of the dresser drawers hung askew. Corvan checked out front. The truck was gone. They never left him at home on a Sunday. He went to the kitchen and looked for a note. Nothing. Wandering back into the living room, he heard Kate call from the back door. He crossed his arms over his bony chest. He hated being seen without a shirt on.

They met in the kitchen, and she shook her head in disgust. "Are you just getting up? Must be nice to sleep in half the day. Mom had me up at six to take the pies out to the station wagon." She placed her hands on her hips. "You should get a shirt on." She nodded to the laundry basket by the back door.

"Have you seen my parents this morning?"

"They drove past our place early this morning." She looked out the window. "So what are you doing today?"

"Nothing," Corvan said, relieved that his parents were okay. He wanted to look at the stuff in the chest, but not with Kate around. He grabbed a T-shirt from the laundry basket and pulled it on.

"I went out to the rock," she said. "What a mess! The fort's gone, and there's a big pile of rocks there."

"The storm flattened the fort. And I piled the rocks. I was making a . . .
monument. Like a pyramid."

Kate scowled. "When are you going to start telling people the truth instead
of making up silly stories? If you don't want to say what you were doing just say,
'Kate, I don't want to talk about it.'"

He hated to admit it, but Kate was right. He did need to be more truthful. "Its
not that I don't want to tell you. Its just that I don't think people will believe me if
I tell the truth this time. This sounds crazier than any story I ever made up. I'm not
sure I even believe it."

"Try me," Kate replied, sitting on the kitchen table.

His grandfather had told him to trust no one. But this was *Kate*. Besides, she'd
already seen the hammer.

"It's all connected to this." Corvan pulled the hammer from his back pocket
and placed it on the table.

Kate stared at it as if she were seeing it for the first time. She touched it with
one finger, then pulled her hand away. "You never did tell me where it came from."

"I thought my grandfather made it for me, but now I'm not sure. Last night the
hammer was stolen."

Kate hopped off the table. "Bill Fry took it?"

"No, it wasn't Bill. It was . . ."

"Who?"

"Aw, forget it. I get enough mocking from the kids at school." He went around
her, out the screen door, and slouched on the porch steps.

She followed him. "You're talking about that lizard again, aren't you?"

Corvan checked to see if she was teasing him, but her face looked serious.

"I'm sorry if I made fun of you about that story. It just seemed, well, far-
fetched, and no one but you has ever seen it." She shrugged. "But I guess not
seeing something doesn't mean you should doubt someone who says he has."

Corvan stared at the rock. He had definitely seen it. His stomach churned at
the memory.

"So why would a lizard need a hammer?"

Corvan dropped his gaze to the ground.

"Come on, I said I was sorry."

"All right, I'll tell you what happened. But if you start to laugh, I'm not telling
you any more."

"If the story gets funny, it's not my fault if I laugh."

"It's not that kind of story. Just do me a favor and let me get to the end before
you ask questions." Kate nodded, and Corvan told her about the lizard stealing the

hammer and his battle to get it back.

Kate listened intently, but as the story progressed, her frown deepened. When he got to the part where the lizard spoke, she interrupted. "Wait a minute. I could imagine a wild animal trying to bury your hammer, thinking it was a bone or something. But everyone knows animals don't talk. That's just crazy."

Corvan jumped to his feet. "You're right. I am crazy. Crazy for thinking I could share this story with someone like you." He stomped off.

"What do you mean, like me?" Kate hollered after him. "You think you're better than me?"

Corvan rounded the corner of the house and broke into a run. He knew she wouldn't believe him. He should never have told her. He bounded up the front stairs, eased the door shut behind him and peeked out the living-room window. Kate hadn't followed. Hopefully she'd gone home. Now he'd finally have a chance to look through the chest in peace.

He climbed the stairs to his room and unlocked the chest's secret panel. Draping the soft cloth over the footboard of his bed, he looked over the various items, but his attention kept returning to the pale green rope. Undoing its clips, he plucked it from its shallow depression and tried to shake it out. One end was squashed flat and wrapped securely around the coils, keeping them fastened in tight loops. Corvan tugged at the flaps, but they wouldn't budge. He pulled as hard as he could on the free end, but the rope only stretched a little.

A low whistle escaped his lips. How could something this light be so strong? It wasn't even woven like regular rope; it was all one thin strand although the free end was a bit thicker, like a short handle. On the tip of the handle was a round button, like an eyeball with a black knobby pupil staring from the center. Corvan pressed on the dark bump, and the flat flaps opened and released the coils.

Letting the soft rope play through his hands, he picked up the flat end that had been wrapped around the coils. It was a wide disk, like the head of a cobra. He held it flat in the palm of his left hand and then pressed his thumb against the dark eye on the end of the handle with his other hand.

An intense prickling sensation snapped his left hand closed around the flat disk. Corvan tried to open his fist, but he couldn't. It was as if the green disk had been coated in glue. He tried harder but the prickling increased, and his fingers shifted about of their own accord. His hand was hurting. He dropped the eyeball end. It bounced off the open chest and his left hand sprang free, spilling the disk to the floor.

Red dots of blood rose to the surface of his palm, as if many tiny needles had punctured his skin. Corvan gingerly picked up the disk, set it on the bed, and picked up the eyeball end. His thumb touched the black knob, and the flat disk twitched like something alive and burrowed into his blanket. He leaned forward to examine it. A thousand miniscule fingers stuck out from the disk, grasping and bunching up the cloth. He flicked the black button again and they vanished.

Corvan turned the disk over and pressed the button. The tiny tentacles extended, waving and seeking something to grasp. The rope grew thicker and recoiled on itself like an angry snake, pulling toward his arm. Corvan let out a yelp and dropped it to the floor, where it spread out on the wooden planks.

He pulled on the free end but the flat disk didn't budge. He pulled harder. The floorboards flexed and creaked. Working the small button, Corvan released the disk from the floor and picked it up. Activating the fingers, he tossed the flat disk at the wall. It stuck. Small flakes of paint fell as the tentacles found the tiniest cracks.

Corvan examined the black knob, pushing it to one side. Slow movement in front of him caught his eye. The disk crawled like a round centipede across the wall. He released the sideways pressure and it stopped.

Sitting on his bed, Corvan discovered he could control not only the direction but also the speed of the disk end of the rope. The farther over he bent the knob, the faster it moved.

He directed the flat head up to where the ceiling met the wall. It made the transition smoothly and slipped across his ceiling, dislodged plaster raining onto the bed around him. He laughed as he sent it in circles around his light socket. When it dropped and landed on his legs, he shouted, jumped against his headboard, and laughed again. He must have released the button by mistake.

He picked up the disk. How would it work on something really smooth? Walking over to the window, he held it up to the glass on the upper section and activated the button. The disk spread out flatter, looking like a translucent green leech feeding on the flyspecks. As he worked the controls, it moved slowly across the smooth surface.

He heard a scream from outside.

Outt the window he caught a glimpse of someone swinging a stick madly about in the castle circle. The person screamed again and disappeared from sight.

He knew that voice. Kate was being attacked by the lizard!

CHAPTER NINE

Blood pounded in his ears as Corvan scrambled into the castle. Kate sat in the dirt. The thick body of a large garter snake stretched out toward her, a long stick from the ruined fort next to its crushed head. Relief flowed over Corvan as he knelt beside her.

"Are you okay?"

"You know I hate snakes."

Corvan grabbed the smashed snake by the tail and carried it over to the edge of the castle rocks. It was a real beauty, one of the largest he'd ever seen. Too bad it was dead; it would have made a fascinating pet. He threw its long body into the field down below. Some coyote would make a nice meal out of it.

He turned back to find Kate on her feet, brushing off her jeans. "It tried to bite me."

"I thought the lizard was after you," Corvan answered, then instantly wished he hadn't mentioned it again.

Kate nodded. "I was going to prove that you imagined it all, that the lizard was just in your mind, but . . ." She pointed to where his pile of rocks had been. They were moved to one side, clearing the spot where the lizard had disappeared. The dark hole beside the central boulder gaped at him.

Corvan's heart jumped. Remembering the lizard's reaction to the hammer, he pulled it from his pocket. "Did the snake come out of there?" he asked, not taking his eyes off the hole.

"No. It was behind the big rock. I was trying to move it so I could see the rest."

"The rest of what?"

"The door."

"Door?"

THE HAMMER

"If you look near the hole, you'll see a row of big rocks jammed into a crack in the ground. They are holding the two slabs of the door apart. That hole is where the dirt has been washed away."

"Did you see the lizard?"

"No. You said it only comes out at night."

"I don't know that for sure." Corvan moved in closer.

"Look where the crack runs under the boulder." Kate pointed with a grubby hand. "I was digging the dirt away when the snake crawled out."

Corvan slipped past the open hole and crouched by the large rock. Kate had scraped away the dirt that had gathered around it and he could make out two parallel lines about ten inches apart. Between them were the bumpy outlines of rocks held in place by sticks and mud. The two lines vanished under the large rock.

"It's just a big crack that the rain has washed stuff into," Corvan said, glancing up at Kate, who stood beside him.

"That's what I thought too. But look on the other side."

Corvan peered over the large rock. The lines continued a short distance, then each bent out at precisely ninety degrees. Someone had cut those lines into the rock.

"It must be something the Indian tribe carved here. Like the rock paintings in the caves by the river valley. My father says this was a sacred place to them."

Kate knelt beside him. "You could be right. I found some symbols carved in the door." She brushed away the dirt at the base of the boulder. "But we need to move this rock to see the rest."

Corvan bent down and inspected the cleared area. The strange marks cut deeply into the rocky floor.

He pushed with all his might against the boulder. It rocked slightly, but he couldn't get it to roll away. "We need a pry bar." He scratched his head. "My father has some long pipes on a rack in the cellar."

As they climbed down the rock, Kate spoke. "I saw some strange tracks when I was moving the dirt. Something must live down that hole."

"Three toes with claws?"

"Yes. Are they from that lizard?"

Corvan nodded.

"It must be big."

"It might not be three feet tall, but that's almost up to your waist when it's next to you."

"I don't want to see it that close." Kate looked back at the rock. "What happened after it . . . talked to you?"

"I told it to go away and held the hammer up in front of me. It's really scared of the hammer. It won't even touch it, so I think we are safe as long as we have the hammer with us."

Approaching the house, Corvan heard gravel crunching in the driveway. "Sounds like my parents are home. Do you think we should show my father the cracks in the rock?"

"It wouldn't hurt. He knows a lot about the history of this place."

Corvan touched Kate's shoulder. "But the hammer has to be our secret."

Kate rolled her eyes. "I'm not a moron."

They met Corvan's mother at the corner of the house. Quickly she wiped the tears from her eyes.

"What's wrong mom? Were's Dad?"

"Let's go inside the house. I need to sit down."

They followed her in, and Mother sat at the kitchen table. "Katie, can you put the kettle on for tea?"

Kate brought the teapot and cups over to the table while Corvan went to the pantry for a tea bag. "Mother," he said as he came back into the kitchen, "this is the last tea bag."

Mother nodded. "Put it back then. We may need it for company. Kate, please bring me a cup of cold water."

Kate poured the water and joined them at the table.

Mother took a sip. "I took your father to the Fenwood bus depot this morning. We got a call early this morning from Fred Simpson. He arranged for your dad to start a job up north at the Langdon mine, but he had to be on the bus right away." She stared into her cup for a moment. "It's a long way from here, and we won't see him for a least a month, but we need the money if we're going to make it through the winter."

Corvan frowned. "Why can't he keep working at the Red Creek mine?"

"The meeting was just to tell the miners they are shutting the mine down. They breached a major underground river and the lower shafts are filling up with water. Now the owners are telling the men the ground is too unstable around here and they have lost too much money. They're going to blow the entry later this month and close the mine for good."

"But harvest is in a few weeks. We can't do that without Dad."

"Fred promised your father he'd take care of our field this year if the Langdon mine won't give him time off." She hung her head and wiped another tear from her eyes. "That rocky field isn't a very good piece of land anyway. We should sell it and be done with it."

Kate slid her chair away from the table and quietly made her way toward the door.

T The Hammer

THE HAMMER

"You don't have to leave, dear. Fred gave us fresh chicken for supper. You're welcome to join us."

"That would be great. Thanks."

Corvan's mother stood. "You two go ahead and enjoy the outdoors while we still have some nice weather."

Corvan rose to his feet. His life was turning upside down.

His mother gave him a hug. "Don't worry. Things will work out. We'll miss your father but we're fortunate that he found work so quickly."

"I know," he said as he followed Kate to the door.

"Supper will be done in about an hour. I'll ring the bell when it's ready."

Kate sat on the porch steps. Corvan jumped past her. "Wait here a minute. I'll grab a pipe." He headed around the house to the steep ramp that ran down to their cellar. It would take a pretty strong pipe to move that heavy rock, but he was sure his dad would have something down there. The cellar was his workshop, where he tinkered on a variety of projects related to mining and metalwork.

The two large doors at the base of the ramp were shut tight. When they were open, his father could back their truck down the ramp right into the cellar.

Corvan descended the stone ramp and pushed one door open. A shaft of light shot through the dusty air to the pipe racks on the far wall. He took a step inside and then remembered he was not supposed to go into the workshop until after his birthday. But if he went straight ahead to the far wall and grabbed a pipe without looking around, surely his dad wouldn't mind. He wouldn't even turn on the light. Besides, with his dad gone they wouldn't be celebrating his birthday for a long time. He swallowed the lump in his throat and moved forward.

He walked between the slender columns that supported the ceiling. The arches between them always reminded him of a cathedral he had seen in a travel magazine. When his grandfather had built their home, he had cut the stone blocks for the walls right out from under the house. He had even cut the workbench from the bedrock, complete with storage spaces and tool racks. This was where his father spent most of his time since losing his job last year.

He kept his eyes forward and forced himself to walk straight ahead and pull a long, heavy pipe from the rack.

He intentionally turned away from the workbench to avoid seeing what his father might be working on. Instead, he saw a door.

Ever since he could remember, the north wall of the cellar had been covered with a set of tall wooden shelves. Now the center section had been pulled away, revealing a metal door. It was at least four feet wide and reached almost to the ceiling. Was this something new or had it always been behind the shelves?

He stepped forward to check it out, and the end of his pipe banged on the door. He jumped back. It sounded hollow behind there, like the door hid a room as big as the entire house. He could hear the echo a long way inside.

Why would his father create such a large storage place down here when Grandfather had cut so many bins and cupboards into the stone? Three sturdy metal bolts locked it from this side. What could his father be locking in . . . or out?

"Did you find one?" Kate's voice floated down from above.

Corvan gave the door one last glance and climbed up the ramp. After dropping the pipe into the grass, he ran back down and eased the cellar door closed. "Don't let my mother know I was down there."

"Why not?"

"My dad said I was supposed to stay out of there until after my birthday."

She frowned. "Then you shouldn't have gone in."

"I forgot."

Kate shook her head. "You sure are good at making up excuses."

Corvan grunted and picked up the pipe. Why did the truth hit so hard the last few days?

By the time they reached the top of the hill, shadows from the rocks almost covered the circle. The dark hole next to the central boulder stared back at him. It would probably be a good idea to block it up, but he was anxious to see what was under the boulder. Wedging the pipe under it, he leaned on the end, and the rock began to tip over. Kate stepped in beside him and added her weight. The rock slowly lifted, then suddenly rolled away, dumping them onto the ground. Kate scrambled to where the rock had been sitting and swept away the dirt.

"I see a couple more figures carved here. Hey, if this is a door, then this must be the keyhole."

Corvan crawled up beside her and stared in amazement. The shallow hole had two circles around it.

"It has to be a door. Listen to this." Kate picked up a rock to tap the insignia. A dull *boom* sounded. "It's hollow underneath."

As the echo died away, Corvan heard the rustling of scales as a shadow flitted across the hole beneath them.

THE HAMMER

CHAPTER TEN

Corvan grabbed Kate's arm and yanked her away from the hole. Eyes wide, she dropped her rock and moved back with him to crouch by the boulders.

"Was that the lizard?" she whispered.

Corvan nodded. "I need to block that hole again." Pulling the hammer from his pocket, he crept forward.

"Be careful."

Corvan chose a good-sized boulder and pulled it to his chest with one hand. It slipped free, and he jumped back to save his toes from being crushed.

"I'll help." Kate bent to the rock, but Corvan stopped her.

"Here." He held out the hammer. "If the lizard comes out, hold this toward it and tell it to go away."

Kate hesitated, then took the hammer from his hand. Corvan bent, heaved the rock to his chest, and stepped toward the gaping hole.

All was quiet. He took another step forward and held the rock out as far as he could over the hole. A claw appeared. Kate screamed. Startled, Corvan lost his grip, and the rock dropped. He heard a screech of pain as it bounced and rolled away. From down below there was a scrabbling of claws, and then silence. He had to find something else to block the entrance to the lizard's den. Fast.

Corvan looked around and spotted a wide board from the fort. If he could cover the hole with the board, he could stand on it while Kate found rocks to pile on top. Keeping his eyes on the hole, he bent over and picked up the heavy plank. It was unbalanced, and dipped down toward the hole. Corvan fell to his knees to stop its descent, but it kept falling and rapped sharply on the door.

The lizard sprang from the hole and sank one of its long claws deep into the wood. It glared at him, its mouth flecked with foam, and muttered something. Corvan couldn't understand the words, but a gasp from Kate told him that she had heard the creature.

It took a step forward, locking its fiery eyes on Corvan. One foreleg and claw extended toward him, the other hung at its side, blood dripping from the end of a claw.

A bell broke the silence. Mother called them in for supper.

The lizard turned toward the house and its eyes fell on Kate. Its eyes narrowed and it took a step toward her. Her hand shaking, Kate lifted the hammer toward it. "Go, go away. Leave us alone."

The lizard's eyes bulged, and it collapsed as if she'd shot it. Covering its head with its good claw, it whined and writhed on the ground, its wounded claw dragging about in the dust. Kate moved toward the creature.

"Stay away Kate. It's a trap!"

Kate kept her eyes focused as she advanced on the injured creature. The lizard stopped moving. Corvan had seen animals feign death and then attack. Kate needed to back away. Instead the lizard stretched out prone before the advancing girl. Kate stood over it and raised the hammer high above her head. The creature lay perfectly still, as if waiting for the fatal blow. Corvan watched in horrified silence as Kate brought the hammer down and then gently touched the lizard on the back of its neck. With a low metallic groan, the black collar around its neck quivered, then fell to the ground.

The lizard pushed itself off the ground, bowed its head to Kate, and spoke a few soft words. As it backed away, she bent to examine the black band. The lizard shook its head and rattled off a string of clicks and hisses. Kate sank to her knees and stared at the object in the sand. As she picked it up, the lizard stepped toward Corvan, hissing and gesturing toward Kate with its healthy claw. What was it saying?

Kate glared at the lizard and thumped the hammer on the ground. The rock shivered beneath them. "Be quiet. I told you to go away."

The lizard glanced at Corvan with a helpless expression on its narrow face.

"Now," Kate barked.

The lizard scurried away and retreated down the hole.

Kate picked up the lizard's black band and stood with it draped limply over her palm like a small black snake. She looked back to the hammer as if weighing both objects in her hands.

The dinner bell rang again. "We've got to go," Corvan croaked. "I'll put a rock over the hole."

"You don't need to," Kate stated. "It won't come back now that I'm holding the hammer."

Corvan stepped toward her. "Let me see its collar."

"There's no time." Kate stuffed the black band into the front pocket of her jeans. Hammer in hand, she strode down the western trail.

He ran to catch up to her. "Kate, the hammer."

"What about it?" She shoved the hammer into her back pocket and sped up, slipping and skidding down the incline.

"I need it back." Stretching his hand out, he raced after her and grabbed at the back of her shirt, but she was too fast; the fabric slipped from his fingers.

As soon as she reached level ground, she broke into a run and hollered, "Race ya," over her shoulder.

Corvan didn't even try. Kate always beat him in a foot race.

She was washed up and inside the house before he even got to the porch. His mother came out to pour the potato water into the washing machine and looked at him out of the corner of her eye. "Aren't you two getting a little old to be playing together on the rock?"

His face and neck hot and prickling, Corvan concentrated on his soapy hands. "We were cleaning up the mess from when the old fort blew down. Didn't want that tarp blowing out into the field."

Corvan's heart dropped. He'd done it again. Another lie.

Kate met them at the door. "I didn't realize it was so late. My mom will be home in half an hour, and I haven't finished the dishes. She'll be furious. I've got to run." She started to move past them, but Corvan's mother put out her hand.

"Wait," Mother said. "I want you to take your mother some of the chicken dinner." She hurried into the kitchen and dished hot food into a tin pie plate.

Corvan tried to catch Kate's eye, but she just stared at the floor. There was no way he would let her leave without giving the hammer back and letting him get a good look at that band.

Mother wrapped the plate in a tea towel.

"I'll carry it for her." Corvan took the dish from his mother's hands.

"Then come right back. I'll wait for you."

Corvan slipped out the door. Kate followed.

As soon as they were out of earshot, he turned to her. "So what happened with the lizard?"

"It was frightened," Kate responded abruptly. "Couldn't you see that?"

"But what did it say? You did hear it talk, right?"

Kate paused, as if thinking back a long way. "It said it could not stand against me. That I had the power to destroy everything."

"What did it say when you touched it?"

"It begged me to let it live. It said I was the only one who could set it free from the band. All I needed to do was touch it with . . ." She swallowed hard.

"Let me see that black band."

"Not now. I'm tired and I need to get home."

"It'll just take a second." He stepped around her and blocked her way.

She snatched the plate from his hands. "I said I'm tired. And I'm not a child who needs to be walked home in the dark. I can take care of myself." She pushed past him into the shadows, leaving Corvan alone in the street.

He turned for home. Girls could be so strange. One minute she was his best friend and the next she was chewing his head off. Maybe he should just leave her alone for a few days. The last thing he wanted was for Kate to pull away from him again.

He let the screen door bang behind him as he slumped down at the table. Mother's eyebrows arched. She retrieved their supper from the oven and sat with him at the table. As they ate, she filled him in on the details of his father's new job. He was one of the fortunate ones. There were ten or more families affected by the mine closure, and very few of the men would be able to find a job. "It's going to be a difficult winter. We'll need to help as many people as we can."

Corvan barely caught what she was saying. His mind was still sorting out what had happened with Kate and the lizard. "Is Father going to sell our field?"

"You mean that rock of yours, don't you? He should have sold that thing to the mayor when he wanted to make it into a tourist attraction. Now with the new highway missing us by ten miles, the only tourists we see are the ones who get lost." Her lips pressed into a thin line.

They finished eating and washed the dishes together. Whenever Father was gone, Corvan figured it was his duty to keep his mother company. After the dishes, they played Scrabble until past eleven. He found it hard to concentrate, with thoughts of Kate and the lizard continually coming to mind. Finally Mother said they should get to bed, although she seemed pleased that for once she was winning the game.

Corvan returned the game to the pantry. As he turned for the stairs his mother looked up. "Did you see the note your father left you?"

Corvan looked blankly at her.

"He left it on your washstand when he went up to say good-bye. He didn't want to wake you."

Corvan ran up the stairs. Sure enough, a folded piece of paper with his name printed across the front was propped up against the water pitcher. Corvan almost ripped it in his haste to get it unfolded.

There was only a short note.

Corvan,

I'm sorry I have to leave without saying good-bye. I will come
home just as soon as I can.

The next four words were crossed out. Call me if anything. Below the scribbled
out words, he had written,

You will be a man by the time I get back. Use your judgment
and do what you know is right.

Take care of your mom while I am gone.

Love, Dad.

Corvan sat on the edge of his bed. He wasn't ready to be a man. And actually his
mom was a whole lot stronger than he was. Still it felt good that his dad trusted him
to look after things.

There was a knock at the front door, then an agitated female voice. It must be
one of the wives of the men at the mine.

As the voices moved into the living room, his mother called from the bottom of
the stairs. "Corvan, can you please come down here for a moment?"

He considered pretending to be asleep but decided he'd better help out since
Father was not around.

As he entered the living room, he stopped short and stared. Kate's mother sat
on the couch, her cheeks streaked with tears and mascara. Corvan had never seen
her look so sloppy. She took great pride in her looks and the fact that she once had a
small part in a movie.

Corvan's mother entered from the kitchen with her teapot and cups. She nodded
at the armchair, and he sat on the edge while his mother poured the tea.

"Mrs. Poley believes you might know where Kate has gone." She fired a glance
at him from beneath her eyebrows. "When you were walking her home, did she say
anything to you about going somewhere?"

Corvan's heart sank. "No."

"Did she say anything about me?" Mrs. Poley asked.

Corvan's jaw tightened. Every time he met Kate's mom it seemed the
conversation turned to her. "She said she was worried that you'd be mad about the
dishes not being done."

Mrs. Poley shook her head. "I was only a little annoyed with her." She turned to Corvan's mother. "I get so tired from working those long shifts, you know, and it's not easy to raise a child on your own." She paused and dabbed at her eyes. "She told me she had been busy too and had made me a chicken dinner. But as soon as I saw the plate, I knew she was lying because the towel matched the one on the bowl of pastry you sent over." She blinked her long lashes, but no more tears fell, in spite of her efforts. "Kate's never lied to me before, but before I could say anything, she ran to her room and slammed the door. I left her alone while I watched my TV." She paused, probably expecting them to be impressed that she owned one of the only TV sets in town. "When I checked on her, she was gone. Took the blanket from her bed and left." She finished the sentence with a grand flourish.

Corvan's mother patted her shoulder. "I'm sure Kate will come back soon. She just needs time to cool off."

"She had better do it quickly." Mrs. Poley pouted. "I'm tired of phone calls about her fighting and her bad attitude. I've always been there for her but now she keeps saying she is old enough to take care of herself." She stood up and looked out the living room window. "Dave wants me to move to Las Vegas with him. If Kate is so sure she can make it on her own, I have half a mind to just leave her here and go."

Watching her reaction, Corvan wondered if there even was half a mind under that dyed blond hair. This had happened more than once in the past and Kate had spent the night in the fort. Now where could she have gone?

Kate's mom turned around. "She even took my outhouse flashlight from beside the back door. She knows I hate going out there in the dark."

Corvan's mom gestured for him to leave, so he headed for the stairway. He wouldn't go to sleep though. As soon as Mrs. Poley left, he was going to slip out and see if he could find Kate.

Mrs. Poley called after him. "Corvan, do you know who gave Kate that lovely black bracelet?"

He stopped in his tracks.

"She was wearing a shiny bracelet, but she wouldn't let me look at it. You didn't give it to her, did you?" She studied his face intently, as if she would be able to read his mind.

Corvan shook his head.

"She said that even though I didn't want her, there was someone who did and I thought . . ." She cocked her head to one side. "Did she say anything about hearing from her father?"

Corvan stared blankly at Mrs. Poley and shook his head again, his mind racing. Why would Kate put that black band on? What had the lizard said to her?

Mrs. Poley crossed the room and knelt before him. "Corvan, I know I haven't been keen on you and Kate playing together. It's just that I know all too well what can come of a boy and a girl spending too much time together."

Corvan felt his face flush. He didn't know what to say. Mrs Poley took his hands in hers. "If she goes to find her father, her feelings will be hurt much worse than if you break her heart. Please don't let her go to him."

The way she said the words and tossed her hair made it look and sound like Mrs. Poley was acting in a movie. But the worry in her eyes looked real.

His mother pulled the woman back to the couch and turned to Corvan. "Run along to bed, Son. We'll sort this out in the morning."

Corvan looked into Mrs. Poley's face. In spite of the way she treated Kate, he truly felt sorry for her. "I'll find Kate and bring her home," he blurted out. "I promise."

She smiled at him, as he left the room to climb the stairs. That bracelet must be doing something strange to Kate. He should never have let her hold the hammer in the first place. He pulled his tennis shoes on and laced them up. As soon as he found Kate he was going to roll that boulder back over that hole and cover it up for good. He didn't really care if anyone else believed him now that Kate had held the hammer and had seen the mysterious lizard.

A chill raced up his spine. Kate still had the hammer!

The Hammer

CHAPTER ELEVEN

Corvan heard the front door close and his mother move back into the kitchen. The kettle scraped across the stove.

A beam of light from the rock played past his bedroom window. Corvan pressed his face against the screen. The shadows shifted as a light flickered on the rock and went out.

Kate! What was she doing out there?

Corvan lifted off the screen and slipped over the windowsill onto the porch roof. At the edge, he grabbed the overhanging branch of the maple tree, and within seconds he was on the ground. Crouching low, he skirted the back porch and cut around the trash pile. The light in the porch went out, plunging the backyard into darkness. Through the kitchen window, he saw his mother turning toward her room. He ran through the wheat field.

In one bound, he leaped onto the rock, stumbling as the stone beneath his feet shuddered and knocked him to his knees.

A scream pierced the night air and was abruptly cut off.

Corvan bolted up the rock into the circle in time to see the two huge stone doors slide back together. "Kate!" he hollered, sprinting forward.

The stones crashed into each other like the doors of a massive elevator. Splinters of shattered rock exploded into the air, raining down around him as Corvan fell to his knees and pounded on the cold granite. "Kate, open up. It's me, Corvan. Open the door!" He grabbed a stone and hammered on the door. The only answer was a hollow boom from below, but Kate was in there with that *thing*. He whirled and found a bigger rock, then bashed at the doors until the rock fell from his scraped and bleeding hands.

His strength spent, Corvan collapsed onto the door. His eyes focused on the thread of a crack that led to a piece of cloth caught in the corner. It was the edge of Kate's flannel blanket. Corvan tugged and it came loose, neatly snipped off by the doors.

Kate was gone. And without the hammer to open the door, there was no way he could get her back.

The clouds parted and moonlight poured into the rock circle, revealing footprints in the slender piles of dirt pushed up by the opening doors. Some were from Kate's shoes; the rest were made by the lizard. It must have been hiding behind the large rock, for he could see the deep prints where it had jumped out when the door opened. Then the tracks came back to the door. And there . . . the prints left in a hasty retreat, the tail dragging behind.

Corvan followed the tracks until they vanished on the hard surface of the rock. Heading down, he searched the soil around the base of the rock and found them leading toward the pile of firewood behind the outhouse. He had to find that lizard. It must know another way to get inside the rock.

A bank of clouds enveloped the moon, and the tracks vanished in the dark. Corvan looked up. There were only a few small breaks in the sky overhead. It was going to be a long, black night.

A small patch of moonlight from a hole in the cloud cover slipped past him toward the woodpile. As it slid over the jumbled logs, the silhouette of the lizard appeared at the top of the pile.

Easing himself down among the stalks of wheat, Corvan crouched onto the soft, warm soil. He needed a weapon of some kind. He couldn't face the lizard unarmed. It was far too quick and dangerous. He'd better go get his slingshot.

Crawling out of the wheat, Corvan crouched low and scurried up the path to the house. Leaving his bedroom light off, he retrieved the slingshot and his pouch of marbles from inside the chest. The slingshot had been a tenth birthday present from his dad, and it was a beauty. Corvan could hit the knot on the outhouse door from his bedroom window. He hit it once when his mother was inside, but she hadn't been impressed with his incredible aim.

Corvan looked out into the deep shadows. If he stayed downwind and came in from this side of the outhouse, he should be able to catch the lizard unaware. If he pulled back only part way the slingshot wouldn't kill the creature, but it should stun it long enough for him to capture it. He would need a long forked stick like he used for catching snakes.

Corvan crept downstairs and made his way out to the backyard. Out in the garden, the scarecrow stood at attention like a lone watchman, a broken pitchfork in its hand. That would work perfectly. It had only two points left.

Corvan pulled the pitchfork from the scarecrow's hand and jumped when its head flopped to one side. Leaving the scarecrow with its cockeyed stare, he crept across the yard and crouched behind the outhouse. Overhead there was an open patch in the clouds; the moon would be out any minute.

He moved deeper into the shelter of the trees and melted into the darkness around the weathered trunks. The plowed soil muffled his approach as he padded silently to his vantage point. Leaning against a tree, Corvan pulled three marbles from the pouch. Two went into his mouth and one into the slingshot. Pulling it halfway back, he steadied his aim and waited. As soon as the light came back, the creature would no doubt expose itself to look around.

A wide path of light came in from the northwest, lighting the prairie in a silver arc. Corvan focused on the woodpile and waited. As the light neared the rock pile, he saw a familiar shape lean out.

Corvan pulled the leather back and let the marble fly. It struck the lizard on the side of the head and it slumped forward, its body draped over a log.

Pitchfork in hand, Corvan picked his way over the loose wood toward the reptile. It stirred and rolled over, eyes springing wide with fear as the points of the pitchfork dropped toward its head. Adrenalin surged through Corvan. He pushed the two tines firmly around the lizard's neck, pinning it against the bark. It gurgled and coughed, its eyes begging for mercy. He eased up on the handle to let it breathe.

"Where's Kate?" Corvan demanded and almost choked on the marbles still in his mouth.

The lizard blinked its eyes and hissed out words that made no sense.

Corvan spit the marbles away. "Where's my hammer? Does Kate have it with her?"

The lizard shook its head as much as the tines would allow.

"Do you know where the hammer is?"

The lizard tried to speak again, its healthy claw pushing on the metal shaft of the pitchfork.

Corvan returned the creature's gaze. Its dark eyes had lost the venomous anger from their previous encounter. They looked almost human now that the black band was gone.

"Can you open the door so I can find her?"

The lizard blinked at him. Then, slowly, it nodded.

What choice did he have but to trust it?

Tugging the points free of the wood, Corvan set the fork beside him.

The lizard sat forward, rubbed its neck, and looked around the jumble of logs.

In an instant, it leaped up and disappeared into a hole between the chunks of wood.

Corvan groaned and plopped down on the end of a thick log that jutted out from the pile. The lizard had tricked him. How would he ever find a way through that door? His stomach churned at the thought of losing Kate.

He heard a noisy scrabble, and the lizard reappeared above him. It gave a yank with its good claw, and a battered pink pencil case popped into view. Slipping down to where Corvan was seated, the lizard pulled on the straps and the case bumped down over the logs, falling into a pile of debris at Corvan's feet. The lizard crouched, its sides heaving from exertion.

Corvan pulled the case into his lap. He remembered seeing it on Kate's desk a few years back. Her father had sent it to her in the mail. When two boys stole it and tossed it back and forth, she'd given one a bloody nose.

As Corvan's hands played over the soft vinyl sides, he felt a familiar outline. Tugging the zipper open, he pulled out the hammer. As soon he touched it, the insignia lit up and the handle seemed to snuggle into his palm. A sense of calm flowed through him.

"She was going to take the hammer back to him," the lizard said. "That would have been the end of everything."

Corvan stared at the lizard.

"When you possess the hammer, you are able to understand my language."

So that was why Kate knew what the lizard had said when he didn't.

"Your counterpart has willingly accepted the rule of the master."

"Her name is Kate. And what master are you talking about?"

"He is not yet aware that she exists. But the command of the shackle compels her to seek him."

"The shackle?"

"The black band that was around my neck. I told her not to touch it, but she wanted it for herself. Now she is wearing it and is under its command."

"But can't she take it off? Can't she just say no?"

The lizard solemnly shook its head. "She has accepted the band of her own free will. Now it will call her to him, to serve him."

Corvan's mind whirled. "Can I use the hammer to set her free?"

The lizard thought for a moment. "Only if she desires to be set free and only if we find her before she gets back to him. Once he sees her, she will be doomed. He will not allow her to go free, for she could destroy all his plans."

The lizard's words were confusing and frightening. "If you're right, I've got to go after her right away." Corvan jumped to his feet and scrambled down off the pile. Hitting the soft dirt, he ran toward the rock. The lizard caught up to him on its swift hind legs and ran alongside like a well-trained dog.

"She is gone, Cor-Van. She will be inside the labyrinth by now. You will not be able to follow without a guide."

Corvan slackened his pace. "What are you talking about?"

The lizard stopped. "Beyond the door is an intricate maze. Only those who are called from within can find their way through. The shackle on the girl will guide her, but without help, you will most certainly be lost."

"Will you guide me?"

The lizard shook its head. "I no longer serve the band. I cannot help you."

Corvan held out the hammer. "What about this? Can it guide me through?"

The lizard stepped away. "Perhaps . . . if you have been trained in its use. Have you studied the writings?"

"I don't know anything about writings, unless you mean my grandfather's book. It's metal, and the hammer unlocks it."

The dark eyes of the lizard widened. It drew in a hissing breath. "Have you discovered what it says?"

The urgency in the lizard's voice prickled Corvan's mind. Maybe this was just a trick to get the book. Corvan grasped the hammer tighter. His grandfather had said not to trust the dark eyes. Was he referring to this lizard?

"Put your hand on the hammer," Corvan commanded.

"My hand?"

"Your claw. Place it on the hammer."

"Oh, I cannot touch it. I tried once, when I wanted to take it to him, but it hurt me badly. I had to wrap cloth around my paws."

"That was before Kate released you from the black band."

The lizard nodded and felt its neck.

"I don't think the hammer will hurt you now, unless you are not telling the truth." Corvan extended the hammer.

The creature shrank back. "I fear it will hurt me again."

"Then you have to decide if you're willing to trust me."

The lizard edged its claw toward the head of the hammer. Its eyes closed as it made contact. There was a moment of silence and then a long sigh. "It is not angry with me any more."

"Try the other claw, the injured one," Corvan suggested with sudden inspiration.

The lizard attempted to lift its bloody claw and let out a low, painful hiss. Crouching lower, Corvan touched the hammer to the damaged paw. A look of astonishment crossed the lizard's face.

"Does it feel better?"

"Oh, yes. Look, I can lift it now, and the pain is almost gone. Oh, thank you, sir, thank you."

Corvan watched the creature bobbing and bowing. It reminded him of the old Chinese man who used to be the caretaker at the mine. "Don't thank me; it was the hammer. If you lie, it hurts you, but when you tell the truth, it heals you. I don't know how it knows, but it does." He pointed the handle at the lizard. "So be sure you always tell me the truth."

The lizard nodded vigorously. "I will, sir. But we must hurry if we hope to get through the door before daylight."

Corvan looked to the eastern sky. "Is there anything else I should bring? What about a flashlight?"

"I do not know the word *flashlight*."

"You touch a switch and light comes out."

The lizard's face wrinkled.

"Kate had one at the rock."

"Oh, yes, the short fire stick. No need. I have much larger ones in the entry."

Corvan wanted to ask for more information, but time was passing quickly. "Is there anything else I should get?"

"Whatever you think you will need for a long journey."

"A long journey?" Corvan's heart dropped. "How long will it take?"

"Many of your days, sir."

"Days? How far down does this cave go?"

"At least four days just to get through the labyrinth. If we can make it past that, there is a long descent before we will arrive at the main cavern."

Corvan's mind reeled. His parents had told him that his grandfather had been gone for up to a year at a time. This must be where he went. If only he had lived to show Corvan how all this fit together.

How could he go into this maze of tunnels unprepared? He needed more time, but there was no time. He would have to just step through the doors and see what happened, it spite of how crazy it seemed. *But then, who am I to say what's crazy when I'm sitting here having a conversation with a lizard?*

"Looking on the bright side," he mumbled to himself, "it will mean missing a few days of school."

"Oh, no, sir." The lizard gazed at him sadly.

Corvan squeezed the hammer, wondering if he'd misheard. "But you said it would take days, didn't you?"

"I'm afraid you do not understand, sir. The cycles of your moon affect the passages. Once we have passed through the labyrinth, the opportunity to return to this sphere will not come again for at least one of your months."

Corvan shook his head. "I can't be gone for a month. Father is away up north, and my mother needs me here to help her."

The lizard turned to gaze at the castle. "The doors will be sealed at sunrise. If you do not wish to go, that is your choice."

The inside of Corvan's mouth felt like sandpaper. "But what will happen to Kate?"

"She will most certainly die."

THE HAMMER

CHAPTER TWELVE

There was no way he would leave Kate to die. "We must save her. No matter what it takes."—he looked sideways at the lizard, who confirmed his fears with a deep nod—"It's the right thing to do." Corvan heard himself speak, but the voice sounded more like his father's.

"It is the only thing to do, sir. If we do not try, all will be lost. If you stay here to protect your world, you will lose it anyway."

Corvan didn't like the sound of that last statement. "Why? What's going to happen to my world?"

The lizard studiously scratched at the dirt with one of his claws. "It will depend on our success in rescuing the Kate. It is best now to focus on the task that is before us."

"I'll need to bring along some food . . . how can I carry enough for a month?"

"There will be food once we reach the boundaries of the Cor. But there is none in the labyrinth. You will need enough for six of your days."

"The Cor? What's that?"

"It is the place where Kate is going, but we must move quickly if we are to find her. Will it take long to pack your food?"

"Not long. Wait for me on the rock. I'll be right back."

The creature looked overhead. "You must hurry. I cannot be outside once your sun is in the sky, and we waste valuable time talking."

"I'll be right back."

Corvan ran toward the house. Should he wake his mother to help him pack? His pace slackened. She would never believe a story about a talking lizard. It would be best to leave a note telling her he'd gone to find Kate. That would cause her the least amount of stress.

Corvan looked at the familiar outline of his home. He was not ready to leave.

THE HAMMER

He paused with one foot on the porch steps and looked back at the rock. Ready or not, Kate was in great danger. He had to try to save her. He slipped into the darkened kitchen.

The house was silent; even Mother's snore was missing. He stood still and waited until he heard faint measured breaths coming from her room. She never slept well with Father away. He would need to be especially quiet.

He pulled the hunting packsack from behind the pantry door. His father would not mind if he took it for such an important task. Closing the pantry door behind him, he lit a candle and placed it on the rough wooden shelf.

After filling one of the side pockets of the pack with jerky, he stuffed some tinned food, bread, and candles into the main section of the pack. As he routed behind a box of soap flakes, he discovered a plastic bread bag full of oatmeal raisin cookies. They fit perfectly into one of the side pockets. A bonus was finding a full package of chocolate chips tucked inside an empty tin of baking soda. He smiled. Mother was getting creative at finding hiding places. He would have to tease her about it.

His heart fell as he dropped the chocolate chips in the pack. There would be no teasing his mother for quite a while. Opening the bag of cookies he took three out and placed them on the shelf. There was no tea left but she could enjoy the cookies with some warm milk.

Back in his room, Corvan set the pack on the bed, opened the chest and checked over the various objects. What should he take? For the first time, he noticed an empty cavity at the back of the tray. It ran the length of the lid and connected to another compartment along one side. It was about the length of the long wooden case his father had shown him on the rock. What could have been there and where was it now? There was no time to look for it.

Corvan touched the metal book. The lizard had been a bit too interested in it. Since he couldn't read it anyway, he should probably leave it in the chest for safekeeping. He passed his hand over it, hoping he was not making a big mistake.

He released the rope and shoes and stuffed them with the gray cloth into the rucksack. He jammed his slingshot and more clothes on top.

After tying the pack cover in place, he hefted it onto his shoulders with a groan. How would he ever manage to carry this around in the caves? On the other hand, how could he know what the journey would require? As soon as possible, he would need the lizard's help to lighten his load.

Taking one last look around, he caught a glimpse of a black handle sticking out under the blankets. The lizard wouldn't be too impressed if he had left the hammer behind. He needed a better way to carry it.

Setting the pack on the bed he pulled an army footlocker from underneath it.

Mother insisted he keep anything that might cause a fire in the metal box. He dug past an unopened packet of Black Cat firecrackers, three stubby bottle rockets on short bamboo sticks, and a Roman candle. Finally he found it: his Hubley Trooper cap pistol with a large Texas star on its holster. He had quit wearing it years ago, after the other kids began calling him Tex.

He pulled out the gun and threaded the empty holster onto his belt. The hammer slid inside, handle down, as if it were made to order. The top flap snapped down neatly over the head. He stepped in front of the mirror, and in one fluid motion released the hammer and pointed it at his reflection. He had practiced that maneuver a thousand times with the pistol and was pleased it worked just as well with the hammer.

Corvan dropped the gun back into the metal box. He wanted to take it along, but there was no real purpose for a cap pistol. He picked up the fireworks. These, on the other hand, might be useful. They weren't that heavy. And you never knew when you might need a good flash or a loud noise. He opened the pack, pulled out the gray cloth and wrapped it around the fireworks, just to make sure nothing went off accidentally. After tying the pack shut, he dragged it up onto one shoulder.

Pausing at the door, Corvan glanced around his room. A dreadful feeling came over him that he would not be returning to his home. He pushed the light switch down and closed the door.

This time he remembered the third step, but with the added weight of the pack, even his evasive tactics resulted in a muted squeak. Mother mumbled in her sleep, the bedsprings squeaked as she rolled over. Seizing the moment, Corvan released the noisy stair and scooted through the kitchen.

Easing the back door open, he let it close softly behind him. As he turned, a dark shadow spoke from the armchair.

"I watched you sit here through the night with the hammer in your hand. But I do not see the advantage of placing one's body in this contraption." The lizard pushed itself out of the chair. "It seems designed merely to keep one awake. It hurts the tail."

Corvan frowned. "I told you to wait for me on the rock."

"I was concerned that you'd changed your mind. I was considering coming inside to find you."

"Well, I'm glad you didn't. The sight of you would have been too much for my mother to handle."

"Sir?" The lizard had a gravely wounded expression.

"It's nothing personal. She just doesn't like snakes."

"But I'm not a—"

"Never mind. Come on, let's get going."

"Gladly, sir. It is well past time to leave."

"Just a minute." Corvan crept back inside the kitchen and found a pencil and paper by the telephone. He jotted a note telling his mother he was going to look for Kate and not to worry. At the bottom, he wrote his name, Cor-van, with a tiny hyphen. His father would understand where he had gone once he checked the castle rock.

After setting the note on the shelf under the phone, he squeezed out the door. He pushed off down the stairs with the lizard following close behind.

"I believe your belongings will be too large to fit through the labyrinth. Some of the openings are quite small."

"I grabbed everything I thought I might need. We will lighten the load as we travel and eat the food."

"Is it heavy?"

Corvan straightened his back. "I've carried more than this before."

The dark bulge of the rock loomed ahead. Corvan tried to leap aboard its rocky decks but misjudged the weight of the pack and crashed back to the ground. The lizard's head appeared above him, an I-told–you-so look on its narrow face.

Corvan rolled over onto his knees. "I guess this pack might be a tad heavy after all. Maybe once we're inside we should go through it and decide what to leave behind."

The lizard didn't answer, but Corvan thought it rolled its eyes before darting up the rock and into the circle. Heaving himself to his feet, he staggered up after it.

The rocks around the circle appeared as mute sentinels against the thin gray light of the approaching dawn.

"Light is coming, sir. We must get inside."

"We have a few minutes." Corvan put his pack down by the stone door and crossed back to the southern gap. A light came on in the kitchen. Through the window, he saw his mother go to the sink. For a moment, he thought of running back to say good-bye. He lifted his hand to wave. She couldn't see him, but it made him feel a bit better all the same. She turned away and the kitchen light went out.

The lizard looked at him as he turned around.

"Why do you raise your hand and shake it back and forth? I have seen others do this. What is the meaning?"

"We are saying good-bye." The lizard looked at him, expecting more. "When

we are leaving someone, and we don't know how long it will be before we see
them again, we wave." He swallowed hard. "It means that we love them and hope
we'll see them again soon."

The lizard nodded. "We do not wave. Love is not permitted when you serve
the darkness." The lizard studied him for a moment, then jumped over to the pack.
"We must get moving. Once this night is over, the door cannot be opened until the
next phase of your moon." It wrapped its claws around the strap of the rucksack
and tried to move it closer to the door. The pack refused to budge.

Corvan stooped and slung it onto his back. It seemed heavier each time he
picked it up.

"Sir."

Corvan turned around, but the lizard was gone.

"I'm here, sir."

Something poked Corvan's side and he twisted to find the lizard's hind leg
hanging beside him.

"My claw appears to be caught in your belongings, sir."

Corvan chuckled as he set the pack down and unhooked the lizard.

"I do not understand that noise you just made. I heard it before when you and
the Kate were together."

"I was laughing. You looked funny hanging there."

The lizard frowned and glanced over its shoulder at the growing light. "Do
you have the hammer?"

"Yes, right here." Corvan slipped it from the holster. "It should work when I
put the handle in that keyhole between the rings." He pushed the handle forward.

"Stop!" The lizard darted in front of him, barring his way to the door. "The
power of the hammer flows through your body. The door will open even if your
feet touch the stone. The Kate stepped on the doors, they opened, and she fell,
throwing her arms up, like this." The lizard mimicked the motion. "The small case
flew from her hand, bounced off the doors, and they closed very fast. I grabbed her
case and carried it away as you approached."

No wonder Kate's scream had been cut short. "How long does it stay open
once you touch it?"

"I think until you touch it again. It shut when the hammer dropped on it from
this side. The Kate was fortunate to not get hit, for it closes quite swiftly."

"Let's test it and see."

Setting his pack down, Corvan tentatively touched the stone. A low rumble
echoed below him, but nothing moved. "Well, that didn't work." As he leaned
forward to try again, the door sprang apart, and the lizard had to yank him back

from the open hole.

"That's incredible. Does it work the same to close it?"

Corvan leaned forward and touched one finger to the exposed edge of the door. All was silent.

The lizard was hissing and clicking. Corvan looked at him. He was pointing at the ground where the hammer lay in the dirt, dangerously close to the door. Corvan's face flushed. As he picked it, up he brushed the frame with his free hand.

Wham! The doors slid back together with the ferocity of a massive stone mousetrap. He looked up into the wide eyes of the lizard. "So how do I get inside without being crushed?"

"If you open the door and drop the hammer inside, you will be able to climb in safely. I will go first and you can follow. I suggest you toss your belongings down behind me to avoid getting caught in the door." The lizard gave the eastern sky another quick glance.

Corvan pulled the pack in close beside him. He placed his hand on the stone, and the doors rumbled open. The lizard leaped inside and disappeared into the blackness.

Corvan called, "Heads up," and threw the pack. It hit the ground. Edging forward, he held the hammer out over the hole. "I'm going to drop the hammer in now." No response. "Here comes the hammer." Silence.

Was this a trick to get the hammer inside the door with him locked outside? His dad always said there was always more than one way to solve a problem. But how could he get the hammer inside without touching the door? Maybe if he jumped down without touching the sides, he could shut it from below. He brought his feet together with his toes just inches from the doorway. It reminded him of the time he jumped off the high diving board at summer camp. That time he'd ended up in the infirmary.

Corvan jumped forward and landed amid a pile of jumbled rocks. He stumbled, and his head grazed the bottom of the door. The massive slabs slammed together with a resounding thunder that tore painfully at the hair on the back of his head.

He jerked the strands free and fell to the ground in the choking dust, his head coming to rest against the coarse canvas of the rucksack. It was so dark he couldn't see his empty hand in front of his face. Empty! Once again, he had dropped the hammer. He felt around the floor, panic rising in his throat. He was defenseless without it.

What if the lizard was waiting in the darkness, its razor-sharp claws ready to tear out his eyes?

"Are you down there—lizard?" His voice echoed in the cavern.

His groping hands encountered a round handle, but it was just a short, thick stick. He needed some light. He fumbled with the pack and pulled out the waterproof tube of matches from the top pocket.

He struck one and it sputtered to life. He tilted it down and waited for it to catch. As he held it aloft, he came face-to-face with the empty eye sockets of a human skull. A sharp cry escaped his lips. The match fell and died.

THE HAMMER

PART II

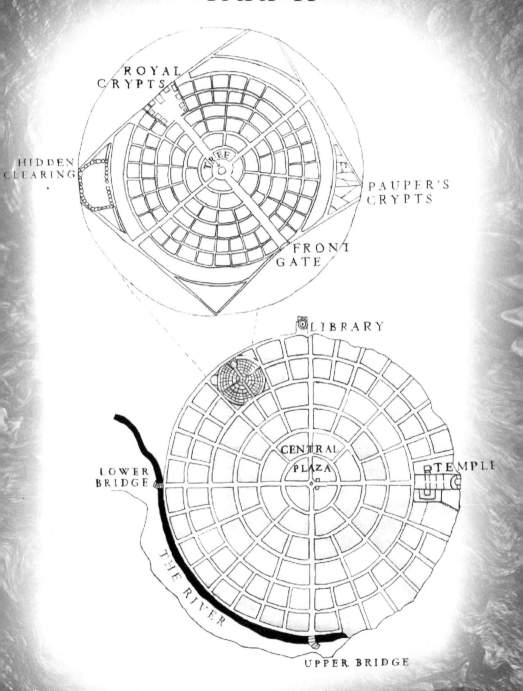

THE HAMMER

CHAPTER THIRTEEN

The rhythmic click of claws on rock approached and a spark of light expanded to a dome of brilliant white flame. As Covan's eyes adjusted to the harsh light, he saw that it came off the end of a long stick the lizard carried. The lizard stopped, cocked his head to one side and rolled his eyes. He pointed a claw past Corvan.

Corvan turned back to find the hammer lying amid the broken ribs of the skeleton, the skull above looking on in wide-eyed disbelief. As he plucked the hammer from between the bones and tattered remains of rotting garments, a piece of mildewed cloth fell from the ribs, revealing the letters IPC embroidered in faded red thread.

The International Power Company was the bankrupt mine with the deep bore problems. How could an IPC miner have ended up under this rock? A shiver ran up his spine. It must have been terrible to die so close to freedom.

"How long has he been here?"

The lizard studied the skeleton as if seeing it for the first time. "For as long as I have been guarding the door."

The hammer pulsed in Corvan's hand as he slipped it back into the holster and fastened the snap. "How long have you been guarding it?"

"Many years, sir. I have lost count. It has been a long assignment, and a tedious one."

"Assignment?"

"I am a Watcher."

"What are you watching?"

The lizard's eyes darted about. "For those who might try to enter our world . . . or leave it. I am to report anything I see back to him."

"Who's him?"

"No more askings," snapped the lizard, then it bowed to the ground. "I am sorry, sir, but my service is a painful memory for me, and I would prefer not to speak of it. Come, we must prepare to make our way through the labyrinth."

Corvan looked at the skeleton. "It doesn't feel right to leave these bones here like this. We should bury them."

The lizard looked at him blankly. "How long does a bury take?"

Corvan looked around the rocky floor. "Well, I guess in a way they are buried, being underground and all. Maybe when we come back I can take care of them."

Apparently satisfied, the lizard moved off down the rocky passageway.

Corvan crawled over the rough floor after it, dragging the rucksack. "Are all the caves this small?"

"Most are larger, but sometimes the doors between them are quite small."

The ground slanted steeply down, and Corvan took to sliding after the lizard. If his sense of direction was correct, they were descending below the western slope of the castle rock. The tunnel became less steep, and the passage opened up to where Corvan could stand upright. They must be under the field. With this much solid granite down here, no wonder their soil was so poor and rocky.

The light from the lizard's stick bobbed away in front of him. Loose stones rolled under Corvan's feet, and he stumbled, cracking his shoulder against the craggy wall. "Hey, slow down, I can't see where I'm going."

The light stopped and came back. "Sorry, sir. After so many times running through here in the dark, I forget there are obstacles in the way. Please take my fire stick, I do not need it. But be careful not to touch the light. It will burn through anything, even rocks." He thrust the stick at Corvan and moved on. Corvan held the strange torch out in front of him. He hoped it would not drip and start his shoes on fire.

The tunnel descended rapidly for a few hundred yards and then branched in two directions. A clear trail cut to the left, but a single set of shoe prints went right. He peered down the right-hand tunnel.

"It is no use to follow the Kate now," the lizard said from the darkness behind him. "The first shifting of the openings has already occurred, and she is in the next cavern. Now that we are through the door, we have some time before we can follow her. Come, I will show you a place where you can rest."

Corvan followed the lizard down a short corridor and into a small room.

"You can cover the fire stick, sir. There is enough light here when your eyes adjust. Just put the cover back on top."

Corvan examined the stick he held. A small black cap hung from a silver thong just below the glowing end. He held his hand over the fire. It was not as hot as he expected.

"Do not touch it, sir. If it gets on your skin, it will burn through to the other side."

Corvan remembered having dripped burning plastic on his arm when he was melting one of his green army men. It had burned into his flesh before it solidified and cooled. This sounded infinitely more painful. He eased the black cap over the flame and it went out.

As his eyes adjusted, he noticed the cave was bathed in a pale blue glow from the ceiling.

"Not enough light for you, sir? Just a moment." The lizard ran onto a low shelf and pushed a claw toward the light, which became stronger and more pinkish as it spread across the room. "They said lumiens would not grow so far from their source, but I kept tending them and they survived."

Corvan found that the entire roof was carpeted with long, silky threads that hung in clusters around the knobby, bulbous globes that were the source of the mysterious light. Near his head hung the largest, about the size of a small pumpkin. He brushed the soft tentacles that hung around it, and the bulb dimmed to a deep blue. The change spread out like ripples in a pool to the other bulbs scattered about the room. Corvan detected an electric smell, as if lightning had struck close by.

The lizard grinned. "Touch it again."

Corvan reached up, and waves of light spread from bulb to bulb, becoming brighter until they were all the color and intensity of the brightest full moon.

"Be careful, sir. Mine are not as strong as those in the Cor." The lizard raised a claw, and the globes dimmed back to a pale blue. "They can expend themselves and never recover. We are not permitted to let that happen." He pointed above Corvan's head. "That is my best one. Not as splendid as those in the Cor, but a beautiful specimen nonetheless."

Corvan inspected the large bulb and discovered that it hung lower than the rest because it was attached to a metal holder that arched out from the cavern wall. Its gnarled stem wrapped along the pipe and spread its roots out onto the rock.

Corvan looked at the large globe. "Are they plants?"

"Yes, like your vegetables, but much better tasting. Here, try one of these, but do not bite the center." The lizard plucked a small globe the size of a cherry tomato from a patch that hung down the wall. "Quick, eat the flesh while it is still blue; that is the nicest flavor I think."

Corvan nibbled on the strange fruit. It tasted sweet like a peach but tangy. The texture was smooth, like a melon but not as juicy. Warmth flowed down his throat and into his stomach. He popped the rest into his mouth.

"Careful, sir." The lizard approached him. "Remember the center. It is not permitted for us to consume its life."

Corvan worked his tongue around the hard pit of the fruit. There was a tiny buzz of electric current as his tongue touched the pointy end of the seed. He spat it into his hand. It was teardrop shaped, with veins that pulsed as if a tiny heart beat inside. The tingle in his tongue was spreading through his head. It was a pleasant sensation.

"Touch the pointed end to the ceiling, sir."

Corvan reached up and felt a small tug as the seed reattached itself to the rock. A translucent skin formed, obscuring the patchwork of veins.

"It is forbidden to eat the center of the lumiens. The penalty is death, for they are our source of light and life."

"Do they only have one seed?"

"I have been told that there is a special mother plant that produces clusters of seeds, but I have never seen it. It belongs to the priests, but it must not produce many offspring, for the Cor is darker each time I return."

A pale blue skin now covered the seed. It twitched and stretched as the fruit expanded.

"They grow quickly at first, but they won't glow until they are larger. If you pick them when they are brighter, they become too spicy for my taste. Would you like to try a brighter one?" He raised a claw toward the globes.

"I feel full. Maybe later." The pleasant feeling from the seed had passed leaving behind a heightened awareness of his body, as if the electricity was trapped inside him. Corvan looked to the wall behind the lizard, where a large, intricate sculpture created from bits of metal hung from the wall. Looking closer, he could see pieces he recognized: a circular saw blade, lids from tin cans, a tie rod from a truck, and a rusty hand-cranked egg beater. "Did you make that?"

A proud smile spread across the lizard's face. "The hole in the portal door permitted me freedom that a watcher normally does not receive. I did not have to go back to the Cor for supplies and was able to learn much of you and your world. This is something I made to help me pass the time. I use the small fire sticks I grow up here to melt the pieces together. Do you like it?"

Corvan nodded. He didn't know much about art, but it certainly looked as good as anything he had seen on his field trip to the art gallery in the city.

Below the sculpture, a row of tall quartz crystals sprouted from the floor. "I've never seen crystals that big."

The lizard nodded. "I have practiced much over the years. It is one of the things that kept me from losing myself. Would you like to hear them?"

"Sure," Corvan said, not certain how you could listen to rocks.

The lizard stepped into the center of the tall crystals. After a moment of intense concentration, he caressed the angular shapes with the tips of his claws. A faint sound like tiny glass wind chimes filled the room. It swelled and invaded the inner recesses of Corvan's head.

Corvan closed his eyes as the tempo of the music increased. Warmth and peace surrounded him. In his mind, he could see a group of small creatures moving in a circle, bobbing rhythmically up and down. Abruptly the music stopped.

The lizard looked up with glistening eyes. "I have not played that one since before I accepted the shackle." He scurried up to Corvan. "It was about my kind in the days before we became Watchers. Did you like it?"

"It was very nice." Corvan's ears still rang with the tune, and his head felt fuzzy. "I think I'd better sit down." He dropped the pack from his shoulder and sat beside it.

"You should rest, sir. We have a short time until the first movement of the labyrinth, and I need to pack. I am not sure what to take with me. I have more things collected than I could ever carry." He moved to the cave wall and pulled back a coarse curtain to reveal a small room carved into the rock. Hanging on the back wall were row upon row of skinned and dried gopher carcasses. No wonder Corvan's father was amazed that his field was not full of gopher holes.

Small sheaves of wheat were piled high in a roughly hewn stone bin. Shelves cut into the rock above it held a variety of glass jars full of dried fruits, nuts, and strange things Corvan didn't recognize. "So that's where mother's canning jars went. She always blames me for taking them outside and losing them."

"You did bring them outside, sir. So in a way she was correct."

"Why do you keep calling me sir?"

"Out of respect. You are the new master, and I am pleased to be your servant."

"But you said you were glad to be free. You can't be free and also be a servant."

The lizard stopped picking items from his shelves and turned to look at Corvan. "That is the best freedom of all. To know I can serve by my own choice and not from fear of pain. I was born to serve, but I can only truly enjoy it when I freely choose my master."

"Didn't you freely choose to accept the black band?"

The lizard's face wrinkled, and he caressed his neck. "Yes. The master offered me much, but in the end, I became his slave. It is true, I made the choice of my own will, but once the bond was on me, I was not free to leave. My choice placed me under his control. But that is not how Tsarek was created to serve."

"Is that your name, *Tsah-reck*?"

"It is the name I was given at emergence. But I have not used it for many years. He forbade us to have personal recognition. We were referred to only by the location of the portal we guarded."

"What does your name mean?"

Tsarek looked down at the ground." It means *pretty face* . . . on account of these blue markings." He pointed to the side of his face and looked away.

The three lines of deep blue scales that swept off Tsarek's face and onto his neck seemed to be more visible than before, as if the lizard were blushing. Corvan felt a bit sorry for him. "You don't have to call me sir. You can call me Corvan if you want."

The lizard shook his head. "Oh, no, sir. If I were to use your title where others may hear, that would be the end of us both. Perhaps I may be permitted to use your personal name?"

"But Corvan is the only name I have."

"I refer to the name your mother used: Kalian."

"My mother never called me that."

"She said it and sang it to you often in her song. Kalian means *my only one*."

Was that the name Grandfather's letter referred to? He liked the sound of it. "That will be fine. From now on, call me Kalian."

The lizard's eyes shone with honor. He crossed to Corvan, placed a slender paw on his knee, and looked into his eyes. "Tsarek promises to serve Kalian and . . . Oh, sir, I am sorry." His paw fell from Corvan's knee, and he pulled back across the cavern floor, leaning heavily against the crystals. A discordant jangling filled the room.

"What's wrong, Tsarek?"

"I cannot serve you, for you must kill me. You must take the right of family blood."

"I don't understand."

The lizard pulled something from a niche in the wall. He turned slowly, placed a heavy object into Corvan's hand, and backed away, bowing deeply.

Corvan looked down. In his palm was an old pocket watch. Crudely scratched symbols covered its back. He turned it over. The front cover was carefully inscribed with the same insignia as the hammer. He flicked the catch, and the watch popped open.

The bezel was cracked, the hands frozen together at midnight.

Noticing something written on the inside cover, he pulled it toward the largest globe and read, "To Grandfather, on the birth of Corvan, September 21, 1937." His mother had told him about this watch. It had been a present from her to his grandfather. He wrapped his hand tightly around it, closing the cover with an audible click.

"Where did you get my grandfather's watch?" Corvan looked down and found the lizard kneeling before him.

"The bones in the entry. I took it from the skeleton after . . . Oh, sir, my life is forfeit to you. You must take it, for I am the one who took the life of your past-father."

CHAPTER FOURTEEN

Tsarek's words hung in the tense air of the cave. Corvan's fingers traced the engraving on the watch cradled in his hand. This creature had just admitted to attacking his grandfather and leaving him to die in the dark. And Corvan had trusted him. He stared at the lizard and his anger boiled. "Why?"

The lizard fell on its face in the dirt before him. "It was the task I was given. I was under the band and had to obey."

"But you said you chose the band. You were responsible for your actions."

"Yes, I was. I am still. That is why you must take my life for his. It is the law of the Cor."

Corvan felt disgusted by the creature groveling at his feet. He wanted to strike out and punish it for what it had done. "We will let the hammer decide your fate." Corvan released it from the holster and held it above his head.

The lizard rolled onto its back, a guttural scream escaping its thin lips. Startled, Corvan stepped back, and the hammer brushed the large globe. A shower of warm blobs of light exploded over his head, plunging the room into darkness as they fizzled out on the floor.

Corvan dropped to his knees in the dark and heard a rasp of scales on rock.

A small voice spoke. "Please, sir, do not use the hammer against me. It searches out my lies and burns terribly inside. Oh, sir, I want to believe that I am pure with the band gone, but I cannot know for certain."

The glow in the remaining globes returned, lighting the pathetic form cowering against the far wall of the storage room. Corvan felt sorry for him. Even if Tsarek had killed his grandfather, the creature before him was different now that it no longer had the band around its neck.

"I will not take your life, Tsarek." He slid the hammer back into the holster. "I am not bound by your laws and I am not your judge. You are free to go."

"Oh, sir, do not send me away." He crawled toward Corvan. "To send me away is to send me back to him." His claws rested on Corvan's right sneaker. "Please, sir, I wish to stay with you. You will need me to get through the labyrinth. I wish to serve the Cor-van and help him remove the band from the counterpart."

The lizard was right. The band was on Kate, and she was heading deeper into the darkness to serve an evil master. To find her he had to work together with Tsarek, dark eyes or not.

"Fine. I will let you be my guide. But only until we find Kate."

Tsarek nodded. "We cannot reach her now, and she can go no farther until the next shift of the labyrinth. I must finish packing and you must rest. You can lie there." He pointed to a low mound on the floor. "It is my special resting place."

Corvan dragged the pack over and sat down. The weariness of the long day and night settled in as he leaned back against his pack. As he relaxed, the mound beneath him grew softer and conformed to his body.

Tsarek watched him with keen interest. "There is a long journey ahead of us. I will wake you in time to repack your things. The first opening is usually quite large, but the others may be too tight for all your belongings."

Corvan watched as Tsarek turned and picked through the alcoves cut into the walls. Each hole contained something from the world above: a small adjustable wrench, a carefully polished bent fork perched on a rock like a thin metal bird, a battered transistor radio with a piece of barbed wire stuck into the broken antenna, and a scruffy baseball with Corvan's early attempts at a signature scrawled across it. The lizard was a tidy version of a packrat.

Tsarek appeared to ignore Corvan, but he saw the lizard's eyes flicker in his direction from time to time. Was he waiting for him to fall asleep? Should he trust Tsarek? His grandfather had warned him not to trust anyone.

He sat up and forced his eyes to stay open. He had to find out more about this creature.

"Tsarek."

The lizard jumped. "You must sleep, sir. Our journey begins soon and it will not be an easy one. You will not find a soft sleeping place like that once we are inside the labyrinth."

"I can't sleep. Too much has happened in the last day. Or has it even been a day? I guess there's no way to know down here."

"We know the passing of time, sir, for the glow of the lumiens ebbs and flows in a regular pattern."

"Like the tide of the ocean?"

"Yes. And just like in your world, we rest in the dark and work during the light. Although I have heard that the settlement workers have to work longer if the production of fire sticks can keep up with their progress."

"What do the workers do?"

"Each group has different tasks to perform. The lowest class are the gleaners. They tend the lumien clusters and the plants people need for food."

Corvan pushed his pack farther away and stretched out. Whatever the soft ground was, it sure made a nice bed. "The people eat only vegetables?"

Tsarek emerged from his pantry, his paws full of wheat sheaves. A dried gopher carcass hung by one leg from his teeth. He scurried over to drop his load by the growing pile. "It is against the laws but some have taken to eating other creatures."

"Like what, cows?"

"Oh, no, nothing like cows. Just a few small animals, like those." He gestured to the gopher carcass lying on the ground. "And just as in your world, in the Cor there are those who take advantage of their position higher up in the eating order."

Was the lizard saying that the high-ranking ones ate those in classes lower than themselves? He thought of his grandfather's bones in the entry above and decided he didn't really want to know.

Tsarek watched him intently, but when Corvan met his gaze, he bustled over to the cubbyholes and began selecting more items. At times he would hold something up to the light of the remaining lumiens, then give a heavy sigh and place it back in its cubbyhole. "Such a wonderful collection," he muttered. "Some they have never seen before. There would have been a great privilege for bringing back such things."

Corvan stiffened. Was there also a reward for turning him over to the master?

Tsarek chose three smaller items, wrapped each one in a scrap of cloth, and placed them by his row of supplies. He turned and his eyes met Corvan's. "Sir, you must sleep."

"I can't. I have so many questions."

"Then ask. I will try to help. I have been observing your world a long time."

"Since I was born?"

"Oh, long before that. I was young myself when I was sent here."

"Were you expected to guard this portal all your life?"

"There is no returning unless the band calls you to report or another watcher takes your place. We must keep the portal safe from all intruders. No one must be allowed to . . ." Tsarek's voice trailed off, and he turned back to his packing.

Corvan flicked the pocket watch open and reread the inscription. "Did my grandfather say anything to you before he died?"

Tsarek turned around. "He did not have time." A look of remorse crossed his face "When we kill, it is very swift." The lizard lifted one claw and glared at it with the angry expression Corvan remembered vividly from that night on the rock. Tsarek frowned at his claw. Then the angry look returned, his dark eyes smoldering with hatred.

Corvan sat up and fumbled for the hammer.

Tsarek's face relaxed, and the lizard moved his claw closer to Corvan's face. In the dim light, he could make out a drop of pale yellow fluid forming at the tip of the longest claw.

"It just takes a scratch, and it is all over. The poison was much easier to produce with the band on. Catching small rodents was simple. I would wait until they stuck their foolish heads out of their holes, and that was it." He made a slashing motion with his claw. "They were dead before they could even pull their bodies back into their burrows. It is a little slower with larger animals, like that dog creature that attacked me. And I can make it slower if I want them to live until I—"

"It's okay, Tsarek, that's all I need to know."

"Yes, sir." A shimmer of light glinted on the lizard's claw. "Are you able to sleep now?"

Any hope of sleep had abandoned him. He would need to keep an eye on Tsarek day and night.

Tsarek stepped up to the crystals. "I know what will help you rest. My mentor used to play a tune for me when I could not sleep. I am not sure I can remember it after all this time, but I will try."

As Tsarek ran his claws over the angular rocks, soft music swirled around the cavern. It surrounded him like a warm blanket, like his mother's song.

Corvan leaned against the pack and closed his eyes. Faint images of small lizards danced in his mind, their claws clicking on the rocks. He forced his eyes open to watch Tsarek's poisonous claws caressing the crystals.

His eyes grew heavy, but before they closed, he caught sight of a line of pale yellow venom dripping down the luminescent surface of the largest crystal.

A sense of imminent danger yanked Corvan from a deep sleep. A shadow fell across his eyelids. Something sharp brushed his cheek. He rolled to one side. Pain shot up his elbow, and his arm went numb. The lizard had scratched him with his poisonous claw!

Tsarek stood beside him. "I am sorry to startle you, Kalian, sir. But it is time for us to go."

Corvan moved his arm. The numbness started to go away, though his elbow ached fiercely. He must have hit his funny bone on a rock.

A faint tremor ran through the cavern walls.

"Sir, the entry is starting to open. I let you sleep too long. We will need to sort through your pack between the next levels."

Corvan sat up and rubbed his sore elbow.

"While you slept, I added a few of my belongings to your pack. I did not have room in mine." The lizard gestured over his shoulder to a small bundle tied to the end of some sticks. "I hope that is all right."

Corvan pulled his pack on. There was no way he could carry it very far. "What did you put in here, rocks?"

Tsarek smiled briefly. "Just one," he said, pointing to the musical crystals.

Corvan twisted around. All that remained of the largest crystal was a broken stump.

"If it is too much for you, I can try to carry it in my bundle."

Corvan shook his head. "It's okay. When we go through my stuff later, we'll decide what we really need."

"Thank you, sir. I have grown attached to my music. I believe it may help keep our spirits up during the long walk to the lower levels."

Corvan staggered as a tremor went through the rock.

"It is opening. Quickly, we must hasten to the entry." Tsarek tugged on Corvan's sleeve "It has been so long since I have watched them open that I am not sure how long we will have." The lizard hurried from the room, Corvan stumbling along at his heels.

The passage was pitch black, and Tsarek was quickly lost to sight. "I can't see anything. Where are you?"

"Right in front of you, sir. No time to stop. Follow my voice; the entry is not far. But watch for the stones on the floor."

Watch? In complete darkness? Maybe the lizard could see in the dark, but Corvan couldn't.

This lizard shouted a word that Corvan didn't understand. "Sir, there is a big rock in the middle of the path. Be careful."

Apparently the lizard couldn't see in the dark either.

An abrupt shift in air pressure caused Corvan's ears to pop. A moist breeze blew, heavy with the powerful odor of burning matches. He held his nose, but it passed quickly.

The soft wind grew stronger with each twist and turn of the passage.

"It's just ahead, sir, and still open. The other entries all open at the same time, so the air from the Cor pushes toward the surface. Let me get some light." The lizard fumbled with his bundle of sticks and presently a brilliant glow fluttered in the breeze.

They stood at the end of a roughly hewn tunnel. On the wall before them was the source of the sour wind: a hole about a foot off the ground and three feet in diameter. The rock around the edges looked like melted blue glass. Wisps of smoke trailed from its edges. Corvan stepped closer.

"Do not touch it, sir. We must wait until it is fully formed or it will close around us." The lizard shuddered. "It is not a pretty sight."

Corvan pictured himself squeezed into two pieces, and he shuddered. "Will Kate know not to touch them?"

"She will be moving forward, sir, as the black band calls her on. The next link in the labyrinth will be formed by the time she gets there. See, this one is ready."

Corvan noticed that the blue glass had turned black and the smoke was gone.

The lizard leaped up through the hole. His head popped back through. "You can touch the side now." His claws clicked on the glossy surface as he jumped back through the hole to Corvan's side. "It will be easier if you throw your pack in first. I will stay here and hold the light for you."

Corvan tossed the heavy pack to the other side of the hole. He put one foot over the threshold and stood straddling the gap in the wall.

This was it. He was leaving his world behind.

Gingerly he touched the surface. It pulsed warmly against his fingers. Blue light rippled out from around each fingertip.

A yell erupted, and the lizard shoved him through the hole to land in a heap on the other side. Darkness fell as if someone had switched off the lights. The smell of burning matches infused the air.

The breeze stopped. In the darkness Corvan heard the lizard grunt softly. "Sir, I need your help, please. You will find more fire sticks attached to my bundle on the floor. The one in my claws is no longer useful."

Fumbling around the floor, Corvan located the sticks, untied them, and exposed the capped end on one. Fire flared, revealing Tsarek hanging from the end of a stick that stuck straight out of a solid cave wall. He looked so funny with his short, thick legs dangling in midair that Corvan had to choke back a laugh. "Was it supposed to close that fast?"

"No. Something odd has happened. I can only think that Kate found the next door very quickly. There is no other way to explain it." The lizard shrugged, bobbing on the end of the stick like a jackfish on a willow pole. "Could you help me down, sir?"

"It's not far. Just let go."

"I would, sir, but when I get frightened my claws lock up on me." Squirming, Tsarek ducked his head and dropped his gaze to the ground. "You will need to rub the spines on my back in order for me to relax enough to let go."

Corvan stepped closer. "These little spikes?" He ran his hand up the lizard's prickly spine.

"Yes, sir. But the other direction. That way just makes me more tense."

Corvan ran his hand downward, as if petting a cat.

"Ah, that's much better." Tsarek dropped from the pole, and the stick twanged in the still air. Muttering a stiff "Thank you, sir," the lizard scurried over to his belongings and tied the sticks and bundle back together. "I think we'd best get ready to find the next entry."

"You said it will be close by?"

"Not anymore. The entries move each time they open and close. That is why we need the hammer to guide us on from here. It will be many hours until the next shifting. Let us find a comfortable spot to sort through your belongings."

Corvan hoisted his pack and grabbed the stick in the wall. "I suppose we should break this off in case we need it later." As he tugged on it, Tsarek's shouts filled the cavern. The stick shuddered in Corvan's hand, and a dull boom thumped through the walls of the tunnel.

"Oh, my, so fortunate it did not break on this side. To break a fire stick is to release all of its energy at one time. Very dangerous, sir. It is good for us that the Cor shield is unbreakable."

Corvan's hand dropped away from the stick. "Sorry. I didn't know."

"No harm done, sir. Though good for us that we are not deep enough for buraks. A vibration like that in their area would have them eating us before we could say *torpy tollig*."

"What?" Corvan didn't recall the lizard mentioning strange, man-eating creatures lurking down here. He peered over his shoulder into the blackness.

"Not to worry, sir. The buraks cannot enter the labyrinth. But let us move down the tunnel in case that fire stick breaks on this side too. Sometimes, when they get as old as these, they can shatter on their own. Very messy if you happen to be holding one."

Corvan thrust the fire stick at Tsarek. The lizard took it and his short legs churned as he moved off, leaving Corvan to keep up as best he could.

The narrow tunnel opened into a cavernous room with a low ceiling. The sound of water echoed in the far corner, and Corvan's parched throat made him realize he'd had nothing to drink for a long time.

Tsarek was already at the pool when he arrived, lapping at the water like a scaly dog. The pool was a good twenty yards across, the water tumbling in from a fissure in the far wall. No stream ran out of the pool, so the drain must be somewhere below the surface.

Corvan stretched out on the ground and sucked greedily from the pool. The water was cool and refreshing but tasted of fish. He glanced to one side. Sure enough, Tsarek had waded into the pool beside him and was washing his scales. "Do you mind, Tsarek? I was still drinking."

"No problem, sir. You do not bother me. Please continue."

Corvan rolled his eyes. Getting to his feet he waded cautiously into the pool. A small bundle of wheat, tied with a leather thong, bobbed past him. He watched it float away and stepped in closer to where the fresh water fell into the pool. Stooping over he splashed water onto his dirty face. The water was too cold for a bath, though Tsarek didn't seem to mind. His energetic splashes sent ripples dancing across the pool in all directions.

The small waves bounced off the rock wall and crisscrossed one another on their way back, like many thin snakes swimming through the water. The ripples moved back toward Tsarek, and then suddenly changed direction and undulated toward Corvan.

He pointed to them. "Hey, Tsarek, why are the ripples—"

A thin rope wrapped around his legs and yanked him under the water. Corvan pulled at the rope, struggling to free his legs. More ropes whipped around, binding his arms and legs together. Panic swept over him as he was dragged like a hogtied calf deeper into the dark water.

As the black liquid closed in around him, a bright light bubbled past him. He caught a glimpse of a fire stick in the claws of a green lizard. The water below him foamed angrily, his ears thundering with pain as the light faded to a narrow point.

The ropes yanked him down even faster. His lungs screamed for air. He had to breathe. *Don't open your mouth.* His head throbbed. Sparks swam before his eyes. Before he could stop himself, his lips parted and water swept into his body.

His energy melted away. His limbs relaxed, and his arms drifted up past his head. A bright light moved toward him, and he knew for certain he would die and Kate would be lost forever.

CHAPTER FIFTEEN

"Breathe, sir, breathe. You are the Cor-van. You must live to set us free."

Corvan heard Tsarek's voice but it was hollow and distant.

Tsarek knelt beside Corvan and pushed on his shoulder. "Wake up, sir. Without you, the Kate will die." The lizard rocked Corvan's body harder.

Water gurgled from his mouth, but he could not pull in any air. Heart pounding, his body arched, and he coughed up brackish water.

Tsarek sat back and patted Corvan's shoulder. "Thank you, sir, thank you."

Corvan pushed himself to a sitting position and managed to choke out a few words between coughs. "What . . . happened? What . . . was that?"

"It must be an offspring from the great water creature in the Cor. This one's arms were smaller. Even so, we were fortunate only its tentacles were in our pool. Even a fire stick is no match for the main body." He pointed to where a floating fire stick was casting its bubbling glow through the water.

"Was it your stick . . . I saw under the water?" Corvan fell into another fit of coughing.

"Yes. They burn well under water." He dropped the pair of unlit ones and waded out to retrieve the one in the water.

A long, black tentacle rose to the surface. Tsarek gave it a poke with the fire stick. It twitched horribly. The lizard yelped, sprinting for shore.

Back on dry land, he stuck the light into a crack. Attempting to speak, Corvan found himself heaving up water until his stomach muscles ached.

"I burned through many of its arms, but they just kept coming. It was not until we came to this pool that I finally burned through that large one and it let you go." Tsarek looked over his shoulder. "I just wish I knew where we are now."

Corvan suppressed another coughing fit and looked around. They were in a different cavern, with a high ceiling and deep black walls. The pool was long and narrow, and there was no water coming in or going out. The surface was as smooth as a mirror, the limp black arm of the water monster reflected in the shallows. The air was much colder here.

Tsarek looked at him. "I believe we are still in the labyrinth, but I doubt we can locate the next opening. I do not know which level we are on or how many entries we skipped. This is not good, not good at all."

Corvan shivered with cold and fear. Would the rest of this adventure be this dangerous? They had just started and already he had almost drowned.

"Oh, sir, I forgot you humans cannot tolerate the cold. I heard your mother say you would catch your death of cold." He pressed his smooth, chilly nose up against Corvan's face. "Are you dying?"

Corvan tried to answer but his teeth chattered too much.

"You must not die. I shall get you warm." He jumped over to Corvan's pack and yanked the top open. A clump of soggy clothes came free along with the slingshot. Tsarek tossed them to one side and dug deeper into the pack. "Here is something that is still dry." He held up the gray cloth from the chest and the fireworks tumbled to the ground.

Tsarek let out a long hiss as he lifted the cloth and stared at it, wide eyed. "I was told only he had one of these, to walk undetected through the Cor." He turned to Corvan. "When you wear it, others see you for whatever is foremost in their mind."

"Wear it?" Corvan leaned closer and discovered it was a tunic of sorts. The center opened into a hood, and the buttons down the sides that held it into the chest could also fasten it together, like a rain poncho. "Is it an evil thing?" Corvan doubled over and coughed up more water.

"No, not evil, but highly valuable. He will surely send his seekers to find it and take it back." He draped it over Corvan's shoulders.

In spite of the cold fear in his heart, Corvan's body was immediately infused with warmth.

"If you do not want to wear it, I can find other dry things." Tsarek stuck his head inside the pack, and Corvan heard a muffled expression of surprise. The lizard emerged again, holding the strange coil of rope in his claws. "Most incredible. I have never seen one so long and thin. There are tales of such that grow in the farthest regions, but I did not think them true. Where did you get a krypin such as this?"

"It was my grandfather's. He left it for me in case he did not return."

Tsarek's face fell. "Most sorry, sir. I should not be touching such things."

Tsarek dropped the rope at Corvan's feet and moved over to the clothes. "The air is drier here. We must be closer to the Cor. Perhaps if I hang your things on the rocks to dry?"

"I have a better idea." Corvan pulled himself forward and grabbed the rope. Pushing on the dark button, he ran the sticky disk out to the wall and tied the other end off at a short pillar of rock near his pack. "There, a clothesline. You can hang up the clothes while I empty out the pack. I need to check on my food."

Tsarek grimaced and Corvan realized that the lizard's supplies had been left behind at the upper pool, tied to the rest of the fire sticks. "I think I have enough for both of us. Do you like canned beans?"

"I have never tried them, but I am grateful for your concern." He started to hang up the wet clothes.

Corvan dragged his sodden pack up the rocky shore so it wouldn't be so close to the dark water. A flat stone slab the size of his kitchen table lay just beyond his clothesline. That would be a safer place to go through his pack. Grabbing its straps, he carried it to the stone table and set it down.

He opened the pocket with the beef jerky. It was a little soft, but it would dry out. He pulled out the cookies. Amazingly, the knot in the bread bag had kept the water out.

In one of the larger side pockets, he found Tsarek's small wrapped bundles. He hoped none of them would turn out to be a slimy gopher carcass. As he piled them by the pack, a small red Swiss Army knife tumbled out. His ninth birthday present. It had gone missing when he left it out by the fort.

He looked at Tsarek smoothing the clothes on the line. The knife had been given to him, but he had left it at the rock. Finders keepers, losers weepers. He rewrapped the knife and placed it on top of Tsarek's pile.

At the bottom of the pouch lay Tsarek's musical crystal. Corvan stood it on the rock. He stroked it lightly with a fingertip and was startled by a soft, clear note.

Tsarek's head jerked up, and he hurried over. "Thank you, sir, but please do not attach it to the rock. I do not want to break it off again."

Corvan leaned the stone down and the soft glow died away. Tsarek tried to gather all his bundles in his fore claws but there were too many to carry. "Do you need a hand?" Corvan asked.

"No, I am fine. I will just move these over by the wall and dry them there. I will be back for the rest; you do not need to help me, sir." Tsarek hurried to the far wall but kept glancing over his shoulder. He sprinted back to the table, loaded up the rest, and ran them back to the wall, where he pawed through them. A sharp hiss escaped his teeth, and he ran back. "One is missing."

"Did you put something in another pocket?"

"No. Please look again." Tsarek leaped up onto the table and peered at the pack.

Corvan felt in the pocket. Sure enough, a small flat bundle lay on the bottom. As he pulled it out the cloth unraveled, revealing a thin silver disk with lines etched into its surface. It was warm.

Tsarek snatched the object from his hands. "Thank you, sir. That is the one I was missing." He bounded off the table with the bundle clutched to his breast. With his back to Corvan, he unwrapped and rewrapped his things.

Corvan shrugged. Crows and packrats always carefully guarded their treasures, no matter how worthless they were.

Tsarek finished fussing with his belongings and joined Corvan, his eyes scanning the food laid out on the rock. Corvan picked up a piece of jerky and held it out to him. "Try this; you might like it."

Tsarek nibbled a taste, nodded enthusiastically, and took a larger bite. "That is very good, sir. What is it?"

"Beef jerky. Dried strips of beef."

"Much better than small rodents. What is beef?"

"It comes from the large black-and-white animals in the field next to ours."

"Cows?"

"They are until you eat them, then they become beef." Corvan laughed. "If they have no legs, we call them *ground* beef, and if they only have two legs we call them *lean* beef." He tilted his body to one side and laughed again. "Get it?"

Tsarek stared at him. "From that strange noise you make I understand you are happy, but I do not know why a cow with only two legs would make it so for you." He bit off another piece of jerky. "Do all cows taste this good or just the black-and-white ones?"

"They're pretty much the same, but beef cows taste better than milk cows."

"Had I realized, I would have taken one of those instead of the rodents."

"You've obviously never been chased by a bull."

"Bull, sir?"

"A male cow. It's big and dangerous."

Tsarek raised a claw. "One does not need to be big to be dangerous."

Corvan looked closely. There was a drop of yellow on the end. Was Tsarek that upset about his things?

Tsarek dropped his claw and took another bite. "Thank you, sir, for sharing your provisions with me."

"We could try some beans if you like."

"No. We need to be careful with what food we have left. We do not know how long we will be here, where here is, or if there is a way out of here."

"Do you think we're trapped?"

"I do not know, sir. Permit me to see if there are any passages. It will not take long." Tsarek scrambled away into the dim recesses of the cavern.

Corvan nibbled at his jerky and opened one button of his cloak to get more comfortable. His clothes were almost dry. Somehow, the cloak was able to pull the moisture away from his body, but his feet were still cramped and cold.

The strange slippers from his grandfather's chest lay beside the pack. After unlacing his sneakers, Corvan struggled to remove his wet socks. He was glad he made the effort, for nestling his feet into the slippers was like stepping into a warm bath after playing all day in the snow. The cloth contracted around his feet like a second skin, each toe showing distinctly through the soft material.

He swung his legs off the table, stood, and walked about on the rough floor. He could feel every ridge through the smooth soles, yet the small pebbles and sharp rocks felt no different than going barefoot in the warm summer sand at Buffalo Lake.

He moved to where Tsarek had vanished into the gloom. The slippers gripped tightly on the rocky surface. He turned a corner and the light from the torch behind him vanished. He slowed his pace.

His knees plowed into something soft, and he toppled headlong onto the ground, scraping his hands along the rocks and losing the air from his lungs. Something sharp pressed against his neck, pinning him to the ground.

"Do not move," a hoarse voice croaked in his ear. "In the name of the Chief Watcher, who are you and what are you doing here?"

Corvan tried to speak, but no sound came out. The fall had knocked the wind out of him.

"Answer me," the voice rasped, "or I will kill you now."

Corvan finally managed a small breath, "Cor . . . Cor . . . Kalian."

"Kalian?" The voice changed. Tsarek's glittering eyes appeared over his shoulder. "It is you, sir. I am so sorry. I did not hear you coming. I thought I was being attacked by someone lying in wait for me."

Corvan's breath returned in a painful gasp.

"Are you injured, sir? Can you stand?"

Corvan croaked out a weak, "Yes, I'm okay."

The lizard helped him to his feet. "Let's get you back to the light."

Corvan followed the lizard's voice. Presently he saw the burning fire stick and the stone table.

THE HAMMER

As they retraced their steps, Tsarek kept looking at Corvan's feet. "Sir, where did you get those shoes?"

"They were with my grandfather's things."

"Listen."

Corvan listened. All he could hear was the drip of water from the clothesline and the occasional click of Tsarek's claws on the floor. He almost tripped over a small rock that clattered away to one side.

They arrived at the table and Corvan sat down wearily. "I didn't hear anything."

"Exactly, sir. Those shoes make no noise. I have keen hearing and I would have heard you coming like a rock slide, but I heard nothing until you bumped into me. These are special shoes, sir."

Corvan pulled one foot onto the table. Not only were they warm and dry, they were silent. He reached to touch one of them, and a drop of blood fell from his fingertip to the table.

"You are hurt, sir. Let me see."

Corvan turned his palm up. A flap of skin was torn back where a sharp stone had broken his fall.

"We must bind it up. I will get a rag." The lizard darted for the far wall and unraveled a cloth from one of his objects. Running to the pool, he stooped to dampen it and then bounded back to Corvan. "Let me see your hand, sir."

Corvan held out the bleeding hand. Tsarek dabbed tenderly at the loose piece of flesh. Corvan wanted to jerk his hand away but forced himself to remain steady as the lizard pushed his skin and tissue back into position.

"Hold this in place while I get more cloth."

Corvan's hand throbbed as he pressed it against the cloth. This hurt much more than burning his finger on the half dollar.

Now why didn't he think of that sooner? He pulled the hammer out and wrapped his wounded hand around the shaft. His palm stretched and pulled, as if army ants were crawling inside and using their pincers to close the wound.

He pulled the hammer and rags away to discover only a faint line remained. He clenched his fist and opened it again. The skin felt a little tight in the center but it did not hurt.

The lizard returned. "Here you are, sir. I have enough now to wrap your—" Tsarek stared at Corvan's hand.

He held out the hammer toward the lizard, who stumbled backward.

"It is very powerful, sir." Tsarek scrambled to his feet.

Corvan stood to help the lizard up, but dizziness caused him to sway and sit back down.

"You must rest while I keep looking for a way out. I shall awaken you if I find a path to follow."

Corvan pushed the pack to the floor and curled up on the stone. He had never been so weary as he was now. His eyelids drooped shut.

In his dreams Corvan found himself at home. Someone was lighting a fire in his backyard, and he could smell the matches. A pale white moon flickered behind him, bobbed along, and came to rest over the clothesline where his dripping T-shirts rippled gently in a cool fall breeze. The moon swung closer, but when he lifted his head to see it more clearly, it bounced away and disappeared. The smell of matches came again, and the moon reappeared, turned blue, and oozed out of sight over the horizon.

Corvan smiled dreamily to himself. How strange that the moon should have Kate's face.

THE HAMMER

CHAPTER SIXTEEN

Corvan opened his eyes. He blinked and then blinked again to make sure they were open. Absolute darkness was a weird sensation. It felt as if he were breathing the black into his body and letting it seep back out his eyes.

A faint glimmer appeared on the other side of the pool and pushed the shadows away. Tsarek walked toward him, the stub of a fire stick hanging limply at his side. He gave the pool a wide berth and shuffled up to the stone table.

"Did you find a way out?"

"No, I did not." The lizard wedged the short fire stick into a crack on the table. "I followed a thin, twisting tunnel for a long way. It kept getting smaller until it reached a narrow crack that you cannot fit through."

"So it's a dead end?"

"No." Tsarek scowled at him. "There is a larger cavern after the narrow place."

"But is that passage the only way out of here?"

"Yes."

"Then we have no choice but to try it."

Tsarek pulled himself wearily onto the rock. "You are the master. But I will need to rest a minute." He peered hopefully at Corvan. "If you could let me eat one of your cows, I would be grateful."

Corvan handed a piece of jerky to the lizard. "My fire stick must have burned out. It was pitch black in here before you returned."

Tsarek talked past a thick chunk of meat. "You must have put it out before sleeping. It should have at least two periods of burning left for us."

Corvan couldn't remember putting the stick out. He moved over to where it had been stuck in the rock, but it was gone. "You must have come back for it."

The lizard stopped chewing and shot him a withering glance. "And how could I do that and be walking down that long tunnel at the same time?"

Corvan pointed to the ground. "Well, it's gone."

Tsarek was beside him in a flash, searching the spot. He dropped to all fours, sniffed at the rocks, and scampered from side to side. He groaned. "Not lost, sir, stolen. The Kate has come through while you slept. Her flower scent still lingers."

Corvan's brows rose. "Kate, here? Why didn't she wake me?"

The lizard's short arms shot up. "Wake you? Be glad she did not kill you. The Kate is under the control of the band. But she must have sensed the hammer about you and dared not come close to . . ."

Tsarek bounded to the wall where he had carefully stored his possessions. "The thief! She has taken it." The lizard stamped back to the rock table, hissing and muttering.

"What did she take?"

"She took many of my things, including the one I value most."

"The silver disk?"

The lizard's eyes blazed as it leaped onto the table. "Who said you could look at my things?" He pointed a sharp claw at Corvan's face. "Is that why you hid it in your pack, because you wanted it for yourself?"

Corvan took a step back. "No. I saw part of it when I took it out for you. It was . . . warm."

Tsarek sank down onto the rock. "All those years I held it to ease the weight of the band." His body sagged lower. "Without the disk I would have been completely lost to the darkness of the band. Every time I held the disk, the band punished me. Burned me. But I did not care."

"Why did you get so angry when I touched it?"

"I knew you would want it for yourself."

"Why?"

Tsarek squirmed. "Because it belongs to the hammer. It is the counterpart."

Corvan sat bewildered. Kate was a counterpart and now the hammer had a counterpart? "How do you know it belongs with the hammer?"

"I saw the carvings on the bottom of the hammer when you were going to punish me with it. They are the same as the ones on the disk."

"Are you sure?"

"Yes." He looked at the ground. "I also know it belongs with the hammer because it was clutched in your past-father's hand when he died."

Corvan's mind reeled. The disk must be the other piece his grandfather had spoken of, the one he'd said he would need to take with him. It was an important part of the puzzle. And now Kate was taking it to the lizard's master.

He leaned back. The hammer was a key for opening doors, but how did the disk fit in?

Tsarek put a claw on his shoulder. "I am sorry to bring up your past-father's death." He spoke softly. "I see it has hurt you greatly."

Corvan focused on the lizard's face. "It's not that. I just don't understand why the hammer needs the disk."

"I cannot say. All I know is that the hammer tells me what I am, but the disk always gave me hope that I could be better."

Corvan tried to figure out why a hammer would be connected to a disk. A hammer should be paired with another tool, like a saw, or maybe a large spike or nail.

As Tsarek slipped down from the table to pull clothes from the line, Corvan slipped the hammer free of the holster. He hefted the stone handle in his hand. It didn't look like it would be good for building things—the handle was too short. It was more like a model you'd see on a shelf or on a desk.

Yes. And he had seen one like this back home. A wooden hammer lying beside a round wooden disk. Closing his eyes, he pulled the faint memory forward. "Of course!"

"Sir?"

"It's not a hammer, Tsarek, it's a gavel. And the disk is what it pounds on."

"Gravel, sir?" Tsarek came closer to the table.

"Not gravel, gavel. It's a small hammer that a judge in a court bangs on a wooden disk to stop an argument. Or an auctioneer, when something gets sold. I saw one at the town council meeting when they tried to take our field away. Old Man Fry was shouting at my dad, and the mayor banged his gavel on a wooden disk to get everyone to be quiet." He held out the hammer, and Tsarek backed away.

"With the band gone, you don't need to fear this anymore."

Tsarek turned away and went back to packing his things.

Holding the hammer in his hand, Corvan thought back to the council meeting and the injustice his father had suffered. It was good to seek the truth, but not without kindness. The words and ideas spun in his mind, coalescing into understanding. That's why the hammer needed a counterpart. It made sure the truth was always balanced with compassion.

Tsarek called from where he was picking through his remaining things. "You will need to collect your belongings. If it is permissible, I need to put a few things in your pack. I no longer have a way to carry them."

Corvan slid off the rock. One of the side pockets of the pack hung open. The bag of cookies was gone. Anger sparked in him, but an image of Kate wandering alone in the darkness struck him. He was glad she'd taken the cookies. He wouldn't even mention it to Tsarek—no use getting him more upset.

The lizard approached as if he were in a funeral procession, his tail dragging limply on the rocks and his crystal cradled against his chest. "There is nothing else I will need, except this."

Corvan wanted to say no. The pack was already heavy enough, but the sadness in Tsarek's dark eyes would not let him. He added the crystal to his pack and walked over to retrieve the krypin rope, leaving Tsarek hunched down by the flat rock. The fireworks lay on the ground where they had tumbled out of the cloak. It was a good thing he had wrapped them inside it, for they were still dry. He tucked them in along one side of the pack. Picking it up, he discovered that his wet sneakers were also missing. Good thing he had the new slipper shoes.

The lizard stood and shuffled around the pool. "Since Kate has already gone through this level, the door will not open here again. I fear this cave will be our tomb."

Corvan pulled on his pack and followed. He didn't even want to think of what might happen if Tsarek was right.

CHAPTER SEVENTEEN

The narrow tunnel wound on for miles. To save their last fire stick, Tsarek insisted they travel in darkness.

Corvan pulled the hammer from under his cloak and found the insignia was giving off a feeble light, like a flashlight with the batteries almost gone. Still, it was enough to keep from stubbing his toes on the rocks, and for that he was grateful.

Tsarek stayed well forward of the pale pool of light, as if he were afraid it would bite his heels.

"Is it much farther, Tsarek? We've been walking for hours."

"Just a bit more, I think. The roof is—"

Corvan's head scraped a rock jutting down from the roof. "Ouch!"

"You should crawl, sir. The ceiling is quite low."

Corvan got down on all fours. Fortunately, the floor was soft and sandy. "How much farther to the tight spot?"

"Not far."

Corvan soon realized that *not far* likely meant something different to Tsarek than it did to him. He tucked the cloak under his belt to free up his legs. His knees ached, and he had to jam the hammer under the straps of the pack so he could use both hands.

Tsarek stopped. "The ceiling gets even lower here. You will need to take off your pack and push it."

Corvan struggled with the straps and managed to remove the pack. "I'm not sure I want to push it in front of me. It might get stuck."

Tsarek turned to face him. "Perhaps if you tied it to your leg and pulled it along behind you . . . No, that's not a good idea. If the pack got stuck, I could not get past you to release it from your leg."

THE HAMMER

Corvan shivered at the thought. His father had told him about a spelunker who'd been exploring a small cave when a rock rolled behind him and trapped his legs. His rescuers could see him, but they couldn't pull him free. They tried to tunnel around him, but after ten days, he'd lost too much body heat and died from hypothermia.

"I think I might just leave it here. If I get through, you can bring me rope, and I can pull it from the other side. Is there enough space to turn around after the tight spot?"

"It comes out in a larger cavern. I think it might be part of the outer edges of the Cor. The shield walls transmit light from our city, and I thought I saw some in the crack. It was very dim, so either we are a long way out or the Cor was in a dark cycle."

Corvan didn't understand all that Tsarek had said, but at least it sounded like there was some hope of getting through. "Let's keep going."

Tsarek moved off into the darkness. Corvan left the pack behind and followed, the soft glow from the hammer in his hand lighting the way. The tunnel got progressively lower, but he could still wiggle snakelike along the floor.

The sleeve of his cloak caught on a rock. He was stuck, his left hand unable to move forward or back. Panic welled up inside him as the passage squeezed in. Everything in him clamored to thrash about and get out of this tiny hole.

Millions of tons of rock above and on every side of him, the musky-smelling dust of it clogging his nose. He gasped and tried to pull in a breath.

Closing his eyes, he forced his rigid muscles to relax.

When he opened them again, he found the hammer's glow casting a perfectly round circle onto the tunnel wall. The words of the script seemed more natural when projected this way. He still couldn't read them, but in a strange way, they reassured him that things would be okay.

Visualizing his cloak and the jagged rock that had snagged it, he rotated his shoulder and body until the trapped sleeve slid free. A huge whoosh of air escaped his lungs.

"Look this way, sir." Tsarek's muffled voice came from Corvan's left, where two gleaming eyes looked at him through a narrow crack in the wall. "This is the spot, sir. You must get through this hole to make it into the chamber I am standing in."

Corvan inspected the crack. The space he was crawling through ran horizontally, but the crack ran vertically. Where the two met, a small square opening had formed. Far too small. His stomach clenched at the thought of wriggling back through the tunnel only to die trapped in that last cave. He lowered his forehead to the cold rock. "My shoulders won't fit through there."

"You must try, sir. There is no other way out. If you do not make it through, you will most certainly die in there."

Most certainly die . . . just like Kate would if he didn't find her. He thought of her face when she had passed through the last tunnel. In his mind he could see her eyes begging for his help.

Corvan summoned his courage and examined the small opening. "There's more than one way to skin a cat," he mumbled.

"It is not worth the effort, sir. I have tried the creature called cat. They are tough and do not taste very good."

Corvan looked at the unblinking eyes. His mother always wondered what had become of her favorite tabby. "Those words are just an expression. It means there are always more solutions if you look hard enough and take the time to think things through. I'm not going to die of hunger in the next ten minutes, so let's look at the problem carefully. My shoulders won't get any smaller, but maybe there's a way to make the hole larger. How about the hammer?"

"That would not be a good idea, sir. I do not think this hole is very stable. There is a large overhang above the crack that could collapse at any time. It may not be the best skinning of a cat to try the hammer. The risk is great and—"

"All right, I get the picture. How about a fire stick? You said it could burn through rock."

"Not all rock. This looks like Cor shield. A fire stick will not burn it. If we try, the stick will explode."

Corvan held the hammer closer to the vertical crack. The rock was shiny and black, like the piece of obsidian rock he had in his collection at home.

"This is the main wall around the Cor?"

"I believe so. The cavern on this side smells like the Cor."

Corvan sniffed at the faint movement of air coming through the hole. It was damp and smelled of rotting compost. "It doesn't smell very good."

The pale eyes blinked rapidly. "It smells like home."

"Then I have to make it through. If I twist diagonally in the opening, that might give me a bit more space to work with. But I need to take the cloak off first. It might bunch up and trap me."

Corvan squirmed out of the cloak and quickly felt just how cool the cave walls were. Pulling his legs up behind him, he dug his toes into the soft sand and rotated his body around until he was heading toward Tsarek. He pushed into the crack and stopped. "If this is a shield wall, will it close and squish me like the blue wall around your fire stick?"

"I don't think so, sir. This one is not soft."

Corvan gingerly touched the hard crystalline surface. Nothing moved. "All right, then. Here goes nothing."

"Excuse me, sir? Where is the nothing and where will it be going?"

Corvan ignored the questions, extended his arms into the opening, and pushed forward.

Tsarek backed away from the hammer's glow. "You are doing it, sir. Keep coming—not far now."

Corvan pushed again, but his feet no longer gripped in the sand. His legs were too confined to offer any advantage. He wiggled and squirmed, and ever so slowly, his body moved through the narrow niche.

"Your hands are through, sir. Keep coming."

The rock surface pushed on his chest and tore at his shoulders. Was the shield trying to squeeze him out of the Cor? He couldn't get a full breath. Panic swept over him again. He jerked erratically in the tiny space, banging his flailing legs and knees against the rocks behind him. Pain swept up his legs, but he gained a few precious inches. His face emerged from the other side of the crack.

"You are here, sir. I am so happy."

Tsarek's face was level with him. The lizard stood on a narrow rock shelf. Below him, a long scree slope of broken rock shards stretched away into the darkness.

Now that his head was free, Corvan's breathing slowed. "My head may be through, but my shoulders don't want to follow. It gets more narrow at this end. But if I can get one shoulder out, my body will follow. Can you pull on my arm?"

Corvan wiggled his left hand. The lizard held out both claws and clasped them together so Corvan could wrap his fingers around them.

"Okay, Tsarek, lean back and pull."

The lizard leaned back. Corvan's shoulder moved forward slightly but then jammed tight. The folds of his shirt bunched and pinched at his flesh.

"I think my shirt is part of the problem. Can you climb up by my shoulder and pull some of the cloth through the opening?"

The lizard scrambled up the wall and found enough toeholds to get close to the trapped shoulder. A sharp yank was followed by the sound of tearing cloth.

"So sorry, sir, but I think I have ruined your garment."

Cool air flowed over his forearm as Tsarek reappeared with Corvan's shirtsleeve draped over a claw.

"I think we must remove the skin from a different cat, sir."

Corvan managed a wry smile. "We have to free my shoulder. Take the hammer and carefully chip away at the rock lip that has it trapped."

Tsarek shook his head so vigorously his scales rattled. "I cannot touch the hammer, sir. It will kill me, and you will still be stuck."

"Wrap my shirtsleeve around the handle, like when you wrapped rags around your claws on the rock."

"That may work. Just a moment." Tsarek bent to the ground. Corvan heard a soft hiss. A harsh light seared his eyes, and he cried out in pain.

"Sir, are you hurt?"

"Put out the light. It's too bright." Corvan clamped his eyes shut.

"Sorry, sir. There, is that better?"

Corvan opened his eyes. All he could see was a milky white orb. His eyes felt gritty. "Is it still on?"

"No, sir, it is out."

Corvan recalled something like this happening to his father when he was welding. He couldn't see for almost a week.

A wave of fear passed through his cramped body. He must not panic. His eyesight should eventually return. Right now he had to get out of the crack.

"Move the fire stick farther away from me on the other side, then light it again. When I drop the hammer, try to chip away the rock by my shoulder."

Tsarek scrambled around as Corvan relaxed his fingers to let the hammer fall. As it left his hand a powerful wave of helplessness coursed through him. Corvan forced himself to relax and concentrate on the milky moons covering his eyes. They had already faded slightly—a good sign.

"I am ready, sir. Please hold still."

A sharp *crack* was followed immediately by a deep *gong* and a rumbling whoosh past Corvan's ears. The air filled with dust. He choked and coughed, his chest squeezing painfully against the rocks. "What's going on?"

The only sound was sliding rock and crashing boulders on the slope below.

"Tsarek?"

Loud echoes mixed with the clatter of small rocks peppering down from above. The acrid taste of panic mingled with the talc in his mouth.

If Tsarek had been killed by the rocks then he would die trapped in this hole, just like the man in his dad's story. Fear rose in his throat.

"That was a close one, sir. I do hope there are not any buraks hunting close by." The voice of the lizard spoke quietly in the dense air. "I barely touched it and the whole wall shook. A large piece of the slab above you came down and just missed your head. We cannot try that again, sir. The rest of the boulder hangs above your head and may come down at any moment."

A small rock clattered down, glancing with a sharp blow off Corvan's head and bouncing down the slope. A low grinding followed.

"The rock is sliding. Pull your head back!" Tsarek pushed frantically on

Corvan's head, but it was no use. He stopped. The cavern was silent.

"Sir," the lizard's tense voice whispered in his ear, "we must push you back or pull you out now. That huge rock balances just over your head. A few more inches and we will both be crushed."

Corvan swallowed. He could think of only one way to rescue a trapped person. He had seen a diagram in one of his dad's caving books. To bring the shoulders in, the rescuers would break one or both of the collarbones and push the shoulders toward the body.

He shuddered. The rock grumbled. Tsarek tensed.

Pain would be better than death. "Tsarek, you must use the hammer again."

"Sir, if I touch the wall, the rock will surely come down on us."

"Not the rock, Tsarek. This time you must strike me."

"Sir?"

It took a while to convince the lizard of the necessity of the operation and the method by which it must be accomplished. The thought of striking Corvan was not palatable at first, but slowly he began to understand. Tsarek refused to use the hammer and went to find a smooth rock.

Corvan was starting to have second thoughts by the time Tsarek came back. "I am ready, sir."

"Make sure you hit me hard enough. I don't want to do this more than once."

The lizard's claws caressed Corvan's skin, making sure of the placement of the long, thin bone. Corvan closed his eyes and waited.

There was a long pause. Corvan was just about to ask Tsarek what he was doing when an intense jolt of pain shot through his body. In the haze, he heard Tsarek talking in his ear, begging him to push with his legs. The lizard tugged at his torn shirt and pushed on his broken shoulder.

Corvan wanted to yell at him to stop, it hurt too much, but no words would come out. He pushed hard with his feet, and a ragged cry escaped his throat. Suddenly his body was free of the confines of the hole. He tumbled forward, bumping and sliding over the rocky slope until he came to rest against a large boulder.

Instantly Tsarek was beside him. "Sir, are you alive?" he whispered.

Corvan groaned.

Tsarek put a claw on Corvan's mouth. "I know you are in much pain, sir, but you must be as quiet as possible. If the buraks have heard, they will come to investigate." The claw patted his head lightly. "Please lie still while I get your pack. I will return quickly."

In a moment, he was back, laying something on Corvan's stomach. "Here is your hammer. I am going to put out our light in case the buraks come."

Light? Corvan could see only the white orbs. If the creatures Tsarek mentioned came, he would be defenseless. Fear mingled with pain and gagged him. His broken bone grated with each convulsion of his chest.

A rock rolled down the slope from above. Corvan's heart skipped a beat. He bit his lip and forced back another coughing fit. He had to move out of the way of the boulder balanced above him. He tried to sit up, but searing pain pulled him back down.

Raising his good arm, he wrapped his hand around the smooth handle of the hammer. It could heal cuts; would its power fix a broken bone? He had to try.

Drawing the injured arm over his stomach, he winced as bone ground against bone. He gingerly traced the path of the collarbone with his finger. Yes, there was the broken spot. The bones were back in alignment.

As he stroked the handle along his shoulder, the pain eased. He lifted his arm, and the ugly sound of bone on bone washed over him in waves of pain. Tears welled up in his eyes. The hammer could not heal him. He was helpless. He savagely wiped his eyes until the handle was slick in his hands.

"Stop it," he whispered. "Crying will solve nothing. You have to take care of your arm a different way." He blinked away the tears and focused on the hammer in his hands. Its circles glowed faintly. Although the hammer had not healed his arm, the white orbs were gone. He could see again.

A pebble rolled down the slope. He turned his head and saw Tsarek picking his way down, the bulky pack balanced on his back. Corvan waited for the lizard to join him.

Tsarek stopped a foot away and leaned forward as if listening intently.

"What are you doing?"

The lizard jumped straight up, and the weight of the pack dropped him onto his back against the slope. He looked like an upside-down turtle, legs and head churning in circles, trying to grab an advantage from the air. Finally, he managed to get back to his feet. "I do not like it when you use your shoes to sneak up on me. Don't do that anymore."

"I didn't sneak up on you."

"I could not see you in the dark, and with the pack on I could not smell you, so I did not know you were there."

"But can't you see me now?"

The lizard seemed to look right past him. "Are you making one of your jokes, sir?"

Corvan looked down the cavern. Even without the fire stick, he could still see, in a murky sort of way. The far end of the tunnel faded to blackness, but he could make out the end, where it turned the corner. He squinted into the gloom. Something was moving slowly in the shadows down there.

"Tsarek, what does a burak look like?"

"They are hard to see. They take on the appearance of the rocks in which they live."

"What do they do?"

"They guard the far reaches of the Cor. Sometimes settlement workers try to escape to the outer edges of the Cor. The buraks prevent them."

"How?"

"They are meat eaters, Kalian."

"How big are they?"

"Very. They have a poor sense of sight, but they hear quite well."

Corvan swallowed. "I think one is guarding the way into this cavern."

"How do you know?"

"The hammer," he whispered. "It touched my eyes." He gripped the handle tightly. "There's a large creature down by the far end."

Tsarek stepped in the general direction of the entrance and stood in silence. "You are correct, sir. I hear something, and there is a faint smell of burak in the air. Can you see only one?"

"Yes. It's moving back and forth."

"Then it is waiting for its partner. They hunt in pairs. They have heard our noise and have come to satisfy their hunger."

Corvan gulped. "Can we get past it before the other one arrives?"

"We could try. But when they sense fresh meat, they can move very fast." He stepped back to Corvan. "Let's get a little closer and see if we can find a way around it."

Corvan bent forward and groaned. "I can't carry the pack. My broken arm doesn't work very well."

"I could carry it for you, sir, but I would not move very fast in the dark."

A low, rumbling growl grew to a grating shriek that echoed through the chamber.

"Its partner has arrived. The hunt has begun. You must wait here while I draw them away."

"But you can't see them."

"I can smell them and hear them. It is the only way, for you cannot move fast enough to get away. If I can get past them, they will pursue me. They do not know there are two of us here and they will not let a sure meal get away. Wait here until they are gone, then move as quickly as you can out of this tunnel. Just keep going down. Always down. When you reach the Cor, seek out the chief family of the temple priests. They stay in the only dwelling with a pointed roof." He made his claws into a sharp point.

"Tsarek, you can't do this. What if you get caught."

"It does not matter. You must escape and save the Kate." He placed a claw on Corvan's hand. "I did not want to worry you sir, but the Kate is not of the Cor."

Anxiety knotted his stomach. "What does that mean?"

The lizard ducked his head. "She cannot live long under the light of the lumiens. If you do not find her soon, she will fall into a deep sleep."

"And . . . ?"

"She will never wake up. But if he finds her while she is still alive, her fate will be worse than death."

Corvan opened his mouth to ask what could be worse than death, but another rumbling growl echoed off the walls. Tearing his gaze away from Tsarek, he peered back down the cavern. The strong odor reminded him of plucking butchered chickens.

Movement caught the corner of his eye. One burak stood high on the slope to his right. He looked back down. The other one must be hiding among the boulders on the floor.

In a burst of movement, a small form darted between a gap in the boulders. Tsarek tumbled down into an open space on the floor, crying out in pain as he fell.

A deep grunt pulled Corvan's gaze to the right. The burak was close enough that he could make out the bulbous eyes on its flat, angular head. It stared at the cavern floor, its head cocked to one side.

A series of clicks from below caught the burak's ears, and its head bobbed up and down. A wide mouth opened to reveal twin rows of jagged teeth.

The creature's throat bulged in and out like a bullfrog's, emitting a series of gulps and clicks. Corvan looked to the floor of the cavern. Tsarek was on his feet, moving slowly but dragging one leg.

More noises came from the burak on the slope. Tsarek stopped.

As Corvan watched in horror, a huge rock behind the lizard shifted slightly. It was not a rock. It was the other burak. Tsarek was heading directly into a trap.

Corvan took a step forward. A pebble broke free under his foot. The burak to his right turned to face him, its flat face swinging from side to side. Corvan froze. If he moved, the burak would know he was there, but if he didn't, his companion would die. The beast stared sightlessly in the dark until a cry from the cavern below grabbed its attention.

Tsarek dragged his injured leg behind him as he floundered about on the rocky floor. He stopped and held both paws over his mouth as if trying not to cry out in pain. He turned his head in Corvan's direction and raised his claws over his head, touching them together. What was he pointing at?

A dark shape loomed up behind him. For a fleeting second Corvan saw the outline of the lizard, and then it was gone.

A moment passed in eerie silence. Then a slow, rhythmic throbbing sounded out. The shadow on the floor rose on its hind legs and danced in a slow circle, pounding its feet on the ground.

The burak on the slope rumbled a response and slid toward the floor, responding with more grating shrieks. The dancing creature turned toward Corvan.

From its mouth hung Tsarek's lifeless body.

CHAPTER EIGHTEEN

Corvan cowered behind a large boulder as the buraks left the cavern, celebrating their successful hunt with loud shrieks. The pain in his shoulder was dulled by an intense ache in his heart. In the few short days he had known Tsarek, they had become more than just traveling companions. He could not believe his friend was gone.

The enormity of his situation began to sink in. He was far below the surface of the earth. No one else knew he was here and no one would come looking for him. Ever. He couldn't go back, yet how could he carry on without Tsarek's help? How could he find Kate on his own? For the first time in his life, Corvan was truly alone.

Tsarek's last words filled his mind with dread. Kate didn't have long to live. He had to forget about his fear and keep moving down to the Cor. The only hope was to locate the pointed roof of the temple priests.

That must have been what Tsarek meant when he raised his arms over his head. He knew he was about to be captured and was giving Corvan one last instruction. No, two, for the paws over the mouth told Corvan to be quiet so he could escape the buraks. Tsarek had given his life to save him.

The cold penetrated his sweat-drenched clothes. If he didn't get dry ones on and start moving, hypothermia would set in. He pulled the pack closer with his foot, trying not to move his damaged shoulder. Both of the leather thongs that had tied the top down were cut. Why would Tsarek have done that? Pushing the cover back he found that Tsarek had put the cloak back into the pack.

With only one arm, it took a while to fashion a crude sling for his broken arm, but once the sling was in place, the pain began to subside. He slipped the cloak over his head and flipped the hood up. It felt wonderful to be warm again.

Faint patches of blue light were showing up around the cavern. Tsarek was right;

they had found a way past the labyrinth and through the Cor shield.

He struggled to his feet and dragged the heavy pack down the slope and into the clearing where Tsarek had been captured. If he didn't lighten his load, he wouldn't get much farther. As he pulled the rest of the clothes from the pack, the smell of wood smoke and beef jerky wafted out. His stomach growled. In this timeless world, there was no way of knowing when he'd last eaten.

The labels had fallen off the tins but he discovered it did not matter—he had left the can opener at home. If only Kate had not taken the Swiss Army knife. He picked out a familiar rectangular tin. A can of Spam—the kind with an attached key to open it. He flipped it over. The key had broken off.

Anger welled up. Why was everything going wrong? He threw the can to the ground. Pain shot across his chest as the can bounced off a rock, cracked, and landed in the dirt at his feet, neatly split open along the seam. He bent forward, placed it between his knees, and peeled the top back with his good hand. Cold, gritty Spam. It had never tasted so good.

Even with the tins out, the pack was too heavy to carry with one arm. Reluctantly he pulled out Tsarek's crystal and set it on the floor between his knees. He wouldn't need it. There would be no more music from Tsarek. A tear fell onto the tapered crystal and slid down its length leaving a phosphorescent glow trailing behind it.

If only Tsarek were here to help. He reached out to the crystal, and a tiny spark leaped out to meet his hand. A sound like miniature wind chimes in a summer breeze made his mind swirl with a jumble of images. A winding path appeared at his feet and led him down to a city of stone buildings. A group of prisoners in chains emerged from a broken gate, singing as they shuffled along.

Though the land is dry and dark,
and nothing more can grow.
In the distance comes the light,
and everyone will know.

The quest of justice pulls him forth,
upon the road of truth.
A heart of mercy makes him known,
as the darkness moves.

Then all will be light, the evil cannot hide.
And with healing of the tree,
We all shall be set free.

The prisoners descended a set of stone stairs to a platform overlooking a deep pit. Red-cloaked guards released the shackled men from their chains, herding them forward at the point of fire sticks. One prisoner tried to run and a fire stick burned into his body. He crumpled to the ground and rolled off the ledge into the pit.

Corvan felt himself falling along with the body. Together they landed with a sickening crunch on the rocky floor.

Suddenly he was looking through the eyes of the dying man at a dark shadow that had detached itself from the side of the pit. The beast from his nightmares! Corvan struggled to pull back, but he was trapped inside the dying man.

Corvan hauled the mangled body to its feet and stumbled away. A roar drowned out the blood pounding in his ears, and darkness swallowed him as the beast's powerful jaws crushed the body.

Gradually coming to his senses, Corvan found himself back in the buraks' cavern. He was standing, his hand wrapped tightly around the top of a crystal that had grown taller than his chest. He pulled his hand away and the chimes died off to a faint sparkle.

His knees shook. Death was waiting for him down the path. He couldn't go on . . . but he would never make it back through the crack by himself. "Please show me the way out of here," he whispered. "I want to go home." His knees gave out and he grabbed the crystal to steady himself.

Sparks exploded in his mind and sparkled into a fog that descended around him. In the cool white mist, two figures walked past. His mother and father. He called out but they did not hear.

Following them through the murky air, he found himself climbing the rock. They must be trying to show him the way home.

As they passed through the gap into the castle rocks, the fog parted to reveal a figure sitting on a black throne. It was Kate. A blood red cape sat on her shoulders, a shimmering crown on her head. Thick black bands encircled both wrists.

Corvan's parents knelt before her, begging her to open the door so their son could come home. Kate smiled at them, raised both hands, and pointed to his home. Lightning arced from the bands and his house melted into a pool of fire, setting the fields alight. The fire roared away, incinerating every house in its path. The flames swirled back around his parents. They cried out in pain, and then they too were gone.

"No-o-o-o!" The cavern walls echoed with his cry as the vision faded away. This couldn't happen. How could Kate become an evil queen capable of destroying his world? Is this what would happen if he failed to rescue her?

A rumbling crash interrupted his thoughts. The rock face where he and Tsarek had entered collapsed onto the slope, and the rocks gained momentum, tumbling and smashing against one another, sending tremendous shudders through the ground as the slide roared downward and ground to a halt. He needed to get out of there, and quickly, for the avalanche was sure to bring the buraks back. A dense cloud of rock dust closed in about him as if it were trying to bury him alive.

The fine dust filled his lungs and he pulled the hood across his face, amazed to find that he could breathe easily through its fabric. He crouched low and waited for the dust to clear. It was difficult to see through the murky air. He pulled the hammer out, and the blue light cast a weak glow at his feet. As the dust settled down he found the circles from the handle sharply reflected in a tiny round pool at the base of Tsarek's crystal.

His tears had flowed down it and gathered in a small depression of the rock. Touching the shiny surface, he found it was as solid as the crystal. He pried at the edges and out popped a thin glass, like the small round mirror his mother kept in her purse. When he touched his finger to the surface, the glass rippled and became dark blue with small points of light, like a starry sky.

Hope. He felt it grow in his heart as he looked at the tiny stars. He had made it this far. He was inside the Cor and now if he could find Kate, they could find a way out and see the stars again.

He slipped the glass into his pocket, picked up the pack by its straps, and turned for the exit.

CHAPTER NINETEEN

With the labyrinth behind him, the journey to the Cor was easier than Corvan expected. Just as Tsarek had said, he only needed to keep moving down. At first, he picked his way around large boulders, but after a time he saw narrow tracks in the dust created by animals he could not identify. Later, rocky paths wound through caverns and tunnels, ever downward.

Tsarek said it would take about six days to reach the Cor, but it was impossible to tell how many days had already slipped past. Patches of Cor shield on the walls and ceiling grew lighter for a while, then faded to black. At times he found clumps of thick purple moss that glowed softly in the dark. He tried sleeping on a large patch but it made his skin itch.

At each rest he gnawed on what was left of the beef jerky and allowed himself a few chocolate chips. At least there was a steady supply of water. It dripped from the roof and pooled in small depressions, sometimes gathering in small streams alongside the path. It tasted strongly of minerals. Corvan soon learned to avoid the brackish standing water and to satisfy his thirst at the streams.

He walked as far as he could while there was light from the Cor shield before stretching out for a rest. Lying on the stone floor would have been unbearable except for the warmth of his cloak. Even so, sleep eluded him. He lay in the darkness, listening to the sounds of dripping water and the pattering feet of what could be small animals or incredibly large insects. He hoped they were not spiders. He hated spiders.

The visions from Tsarek's crystal haunted his thoughts. Most of the time he managed to banish the monster from his mind, but he couldn't escape that image of Kate. Was it possible for someone to change that much? Could the pursuit of anger consume your whole being? Sure, Kate sometimes got angry, but how could that grow to where she would want to kill everyone around her?

He tried to sleep and find temporary relief from his fear and loneliness, but rest eluded him. His father was right. It was terrible not seeing the moon and the stars. Without their light, the darkness was overwhelming, crushing Corvan with its vacant weight.

He found some comfort in the ice disk from the base of Tsarek's crystal. The patterns in the tiny pinpoints of light reminded him of the constellations he'd studied while lying out on the rock on warm summer nights. It almost seemed he could make out Orion and the Big Dipper. At his last rest he had noticed a brighter glow over the handle of the Big Dipper. Now the glow was a tiny full moon, making its way along the edge of the glass.

He puzzled over this for a while, and then it came to him. Tsarek's crystal showed him the future—at least a possible future. In a similar way, the ice glass reflected what was on his mind in the present. It showed him the stars because his first thought when he touched it was of a starry sky. Maybe it could also reveal his home.

Holding it in his palm, he concentrated on walking in his mind from the rock back to his house. The stars in the ice glass spun, and his home came into view. A tiny yellow square flickered, and his mother appeared in his bedroom window. He focused on her. The window grew larger in the glass until he could clearly see her face. Tears lay on her cheeks but she was singing. Her hand rose toward him as if she knew he was watching.

"I'm here, Mom," Corvan said. A tear slipped down his cheek and splashed on the glass.

His mother stopped singing and stared out the window. A puzzled smile flickered across her face. She wiped her eyes with the back of her sleeve and disappeared. The light went out.

Loneliness welled up and choked him. This was so unfair. Why should he be trapped in the earth, far away from his home? He doubted he could even reach Kate in time.

Kate. Would the glass reveal her whereabouts?

He turned his thoughts to her, and memories flooded back. Days of building forts and riding bikes and hiking through the coulees. He smiled. Kate was his best friend in the world. At least in the world above. Down here, he wasn't sure he knew her anymore. Pushing that thought aside, he concentrated on the Kate he remembered.

A fond memory stole into his heart. He and Kate were lying on the rock, watching for falling stars. A coyote barked in the field and Kate jumped and reached for his hand. It barked again, then all was silent. They stayed there, hand in hand, looking up at the stars, until his mother called him in. Neither of them had ever talked about it.

As he thought about this memory, the glass grew warm. He caught a glimpse of Kate in the darkness, tears trickling down her cheeks. "Hang on, Kate, I'm coming for you."

The image of her in the mirror looked at him in shock, calling his name so clearly he almost dropped the glass. He tried focusing his thoughts on Kate again, but the glass remained black.

The light from the Cor rocks had ebbed away. There was no purple moss in sight. Everything was dark. Corvan lay back down on the ground and pulled the cape over him.

There were times he was certain this must be a dream. A sharp rock poked into his ribs as if to remind him that he was not asleep. He wondered if it were possible for things to get any worse than this. His father used to say, "Cheer up, Son, the worst is yet to come." His dad wanted him to learn to be thankful for what he had right now instead of focusing on what could go wrong in the future.

Lying on the rocky floor, with the rhythmic drip of water falling in the darkness, Corvan tried to come up with something positive. The only thing that came to mind was that his collarbone had healed quickly and he didn't need the sling anymore. The hammer had an effect on bones after all; it just took a bit longer.

Sleep did not come easily, but when it finally settled on him, he found himself in a disturbing dream. The Kate he knew in the world above repeatedly battled the Kate in the red cape. Each time, the evil Kate won and she would raise a jagged blade over her head to bring death to her defeated foe. Corvan would cry out, and both Kates looked at him as if neither of them knew who he was.

He sat up. It was no use trying to sleep. He might as well walk on a little farther. Pulling his pack onto his shoulder, he unclipped the hammer and followed its glow around a corner to where another cavern joined the main trail. Corvan pointed his light up the steep slope. The toes of Kate's dirty running shoes stuck out from behind a rock.

"Kate?" He jumped forward, only to find the shoes were empty. The toes were separated from the soles and gaped at him as if they had something important to say. Behind the boulder he found an empty bread bag. The smell of oatmeal wafted out at him, along with a trace of her lilac perfume. Kate must have just been here. It had actually been her calling when he saw her in the glass.

There was a keen sense of disappointment but at least now he had something to be thankful for: Kate was alive and somewhere just ahead of him. Whipping around, he called her name. The only response was his voice echoing off the rocky walls.

T THE HAMMER

Hurrying down the path, Corvan saw a soft blue glow behind an outcrop of rocks. As he approached, the light grew steadily stronger. Whatever was down there was right on the path. He crept off to one side of the tunnel, keeping larger boulders between himself and the light. Picking his way along the rock wall, he approached a gap between two columns of rock. Up ahead, the small cavern he was in emerged into an open space full of light. Moonlight? Yes! Somehow, he had managed to find a way out of the tunnels and back to the surface.

Corvan's heart soared as he ran down the path toward the light. This meant Kate was out as well. They had both escaped from this terrible maze of tunnels.

The cavern narrowed down to a uniform arch. This must be the door to the tourist cave in the canyons near the city. His dad had taken him there once but they couldn't afford the entry fee.

He drew nearer and saw a thick stone door. His heart sank. This wasn't the tourist caves. They had iron gates to keep out non-paying customers.

Corvan moved closer to the entrance and peered out. High overhead shone a full moon and a few bright stars. He blinked. What had the fire stick done to his eyes? The moon was blue, and the stars in the sky pierced the black sky with a pinkish light.

Corvan took another step forward and tripped on the threshold of the doorway. He put a hand on the door to steady himself, and it opened wider. Carved across the middle of the door was a row of the strange script from his grandfather's book.

A wave of despair crashed down upon Corvan. Instead of a way out, he was going to have to go through another door and follow Kate deeper into the darkness.

He was about to step through when he heard angry voices approaching. Two men were men arguing about who had checked the door last. He ducked behind the thick slab and wedged his body in along the wall. As he slipped into the corner, the pack crowded his head forward under a large metal hinge, but there was no time to take the pack off. He looked through the crack that ran down the length of the door. Hopefully the men wouldn't see him in the shadows.

The first man entered his field of vision. He was short and thin, like Corvan. He was dressed in a green cloak, his face hidden in the dark recesses of his hood. In his hand was a staff that reached as high as his shoulder. At the top was a carved red globe with a deep black center. He stopped before the door, his head shaking slightly. "You're right. The door is open."

An even shorter man appeared. A deep rasping voice responded from the depths of his hood. "I can see that, Tarran, but why is it open? The priests hold the only key, and you are the only priest I know who bothers to come up here." He folded his arms over his chest.

Tarran threw back his hood revealing the sharp features of a young man with thick black hair. "What are you trying to insinuate, Harmon?"

The heavy set man didn't reply.

Tarran turned away and carefully examined the far side of the door. Would he examine this side as well? Corvan tried unsuccessfully to push himself away from the crack.

Tarran pulled a notched cylinder on a red cord from around his neck, inserted it into a hole, and twisted. Three sturdy bolts clicked out from the doorjamb. When he twisted the key and removed it, the bolts sank back into the rock.

The green cloak swished as Tarran crossed over to inspect the hinge side of the door. Corvan slowly pulled out the hammer. Warmth flooded his arm as its blue symbols glowed fiercely in the darkness. He quickly covered it with his free hand, but too late. He looked up into Tarran's wide eyes.

"Find something?" Harmon asked.

"Just checking the hinges," Tarran said, not breaking eye contact with Corvan. "The door was not forced open." He gestured to the left. "I have seen all I need to see here. Let's head back down. You can file a report tomorrow."

"Too late for that," Harmon sneered. "I already reported it to the Chief Watcher."

Tarran's eyes grew wide and he whirled about to face the stocky man. "You what?"

"The law states that he is to be informed any time this door is opened. Since it could only be a priest who opened it, I suspected that you wouldn't tell him about it and put your friends and family in jeopardy."

Tarran pounded his staff on the ground and the red globe filled with light. "You're a fool, Harmon. You know little of what is happening. All you care about is trying to advance your own career."

"What else is there? With the bad blood between the Watchers, the priests, and the rebels, this is the perfect time to get on the side of those who have the most power."

Tarran pointed the staff at him. "Power is not a toy for our amusement. Remember, if you play with power, you will pay the powerful."

Harmon snorted. "You priests and your proverbs. The way you talk, you'd think you were part of the rebel cells, not the city. Don't think for a moment that the Palace doesn't know what you and your father are planning."

Tarran stared at the stocky man. "You don't know what you're talking about."

"I know that Morgon has uncovered a plot to overthrow the palace, and I know that the sources all point to the high priest." Harmon turned his back on Tarran and swaggered away.

Tarran gripped his staff in both hands and took a step toward him.

Harmon whirled around. He looked past Corvan's hiding place down the narrow path beyond the door. "He's here," Harmon whispered in a hoarse voice.

Tarran turned. Both men stood frozen at attention. Tarran fumbled with the staff, and its light faded away.

In the thick silence Corvan caught the hollow sound of rhythmic chirps, as if a quartet of wounded crickets were limping in his direction. The soft slap of bare feet on rock overpowered the eerie sound as four incredibly thin men appeared on the path, a palanquin slung below poles on their shoulders. Red curtains embroidered with golden symbols hung around the cabin.

The men's necks and arms seemed too long and slender for them to be human. Blue veins pulsed under transparent glistening skin, reminding Corvan of the pictures he'd seen of cave salamanders that lived all their lives in total darkness. Their deep red robes accentuated milky white faces.

The tallest one at the front of the poles turned toward Corvan, empty eye sockets sealed under sunken eyelids. Its thin white lips pursed and its blue tongue worked to produce the strange, high-pitched chirps as its head scanned from side to side. They must navigate like bats, finding their way using echoes.

Corvan held his breath. Could their sonar find him through the narrow crack?

The palanquin's curtains parted, and a dark body oozed onto the ground. Corvan stifled a gasp. It was a lizard, like Tsarek, but much larger—almost Corvan's own height. Its head bobbed as its long, thin tongue whipped in and out, tasting the air that flowed from the cavern's open door. Powerful biceps strained against twisted silver bracers wrapped around each arm. The muscles in its thick legs bulged and rippled under a scaly black skin as it moved with measured steps into the doorway and out of Corvan's line of sight.

When it spoke, Corvan's blood ran cold. The voice was high and thin, piercing the stone door between them. He did not catch what it said, but Tarran responded affirmatively.

Harmon muttered something, but a command from the lizard silenced him.

Corvan held his breath and listened. He heard the hiss of cold breath. The lizard's snout poked past the door frame, nostrils flaring as it pulled in the scents around it. If the lizard came any closer, it was sure to smell him.

Tarran coughed. The black creature turned toward him.

"Most honorable Chief Watcher," Tarran said, "I checked this door personally, and all the seals were intact. I do not know—"

Harmon pushed Tarran aside. "I'm the one who found the door open. I've been keeping an eye on it for you, just as you ordered me. I'm the one who deserves a reward for—"

A blur moved past the crack and the next thing Corvan knew the black lizard was standing on top of Harmon's still body. He held his right claw up to the dim light and Corvan could see it was badly deformed, leaving only one long curved claw and a small twisted stump. The lizard's tongue shot out and tasted the blood dripping down the long claw. The black face wrinkled in distaste, and he stepped down to wipe the blood on the dead man's cloak. He gave the body a contemptuous kick and twisted his sinuous neck to leer at Tarran.

"Some people don't know when to be quiet, do they? I do not trust those who cannot keep their lips shut." The creature moved in closer to Tarran. "But I also have a hard time trusting a priest who cannot keep his door shut. It smells of treason, of trying to start a rumor that the Cor-Van has come to overthrow the palace."

Tarran pointed to the lock. "The priest's key was not used. The door must have been opened from the other side by the portal watcher."

The black body flickered toward Tarran, words spitting past the forked tongue. "If the Portal Watcher had been called, I would have been told. I am the chief of the Watchers."

The lizard circled around the man. "Do not think I am unaware of why the high priest assigned you to represent the temple in my palace guard. He tried the same tactic with Morgon and failed. That was a terrible outcome for all concerned, especially your sister, would you not agree?"

Tarran stiffened but did not answer. The black form turned back to the door. "Someone opened this door without informing me." The lizard extended a claw toward Tarran. "I will take the key now."

Tarran took a step back. "The key is the responsibility of the priests, not the palace."

"Yessss." The lizard's tongue darted out. "But only as guardians of the entry. The door has been opened without the palace being informed; therefore, your position is forfeit."

Tarran gripped the staff in both hands and held it up like a great sword. The four pale men holding the palanquin dropped it to the ground and spread out behind the lizard. Tightly coiled krypin ropes appeared in their hands.

The lizard extended his long claw and touched the staff. "Do not resist me, Tarran." The lizard pushed the staff aside, then turned his back on the man and walked toward the door. "You cannot win."

Tarran looked over at the four white creatures, who tensed in anticipation.

"You would be wise to consider joining me, as Morgon has done. The priesthood is dying. My new religion is poised to take over. Join me, and I will make you my captain instead of Morgon."

⊤ THE HAMMER

The staff sagged, and the tip hit the ground.

The lizard held out his claw again. This time Tarran reached into his cowl and pulled out the cord with the notched cylinder. The Chief Watcher took it and looped it around his own neck.

"A wise choice. You are a perceptive young man. One who could play an important role in restoring the Cor to its former glory."

One of the men with unseeing eyes bent down to speak in the lizard's ear, his long arms touching the ground.

The lizard nodded. An evil smile parted his lips. "A company of my men is on their way, Tarran. You have until tomorrow to give me your answer. Think it over carefully." His voice lowered. "Your sister's life depends on it."

The lizard slid through the curtains into the palanquin. His voice cracked out a command, and the four men picked up the cabin and disappeared from view, their strange chirps fading into the distance.

As Tarran watched the entourage move down the path, Corvan turned from the crack. He had to get some answers from the man who had just saved him from the black lizard.

He pushed on the door and saw a burak bounding down the pathway in long loping strides. Its broad shoulder slammed into the door, knocking Corvan back against the hinges.

Tarran cried out in pain. Through the crack Corvan saw the huge animal toss the man in the air and catch him again, like a cat playing with a mouse before killing it. Tarran's body flew in a wild arc and landed in a crumpled heap near the door.

Terror-filled eyes looked up through the crack. "Help me," he croaked.

The hammer throbbed in Corvan's hand. Power surged through him. He tried to push on the door but the weight of the creature held it tight against the wall.

The beast roared, and a blast of sour breath slammed into Corvan. The hinges creaked as the burak forced its snout into the crack. Its deafening shriek ripped at Corvan's eardrums, and he dropped the hammer to clench his hands over his head. The door banged again and the horrible shrieks stopped.

Tarran's bloody face was just a foot away. "Help me, Cor-Van."

The pitiful face was suddenly dragged away. A final cry echoed in the cavern. In the silence that followed, Corvan heard the snapping of bones. His stomach heaved.

The great door boomed as the beast smashed into it. The stone slab bounced away from the wall and Corvan caught sight of the burak retreating up the slope, a broken body dragging in the dirt beside it.

Corvan put his head in his hands. He had let the man who saved his life die before his eyes. He had given in to his fear, and the young man had paid the price.

He fell to his knees in the dirt. Blue shafts of light from around the nearly closed door illuminated the dust-filled air around him.

The distant shriek of a burak jerked Corvan's head up. Tsarek had said they always hunted in pairs, but Corvan had not heard the second one during the attack. He held his breath and listened intently. He detected no sound, but he had seen how quickly the large beasts could move.

He scrambled around the floor and found the hammer lying next to the wall. The handle felt cold and the light from the symbols was gone. He stuffed it into the holster.

The great stone door was jammed against Tarran's staff. If it hadn't been there, Corvan might be locked in this passage forever. Pushing the door away, he picked up the staff.

Who was this priest who had saved Corvan from the black lizard yet given up the valuable key? As Corvan ran his hand over the staff's red globe, rays of light shot out, throwing a kaleidoscope of muted patterns around the tunnel.

Movement up the pathway caught Corvan off guard. The other burak was coming! Corvan yanked the door shut. He heard a sigh of air, like a refrigerator door shutting, then three sharp clicks. Muffled blows hammered on the other side of the door. Corvan slumped down against it and leaned his head against the cold stone.

High above him the blue moon shone brightly, but now he could see it was a massive lumien. Scattered around it were smaller ones, the pink "stars" he'd seen earlier. This must be the Cor that Tsarek had referred to.

As the muffled blows against the door fell away, Corvan realized that he had just locked his only exit out of this violent underground world, and the black lizard had the only key. Now there was no choice but to go down into the huge cave and look for the Cor, whatever that was.

Corvan looked across the cavern to the far wall, but it was lost in a brown haze over what looked like jagged mountains.

He pushed to his feet, drawn forward by the sheer size of this new cavern. It was hard to judge distance in the dim light, but it had to be miles to the other side. As he stepped forward, his foot slipped, and he recovered to find himself at the edge of a precipice that ended in a steep slope hundreds of feet below.

He scrambled back and looked down. At the bottom of the cliff, he could make out the tiny figures of the pale men as they carried the lizard over a narrow bridge.

Corvan blinked. Beyond the ribbon of dark water was the largest city Corvan had ever seen. It was also the strangest for it was laid out in concentric circles from a central hub. Each circle joined the next one at periodic intervals making the streets look like the web of some incredibly large spider.

THE HAMMER

A few larger buildings, some missing their roofs, were scattered about the center of the city, but nowhere could he see a building with a pointy roof.

He scanned both sides of the main street that ran toward the far wall. The left side of the city was in ruins, but the right side looked relatively undamaged. A thick wall ran between them.

When the lizard's pale servants reached the central plaza, they turned right and proceeded through a gate in the dividing wall. They marched up a wide street through wisps of fog that flowed down from a wide gate.

Corvan looked ahead of the tiny travelers. His eyes opened wide in amazement. Rising above the city, almost to the top of the cavern wall, was a stone figure sitting on a massive throne. Corvan inched closer to the edge of the cliff, his eyes wandering over the broad chest. Tiny squares of light shone through the stone robes. The statue must be a temple of some kind, like the temple of Ramses in Egypt. Topping the wide shoulders was a rough block of stone. The face was not yet finished.

Corvan's gaze swept down over a powerful stone bicep overlaid with writhing snakelike creatures. The arm lay on one of the wide armrests of the throne, its hand gripping a tall staff similar to the one Corvan now held.

At the bottom, surrounding the huge stone feet, tiny figures crawled like ants around a circular stone wall. Great stone blocks were being moved into position with cranes and rollers. Hundreds of fire sticks burned around the construction site, casting their hazy heat waves into the air around the statue and making it look almost alive, like it might leave its throne and crush the city beneath its feet.

Corvan peered into the gloom off to the left of the statue. Was that a pointy roof?

A rough shove from behind pitched him over the edge. Before Corvan could scream, two powerful hands gripped his shoulders and held him dangling in air.

CHAPTER TWENTY

"So, Tarran," a deep voice growled in his ear, "once again you have proven yourself to be as inept as your father. Only this time he cannot save you from the Chief Watcher. Perhaps it would be best for everyone if you accidentally fell to your death." The hands on his shoulders relaxed, and Corvan's body slipped down.

"Kharag," a soft voice spoke. "Our orders were to relieve them, not kill them."

"Shut up, Rayu, or you will be next. It would be a relief to not have any of you priests hanging around the barracks"

Corvan slipped another inch, then was hurled back toward the door. He lay still and looked out under the folds of his hood. Men in black cloaks moved about. A boot caught him in the leg.

"Get to your feet," Kharag growled.

Using the staff in his hand, Corvan stood, keeping his hood down low and his eyes on the ground. Two large boots planted themselves in front of him.

If these men were from Tarran's temple, they might take him to the very place Tsarek had told him to go. A spark of hope lit within him.

"Why is your staff lit?" It was snatched from his hand. "And why is there blood on it?"

"Kharag," another voice called, "look over here."

Corvan raised his eyes and watched Kharag move to where a small knot of soldiers stood around Harmon's body. An old man in a green cloak pushed in to crouch over the corpse. "This wound was not made by a staff," he said.

Kharag shoved the man away from the body.

"We don't need your help, Rayu. This is not a temple affair. The body and the prisoner are under the jurisdiction of the Chief Watcher."

The large boots returned. "Tarran, you are under arrest for the murder of

Harmon. You will immediately be taken before the Chief Watcher for judgment."

Hemmed in by soldiers on the narrow pathway, Corvan had no choice but to keep walking. There was something odd about his guard. He couldn't figure it out at first and then it struck him. Among these grown men he was of average height. Either the guard was chosen specially for their short stature or the people here did not grow very tall.

The light from the lumiens grew dimmer, and with his hood low over his eyes, he felt safe from discovery, at least for the time being. Once he was taken to the Chief Watcher, he would be exposed as an impostor. Beads of sweat broke out on his forehead at the thought of meeting the black lizard face-to-face.

He felt under his tunic and touched the hammer. It was cold and lifeless. Something had changed when Tarran died. The man's frightened face filled his mind. He pushed the image away, but the voice in his head kept pleading, "Help me, Cor-Van."

Silently he responded, *I couldn't. I'm not strong enough. I don't even know how to use the hammer.*

The eyes kept pleading. "Please, Cor-Van."

He tried closing his eyes, but the voice would not quit. It grew louder and more desperate.

"Stop!"

The men around him jostled to a halt and turned to face him. Kharag pushed through their midst and grabbed him by the collar. "Why should we stop? Are you too tired, Tarran? Did killing Harmon take too much out of you?" Kharag dragged him across the path to the edge. "If you are so tired, let me help you get to the bottom a little faster."

The old man named Rayu pushed passed the soldiers. "The Chief Watcher will not appreciate it if he does not have a chance to question your prisoner, Kharag. There is no reward for a dead body. I suggest we keep moving and get off this path before it gets too dark."

Kharag's face contorted into an ugly sneer. He tossed Corvan back toward the guards and gave Rayu a shove. "Keep your thoughts to yourself old man, or you will be the one taking a quick trip down."

Kharag stomped away as the soldiers formed an impenetrable wall around Corvan and plodded downward. There was no way out of this nightmare. Everything just kept going from bad to worse.

Someone gently squeezed Corvan's hand. Rayu looked up into Corvan's hood and smiled. Corvan nodded and swallowed a lump in his throat. At least he had one friend in this place. A soldier behind them coughed, and Rayu released his hand.

Weariness settled in, and Corvan fell into a trancelike state, stumbling down the winding path. The sound of rushing water brought him back to his senses and awakened his thirst. It had been a long time since he last ate or drank.

His guards pressed in against him as they approached the bridge. Although it was protected with a stone wall on either side, the soldiers stayed as close to the center as possible. A few glanced nervously at the water rushing below them. Corvan looked down. High levees kept the water from overflowing its banks. On the far side of the river, the wall of the channel climbed even higher to become the outer wall of the city.

The company passed through a broken gate and marched down the wide street Corvan had seen from above. The buildings on the left looked like empty shells, their doors broken off and roofs crumbling. On his right loomed a tall wall made of stone blocks of various sizes.

The road was uneven, and the soldiers stumbled in the near darkness. The few people they met pressed against the wall on the right side of the street until the soldiers passed, and then scurried away. Corvan could not see their faces, for everyone wore a hooded cloak—likely the only way to stay warm in the damp air.

Kharag led the procession through the city by the light of the staff's glow. The red globe cast strange, elongated shadows onto the wall beside them. Some of the figures looked like those on the hammer. He resisted the urge to pull it out and look.

The company reached the central crossroads. In the middle of the round plaza, Corvan saw a statue topped with the head of a man but having many arms sticking out of a convoluted body. Something moved in the shadows beyond it, and in the half light he caught a quick glimpse of a shrouded figure heading into a street beyond the statue. A whiff of lilacs reached out to him. Was that Kate? He stooped to look under the legs of the statue. The figure turned and looked in his direction.

Yes. It was Kate, with her blanket wrapped around her shoulders. Corvan jumped forward and stumbled over the soldier in front of him. They both crashed to the ground and in a flash Rayu was kneeling at his side, pulling his hood back over his head.

Corvan grabbed the old man's wrist and pulled him close. "There's a young girl in the street behind the statue," he whispered. "You must go and help her. She's wearing . . ."

"Are we going to have to drag the two of you up to the palace?" Kharag's angry voice echoed in the confines of the walled plaza.

Rayu leaned back and pulled Corvan to his feet. "We are all right. Just tripped over the loose cobblestones."

"Don't let it happen again," Kharag barked.

The Hammer

The soldiers moved on along the circular wall that curved around the right side of the crossroads. They came up on a tall structure that looked like a thin metal tree, its branches terminating in metal rings. Rayu gave his hand a firm squeeze, then disappeared behind it. Corvan wanted desperately to look over his shoulder and confirm that Rayu was going after Kate but he dared not stumble again.

At the top of the plaza, a pair of fire sticks framed a narrow iron gate. Kharag strode up and shouted out a command. It creaked open a few feet and the soldiers squeezed through. Just inside, a soldier stood yawning; his hand on the windlass that controlled the gate.

Prodding Corvan to keep up with them, the soldiers marched along the wide street toward the huge faceless statue that brooded over the decaying city. The street became a wide stone stairway, its balustrades crumbling and broken off like rows of rotten teeth. The climb exhausted Corvan. It was all he could do to force his feet to take the next step.

Just when he feared he might collapse and be discovered, Kharag commanded the company to halt.

Corvan raised his eyes and found himself in the gateway of the expansive walled courtyard that faced the statue. Kharag led them to the right and up a wide stairway.

They crossed an open area to stand before a massive wooden door set into the courtyard wall. Above them successive ranks of stairs, broken by large open landings, climbed toward the feet of the statue. Spread throughout the landings were more of the fluted metal trees, sprouting from circular stone platforms.

Kharag ordered the men to stand down and the soldiers sank wearily on the first set of steps. Corvan peeked out from under his hood and watched Kharag enter a small door next to the large gate. He tried to keep watch to see what might happen, but his head sank to his knees. He dozed for a moment, then jolted awake when two men pulled him to his feet.

Kharag swaggered toward them. "The Chief Watcher does not want to be disturbed tonight." The small door slammed behind him and Kharag glanced over his shoulder. His voice lowered. "I have been ordered to leave the prisoner in one of the cells. The Chief Watcher will decide his fate in the morning."

Kharag led them through the main gate, turned left, and entered a narrow street. A light glowed in a window next to an open gate. Two red-cloaked guards, armed with tall axes, stepped out. Kharag approached them and held out the staff, speaking in important tones.

One of the guards ripped the staff from Kharag's hand and pushed him aside. The soldiers around Corvan fell back as the red cloaks swept around him and ushered him through the door and across a small courtyard toward a row of short, round towers that stood in front of a tall building. A shove sent Corvan stumbling inside one of the towers. The door slid closed behind him.

The cell was about five paces in diameter. Other than the faint outline of the door, the walls were smooth as glass. Pale lumien light shone down through a round opening high overhead.

Corvan crossed the cell to a low stone bench that jutted out from the wall. To the right was a shallow depression with a hole in the middle. Corvan wrinkled his nose at the smell. Obviously, this was their version of a toilet. Above the depression, a short, round knob protruded from the wall. When he touched the tip, clear water gushed from the underside and ran into the hole. After drinking his fill of the cool water, he sat on the bench. There was a lot to think about but he was too tired to keep his eyes open. Dropping the pack on the floor, he stretched out on the cool stone.

It seemed he had just closed his eyes when hushed voices pulled him from his sleep.

"Just let me make sure he is all right," a woman said. "The law allows an untried prisoner to have visitors."

"That law is only for those who have been charged," a man's voice responded. "He is not yet officially charged with a crime against the palace."

"All the more reason not to deny my visit."

"That is true, Tyreth, but you and I both know it is only the Chief Watcher's interpretation of the law that counts. I would be in a difficult position if he decides this visit was not in his best interest." He paused. "Whatever we do must also be good for us, if you understand what I mean."

"There is no 'us,' Morgon," Tyreth responded crisply. "Those days are over. You made your choice."

"I had no choice then. But now there are new decisions to be made."

"What are you talking about?"

"Major changes are about to take place. I cannot say more, but I need you to consider what could be if things were resolved between the palace and the priests. If I were able to take over the palace and rule the Cor, I would need a worthy counterpart. Together, we could restore our world to its former glory."

"After what you've done to the priests and to my family? I would rather go to the Wasting before I would agree to marry you."

"Things are not as they seem." Morgon's voice lowered, and Corvan had to strain to hear him. "Soon I will be able to make it all clear to you. Promise me you will attend the ceremony with me, and I will assure you that you will see things differently."

"The high priest's daughter cannot be seen at that ceremony."

T THE HAMMER

"She must not be *seen* there . . . but she will *be* there if she wants to visit her brother before he goes to trial."

There was a long pause. "Fine. I will attend the ceremony with you. Now let me in to see Tarran."

The man's tone softened. "Thank you, Tyreth. You won't regret it. I will awaken him and then wait for you by the door. I still have to fulfill my duty as his guard."

Heavy-booted feet crossed the room, and a hand roughly shook Corvan's shoulder. "Tarran, wake up. Your sister is here to see you."

Corvan sat up. Morgon strode back to the door like a matador going out to defeat a bull. He raised one hand, and a band of amber light encircled the cell, illuminating the form of a woman standing just outside the door. "Be quick. The next guard will arrive shortly."

The woman entered the cell and walked toward him. She wore a long, pale blue cloak with silver tassels hanging from the hood. As she approached, she swept the hood back, revealing an intense face framed by long black hair that moved like silk with each step. She was not much older than Corvan, nor much taller. Her complexion was smooth and brown.

She smiled at him, and his heart warmed until he reminded himself that she was under the impression he was her brother—the brother he had let die. He dropped his head and looked at the floor.

She pulled him from the bench into an embrace. "Tarran, I am so glad to see you." The words were full of concern, but the embrace was cool and aloof. "Have they been treating you well?"

Before he could stop her, she pulled his hood back and looked into his face. He waited for her expression of surprise, but she looked right through him. Her eyes were as blue as a prairie sky in winter but they were cold and expressionless.

"How can they accuse you of killing Harmon? You two went through training together. This must be a terrible mistake."

Corvan opened his mouth to speak, but she touched his lips. Her fingers were soft and smelled of sweet spice.

"Tarran, you look terrible. I have never seen you so sick. These cells are so cold. Here, take my scarf. And make sure you keep your hood on." She pulled off her white scarf and looped it around his neck.

The kindness of her gesture brought tears to Corvan's eyes, and he lowered his head again.

The girl put her fingertips under his chin and raised it up, her eyes brimming with tears. "Don't give in to fear," she whispered. "Be brave." She tugged on the back of his hood, then spoke loudly again. "Keep your hood on at all times and stay warm. I will try to come back to see you before your trial begins."

She stepped back. "I loved you . . . Tarran." Her voice faltered and her tears fell freely as she flipped her hood up over her head and turned for the door. She said something to Morgon about her brother being ill. The door clicked shut behind them.

Corvan sank down on the bench. She knew he was not Tarran, and she apparently knew her brother was dead. He touched the scarf and released its soothing scent. Had she come just to tell him to keep his head covered so his face could not be seen? But why had she uncovered it in the first place? He hoped Morgon had not been watching while she left.

He whipped the hood back over his head and a small packet fell into his lap. A soft piece of cloth tied to a stubby stick, like a short pencil with a hard brown eraser. He untied the cloth and discovered a tiny pebble inside. He held both items up to the band of light on the wall. Pressing the bump near the top of the stick, he heard a tiny voice. He held the stick to his ear.

"We must get you away from the guards before the morning comes." A man was speaking in clipped phrases, like a scratched record. "Your only chance is for the guards to think you have died of some sickness. Swallow the pill we have given you. It will cause you to appear as if you are dead and then they will allow us to come get your body. You must do this immediately, or the next cycle will begin and the Chief Watcher will start your trial. Make sure you drop this message and the cloth down the waste hole. Act immediately. We shall speak with you after we give you the antidote and bring you back to life."

Corvan pushed the knob again, but the stick remained silent. Bring you back to life? The girl was obviously not one of the dark eyes his grandfather had mentioned, but how could she know this pill wouldn't accidentally kill him? Placing the pill onto the cloth on the bench beside him, he dropped the stick down the hole.

His stomach growled as he sat back down. Even if he were to take the pill, he shouldn't do it on an empty stomach. He opened the side pocket of the pack and took out the last piece of beef jerky. It was softer than usual and the salt had risen to the surface in a white crust, but it was the most delicious thing he had ever tasted. He washed it down with a long drink from the stone tap.

Hunger still gnawed at his belly. He dug to the bottom of the pack and found a tin of beans he'd missed when he'd lightened the pack. He was about to throw it down the hole but changed his mind. Kate still had the Swiss Army knife and she would be hungry if he ever caught up to her.

The can went back into the pack, and he pulled out the last of the chocolate chips. He poured half of them into a small pile next to the pill, then rolled down the top of the bag and stuffed it back into the pack. He would save some for Kate. She loved chocolate.

"Don't move." Morgon's deep voice growled in his ear. A sharp point pressed into his back. How long had the man been standing there?

"So, you've been holding out on us, have you, Tarran? These days, when there is so little food, it's a crime to not share with others." The knife dug deeper. "Punishable by death, if you recall. Move over to the wall."

As Corvan slid against the wall, Morgon moved around the bench and sat at the far end, keeping a long black knife between them.

"I regret that it has come to this, Tarran. You and I should have been brothers, not enemies." Morgon looked closer, trying to see into the recesses of Corvan's hood. "I have to ask you something, and I need you to answer me truthfully. Have you defected to the palace? Or is your presence here just another one of the high priest's insane plans?"

Corvan stared at the floor.

"Your silence says it all. The high priest is a fool, and you will be destroyed by his schemes. The Chief Watcher does not tolerate treachery. He will not let you live."

Corvan remained mute.

"So, what are these?" He poked at the chocolate chips with the tip of his knife. "Something your sister brought you? She is as clever as she is beautiful." He picked one up and rolled it between his thumb and forefinger.

Corvan shifted his weight, and Morgon raised the knife to Corvan's chest. "Don't try anything, Tarran. I don't believe you are really ill. You've never been sick a day in your life."

Morgon sniffed at one of the chocolate chips, then nibbled at it. "This is sweet. Just like your sister."

He reached out and pulled the white scarf from around Corvan's neck. "You won't need this in your crypt. Nothing will keep you warm there." He laid his knife by the chocolate chips and looped the scarf around his neck. Then, picking up the chips one by one, he dropped them into the palm of his hand.

Corvan glanced at the knife. Should he try to grab it? Morgon seemed intent on picking up the chips. Corvan raised his eyes and found a smirk twisting at the corners of Morgon's mouth. He was baiting him into a fight.

The man plucked up the last three chips along with the small pebble. As Morgon added the pill to his handful of chips, Corvan twitched. In an instant Morgon swept the knife off the bench and pointed it at Corvan's heart. "A little too slow, Tarran. Perhaps you are sick."

Standing, he stuffed the chips and the pill into his mouth.

"The night guard will be here shortly. If you will not answer my questions . . ."

Something crunched in his mouth. He grimaced, jabbing his tongue into his upper molars. Morgon flinched and grabbed at his stomach, drops of sweat breaking out on his face. "What have you—" He put the knife to Corvan's throat, his hand shaking.

Corvan jerked away, his hood falling back off his head.

Morgon's eyes widened. As he stepped back, his foot caught in the toilet hole and he crashed to the floor. The knife slipped from his hand and skittered across to the wall. His mouth moved but no words came out.

Corvan stood, and Morgon pushed back from him like a crippled crab. His hand flailed toward the door, then he collapsed onto the floor, motionless.

The door slid open and Corvan looked out into the courtyard. Nothing moved. He ran to the bench and snatched up the pack.

There was a whisper of sound behind him. As he whirled around the door closed tight.

THE HAMMER

CHAPTER TWENTY-ONE

No matter how much Corvan waved Morgon's limp hand around, the door remained locked. He searched the man but found only a leather scabbard strapped to his leg. Corvan removed it, slipped the knife back into it, and dropped the sheathed blade into his pack.

As he stooped to pull the pack to his shoulders, two wavy tentacles poked out from the toilet hole. Long, thin legs appeared, followed by the hugest spider Corvan had ever seen. Its bulbous body was bigger than his fist. A shiver ran through Corvan's shoulders as the spider pulled itself from the hole and walked stiltedly to the wall. It climbed, finding minute footholds in the smooth black surface.

That was the answer! Corvan dropped the pack onto the bench and pulled back the top. He searched through all the pockets for the rope. Surely he hadn't left it in the labyrinth. Finally he found it, coiled up inside the top pouch.

Releasing the thin strands, he set the disk on the floor and used the control end to move it up onto the wall. He watched it climb slowly up the glossy surface into the gloom. Would it be long enough?

The rope stretched and became thinner, but it wasn't pulling out of his hand. It reached the ceiling and moved away from the wall toward the circle of light. Suddenly it fell back, glanced off his head, and landed in his hood. The hole in the roof must be just out of reach. But the rope was still in the air, and his hood twitched like a thing possessed. The spider! Corvan flailed around, shaking and jumping to dislodge the creature. It scrambled free and scrambled frantically through his hair. A scream pushed past his lips as the spider flipped past his face and dropped to the floor with a plop like a deflated rubber ball. It pushed up onto its twiggy legs and staggered back down the hole.

Someone must have heard him scream. He had to move fast.

The thin rope still hung near the middle of the room so it had to be anchored close to the opening in the ceiling. Images of the dream where the rope slipped through his hands played out in his mind. He tied the knob end around his waist and gripped the rope tight.

He tensed his muscles and pulled himself off the ground. The rope stretched and gently lowered him back down. Was it coming loose?

Voices drew near the door. He reached up and gave the rope a quick jerk. It tightened like a rubber band and yanked him off his feet. Air whipped past his ears. A circle of light shot past him as he rocketed out of the opening into the cool air. His ascent peaked and he fell back down, sprawling across the roof of his prison cell.

He lay there for a minute, catching his breath. This rope was truly amazing. No wonder Tsarek had been so impressed with it.

Crawling forward, he peered over the parapet. The guardroom was open, and two red cloaks searched the courtyard. No going down that way. He would need to climb onto the main building that towered over the cells.

He pulled back from the edge and crossed to the back wall, sending the green disk up to the top of the building. After gently stretching the rope out, he gave it a small tug. Immediately he found himself being dragged and bumped upward like a sack of potatoes. He swiveled and managed to get his feet against the wall. The slippers gripped the stone, and Corvan climbed effortlessly, just like the spider in the cell below.

The flat roof of the building was much larger than he'd expected. This must be the palace of the Chief Watcher. Corvan tiptoed across the roof to the far edge and looked down into the large plaza he had entered as a captive. To his right the dark statue loomed high over the city. Even without a face, it seemed to be watching him.

Thick fog puffed up from behind the stone wall, sending tendrils through its arched gate. An eruption of white vapor overflowed the wall, creating dense waves of luminescent fog that swept down into the plaza, surrounding the round pots with their tall metal trees. From up here it was clear that at some point in the past, each of the curved posts must have had a lumien attached to the ring on its end.

Across the plaza, a peaked roof rose high above the mist. Finally he had found the priest's building. But he was trapped inside the Chief Watcher's complex. If he dropped down into the courtyard, he would still need to get past the guard standing at the small gate.

What if he didn't go down at all? He could walk the wall to get to the priest's side of the plaza. He'd often walked along the fence rails on his way to school when he and Kate competed to see who could go the farthest without falling off. The fence rails back home weren't forty feet off the ground, but the wall was wide and the slipper shoes would grip well.

But the wall was at least ten feet away. It was a bit lower than the roof, but there was no way he could jump across to it.

The guard at the gate below coughed. Corvan peered over the roof and discovered that an iron girder had been bolted onto the wall and secured to the building to reinforce the main gate. Corvan eased himself over the lip of the roof until his feet touched down on the narrow iron rail. He stepped forward and worked his way into the center. The guard coughed again and Corvan stumbled, sending a shower of dust floating down toward the guard's head.

A shout came from around the corner of the building where the cells were located. As the guard ran off, Corvan scurried over to the plaza wall.

As he made his way along the wall he discovered a flaw in his plan. Soldiers were rushing about in the prison compound below and he was plainly silhouetted against the dim blue glow of the lumiens. The shouts below were being answer by lights coming on in the windows of the palace above. If anyone looked his way he would be trapped.

Looking ahead, he concentrated on walking the wall. He hoped they were preoccupied looking for their escapee on the ground. Wisps of fog climbed into the air and floated past, partially hiding him from view. By the time he rounded the corner near the gates, the thick cotton of rolling mist had risen to the full height of the wall and was squeezing like toothpaste out through the main gate. It seemed he could almost step out on top of it and cut across to the priests' dwelling. It swirled higher, making it tough to see where to put his feet.

The pointed roof was set back from the plaza wall. Light shone from triangular skylights set into the roof. He considered using his rope to drop down into the fog so he could knock on the priest's gate, but decided against it. He didn't want to run into any of the soldiers who might be searching for him.

The wall of the plaza was connected to a thinner wall that surrounded the courtyard in front of the priests' building. Corvan turned onto the thinner wall and made his way over to the large peaked roof. Pulling himself up onto it proved easy, for the walls of the compound became the walls of the building. His slippers gripped flat slate and he tiptoed up to the skylight. The glass was smeared with droppings that must have come from bats—enormous ones.

He peered around the edge of the murky glass. A large lumien hung from a metal ring suspended from the center of the high ceiling, its thick vines twisting over the walls. Corvan tried wiping the glass with the edge of his cloak and the skylight swiveled silently open.

An angry voice spoke from the floor below. Corvan slipped over the sill onto a wide ledge that encircled the room.

A bearded old man in an embroidered green robe stood alone at the far side of a large table in the center of the room. But the angry voice came from beneath the pale blue cloak Corvan had seen earlier that night in the cell.

"I had no choice, Father." Tyreth was almost shouting. "If I hadn't given my word, Morgon would not have let me see him."

The old man slapped both hands down on the table. "That ceremony is an abomination—the opposite of everything we believe."

Tyreth tossed her head. "What other choice did I have? You told me that we have to play this out carefully. Besides, Morgon hinted at an alliance."

The bearded man glowered at her from under thick eyebrows. "Morgon can no longer be trusted. Why are you even listening to that man? That relationship—"

"Is over, Father. Do not be concerned. I had to listen to Morgon in order pass on the message to that . . . that boy."

"Tyreth! You are speaking of the Cor-Van."

"All I saw was a boy, a small child not yet of age to grow out his hair."

The old man pointed out the door at the far end of the hall. "Rayu told us he came from the passages. How could anyone come from the outside unless he is the Cor-Van?"

Tyreth shook her head. "If this one is the Cor-Van, it will be a long time before he is mature enough to lead anyone." She threw up her hands. "He was so afraid he was crying. I feel sorry for him if the Chief Watcher gets hold of him."

Corvan slumped down on the ledge. She was right, but he didn't want to be a leader. He didn't even want to be here. He just wanted to find Kate and get as far away from this awful place as possible.

The old man spoke in a cajoling voice. "We must give him a chance. With Tarran dead, my plans have failed. The Chief Watcher is onto us, and all the priests are in grave danger. This boy is our only hope. I need your support in this."

"If he is the Cor-Van you have waited for, why did he allow Tarran to die?"

"What makes you think he was there when Tarran died?"

"I felt my brother die and I know that boy was there with him. He had Tarran's staff." She paused, twisting the tassels that hung from her hood. "But where is Tarran's body? You know what they do to the dead." A tear slid down her face as she dropped into a chair.

Tyreth's father watched her for a moment. "We will ask him once he is here. Are you certain he understood the message? Does he have it with him?"

Tyreth fiercely wiped the tears away with the sleeve of her cloak. "I did my best. Morgon would not leave the doorway. He listened to every word." A frown creased her brow. "If that boy does have the hammer, it is obvious he doesn't know how to use it. We should rally the priests and follow through with Tarran's plan to take over the palace."

"And risk alerting the darkest powers to the existence of the Cor-van? Put the hammer into his hands? If the death of your brother did nothing else, it gave us the opportunity to get the boy out of the cell without anyone discovering who he is." He looked toward the door. "Why is this taking so long? We heard the signal for the end of the shift."

The old man strode over to the main doors and peered out into the small inner courtyard. Thick wisps of fog coiled around his ankles. He shook them off and shut the door. As he returned to the table he looked hard at Tyreth. "Why was a man of Morgon's rank taking guard duty?"

She rolled her eyes. "Because he knew I would be coming. He still believes you have misjudged him. He wants you to give him another chance."

The old man grunted and stepped in front of a large tapestry hanging on the wall, his gnarled fingers tracing the markings in its center.

He jumped when the door burst open. A young man with shoulder-length brown hair and sharp features burst into the room. Running forward, he stopped and bent one knee before the old man.

"Something has gone wrong, sir. They have found a guard dead in the cell, and the man they think is Tarran has disappeared."

Tyreth stood and smoothed out her cloak. "You see, Father? Your new Cor-Van has no sense whatsoever. He can't even follow simple instructions."

"Then we must find him. The Cor can only be ruled by the Cor-Van. Once we located him, I can prepare him for leadership with his counterpart."

Tyreth glared at him. "Do not think I am unaware of your schemes, Father. You can dismiss any thoughts that I would become the counterpart to this young Cor-Van. I am not willing to let you set me up for another marriage." She flicked the silver tassels on her hood. "When these are gone and I am allowed to marry, I will be making my own choice. I will not be used as a pawn."

The young man jumped to his feet. "Tyreth. The Chief Watcher has issued a warrant for your arrest and is on his way to personally carry it out."

"What?"

"Your scarf was found on the body of the dead guard."

Corvan almost groaned out loud. How could he have been so careless?

The old priest grabbed the young man's shoulder and spun him around. "Are you certain?"

"Yes. I was in the barracks when the orders came through."

"Then you must take Tyreth and hide her in the settlements." The old man walked to the tapestry and pulled on a looped cord. The wide cloth rolled up against the wall.

Tyreth shook her head. "That won't work, Father. If I'm gone, the Chief Watcher will tear the compound apart looking for me. Many priests will die."

Her father tied the tapestry in place and pressed his palm against the wall. A section slid back, revealing a narrow passage. "The Watcher knows the law prohibits civilians from entering the priest's area. This hall is as far as they may go."

Tyreth shook her head. "The Chief Watcher decides which laws must be obeyed. He has plotted to break your power for some time, and this is the perfect opportunity. He will not let an old tradition stand in his way." She turned to the young man. "Tell him, Jorad."

"Tyreth is correct, sir. We have reports of the Chief Watcher's men inside our compound during the night." His jaw clenched as he looked at Tyreth. "But I will die before I let them take you to the palace. I vowed I would never let that happen again to someone I—" He pulled out a long knife from within his robe. "If it's a fight they want, they shall get one. Let us quickly gather all the priests we can find. Even with all his power, the Chief Watcher won't be able to get the soldiers to move until the fog lifts."

Tyreth took the young man's hand and pushed the knife down. "No, Jorad. You have told me many times to choose my battles wisely. Now you must do the same." She released him and approached her father. "The Watcher will not dare sentence me without a trial. This Cor-Van must be somewhere in the city. You need to find him and ask him to help us. Now he truly is our only hope."

Corvan wiped a hand over his brow. He needed to do something. At least show his face so they wouldn't have to look for him.

As he pushed himself up on the ledge, Rayu appeared in the open doorway. "Sir, the Chief Watcher and a group of soldiers approaches our gate."

"In the fog?" Jorad asked.

Rayu nodded. "The Rakash drive them forward."

A steady pounding rocked the walls. The old man pointed to the secret passage. "Jorad, get inside before they break the gate down. Find this young Cor-Van and do whatever he asks of you."

Jorad shook his head. "No. Let me hide behind the door and kill the Chief Watcher when he enters." He waved his knife in the air. "It is the only way the Cor will ever have peace again."

The high priest did not drop his hand. "If you were to murder the Chief Watcher, you would forfeit all your rights in the Cor, including the right to marry."

"That law applies only to humans." Jorad snapped back, glancing over at Tyreth.

"No, it applies to all sentient beings. It was through our own devices that the Watchers have become like us. Now it applies to them as well."

Tyreth grabbed Jorad's shoulder. "I understand how hard this must be for you. But we cannot change the past; you must look to the future."

The knife fell to his side. "You are the only future I have left."

The pounding thundered as if a battering ram were smashing through the gate.

The old man seized Jorad's arm. "Swear to me you will teach the boy to be a Cor-Van, even if it means leaving Tyreth to face the palace alone."

Jorad wrenched his arm free and stepped back. Tyreth moved in close and put both hands on his shoulders. "Do as he tells you," she said softly. "If you help this young Cor-Van, we may yet see each other again."

The walls shook with another round of blows. The old man pulled Tyreth away. "Swear to me, Jorad. Fulfill your vow to me and the priesthood, or relinquish your green cloak."

Jorad's eyes flashed. He growled out the words, "I so swear," and stalked into the secret passage. The door slid shut behind him as the old man dropped the tapestry back into place.

Rayu gasped. "Sir, you have brought out the great tapestry. Why?"

The old man waved him off. "I thought the Cor-Van would be here tonight. I hoped he could tell us what it means. Let's hope the Watcher cannot read the Old Language. Go open the gate."

Rayu nodded and retreated. A moment later the pounding ceased.

THE HAMMER

CHAPTER TWENTY-TWO

Corvan expected to see a squad of soldiers burst into the hall, but instead the large black lizard slipped inside the door with a rustle of scales, its keen eyes searching the room. Corvan pushed farther back on the ledge.

Tyreth's father moved away from the tapestry. "Chief Watcher, we are honored to have your presence in our quarters. May you find the truth you seek."

A chortling hiss of a laugh slithered across the room. "High priest of the Cor, this time your pious religious greeting is most appropriate, for what I seek is standing right before me." He gestured with his damaged hand, the long polished claw glinting in the light of the huge lumien. "The most lovely Tyreth."

"Why would you seek me, most *honorable* Watcher?" The sarcasm in Tyreth's voice was thinly veiled.

The black spines on the lizard's neck stiffened. "I think you know my purpose here. I am certain your spies have already announced my arrival."

The high priest folded his arms. "If you have business in our quarters, you are required to state it clearly, Chief Watcher."

"Oh, yes. Your precious laws. We must keep all the laws and obey the priests. Then the light will come again to the Cor, and truth and justice will reign from the palace, just as it shows in your beautiful tapestry."

The black lizard approached the large wall hanging. "It's a wonderful thing, this religion of yours. False hope is so useful in keeping you humans in line."

As the Chief Watcher examined the tapestry, the high priest stepped up behind him. "Hope is all the people have these days. In your greed you have taken everything else away."

The lizard whirled around, his thick tail slapping the wall.

"Do not abuse your position by insulting me, High Priest. It is only by my permission that your religion still exists. Most of the people find my ceremonies much more satisfying, perhaps even more 'hopeful.'"

"Yes," Tyreth said coldly. "First you take away their food, then you have them worship gods who will give it back, as long as they sacrifice the best and brightest of their youth—the only ones who might stand up to you."

The black face contorted, the sharp spines around its neck pushing out like an angry porcupine. It studied Tyreth through narrowed eyes. "You are the brightest I have seen for a long time, Tyreth. I understand why Morgon was so determined to acquire you for himself." He smiled. "But I do not have the same use for you as he, so I believe the next Wasting will be your last."

The old man shook his finger at the Chief Watcher. "I demand a trial by the elders. She is the high priest's daughter."

The black lizard leaped forward and shoved the elderly man to his knees. "Do not demand anything from me, priest." He yanked the old man's head back and dragged the lone claw across his wrinkled neck. "I hold your life in my hands and will do as I wish." The long claw gestured to the door. "Does it not seem strange to you that I am here without my men? They know I am here to arrest your daughter. If I tell them you attacked me and I had to kill you, that is what they will believe."

"You can't fool everyone." The high priest tried to pull away. "The truth will eventually be made known. You can't kill the truth."

The lizard pulled the old man's head closer and looked into his eyes. "I rule the Cor, and it is time you embraced that truth." It gestured toward the tapestry. "Even your precious Cor-Van could not—" A long, slow hiss filled the chamber, as if a nest of snakes had been disturbed from hibernation. "Impossible! No one has ever been there and lived to tell about it."

He dragged the high priest toward the wall. "Where did you find this tapestry?"

Tyreth's father raised his head. "It has always been here. It is considered a valuable work of art. The legends say that only the Cor-Van can tell what it means."

"Legends!" The lizard spat the word in the old man's face. "When I am finished, that is all your kind will be, legends." He pressed the point of his claw into the taut skin of the old man's neck. A droplet of blood appeared and trickled down into the folds of the priest's robe. "Your foolish plans to overthrow me have failed." The Chief Watcher pulled the old man's head back farther. The high priest's gaze fell on Corvan's face. His eyes grew wide.

The lizard pushed his long claw deeper.

The chair that broke over the lizard's back came from nowhere, toppling his scaly body into a heap by the wall. Tyreth stood over her father, her shoulders heaving, two legs of a shattered chair clutched in her fists.

The dark reptile uncoiled like a charmed snake rising from a basket and slipped toward the young woman. Brushing the chair legs aside, he lifted her struggling body over his head, strode to the huge table, and slammed her down on top of it.

He pushed his nose against her cheek. "If you were not so useful to me in destroying this foolish religion, I would kill you now. Fearless ones like you are most dangerous, especially beautiful ones whom the people will follow." The black head pulled away and studied her face a long moment.

The long claw flicked out and ripped a jagged gash across her right cheek. Tyreth cried in pain and clasped her hand over the wound. Blood squeezed past her fingers and flowed onto the table.

The thin forked tongue of the Chief Watcher whipped out and licked the claw clean. He looked down at Tyreth writhing in pain, and clicked his teeth. "Such a waste." He turned to the high priest. "Your daughter has saved your life. I did not use enough poison to kill you, old man. Perhaps you will live long enough to see her sacrificed to the Cor's new gods at the next Wasting." He looked back to Tyreth, his neck muscles twisting. "Yes, this will be a special event. I will have all the priests join us for your trial. I do hope you live to see this, High Priest. It will be a fitting end for your family and your hopeless faith."

The lizard jumped from the table and clicked its claws on a silver disk that hung around his neck. In an instant, the hall filled with soldiers.

"Take these two to the cells," the Chief Watcher commanded. "When I questioned them on the whereabouts of Tarran, they attacked me." He pointed to the pieces of chair scattered across the floor. "The punishment for such treason is death."

The soldiers stood still, looking at the high priest and the scene before them. "I said take them!"

The men scurried to help Tyreth and her father to their feet, ushering them toward the door as if something terrible might happen to them at any moment.

Tyreth shook off their hands and walked with her head held high. The blood ran down her forearm and dripped from her elbow, marking her path as she exited the hall.

The high priest reached the doorway and turned around. "This is not over, Chief Watcher. The Cor-Van will put an end to your tyranny."

The black lizard dismissed the captives with a contemptuous wave of his arm and turned back to the tapestry.

THE HAMMER

The high priest pushed the palms of his hands together as if praying and pointed them up toward Corvan's hiding place.

Corvan watched transfixed as the high priest bowed and backed slowly from the room, the soldiers following after him. Was the old man giving him a signal? What did it mean?

As the noise of the soldiers faded away, the Chief Watcher remained motionless, studying the tapestry for what seemed an eternity. Finally he extended the long claw and cut out the center. The sound was like fingernails on a chalkboard and sent shivers down Corvan's spine.

The jagged piece of tapestry fell to the floor. The lizard picked it up and folded it into a neat square.

"It *is* over, high priest. Your Cor-Van could never beat us now." The black creature turned on his heel and strode toward the door.

Suddenly he whirled about and looked past the glow of the lumien, staring directly at Corvan. "I almost forgot about you."

Corvan froze in terror.

"I cannot allow you to live. There is far too much hope in this world."

The lizard dropped the folded tapestry on the unbroken chair and pulled a short curved blade from a scabbard at his waist. He gave the blade a twist and it opened to a circle of four curved blades. With practiced ease, he lifted his arm and released the weapon.

Corvan had no time to move. A flash of silver whirred past his ear, then returned to its owner. The lizard caught his weapon in midair. Then he stepped back, his cruel face full of anticipation.

In the stillness, Corvan heard the dripping of a tap. Splashes of light shimmered on the table under the large lumien. The large globe shuddered and fell a few inches, its main cord almost severed by the lizard's blade. Its life juice trickled onto the table as the long tendrils around it reached out to keep the heavy globe from falling.

With a loud tearing sound, the stem snapped, dropping the lumien with a sickening *splat* on the table. The huge globe exploded into pieces that rained down over the stone floor.

The lizard leaped up into the quivering mass that remained, flicked his weapon back to a single blade and cut out the center of the smashed globe. As the light ebbed from the shattered lumien, he pulled out a pulsing red core. He clutched it to his chest and poked about greedily in the pulpy flesh, sloshing his way around the table. Stepping down, he slipped his knife away and kicked aside a chunk of the lumien's thick skin. "Just like everything else in this foolish religion. The mother plant was also a lie. Only one heart."

He held the glistening red pod up in his claw and stared at it. A look of fear crossed his face, his eyes narrowing in anger. "I won't become an animal again." He spat the words out. "You gave them to me. You needed me to understand, and now I know more than you could ever comprehend. You will pay for doing this to me."

He dropped the lumien heart into his mouth, chewing and exhaling in ecstasy. Blood red juice trickled out between his pointed teeth. The dark eyes closed in satisfaction—then bugged open as if they would pop right out of his head. Every vein in his thick neck bulged and jerked as the lizard fell to the floor, writhing in agony and gurgling in the back of his throat. Was it choking on the lumien's seed?

A pool of dark shadows spread out from around the contorted body as if the creature was bleeding darkness. The light streaming into the room from the skylights dimmed, as if the black from below was rising to push it away. The temperature of the air plummeted. The Chief Watcher's breath shot from his nostrils in spasmodic jets of vapor as he whimpered on the floor. Corvan pulled his hands and feet into the cloak and huddled on the ledge.

The Chief Watcher gave one last terrible cry and was still. In the dead air, the light from the lumiens outside the skylights pushed back into the room, flowing around the dark creature. The lizard groaned and rolled onto his knees. The black eyes narrowed, and an ugly sneer spread across the scaled face. "Such amazing power in this one. So much pain . . . but it was worth it. Now I see clearly what I must do. "

The Chief Watcher stood to his feet and put his good claw under the thick black collar around his neck. "If I play this right, I can be free from you as well." As soon as the words left his lips, he hunched low and looked about the room.

Satisfied that no one had heard, he raised his head and sauntered out the door, banging it shut behind him.

THE HAMMER

CHAPTER TWENTY-THREE

Corvan lay still, waiting until the echoes faded and the silence fell thick around him. He had made a mess of everything. Kate was dying, Tarran was dead, and now Tyreth was being taken to the castle. Rolling onto his back he pulled out the hammer and held it up to the skylight. "Please, just get me out of here," he whispered.

The hammer lay cold and heavy in his hand as tears rolled down his cheeks. It was no use. The hammer had lost its power when Tarran died, abandoning him in a brutal world that he did not understand. The hammer was a curse. He should just leave it behind, find Kate, and get out.

Corvan sat up and peered through the skylight. The dense fog had dissipated, and a pale light filtered down. His gaze wandered up the cavern wall. There must be some way to get that door opened again.

His father would know what to do. He pulled out the ice glass and the twinkle of stars spread over the surface. His father's face did not appear, but the memory of what he said that starry night at the rock came clearly to Corvan's mind.

"*Your grandfather made me promise I would give it to you before your birthday. He said you should be old enough to choose between fear and duty by then.*"

His birthday had come and gone since he'd left home. Why would his grandfather think he would be ready to choose between fear and duty by the time he was fifteen?

More of his father's words came back. "*A good leader must do what is right by others, no matter what the cost.*" But he wasn't a leader and he didn't want to become one. He just wanted to go home. A falling star arched its way across the tiny sky and disappeared.

A creaking door startled him so badly the ice glass fell from his hand and rolled toward the ledge. Corvan grabbed for it, but he was too late. A long silence was followed by the sound of shattering glass from down below.

Corvan looked around the darkened room. Where was the door and who had opened it?

"I'm over here," a hollow voice called from directly across the room, where a shadowy figure waited. "You need to make your way around the ledge. There is a door here into the passages."

Corvan shielded his eyes. "Who are you?"

"Jorad. The high priest sent me to help you."

Pulling on his pack, Corvan crawled around the room. That explained the high priest's signal. He was showing Jorad where to find him.

Jorad squinted at him, and Corvan realized his hood had fallen back. "How old are you?"

This was not just idle curiosity. "Fourteen. No, fifteen now, I guess." He studied the young man's face for a reaction. His expression was similar to the look the bigger boys always gave him at school.

Jorad pointed to the main door below. "The Chief Watcher will still want to find the one he thinks is Tarran. I suspect the soldiers will be back as soon as it is light enough to search the priest's quarters. We must leave here immediately . . . Cor-Van." He jerked his head to the door behind him where a circular staircase wound up from below.

Corvan looked away from the man's searching gaze. "I'm not the one you are seeking. I don't—"

Jorad cut him off. "I'll need your help if I am to get Tyreth out of the Watcher's prison."

Corvan shook his head. "I can't help you. I have to find Kate and take her home."

"Kate?"

"The girl I followed down here. She is from my world. She has short brown hair and—"

"I have seen her."

Corvan stepped back, and Jorad grabbed his arm to keep him from falling off the ledge. "Kate is here?"

"Fortunately, Rayu found her before they did. She is being held in the broken side of the city. She is very ill."

"I need to see her."

Jorad frowned. "But Tyreth and her father will die if we do not help them."

"Can't your men rescue them?"

"There are few left and they are all old. The priest's compound is almost empty.

The Chief Watcher ordered all the priests to the outlying settlements to 'inspire' the workers who are harvesting food. He has scattered us throughout the entire Cor. Tarran was working to bring us together but now . . ."

"Don't we have some time before that ceremony the Chief Watcher talked about?"

Jorad sighed heavily. "A little, but the high priest might not live that long."

"Jorad, I promised to take Kate home. She can't survive down here."

Jorad was silent for a moment. "I understand what it means to feel you have abandoned someone you love. Besides, if you do not fulfill your vow, you will forfeit all possibility to be the Cor-Van." He turned to the door. "Come, I will take you to your Kate."

Corvan followed him. "I'm not your Cor-Van, Jorad. I'm just a kid who fell into your world."

Jorad shot a questioning glance at him over his shoulder as he stepped into the tight stairwell. He didn't respond.

Following a narrow tunnel at the bottom of the stair, they opened a door and emerged through the hole the Chief Watcher had cut into the tapestry. Jorad turned to examine the torn fabric while Corvan walked around the smashed lumien to where his glass had hit the marble floor. Instead of shattered bits, he discovered a spray of water droplets radiating out from two small pebbles, one as black as the hammer and the other brilliant white, like a newborn star. They were warm and stuck to each other with a magnetic charge. Corvan dropped them into his pocket and walked back to find Jorad sitting in the chair, gazing at the pulpy mess on the table.

"She was our only hope against the growing darkness. Now we will never be able to replace the ones the greedy beasts have consumed." Anger flashed in his eyes. "If you are to be a great Cor-Van, you must learn that if your pleasure causes others pain, your pleasure is evil. Selfishness is the source of all evil." Jorad pushed the chair away. "Come, it is light enough for us to move freely in the streets. It is a good thing you are wearing Tarran's green cloak. The Broken do not attack priests."

Corvan didn't understand everything Jorad said, but he was amazed at how differently everyone saw the cloak he wore. It was like they made a decision about it when they first saw it and then afterward could not change their mind.

As he turned to follow Jorad, a small flash of light from the table caught his eye. Peeling up a piece of the blackened lumien skin, he found three bright red gems sparkling on the table. "What are these?"

The young man returned to his side. "I'm not sure. They look like seeds from a tiny lumien, but those are always blue."

Corvan touched the wet spot surrounding the gems. "This is where drops from the severed stem of the lumien fell into Tyreth's blood."

Jorad's face brightened as he carefully gathered the small red objects. "I think each of these may be seeds to a new mother plant. But why are they red? It would only make sense if Tyreth . . ." His voice trailed off as he nodded.

Pulling a small cloth pouch from inside his cloak, Jorad poured the seeds inside and pulled the drawstring shut. He started to tuck them into his own cloak, then paused and placed the pouch in Corvan's hand. "As the great tapestry predicted, the Cor-Van becomes the guardian of light. Do not protest, for if you do not accept this responsibility, the only future for the Cor is eternal darkness."

CHAPTER TWENTY-FOUR

Jorad led Corvan through a maze of tunnels and out a concealed door into the empty streets.

"Where are all the people?" Corvan whispered.

Jorad glanced over his shoulder. "The palace has sent most of the population out to harvest food in the settlements: it's the only place left that we can grow our crops."

Wisps of fog snaked across the cobblestones and Corvan noticed Jorad went out of his way to avoid touching them.

"Is the fog poisonous?" He asked the priest.

"No." Jorad replied as he skirted another patch. "But when you live in the Cor, you learn to avoid the water at all costs. It is the harbinger of all things evil."

"I used to be afraid of the water until I learned to swim," Corvan bragged, hoping the young man would think more highly of him.

"Swim?" Jorad studied him.

Corvan was glad for the hood to hide his blushing face. "Well, I really sort of dogpaddle. But I do jump into water that's over my head."

Jorad stopped short and grabbed Corvan's arm. "Never make jokes about the water. The only ones who jump into the water are those who practice sorcery or who wish to die." He squinted into the dim recesses of Corvan's hood. He was going to say more but apparently thought better of it and turned away.

They walked in silence down the long stairway toward the center of the city. As they neared the gatehouse, Jorad swiveled around and motioned for him to stay quiet. There was no need, for the guard saw them coming and opened the gate.

"Priests," he snarled as they passed by. "A waste of lumien light."

Jorad marched straight ahead. The gate clanged shut behind them.

As they crossed to the right side of the square, Corvan could see that the statue in the middle was actually of a man, a woman, and a young child, their hands raised toward the ceiling of the cave. It had looked strange in the dark because the woman's head was broken off, her unblinking eyes staring at him from the muddy water of what was probably once a fountain.

Leaving the statue behind, they turned up a street across from where Corvan had entered the night before. The street Kate had vanished into. He was relieved that Rayu had found her and hidden her away.

"Tyreth is the only girl I've seen," Corvan said. "Are all the women working in the settlements?"

"No." Jorad put a lot of anger into that one word. "Since the rise of the Watchers, many females who come of age are taken to the palace. Some are lost at the Wasting to appease the new gods. We don't know what happens to the rest of them."

His pace slowed. "It is a curse to bear a child these days. Even young boys become slaves to the palace." He looked up. "It may be a blessing that as the lumiens have faded, fewer children have been born."

Corvan wanted to ask more questions, but the young priest squared his shoulders and walked away so fast Corvan had to jog to keep up with him.

They left the main road and took to narrow back alleys clogged with rubble from the crumbling buildings. In the early light, it was even more clear that this side of the once-great city was now an expansive ruin. The stench of decay floated thick in the air. The cobblestones of the alley were slimy with green and black mold.

Jorad stopped where the alley came out onto a wider road. He listened for a moment, then turned right.

"Jorad," Corvan whispered as he followed, "does anyone live on this side?"

"Most of the remaining citizens of the city live inside the walls and close to the palace for protection." He glanced down a side street. "Some live in these ruins. We call them the Broken."

"Why?"

He stopped and faced Corvan. "They lost their minds in the anarchy following the rise of the Watchers. Now they live here like wild animals."

Corvan cast a quick glance over the ruins. The deep shadows and rubble could provide ample hiding places for an ambush. "Are they dangerous?"

"Some say they practice abomination and eat flesh. The Chief Watcher uses that as an excuse to hunt them down. But lately the Broken have fought back and killed the soldiers. Now none of the palace guards come to this side except under direct orders."

A rock tumbled off a heap of stones behind them. Corvan looked nervously over his shoulder.

Jorad frowned. "You shouldn't be afraid. A Cor-Van does not give in to fear."

"Do you think you should call me that? Someone might hear you."

"Is there another name I should use?"

"My mother called me Kalian."

Jorad snorted. "If you wish to use a child's name, that is fine with me. Kalian you shall be until you earn your title." He turned on his heel and headed up the wide street.

Corvan lowered his gaze to the ground and followed behind the priest as he navigated the debris-clogged street. When Jorad stopped short, he walked right into him.

"Watch where you're going.," the priest snapped, and turned to one side, leaving Corvan standing before an ornate iron gate set into a high stone wall. The lock was rusted shut, but off to one side was a smaller opening, its metal door twisted off its hinges.

Corvan stepped up to the main gate and looked inside. Beyond the corroded bars was a miniature replica of the city they had just walked through; each of the buildings meticulously recreated in white stone. A wide boulevard of smooth stones headed up the centre. Towering over it all were the first of the dark mountain-like spires he has seen from the entry. "What is this place?"

Jorad examined the smaller door. "It is the city of the dead. That is why it has been spared destruction by vandals. Until now. Someone has broken down the door the priests use."

As Jorad stepped over the threshold, a commanding voice called out, "You there, stop in the name of the Watcher."

Jorad pulled his hood low over his eyes. "Keep your head down and let me do the talking."

Corvan stole a quick glance as he turned around. Three soldiers emerged from the wide road leading toward the gate. Two carried a body on a litter. Their hoods were thrown back and sweat glistened on their flushed faces. The third, an older officer in a hoodless black tunic, spoke as he approached. "What are you doing out here, priest?"

Jorad spoke in a disguised voice. "This man has a loved one who is kept here. It is important for him to pay a vow to come and see her."

The older man grunted. "Love, eh? Precious little of that these days." He stepped into the doorway. "Was this door torn down when you were here last?"

"No," Jorad replied. "This has been done recently."

"I thought as much. We were told the rebels have been raiding tombs for weapons and valuables. I will need to report this to the palace. Carry on."

Jorad nodded and turned to guide Corvan through the doorway.

The youngest of the two soldiers spoke. "Captain, this body is heavy. Can you order these two to help us get him stowed away?"

The captain nodded and turned to Jorad. "Before you fulfill your vow, you will help us carry this body to its final resting place."

The soldiers placed the litter on the ground, the young one groaning as he straightened. "Can we rest for a minute? My back is killing me."

The captain shrugged and the young soldier sank wearily to the ground. "You young ones just don't have what it takes."

The young soldier curled his lip. "I'm tired of hearing about the glory days of old. I don't care that you had food to eat, a home to live in, and a woman who loved you. We have none of those things, so I think we are the ones who are tough."

"Would you like me to lodge a complaint about conditions in the barracks, Private?"

The frown left the soldier's face. "No, sir. I don't blame the palace for what has happened to our world. If anything, it is the fault of the priests." He spat the final word in Jorad's direction.

The captain looked to Jorad for a response. He gave none.

The angry soldier pointed a dirty finger at Jorad. "The rebellion wouldn't have happened if it wasn't for all the rules you priests heaped on us. If you had allowed people to eat a few lumien seeds or enjoy other pleasures, their anger would not have spilled over to where they consumed every seed they could get their hands on. With all the fighting over food and women, the palace had no choice but to take over. Things may not be great now, but at least we are alive."

"Sure, *you're* alive," Jorad said, his disguised voice thick with disgust. "But how many die at the Wasting and in the settlements?"

The young soldier jumped to his feet and stood toe to toe with Jorad. "If the Chief Watcher believes a man is a threat to our society, why not let the water judge him?"

Jorad stepped back and turned to one side. "And what about the women and children who are taken to the palace?"

The soldier shrugged. "The palace keeps the rebellion in check and that makes all our lives easier. What do I care about the children of the rebels?"

The officer pointed at the young man. "That's the problem. Everyone wants an easy life, so we do whatever we are told to get it. At times I wonder how long a civilization this selfish can survive."

The older soldier, who had been silent during this exchange, finally spoke. "I still remember the days when our city was full of light, and lumiens hung over every doorway. Now our light grows dimmer each day." He glanced at Jorad. "But if we abandon hope, what reason is there to keep living? Tell us, priest. Is there still hope for a brighter future?"

The angry man pointed at Jorad. "Why ask him? All the priests do is offer false hope to control people for their own advantage. The priests belong in the water. I hope they drown them all at the dedication of the new temple."

"That's enough," the captain barked. "We have a job to do." He pointed to Jorad and Corvan. "You two bring the body and follow along."

The soldiers moved through the broken door. Corvan stooped to grab the poles. His hand snagged the burial shroud and pulled it off the body.

He looked down into the ashen face of Morgon.

THE HAMMER

CHAPTER TWENTY-FIVE

Corvan gingerly covered Morgon's face. Without the antidote for the pill, the poison must have killed him.

"Hurry up, Kalian." Jorad crouched between the poles, looking back over his shoulder. Corvan lifted Morgon's heavy body. No wonder the soldiers had complained.

If the city of the dead was any indication, the Cor city must have been beautiful in its day. Each small structure was ornately carved in white stone. For the first time in his life, Corvan felt like a giant, walking the streets of a city built for people a quarter his size.

"Jorad," Corvan whispered, "is each of these little buildings a gravestone?"

"Not exactly. Our people would not be buried in a hole that could fill with water, so we build crypts above the ground." Jorad's subdued tone made his words difficult to hear. "The top of each crypt lifts off, the dead are placed inside and the airtight lid is fastened back down to keep the smell of decay inside. When the next person in the family dies, the bones of the first person are moved to the bottom compartment with their ancestors. Some wealthy families construct a separate crypt for each family member."

Corvan looked up a cobblestone path that curved away from the main boulevard. "Why did they copy the layout of the main city?"

"Your crypt is in the same place here as your home is in the city streets."

"Does each person's crypt look the same as his home in the city?"

Jorad shook his head. "People put more energy into the creation of their tombs than into the houses they live in. These are much more elaborate than those in the city, but they give you an idea of what Kadir looked like before the destruction, when you could clearly see her beauty."

"Kadir?"

"Yes, we have other small settlements in the outlying areas where the workers live, but Kadir is our only city."

They approached the small circular plaza that marked the center of the crypt city. A gnarled old tree stretched its gray branches toward the roof of the cavern. It looked as if a bolt of lightning had split the trunk right down to the roots. Pale leaves decorated one half of the shattered tree while the other side was blackened and dead. Shriveled fruit still hung from its twisted branches. Jorad stopped short and Corvan stumbled and caught his balance against Morgon's body.

He straightened and noticed they were alone. "Where are the soldiers?"

"Weren't you listening? They said to wait while they checked out a crypt. Here, let's set the body on this bench."

It was a relief to be free of the litter. Shaking the cramps from his hands, Corvan crossed the tiles of the plaza, drawn in by the half dead tree.

Jorad joined him at the stone railing encircling the tree. "Legend says it was here long before our people entered the Cor. The living side was much greener before the light began to fade. I'm not sure why our forefathers built the city of the dead around it, but for people today it symbolizes the choices we make before we come here."

"Does the living side ever bear fruit?"

"No. But in the center of the great tapestry, there was a picture of a living tree with many fruits on it. It could have been this tree before it was damaged."

"Are the statues part of the legend?"

"What statues?"

Corvan pointed past the railing. "The two gray men looking at the tree."

Jorad peered past the split trunk. "I don't think it's the tree they're looking at." He stepped back from the railing. "I hear them coming back. Let's pick up the litter so we're ready to go. We don't want any trouble."

Corvan paused, struck by something odd about the dirt around the living side of the tree. He leaned over the fence for a closer look. Radiating from the shattered tree trunk were lines of footprints made by a child's bare feet.

"Kalian," Jorad hissed, "quickly!"

They had no sooner picked up the body than the three soldiers emerged from a street off to the left.

"But all the rest of his family is there," the older soldier was saying. "Perhaps he was to be placed in his father's crypt."

"No." The captain replied. "The order said to look for a large crypt with Morgon's name on it. Let's look up toward the rulers."

They marched away around the tree.

Jorad abruptly dropped his end of the litter back on the bench and pushed Corvan away from the body. With trembling hands, the priest uncovered the dead man's face. The shock on Jorad's face was replaced with such intense anger that Corvan stepped back farther.

A sharp whistle from the captain broke the tension.

Shaking his head vigorously, Jorad returned to the front of the stretcher and yanked it off the bench with such force that Corvan had to dive to grab the poles. He stumbled along after Jorad as the priest towed him after the soldiers.

The captain led them around the tree and up a wide street across from where they had entered. They passed between the two statues that stood on either side of the entrance. The gray eyes seemed to follow Corvan's every move.

The street was lined with grand tombs. It seemed to Corvan that in this replica city they were heading toward the location of the palace plaza. Sure enough, a few streets later, a walled area appeared before them, and beyond its gate, an open courtyard filled with tall tombs. Pointed roofs to the left and flat roofs to the right.

Jorad stopped beside the soldiers and looked up in silence. Corvan followed his gaze to the largest crypt he had seen so far. It was built up against the outer wall of the city and had a door in front large enough for a man to walk into without stooping. Ornate letters were carved into the stone over the door.

"This isn't right," the captain said. "There used to be two or three crypts here belonging to the ruling families."

"They have all been destroyed to make room for Morgon's tomb," the older soldier said. "They even used stones from the previous crypts to build it."

The captain stomped over to the litter and leaned over the shrouded face. "You were always working your way closer to the Chief Watcher. I suppose you thought you would someday become the new ruler of the Cor."

The captain shook, and Corvan wondered if he would strike the dead man. Instead he shoved the body away, almost knocking Corvan to the ground. "I refuse to dignify the memory of this man by putting his remains in this tomb."

"Then let us use one of the pauper's crypts," Jorad suggested in his disguised voice. "A tomb without a name for one who erased the names of others."

"Done." The captain turned from the ornate mausoleum and marched back toward the main gate. The soldiers and litter bearers had to run to keep up with him. In a short time Corvan was so out of breath he thought he was going to drop in his tracks.

At the tree, the captain turned down another road, then took a narrow track strewn with rocks. "Put him in there." He pointed to a large, plain box that rose sloppily from the ground. "A pauper's burial for the man who would be our king."

He turned to his soldiers. "Seal him up and get yourselves back to the palace. I have no more time for this nonsense." He pushed past them in the narrow passage, knocking Corvan off his feet.

As Corvan fell backward, the body slid out from under its shroud and slumped against his chest. Morgon's eyes popped open, and the pupils tilted back to focus on Corvan's face. Corvan tried to scream but only a gurgle came out.

"Don't let that bother you." The younger soldier brushed the eyelids shut. "Sometimes it happens." He bent close to Corvan, and his voice dropped to a whisper. "Get as far away as you can from this priest. Bad things are about to happen to them. You won't have to be a slave to the green cloaks any more." He straightened up, patted Corvan's shoulder, and spoke out load. "Just rest there until we get this thing opened. No doubt the priests are overworking their servants." He shoved Jorad aside and joined his partner in working the rusty metal latches that held the lid of the crypt in place.

Jorad set his side of the litter down and sidled up to Corvan. "Put your hood back on."

Corvan whispered frantically, "He's still alive. Morgon is still alive."

Jorad yanked Corvan's hood back into position. "Don't fall apart on me. The soldier is right. Sometimes that happens if you give the body a jolt."

"But Morgon was my guard at the prison. He took the pill the high priest sent but it didn't kill him."

Jorad grabbed him roughly by the shoulders, "How do you know?"

"His eyes focused on me."

Jorad crouched next to Morgon, straightening the shroud and wrapping it around the body. "You're right. He still has life in him. He was always much stronger than others."

With a loud creak, the rounded lid of the crypt eased up and out of the way. The soldier peered inside. "What luck, it's an empty one. Bring him over."

Corvan and Jorad straightened Morgon's body on the litter, and the two soldiers helped them lower it into the crypt. They must have expected the poor to die in groups, for there was room for three or more inside.

An eerie wail, like a rabbit in its death throes, floated over the cemetery walls. The soldiers looked anxiously at one another.

The younger one turned to Jorad. "Do your priestly duties, and then seal it back up. We want to be out of this part of the city well before dark."

The soldiers hurried away. Jorad bent down to scoop up pebbles and dirt. "Are they gone?" he whispered.

Corvan pretended to stretch. "Just another minute." The strangling sound came again, and the soldiers quickened their pace. "What is that noise?"

Jorad continued picking up pebbles. "That is the sound of the Broken. They are beginning to move about and hunt for food."

"They hunt people?"

"I believe that is why the soldiers are leaving. Are they gone?"

"Yes."

Jorad straightened, dusted off his hands, and dropped the lid of the crypt into place. "Farewell, Morgon. This is not how it should have ended, but everyone must live, and die, by the choices they make. You almost cheated death, but I can guarantee you it will not be for long. There is not much air in a sealed tomb." He lifted the first of the clasps and twisted down the large turnbuckles.

Corvan watched in shock, then put his hand on the rusty metal. "We can't seal a living man in a tomb."

Jorad shoved his hand away and turned fiercely toward him. "I know things about him that you do not. It is best if we seal his tomb and make certain it is all over."

"But it's not right."

"I am a priest of the Cor and I know what's right for my world. If you want my help to get yourself and the girl back to your own world you'll mind your business."

He stared at Corvan through narrowed eyes as he cranked down the second turnbuckle.

Corvan stared at the metal clasps as Jorad stomped off.

"Come on! We must hurry if we are to get to your counterpart before dark."

Corvan turned away from the tomb, a shiver running up his spine as he hurried to catch up.

Jorad strode ahead of him through the narrow paths, turning this way and that, always staying a few paces ahead.

"Jorad," he called out. "Is Kate here in the cemetery?"

Jorad slackened his pace. "Yes. This has always been a secure place for the priests to keep our business hidden from the prying eyes of the Watcher. We are expected to come and go regularly, and we can arrange meetings with other priests and our allies from the settlements."

"Are the rebels the captain spoke of your allies?"

"Many of the rebels were palace guards who lost family in the anarchy that followed the rise of the Watchers. In those days, everyone was betraying friends and family." His voice sagged with the memory. "The rebels fled into those crags up behind the graveyard."

He pointed to the jagged mass of rocky spires that climbed from behind the wall to meet the far side of the cavern. "I used to think they could be a good ally against the Watchers, but a new leader has come into power by claiming to be a Rantellic as well as the promised Cor-Van. He has taken to raiding the settlements for food and recruits. His foolish plans are going to get a lot of people killed."

"What's a Rantellic?"

"It was an ancient order of wise men. It does not matter, for they no longer exist. This new leader is a fraud in every way." Jorad sped back up. The conversation was over.

Corvan lost all sense of direction as they moved on through the maze of narrow streets and alleys. Jorad left the marked paths and threaded his way between the crypts to emerge on a street before a long, curving section of crypts that were very plain in design. They were much taller than most of the others, with short doors in front. Built side by side, the row of crypts looked a bit like the old motel near the city of Fenwood.

Jorad stopped and motioned for Corvan to stand still. He checked the streets around them, then inserted a short cylinder into a round hole in the front of a crypt. The entire wall opened inward, revealing a narrow alley that led into an open space beyond.

Jorad gave a shrill whistle and waited. He whistled again. "Something is wrong. Our guard does not respond. Follow closely and keep a sharp eye out for anyone coming up from behind." A long knife appeared in Jorad's left hand. They walked through the narrow alley with Corvan glancing nervously over his shoulder.

The secret entry emerged into a wide-open space walled by the backs of the tall crypts. Jorad scanned the roofs around the perimeter. Pulling Corvan close, he pointed to one of the walls across from them. "Kate is inside that one. Take this rod, push it into the hole, and the door will open for you. I will remain here and keep watch." He thrust a notched cylinder into Corvan's hand and pushed him out into the open.

Corvan half stumbled across the rocky ground to the back wall of a cracked and weathered crypt. He fumbled with the cylinder, almost dropped it, then managed to push it into the hole. Nothing happened. He twisted it from side to side, but still nothing. He turned to look over his shoulder at Jorad and a narrow section of the wall under his left hand slid to one side, twisting him around and dumping him inside the crypt; the round key rolling across the floor.

He jumped to his feet. The stone benches on either side of the musty room were empty.

Corvan turned to signal Jorad, but the door slid closed and the room went dark.

A loud bang overhead made him jump. Someone shouted just outside the door and he heard footsteps cross the roof.

A round light flickered in front of Corvan. He crept forward and bent down to look through the keyhole. Across the courtyard, Jorad stood talking with two armed men. Someone moved in front of the tomb, blocking his view. When he could see again, Jorad and the men had vanished.

A man in a dirty cloak marched into view and stood with his back to the door. His long hair hung in two braids down his back. He carried a staff with a long curved blade on top. At his waist was a short sword.

Corvan felt his way over the closest bench and leaned against the stone wall. These must be the rebel fighters Jorad mentioned. But why was Jorad working with them? He tried to think it through, but found it hard to concentrate. His last sleep had been in the jail cell. He had no idea how long ago that was. There was no point in trying to open the door with the warrior standing guard outside.

Corvan pulled off his pack and lay down, but his mind kept turning over the possibilities. Maybe Kate had never been here in the first place and this was a trap. His hand fell on a smooth object next to the wall. He felt its familiar shape and breathed a sigh of relief. Jorad had told the truth about Kate for in his hand was the Swiss Army knife she had taken from Tsarek.

The Hammer

CHAPTER TWENTY-SIX

A loud thump awakened Corvan. He rolled over and fell with a crash on the cold stone floor. A rhythmic pounding shook the room as if someone were using the roof of the crypt for a drum.

Red light flickered at the keyhole, and he crawled over to investigate. Darkness had fallen, and a fire leaped from an enormous metal brazier on the far side of the court. A large crowd sat on the ground around the fire.

A horn sounded in the distance and everyone jumped to their feet. Men standing on the roofs of the crypts jumped and pounded rhythmically with their staff blades.

Corvan crawled across the floor and felt along the wall until he located the round key. Taking it back to the door he slowly turned it in the hole and eased the door open a crack.

The pounding ceased as three older men entered through the alley to stand on a low mound of dirt behind the brazier. Another man entered. He was dressed in a long, flowing black coat that looked like leather or oilskin. He was the tallest person Corvan had yet seen, outside of the Sightless. His height was augmented by a head covering made of an animal skin with the head still attached. Teeth bared in a frozen snarl, it perched on top of his head, its glistening skin wrapped tightly around the man's head and down over his ears. As he stepped toward the fire, some among the crowd chanted, "Cor-Van, Cor-Van" and rose to their feet.

From his vantage point Corvan could still see the man over the heads of the crowd. His suspicions were confirmed. Most of the people of this underground world were short. It was about the only part of this place that he didn't find disagreeable.

Corvan looked at the man they were cheering. His posture was that of a person used to being out front and giving orders. The firelight highlighted the angular features of his face. Keen eyes shone from the shadows beneath his high brow as he surveyed his subjects. His audience cheered louder, and in spite of what Jorad said, Corvan found himself wanting to believe that this man might be the true Cor-Van.

The man soaked up the praise, standing even straighter in the flickering light. He motioned discreetly to the three men behind him. One picked up a container shaped like a Greek amphora and poured a thick black fluid into a hole at the edge of the metal brazier. The flames leaped up along with clouds of sticky black smoke.

The crowd cheered and men pounded on the crypts.

Corvan opened the door a bit wider. He wanted to hear what the man was going to say.

The man raised his arms, and the crowd grew quiet. "Our time has finally arrived. For too long we have been reduced to living in holes, our days growing darker as the rulers consume our light for their own pleasure. But the end of these evil days is in sight. As your Cor-Van . . ." He waited for more cheers but the crowd did not respond. "As your Cor-Van I am pleased to tell you that the final sign of our victory against the palace has been confirmed." He strode closer to the light of the fire, revealing a wide forked tail hanging from the back of the animal skin on his head. "The legends tell us that to rule effectively the Cor-van must have a counterpart. But since the rule of the Watchers, all possible counterparts, your wives and daughters, have been taken to the palace."

The crowd rose to their feet, shouting and pressing forward. Unchecked, they would have overrun their Cor-van and attacked the palace immediately. It took some doing for the leader and his men to calm them down and get them seated again.

"Men, we will have our revenge, for the miraculous has occurred. A counterpart worthy to be joined to your Cor-van has been brought to us by the priests. They have seen the light and have acknowledged that I am the rightful ruler of the Cor."

A murmur of questions rose from the crowd, but the leader pressed on.

"The priests have suffered for their support of our cause. The Chief Watcher has murdered the high priest. Tarran is dead, and Tyreth will be sacrificed at the next Wasting."

Tyreth's name rippled through the crowd. The men were not happy with this news.

"The priests have come to us in their hour of need, and we have agreed to help them save Tyreth from certain death."

He turned to the alleyway and Jorad entered to join him at the fire.

Corvan studied the priest's face. He could not tell if Jorad was pleased to be helping the rebel leader or not. It appeared the leader expected Jorad to speak, but the young priest just looked out over the crowd. He didn't look in Corvan's direction.

The silence was broken by a few catcalls. The leader raised one hand. "Men, listen to me. Jorad is here tonight as our new high priest. He has arrived just in time, for he is the only one who can lawfully join a Cor-van and his counterpart in everlasting union." He pointed to the alley, where two men appeared, bearing a chair between them. A veiled woman in a long white cloak sat on it.

The bearers stopped. Jorad held out his hand to help the woman down.

The leader stood beside her. "With the blessings of the high priest, and to fulfill the legends of the Cor, tonight, in your presence, I take as my counterpart the woman Kayat."

An assistant pulled away the veil, revealing Kate's face.

Corvan leaned forward and almost fell through the door as it slipped open even wider. He had finally found Kate, but with the sea of bodies between them she might as well still be lost. How could he possibly get to her?

A man in the crowd whistled at Kate and others joined in. The leader's head snapped around to squint his disapproval, the beady eyes of the stuffed animal head glinting in the light. The whistles died off.

The men were right. In the brilliant white cloak and with her short brown hair pulled back into a tiara that sparkled in the firelight, Kate was beautiful. But there was no smile on her face. Her eyes were sunken and vacant.

The leader said something about his counterpart and the men jumped to their feet, almost blocking Corvan's view. They repeated one phrase of a song over and over, working themselves into a frenzy.

Corvan pulled back from the door. He must do something quick, or Kate would be taken away before his very eyes, and she would die under the light of the lumiens. She looked like she was barely alive already.

"Come on, Corvan," he muttered to himself, "there has to be something you can do."

He pulled the hammer from the holster. "I was too afraid to help Tarran. I won't do the same thing to Kate."

He held the black handle in front of him, but there was no sense of power or direction. Annoyed, he snapped it back into the holster. Morgon's black knife would be more useful than a dead hammer. He dug into his pack and pulled out the blade, along with a bright red cylinder on a stick. That would be even better.

With the fireworks to create a diversion, he might be able to help Kate and Jorad escape. Digging through the pack, he retrieved the rest of the fireworks, the tube of matches, and a stubby candle.

With the Swiss Army knife, he poked three holes around the edge of his last tin of beans. Sticking the three bottle rockets into the holes, he placed the can just inside the door. With the smallest blade, he drilled three holes just below the top of the candle, placed it on the top of the can, and inserted one rocket fuse into each hole. If his crude calculations were correct, by the time the candle burned down to the fuses, he should have reached Kate and Jorad.

Corvan slid the door half open. The noise of the crowd was deafening in the enclosed space. Corvan tried to get a glimpse of Kate through the mob and a shower of dust fell past the open door. He had forgotten about the men on the roofs. Those off to the sides could easily see him if they were to look his way. Corvan stepped back, battling the rising fear. Morgon's knife lay on the ground next to the roman candle and the pack of firecrackers. He lashed the knife to his forearm along with the roman candle and stuffed the firecrackers into the back pocket of his jeans. It was time to act, not think about everything that might go wrong.

He crouched to light the candle. There were three matches left. He struck one. The head broke off and fizzled on the ground.

His hands shook as he pulled out the second. He needed to have at least one left to light the firecrackers. The next sputtered and caught. He touched it the wick and a flame sprang to life. As he dropped the match to the floor, the candle wavered and died to a smoking ember.

One match left. He would have to find another way to light the firecrackers once he got close to Kate. Striking the last match, he held it to the candle until it singed his fingers. This time the flame flickered and grew strong. He slid the can closer to the edge of the door, pushing some dirt under and around the bottom so that the rockets pointed out into the dark sky.

Corvan stepped out the door. Moving off to the right, he kept his back tight to the walls of the crypts. He had room to move at first but soon discovered that the men had spread to the sides and were blocking his way. He backed into a crevice between two crypts. Something was missing. He felt for the knife; still there. The krypin was still attached to his belt. The pack. He had forgotten his pack in the crypt. The slingshot. It was still at the very bottom of the pack. That would have been more valuable than the black knife. But there was no time to go back; the rockets would be flying any second.

The crowd shifted and he caught sight of Jorad and Kate, just twenty feet in front of him through the tangle of bodies. The alley behind them was empty, but armed guards stood watch on the crypt roofs that flanked the narrow channel. One peered over the crowd and then jumped across the gap to his companion, pointing toward Corvan's flickering candle and shouting over the din. The other man nodded, and they moved out over the tops of the crypts toward the light.

Corvan pushed out of the crack and entered the mass of bodies, bouncing with them in their frenzy but making sure he moved steadily in Jorad's direction. He bumped into a stout man, who responded by shoving him into someone else. Corvan evaded another body check and stepped in close to Jorad. The man's eyes widened in recognition as Corvan put a hand on his shoulder.

Corvan shouted over the din. "There is going to be a bright light and then loud noises. Take Kate and meet me by Morgon's grave."

Jorad hesitated, looked intently at the rebel leader, and then nodded. Corvan thrashed away from them and sat down at the wall next to three older men who watched the crowd in disdain.

The rebel Cor-Van stood close to the fire, hollering and motioning for silence. Over his head, Corvan saw the two guards peering down at his flickering candle. "Come on, come on, do something," Corvan urged aloud.

Someone kicked his side. He looked up to see one of the older men looking down in disgust. Corvan grinned at him sloppily. Not wanting another kick, he slid away, bumping against two full jars of fuel leaning against the wall. The jars scraped along the wall and tipped over on their pointy bottoms, the contents oozing down into the alley.

The energy of the crowd was dissipating. Those closest to the fire were standing still and staring at Kate.

"Come, high priest," the rebel leader cried out. "Come and bless our union."

The din subsided.

Jorad raised both hands. Silence fell on the crowd. "God of the Cor, we seek your will tonight. We ask you to give us a sign if you are unhappy with us. Show us if we have moved forward without understanding your will."

The crowd shifted uncomfortably. The false Cor-Van waved his three comrades forward. Jorad continued to pray, asking in more fervent terms for the gods to demonstrate their displeasure if this were not the right time for the Cor-Van to unite with this counterpart.

As the three men moved toward Jorad, Corvan crawled along the wall behind them and closer to the fire. The rockets in the crypt door must have failed. The firecrackers would have to provide a diversion. Carefully taking aim, he lobbed the entire packet of firecrackers toward the brazier.

THE HAMMER

As the packet tumbled through the air, a shaft of light tore through the darkness, followed by a blast that shook the ground. A guard cried out as he fell off a crypt. Men threw themselves on the ground and covered their heads.

Two more bright lights screamed into the sky. Corvan glanced over to see Jorad leading a docile Kate out through the passage.

Bang! Bang! A pair of explosions cracked the night air, and then darkness dropped back onto the crowd. The rebel leader called out for more light. One of his men poured more oil into the brazier. As the flames leaped up, the firecrackers went off in rapid succession, spitting flaming balls of oil in all directions.

The man with the oil jar jumped back, sloshing oil on his robes. In a flash, he was on fire. Screaming, he ran through the crowd, who climbed over one another to get away.

Corvan backed up to the wall and slipped along it toward the alley.

The crowd was awash in confusion. All except the counterfeit Cor-Van. He was shouting to his two helpers and pointing at Corvan, hatred twisting his narrow face. Somehow Corvan's special cloak had failed him. Whatever the false Cor-Van saw in him, it wasn't good. The two men turned toward Corvan.

The last of the firecrackers spit a blob of flaming tar at Corvan's feet. Whipping the Roman candle out, he stooped and lit the fuse from the bubbling flames.

The two men stopped short at the sight of the firework sparking in Corvan's hand like a magician's wand. Their leader shouted a command, but before they could move, a flaming ball shot from the cardboard barrel of the Roman candle with a soft *fwoop* and hit one in the shoulder. He fell back into the crowd.

Corvan shuffled sideways, keeping his back against the wall and his eyes focused on the next man.

Fwoop, fwoop, fwoop. Three green balls whizzed past the man's head and he also disappeared into the crowd.

Corvan turned to enter the alley, but the rebel leader stood there, blocking his retreat. Up close Corvan could see that the animal skin the man wore on his head was from some sort of large bat. Its wings and body clung to the man's head like a leathery skullcap. Small bony claws curled around the man's ears. Corvan pointed the candle at him but all that came out was a small blue dud. It rolled up to the tall man's feet. He crushed it under his foot and pulled out a long, gleaming sword.

Corvan backed away, slipped in the black oil, and fell against the wall, his hood falling back from his head. As the leader's eyes grew wide, the smoke from the brazier billowed around them, and he vanished. Corvan scooted to the side and pushed himself back into the narrow channel.

A sword pierced the curtain of swirling smoke, revealing the angry face of the rebel Cor-Van. "Die, you evil sorcerer, you servant of the darkness." He raised his sword high over his head and Corvan found himself looking into the black eyes of the bat-like creature.

In desperation, Corvan lifted the Roman candle toward the man's sword. The leader snorted. "Your tricks won't work on me, evil one."

The creature on his head pushed itself toward him and hissed past its pointed teeth.

Corvan hollered and desperately shoved the faulty Roman candle toward the man's head.

A blazing red ball exploded in the rebel's right eye. The creature on his head leaped up into the air and flapped off into the night. The sword splashed into the pool of oil. Another dazzling ball hit him square in the chest and then rolled down his robe toward the gleaming pool. Fire leaped up and he disappeared behind a tower of flames that raced toward Corvan.

Jumping to his feet, Corvan ran ahead of the fire, slipping through the black goo and out into the maze of streets, a trail of flaming footprints in his wake.

A ball from the Roman candle arced off into the darkness, giving him a quick look at his surroundings. He aimed the cardboard tube higher as he ran. Another light hit the sky.

Was this the right way? He turned and moved forward.

A final yellow ball sailed through the sky. Yes, just ahead was the half-dead tree.

THE HAMMER

CHAPTER TWENTY-SEVEN

The commotion behind Corvan faded as he raced toward the tree. He figured he could get his bearings from the statues, but he couldn't find them. His ability to see in the dark must be waning. He ran around the tree until he found the right pathway and then retraced his steps back to Morgon's crypt. No one was there. Jorad must still be finding his way in the darkness. Corvan sat down against a crypt to wait.

A hinge creaked, and a faint green line appeared along the lid of Morgon's crypt. Corvan shrank back. The light grew brighter as a hand pushed the lid higher. Corvan slipped to the side and backed away. A face rose in the ghostly green light. It was Jorad.

Corvan jumped up, and the man yelped, dropping the lid and knocking himself back into the closed tomb. Corvan flipped the lid up and out of the way. Jorad lay sprawled on top of Morgon's body, while Kate lay curled up by their feet, pale and still. Her chest rose a fraction of an inch, then fell. Corvan leaned in and stroked her hand.

"Kate, can you hear me?" She didn't respond.

Resting in her limp fingers was the source of the green light: the disk she had taken from Tsarek. It was much smaller than Corvan would have thought but its markings were clear and bright; a seven-sided star with sharp points around the outer edges.

Jorad sat up and rubbed his head, groaning. "Next time warn me before you jump out of the darkness."

"Sorry. Is Kate all right?"

"She's alive, but we barely made it in here before she collapsed." He stood and came close to Corvan. "We were fortunate she had that light along. There's not a speck of lumien light tonight." Jorad looked at him closely. "How did you find your way in the dark?"

Corvan shrugged.

Jorad wrinkled his forehead. "We need to get out of here, but I don't think the girl can move. She doesn't respond at all."

Corvan reached into the crypt and touched Kate's hand again. It felt cool and clammy. "Kate, it's me, Corvan. Wake up." He lifted her hand and grimaced as the black band slipped back, revealing a ring of crusty red blisters.

Jorad leaned down. "We'll have to carry her, Kalian. Once we get her out of there, we can use Morgon's litter."

They gently removed Kate from the crypt and laid her on the rocky ground. Her cheeks were sunken and pale. She had lost a lot of weight since leaving home. Corvan hoped the cookies weren't all she'd had to eat since then.

Kneeling beside her, he held her hand. It was cold and lifeless. He squeezed her hand gently and felt a faint squeeze in return. He let himself breathe again.

Jorad climbed into the crypt, muttering to himself as he worked at wrestling the litter out from under Morgon's body.

Corvan reached under his cloak for the hammer and brought it down to touch the black band. "Release her," he whispered. Nothing happened.

Corvan pressed his face next to Kate's. "Let it go, Kate. Please." Her head shook ever so slightly. Her eyes fluttered beneath closed lids, and a faint sigh escaped her lips.

"If you let it go, I promise I'll take you home."

A faint smile tugged at Kate's cracked lips.

"I want to see the stars again, don't you?"

Kate nodded, just once, but the band quivered under the hammer, opened slowly, and fell to the ground.

Jorad pulled the litter free from the crypt. He jumped out and set it down next to Kate. "That light disk is still in there with Morgon. We'll need it to see where we're going."

Corvan scooped up the black band. He didn't want Jorad to see that Kate had been wearing the evil thing. Putting the hammer away, he climbed into the crypt to get the medallion.

As he picked up the disk with his free hand, he felt a warmth and peace envelope him. He lifted it to his eyes. The words glowing in the center were the same as those on the hammer. A sharp pain pricked at his other hand, as if the black band had bit him. He raised the band for a closer look and found the hand holding the bracelet was nothing but bones, a dead man's hand.

A thought forced itself into his mind, blocking out everything else. *Accept it and you will live forever; refuse and you will die.*"

Intense cold crept up his dead arm and was answered with heat moving up from the medallion. They met at his shoulders. Pain seared through his head. Snippets of images played in his mind, truth and lies, love and hate. He had to choose or he would be split in two, just like the tree.

A thump on his shoulder sent the black band tumbling across the crypt. Jorad's anxious voice broke the silence. "Hurry, Kalian. They'll be looking for us. Let's get out of here."

Corvan looked at his hands; they were both whole. He took a deep breath and then clambered over the crypt wall.

As Jorad pulled the lid down, Corvan saw the black band slither toward Morgon's leg like a glistening leech looking for fresh blood to feed on.

Jorad lifted the first latch.

"Don't lock him in," Corvan said. "If he's already dead, it won't matter, but if he's not . . ."

"I told you before, this is not your business," Jorad said firmly.

"Yes it is. I'm part of this and I can't walk away again and leave him to die."

"Not even if he is a murderer?"

"Are you allowed to decide his fate? The high priest said if you kill someone, you can't be a priest and you can't get married. Is making sure Morgon is dead worth that?"

The light of the medallion cast a glow on Jorad's tense features. He studied Corvan for a moment, then let the latch drop with a dull clank. Crouching, he grasped the poles of the litter. Corvan did the same.

They passed out of the cemetery and made their way up the dark city street. A thin, wailing voice from a building off to the right interrupted their shuffling walk. It warbled and settled down to a low cackling laugh.

The tension on the litter poles increased as Jorad urged Corvan on from behind. "Keep in the middle of the street," he whispered. "Even if they come out, keep moving. I don't believe the Broken will attack a priest."

Another wail came from up the street, and it was answered by two more behind them. The voices were close but even with his keen eyesight, Corvan could not detect any movement.

"Turn right," Jorad urged. They started jogging, the haunting voices pushing them forward. Jorad directed him from behind, but it seemed to Corvan that the unseen cries were herding them through the narrow streets.

Rounding a corner, they found the way ahead of them blocked by a massive pile of rubble. The cavern wall had collapsed and smashed the front portico of a great building. Tall fluted columns of rock were piled like a giant's game of pick-up sticks. There was no choice but to turn into a square tunnel that opened into the cavern wall.

It was a dead end.

Jorad turned them around just as a tall metal gate rumbled across the opening, cutting off any chance of escape.

"I am a priest of the Cor," Jorad shouted at the gate as it clanged shut. "I bring no harm and seek only your peace."

As the echoes of his shout faded into silence, a small door set into the stone wall opened inward. A gentle push from behind signaled Jorad's intentions, and they walked inside. Instantly the door slammed shut.

They stood still a moment, listening to the reverberations of the immense space before them, then Jorad pushed on. They walked out into a great hall, dwarfed by massive pillars that soared into the dim recesses high above them. The air was dense with mold and the stench of human waste.

Up ahead, in the center of the room, a steady light shone. They walked toward it, past heavy stone tables piled high with stacks of rotting scrolls. Each table was presided over by small versions of the lumien lamp stands Corvan had seen in the square. The rings at the ends leaned over the scrolls like empty eyes.

The glow ahead came from four statues on short pedestals, each holding a fire stick in front of it. In the area bounded by their lights, a thick round table squatted on a massive carved column.

"Let's put her down on the table." The dense air swallowed Jorad's words.

They slid the litter onto the stone surface, and Corvan turned around to look into Kate's pale face. He held his hand near her lips and felt a faint wisp of breath against his wrist.

The band of gems had fallen off her head onto the stretcher. He stuffed it into his pocket. It was pretty and might cheer her up later on. He pushed away the thought that she might not live to see it again.

Corvan brushed the hair away from Kate's hollow eyes. It would be his fault if she died in this terrible place. He never should have let her use the hammer. He wished now he'd never even found it. But maybe . . .

As he unclipped it from the holster, thoughts of how it had healed him jumbled in his mind with the pain from when it punished him. Since Kate had chosen the black band, it might hurt her, and she was far too weak to risk it. He snapped it back into place.

A shallow breath rattled from Kate's lungs. The power of the hammer might be too much, but the comfort of the medallion would help her. Pulling it from his pocket, he laid its glowing face in the open neck of her tunic.

Kate took a deeper breath as the warm glow touched her skin. Corvan raised his eyes. "Please let Kate live . . . even if I . . . ."

The words seemed to float high overhead into the vaulted ceiling, where large painted faces gazed down in rapt attention. Although blackened by generations of smoke, their eyes remained focused on the center of the room. All around the faces were smaller paintings of people and animals. Most were obscured by the dark smudge, but off to the sides the murals were clearer. Was that a blue sky and a golden sun? People in small boats on the water? Corvan stepped back to get a better view, stumbled on a loose brick, and fell backward onto a pile of damp scrolls piled against a statue's pedestal. He pulled himself to his feet and looked up into the stone face. It gazed back at him in unblinking silence.

A hand grabbed his arm and pulled him aside. Jorad looked fiercely into his eyes. "Don't touch anything. They are watching every move we make." He turned away, and Corvan could see that he was not taking his own advice, for he had cleared off a table and spread out a large scroll, which he studied intently.

Corvan stared at it. The markings looked like the tracks chickens left in the mud.

Jorad traced a finger backward along a line of characters. "Unbelievable. And this is only one scroll of thousands still readable." He gestured around the room, and Corvan saw that the walls of the chamber were covered in cubicles of various sizes, many containing one or more rolled-up scrolls. Around the perimeter ran a balcony that housed a second tier of scrolls.

"I'd heard stories of a library in the broken city, but I never believed it could be this vast. It would take many lifetimes to read all this." From the tone of his voice, Corvan knew Jorad wanted to start immediately and would not be easily distracted from the task.

The priest moved along the wall, tugging out scrolls, reading the identifying marks, and reluctantly pushing them back into place. "I don't understand. Look, you can see where the water rose this high." He pointed to the wall where a line of black mold encircled the room about three feet from the floor. "All the documents below this point are hopelessly ruined, and the dampness in the room will eventually destroy even those the water did not touch. And this." His voice choked in anger as he checked the remains of a campfire made from the scrolls. "They used scrolls for a fire! Fires are not even permitted in the Cor. Our air is much too precious. And that." He shook in wrath, pointing to where pieces of scrolls had been used for toilet paper. "Animals. The Broken have become nothing but animals!"

"Who are you to judge these people?" a voice called out.

Jorad and Corvan whirled about.

An old woman glared at them from beside a stone column. She wore a bright orange shawl and large black boots. Her frizzy red hair was tied back in a checkered scarf, and wide silver hoops hung from her ears. Corvan wondered if this strange world was also home to a race of gypsies.

Jorad stepped back. "Madam Toreg, I did not know you were still—"

She waved a carved staff in his face. "I wonder what you do know, Jorad. What you know of those who have lived in the broken city for longer than you and your fathers have lived in the priest's compound, filling your bellies with food supplied by the palace, food bought with the lives of those who die in hard labor out in the settlements. What gives you the right to look down on those who refuse the yoke of the oppressors and choose to live off what little they can find here?"

Jorad bowed low. "I am sorry, madam. I was overcome by the loss of such treasures. I had no right to lay the blame for this on those who live here now."

The old woman's face softened. "I understand how you feel, for my mother was once curator of this library." She leaned on her staff. "It is a great evil that is willing to destroy this precious heritage in its rampant pursuit of power."

Jorad pointed to the walls. "But the water. How could the rulers—"

"We do not know, but we have no doubt they will try again. Come, I will show you." The old woman stepped away and motioned for them to follow. As they walked away from the torches, the floor became more uneven. She held out her staff. At their feet, the floor of the building ended in a jagged hole above an open space far below.

"The pool beneath this room had been still and silent since the founding of the city. But some time back it began to bubble and froth, becoming brackish and undrinkable. One day it erupted in a geyser that reached the ceiling. Everyone ran as the water rose higher and higher, flowing out into the streets and into every burrow we had created to hide ourselves from the ruler and his forces. Many drowned." Her voice cracked.

She extended her hands, palm up, striking them together. Then she lowered her hands until the fingers pointed down. Jorad made the sign back to her.

"You cannot see it in this darkness," the woman went on, "but the collapse of the floor was our salvation. The geyser weakened the ceiling, and it fell in and shut off the flow of water. But we live in constant fear it may start again."

Corvan gripped the stump of a broken pillar and leaned out over the edge. An island of broken stones rose from a lake that extended from wall to wall in the room below. The water swirled slowly in dark eddies.

He was turning away when a shadow crossed the lake just beneath the surface of the water. Something or someone was down there.

Jorad pulled him back from the edge and beckoned for him to follow as the old woman stumped her way back to the table where Kate lay.

Kate's hands were clasped around the disk on her chest. The peaceful look on her face made her appear ready for her own funeral.

The old woman caressed Kate's cheek and then put her hand under the girl's wrist, feeling for her pulse. She turned sharply toward him. "Where did you find it?"

Corvan stepped back, unsure what she meant. The old woman backed him against a stone pillar, her cane pushing hard into his chest. "The medallion you put on her, where did you get it? Answer me truthfully, for your life depends on it."

Corvan put his hands on the shaft of the cane. She pushed the tip harder into his chest. She was much stronger than she looked. He was certain the metal tip of the cane could pierce right through him.

His forearm tightened against the lashes that held Morgon's knife in position. In desperation, he pulled out the knife and slashed at the cane. Sparks arced through the air. Her carved staff fell to the ground, cut cleanly in two. The old woman gasped and fell against the table.

Corvan held the black blade out in front of him. "I'm sorry, I—"

He never got a chance to finish, for in an instant the four statues came to life. One struck the knife from Corvan's feeble grip. Two pulled the old woman to her feet. The fourth dropped his torch and pulled Corvan's arms behind him in an iron grip.

The old woman released herself from the protection of her gray guardian. She approached Jorad and struck him across the face. "You have betrayed us by bringing a servant of the Rakash to our dwellings."

Jorad licked at a trickle of blood that oozed from the corner of his mouth. "It is not as it appears. I do not know where he came upon the black knife, but he is not of the Rakash."

"Silence!" the old woman commanded. She moved in on Corvan and pointed to the blade on the floor. "If I dared touch that foul thing, you would die now by your own blade."

Jorad raised his hand. "Madam Toreg, you warned me not to judge people too quickly. Do not make the same mistake."

The tallest of the gray men stooped to whisper in the old woman's ear. She cocked her head to one side and looked quizzically at Corvan, then commanded that he be released. "Your treatment of this young woman is not what the Rakash would do. But I have seen much deception and betrayal in my life. What can you offer as a pledge that will remove any doubt as to your intentions?"

It took Corvan only a second to decide. "I promise that I will not betray you to the palace. I swear to you upon this." He slipped the hammer from its holster and extended it toward her, its insignia throwing shafts of blue light around the room.

PART III

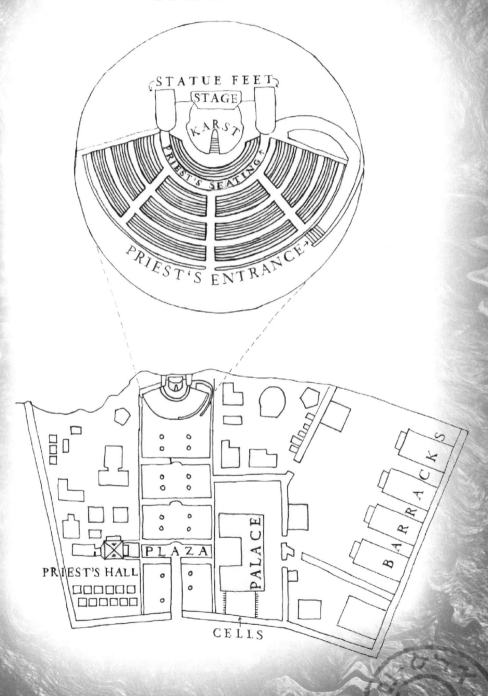

STATUE FEET

STAGE

KARST

PRIEST'S SEATING

PRIEST'S ENTRANCE

BARRACKS

PALACE

PLAZA

PRIEST'S HALL

CELLS

THE HAMMER

CHAPTER TWENTY-EIGHT

Madam Toreg reeled, and the two living statues barely managed to catch her before she hit the floor. The old woman brushed the gray men back and stepped forward to take the hammer from Corvan's hand. "So the legends are true. It does exist as a real object and not just an idea."

She looked at the blue markings the hammer was projecting on the floor between them, then pointed the handle up to the ceiling, throwing its light onto the paintings. The same marks ran between two bands that surrounded the faces above them. "The words up there were painted from memory long after the hammer was lost to us. I often wondered if they were correct."

He stared at the markings. "What do they say?"

"Three words flow between the circles; Truth, Mercy and Justice. These are the attributes that a great Cor-Van must possess to rule the Cor." She looked at him from under thick eyebrows "The legends also say these are the qualities of the one who will return the hammer to us."

Corvan avoided her eyes. "But I don't even understand how it works. Sometimes it heals me and other times it hurts me. Sometimes it does what I want and then suddenly it does nothing at all."

Madam Toreg directed the blue glow onto Corvan's chest. The light reflected off the gray cloth of his cloak. "The hammer judges truth. It has power when held by those who have integrity, those who uphold the truth and stand against injustice. But it cannot be used as a weapon. It helps people know what is right and supports them in their choice to follow truth, but it does not give love. That is the responsibility of each individual."

"Then why would the Chief Watcher want it?"

"People are easily led; they want to believe someone is telling them the truth so they don't have to decide for themselves. If the Chief Watcher can convince the people he possesses the truth, he can easily manipulate the masses."

"But how can he hold the hammer? It punishes those who lie."

The look Madam Toreg gave Corvan reminded him of Mrs. Thompson repeating a simple math problem he couldn't grasp. "If an evil person shields himself from the truth in some manner, he will appear to others as if he's touching it, but that is just another deception. You have to examine people closely to see if the hammer is freely held in their hands. But deceivers never let others get that close to them."

Jorad stepped into the blue glow. "He needs the hammer to destroy hope. Hope gives people ideas, and they search for the truth themselves. If he can destroy hope, the people will willingly follow his plan for the Cor."

Madam Toreg nodded. "You are right. I have seen changes lately that suggest larger plans and forces are at work. Deeper things are coming to the surface. None of my mentors ever thought the Rakash would walk freely through our world."

A chill went through Corvan each time they said that word. "Who are the Rakash?"

"Some call them Sightless, others call them Seekers. Not many use their real name, Rakash, for we all avoid the truth that we are not alone in this world."

"I have seen them," Corvan said. "They are the blind ones who serve the Chief Watcher."

"No," Jorad said. "A greater evil has sent them to keep an eye on the Chief Watcher and they have their own way of seeing."

Corvan's head swam. Too many bits of information that he couldn't fit together. Truth, mercy, justice. . . if the hammer was truth, what was the medallion? Earlier, he'd thought it was compassion, and that was something like mercy. But where did the justice part fit in? He was about to ask when a young woman came running in from the shadows. The hem of her blue tunic brushed the floor, and a short sword hung at her waist.

"Madam Toreg," she said, "a company of palace guards approaches the upper gate."

"In the darkness?"

"They are being guided by one of the Seekers."

"Then someone here is drawing him to us through a special possession, something lost that the person desires found. I do not see how it could be any of us in this room, unless . . ."

They all turned to Corvan. The old woman's eyes bored into him.

The woman bringing the report spoke up. "The Seeker carries a white scarf."

Corvan swallowed. "It was a gift from Tyreth. I left it behind when I escaped from the prison. I didn't have time to go back and get it."

"If you are able to cast it from your mind," Madam Toreg said, "and deny any connection to her, the Seeker will be lost. Can you do this?" She studied his face.

Corvan turned his thoughts to Tyreth. He saw her pain when the lizard slashed her cheek, and his heart ached for her. He remembered how she had touched his face and the scent of the scarf.

Madam Toreg patted his cheek. "I see you cannot. It is a good thing to care for others. We shall talk of this later." Madam Toreg turned to the messenger. "Go wake the mayor and have him come to me. We will have to fight them in the streets of Kadir and draw them away from the new city. How long before the light?"

"One more segment," the messenger replied.

"It may be enough. Tell the mayor to meet me at the upper gate."

The messenger ran from the room as Madam Toreg turned to the tallest of her gray men. "You must act quickly. We need the soldiers' fear of the dark and the Broken on our side."

The gray man shook his head. "Our tricks will not fool the Seeker."

"Then we may have to kill him."

"That's not possible," the tall gray man replied. "Nothing can kill one of the Rakash."

"That can." She pointed to the black knife on the floor. "It has been done in the past, for the five became four, and the cloak of deception that allows their leader to move undetected among us vanished. Our city of refuge was saved from certain discovery and ruin at that time by a great man." She glanced at Corvan. "I have been told the remaining four Rakash have chosen a new leader. Perhaps he is seeking the cloak."

Corvan resisted the urge to twist the buttons on his garment. If the cloak was that important, the leader of the Rakash wouldn't rest until he got it back.

He broke Madam Toreg's steady gaze and bent to pick up the knife. Everyone took a step back. Corvan pulled the sheath from his arm and put the blade back inside. Madam Toreg looked on in admiration until he stepped forward and laid it on the table. Corvan stepped back in embarrassment. Surely they didn't think he would fight the Seeker?

"There is another way." Jorad stepped up to the table. "The Seeker believes he follows Tarran, but to capture him he needs the help of the palace guard. Send your gray men to frighten the soldiers and buy us some time. I will lead Kalian out to the settlements along the river road. We need to take him far beyond where the Seeker can sense him."

"Then we must send this with him." Madam Toreg put the hammer back into

Corvan's hand. Her blue eyes searched his face. "None of us here can protect it. Since you brought it to us, you must carry it on from here. In time it will reveal your true purpose."

Corvan reluctantly took the hammer and put it back into the holster. Ever since he'd found the hammer, it had taken him farther from his family and from safety. How could he and Kate escape from this nightmare unless he could get someone else to take it from him?

"Jorad's plan has merit," the tallest gray man said, the coating on his face crinkling as he spoke. "But let us make use of our preparations at the lower bridge. We have weakened it so that we might collapse it in the event of an attack from across the river. Instead, let us pull it out from under the Seeker and his soldiers. We will drown his men and perhaps the river will sweep the Rakash back to his source."

Madam Toreg looked at Corvan. "Is it permitted to do such a thing to defeat evil?" They all turned to stare at him.

Was he expected to decide just because he held the hammer? "I would think that . . . since these people sent the water to kill your families and children . . . maybe falling into the water themselves might teach them a lesson?" It was more a question than an answer, but the expressions on their faces indicated it was the decision they required.

"So let it be." Madam Toreg turned to the gray men. "You four go frighten the soldiers as best you can. I will take these two through the new city to the water outlet below the bridge. Signal us when the Sightless senses him and begins moving toward the lower bridge."

Three of the gray men turned toward the small door and vanished against the stone wall of the library. The door seemed to open and close of its own accord.

The remaining gray man lightly touched the old woman's shoulder. "Madam, you are the appointed leader of our city, but if you bring untested strangers through, the mayor and the elders will rightly accuse you of breaking the code of the remnant."

She smiled and patted his hand. "I will bear that responsibility. But I thank you for your warning and your concern."

He bowed low and melted away toward the exit.

The old woman pointed at Kate. "You two will need to carry her below. Our healer will attend to her while you are gone."

Corvan shook his head. "I won't leave her behind and risk losing her again. She comes with me."

The old woman searched his face. "I will allow this, for I understand that this girl does not belong in this world. I know that if she does not soon return to her sphere, she will most certainly die." Her eyes narrowed. "You, on the other hand, may yet belong to this world, or perhaps this world will belong to you."

"But I'm not—"

She jabbed her thick finger into his chest. "Do not think for a moment that I do not understand what it is possible for you to become, either for our good or for our final destruction. That choice you have yet to make. May your desire for the truth be guided by love."

She moved past him to pick up the broken pieces of her staff. As she headed for the door, Corvan noticed she walked just fine without it. He picked up the front of Kate's litter and pulled it toward the edge of the table. Jorad hesitated for a moment before he picked up his end. Corvan glanced back. The black knife was gone.

Corvan followed the old woman out the main doors into a dusty lobby. The remnants of vines twisted around the rusty lumien lamp stands that sprouted from the tiles. The stair to the balcony lay in pieces on the floor. The front of the building was completely collapsed.

They entered a grand stairwell that swept down in a wide arc. At the bottom of the stairs, a passage ran a short distance in either direction and then ended in piles of rubble.

Madam Toreg marched straight ahead and inserted the tip of her broken cane into a hole in the rock wall before them. Concealed doors sprang open, revealing armed guards waiting within. A stocky balding man rushed forward and engaged Madam Toreg in a heated conversation, all the while gesturing furiously toward them. Finally, he saluted Madam Toreg in a cursory manner and ran off into a tight passage.

Madam Toreg moved after him and they followed her into a crevice so narrow only one person could go through at a time. It twisted back and forth on itself like a snake, and the corners were so sharp they had to tilt Kate's litter at a steep angle to get around them.

There were openings in the ceiling, from which guards watched their progress. The narrow entry was part of a sophisticated defense system.

The channel finally opened into a wide chamber, where Madam Toreg waited for them before an arched double door. As they stepped beside her, she pushed firmly on the doors and swung them wide.

Corvan stopped short. After many days in near darkness, the scene before his eyes brought one word to mind—paradise. Stretched out at his feet was a deep cavern that housed a compact city. Each building glowing softly in the muted light of a ceiling so crowded with lumiens it was impossible to distinguish any one globe.

The main streets ran around the sides of the bowl in tight rings. Smaller lanes

connected the circular roads winding down the steep sides in tight curves, like snakes
slithering toward the central plaza at the bottom. Small dwellings were evenly spaced
along terraces cut into the floor of the cavern, their whitewashed walls making the
scene look more like a painting than something real.

"This is our city of refuge," Madam Toreg said. "We welcome those who would
escape the tyranny of the palace."

"Its beautiful." Jorad spoke quietly. "It gives me hope that Kadir may again
shine in all its glory."

Madam Toreg frowned. She pointed to the left, where a creek ran along the
bottom of a deep channel next to the cavern wall. "That is what remains of the water
that flows from under the library. The water sent by the palace in Kadir. They filled
our city with water and many of our people drowned." She made the special sign
with her hands. "But we have prepared a deep channel and outlet in case the water
rises again."

"Have the people returned?" Jorad asked. "I don't see anyone."

"The day has not yet begun, and those along our path were instructed to stay
indoors. For your safety and ours, it is best if you pass unseen. Come, we will follow
the water channel."

The road circled the edges of the cavern behind the outer ring of dwellings.
Behind each home was a small patch of vegetation. Some had vines with clusters of
yellow fruit trailing over their walls.

A baby's cry rose above the burble of the water running alongside the road, and
a woman sang a lullaby. "Those are sounds I have not heard for a long time." Jorad's
voice choked with emotion.

Madam Toreg looked back. "I know of your great loss, and I offer you my
sympathy. Perhaps you should consider staying here with us."

Jorad's response was cut off by strains of music that drifted in from around the
corner. They rounded the bend and found a small boy in tattered clothing sitting
on a high wall. His grubby legs kept time to the music as he blew across a set of
graduated pipes. The mournful sound wrapped them in its melancholy strains.

"Gavyn, come here." Madam Toreg looked stern, but Corvan heard compassion
in her voice.

The boy jumped down and landed lightly in front of the old woman, all the
while playing his pipes without missing a note. Madam Toreg gently pushed the flute
down from his lips. He smiled at her, but his blue eyes betrayed an abiding sadness.

"Gavyn, did you not hear that everyone was to remain out of sight for a while?"

The boy looked at the ground and ran a soiled hand through his damp, matted hair.

Jorad gave a soft whistle and smiled at the young boy. Gavyn's eyes brightened.

He ran back to the priest and hugged Jorad around his waist. Jorad bent his knees and said something quietly to the lad. Gavyn reached into the priest's cloak and fished out a small object wrapped in bright yellow paper. Jorad straightened and looked at Madam Toreg. "We must allow the little children that suffer to come to us for comfort."

Madam Toreg nodded but shot Gavyn a warning look. The boy ignored her and came up beside Corvan, his hands patting the side of Corvan's cloak and tugging at the hammer. Corvan tried to pull away from his probing fingers.

"Gavyn." Madam Toreg stepped toward them. "I have warned you about taking things that do not belong to you."

The boy looked at Corvan, a puzzled expression on his face. Madam Toreg stamped her foot, and the child whirled and disappeared over a stone wall, grabbing a yellow fruit off a vine on his way.

"He means no harm," Madam Toreg said. "Some people have broken under the strain of the Watcher's oppression. They live wild, up in the ruins. This one has found a way to come and go as he pleases. Some say he lost his family in the flood. No one knows for sure, for he has never spoken." She turned and headed down the road. "Come along, now. We must keep moving."

Ahead the road branched off into an enclosed passage that followed the watercourse. The sound of the creek grew louder. They rounded a corner and found themselves at the top of a steep flight of stairs, slick with the spray from a waterfall that plunged alongside to the rocks below.

"We have much to do here to complete the outlet channel, so these steps can be slippery. You'd best turn sideways and carry her down together. Let me go first and caress the light."

She descended the stairs and pushed a long pole up into the shadows. The lumien hanging from a ring over her head began to glow as Madam Toreg gently stroked the tendrils that hung around the globe with the soft flaps at the end of the pole. Satisfied, she leaned the pole back against the wall, and motioned for them to join her.

Large stone blocks were stacked near the base of the stairs where they had been cut from the side of the cave. A deep lagoon swirled behind a partially completed wall. They followed the path down and around to where a wide sluice gate allowed water from the lagoon to rush out through a low opening in the cavern wall.

Madam Toreg turned to speak to them, but Corvan couldn't catch what she was saying over the sound of the rushing water. She motioned to them to wait and disappeared around the lagoon. A low rumble, as if a train was passing, coursed through the rock. The water ebbed to a trickle.

Madam Toreg reappeared. "There is not much time before I must release the water. Follow the channel to its end, and you will find yourself directly under the lower bridge. A stairway will take you up to the road. Jorad, you will know where to go from there."

Jorad spoke up. "Thank you, Madam Toreg. Your kindness will not be forgotten. We will hold your well-being in good faith."

"I know you will, Jorad, thank you." She turned to Corvan, put a hand on either side of his face, and pulled him close. "I understand that you must fulfill your vow to this girl, but I ask you to do whatever is in your power to rescue Tyreth. It is important to the Cor." She glanced back at Jorad and whispered, "It is important to me as well, for Tyreth is the only relation I have left in the Cor." She pulled back to look at him, eyes full of tears.

Corvan nodded. "I promise, Madam Toreg." He patted the holster. "I promise on the hammer."

Her bushy eyebrows shot up, then she smiled. "Thank you . . . Cor-Van."

She looked to Jorad. "Take the girl to Jokten in the Molakar settlement; his counterpart is gifted in healing, and he is the only one left with an understanding of the outer passages." She gestured toward the empty watercourse then touched Corvan's arm. "Do not lose the medallion the girl holds. When you become the Corvan you will need it to complement the hammer."

Corvan tried to respond but she waved them on. "Move quickly now. The lagoon walls are not completed, and the water will soon overflow the gate."

Holding tight to the front of the litter, Corvan stepped down into a channel still broken and rough from the cuts of fire sticks. He felt Jorad's reluctance through the poles. Water dripped from the ceiling, which was getting lower as they progressed. Corvan crouched to avoid hitting his head.

"How much farther?" Jorad's anxious voice reverberated in the tight space.

"I can't tell," Corvan responded. "But we need to keep moving before the water comes back and drowns us in here."

It was the wrong thing to say. Jorad pushed so hard Corvan had to run to avoid being driven to his knees.

It was a good thing, for just as they cleared the tunnel's end and climbed out of the channel, water roared from the hole and out into the main river. Corvan glanced back and found Jorad's white face dripping with water and sweat.

A long flight of narrow steps brought them up to the low wall that kept the travelers on the main road safely away from the water. Setting Kate on the wall, they climbed onto the road. Corvan had just grabbed the poles when they heard a familiar warbling cry from the edge of the city.

"They are close," Jorad hissed. "To the bridge, quickly!"

Kate's body bounced roughly on the litter as they ran forward. Ahead, the entrance to the bridge was flanked by two large stone pillars. A shadow moved out to meet them.

There was urgency in the gray man's voice. "Quickly, run across. The bridge will shake but I promise you it will not fall. Do not stop." He pushed Corvan past him out onto a metal suspension bridge that curved gently upward toward the center. The metal panels of its floor snapped and sprang as they ran. They were nearly to the middle when a trumpet blast rolled out over the water.

"Stop in the name of the Watcher!" A deep voice boomed out.

They kept running over the center of the bridge, its panels slipping beneath their feet and pitching them toward the chain railings.

"Stop, Corvan. Stop in the name of the Rakash." The rasping voice crawled up Corvan's spine and into his head. How did it know his name?

Something moved in the shadows ahead. The bridge pitched and rolled beneath their feet as they staggered off the end. Another of the gray men stepped out to steady them.

Corvan looked back. Two guards had reached the crest of the bridge, the gangly form of the Seeker just behind them. The guards slowed as the shifting panels below their feet threw them from side to side. The Seeker staggered against the chains.

Suddenly all three disappeared. The screams of terror from the soldiers lasted only a moment, then were silenced by the splash of water.

Jorad spoke into the heavy silence. "Did they all . . . ?"

"Yes," the gray man replied.

"The Seeker?"

"Gone into the water. May it sweep him into the abyss." The gray man slipped away into the gloom.

A light push on the poles of the litter was all Corvan needed to get him moving. The evil voice still echoed in his head.

They walked in silence along the river wall. Corvan looked down into the dark water rushing by. For a brief moment, he thought he saw a pair of white eyes moving along in the current and staring back at him.

T THE HAMMER

CHAPTER TWENTY-NINE

Corvan scanned the surface of the water. There was nothing there but patches of white foam. His stomach churned at the memory of that voice calling his name.

Jorad pushed firmly on the poles and Corvan plodded forward on shaking legs. Ahead of him the wide stone levee curved out into the distance. Wishing to avoid looking at the water, Corvan concentrated on the road at his feet. He didn't like this feeling of being pushed from behind. He didn't really know Jorad, yet his life and Kate's fate were in the man's hands.

He stepped over a crack in the road. He had seen pictures of the Great Wall of China. If the Chinese used stone blocks as large as the ones on this road, it must have been quite a feat to get them into position. It took three of his paces for each block on the roadway. He began to count them, hoping that would help take his mind off his troubles. He was almost at three hundred blocks when the road took a sudden turn to the left.

Looking up he found they had drawn close to the high crags of rock on the other side of the river. The road turned almost at right angles, then swept downward to meet the farthest point of the cavern. Where it terminated, a dense mist hung in the air with the faint roar of a waterfall.

"This road ends by the falls at the edge of the Cor but we must go down to the fields and then climb up to the settlement passages." The tone of Jorad's words was that of a man resigned to something he dreaded.

"Is there another way?"

"Not to save your Kate." The words were bitter. "But each step we take away from Kadir decreases our chances of rescuing Tyreth."

Corvan walked on in silence. He wanted to ease Jorad's worry but he couldn't make a rash promise. It had to be honest.

Just ahead, a low building at the edge of the road stuck out over the river on sturdy pylons. Below it, the water rushed through a narrow gap in a high stone dam. The poles in his hands twisted as Jorad directed him away from the river and toward an opening in the wall on the field side of the road. Stepping through they descended a narrow stair onto the raised side of an aqueduct that used to carry water down to the fields and across to the terraced hill on the far side of the cavern.

The watercourse on top of the stone arches was dry. The sides that formed the aqueduct were narrow, and the fields a good twenty feet below. Corvan was glad when Jorad suggested they step down into the empty waterway. Walking its smooth bottom, they passed sluice gates that would have allowed water to flow into the secondary channels that fanned out over the valley floor. These, in turn, led to even smaller channels, separating the fields below into a patchwork of irrigation lines. Between them were rectangular fields ploughed in neat rows where small plants lay withered in the dusty earth.

"What happened to the crops?" Corvan asked.

"Nobody noticed at first that the light was fading, but once people realized the seeds of the lumiens were being eaten, everyone tried to get a share for himself. Soon the light was too dim to support the crops. Lumiens need a critical mass to sustain themselves. There are not enough of them left now here in the Cor. Unless there is a miracle, soon all will be dark. Maybe the people who face the Wasting are the fortunate ones."

Corvan heard hopelessness in the man's voice. There had to be some way to help him rescue Tyreth. "Jorad, I really don't know how to use this hammer or what I can do to help. But if the healer can make Kate better, keep her alive longer . . . I would be willing to help you rescue Tyreth."

Jorad did not answer. They walked on, Corvan wondering whether Jorad's continued silence meant he didn't think Corvan would be much help . . . or that it was too late to help Tyreth.

The aqueduct ended at a dry pool at the base of the hill. Walls separated the incline into terraces full of dead vegetation, the path snaking its way up over short sets of stairs at each switchback.

They had climbed for what seemed like half a day when they encountered a stairwell that rose through an enclosed passage in the retaining wall. Corvan put his head down and struggled up the steep flight of steps.

Reaching the top, he looked up again. A tall man armed with a bow stood waiting for them. Corvan tried to run, but Jorad didn't budge.

"It's not real," Jorad said dryly. Corvan looked again. It was only a mannequin, its face painted onto a cloth bag stuffed with dried vegetation. Its mouth twisted to one side in a sloppy grin, and he seemed to laugh at them as they passed.

"He was there to keep the rantels away from the crops."

"Are rantels birds?" Corvan asked.

"I do not know this word *birds*. Rantels were fierce creatures with arms covered in skin that could soar on the air. They would eat our crops, so we had marksmen shoot them out of the air. The same fools who discovered they could use arrows to cut down the lumiens within range. Now all that's left is that patch high in the center."

"Were the rantels large?"

"I have heard that some had wings longer than a man's arms, but I have only seen one as big as my forearm. They died out with the crops."

"Did they have long forked tails and beady black eyes?"

"Who told you that?"

"The rebel leader had one on his head."

"Right." Jorad said. "I saw that. It was a fake. He claims to be a Rantellic to impress his followers."

"What's that?"

Jorad sighed as if the conversation was tiring him out. "Supposedly the Rantellics were a race of men who could communicate with the rantels. The flying creatures would spy on the Cor and then show what they saw by connecting to their Rantellic masters. Personally I think it was superstitious nonsense. Besides, the rantels are all dead."

He sounded so sure that Corvan thought it best to avoid another argument. Maybe the rebel leader's headpiece had just fallen off when the Roman candle hit him. Somehow he didn't think so.

Leaving the terraces behind, Corvan and Jorad carried Kate over rocky ground that sloped gently up toward a series of dark entrances cut into the cavern wall.

"Those are the tunnels which lead to the settlements. The rantels used to roost in the caves, so the ground is fertile with their guano. The palace has moved some of our best lumiens to where the ceiling is low enough to grow food. Now our people work in the fields, tending the plants under armed guard."

"Why do they need guards?"

"Because the penalty for eating food without permission is death."

The journey to the tunnel entrances took much longer than Corvan expected. Distances were deceiving without any landmarks by which to judge the size of things. Small rocks in the distance turned out to be huge boulders. Even with his grandfather's slippers, his feet were killing him by the time they arrived at the settlement entrances.

"We will take the one farthest to the right," Jorad said. "But first let's put the girl down and rest."

It felt wonderful to stretch. Without the weight of the litter, Corvan's step was so light he thought he could jump right over the wall beside the path. As he drew close, he saw it would not be a good idea, for on the other side was a cliff that dropped to the fields below. He leaned over the wall. At the base of the precipice, a stream rushed out to join the main river just above the falls. Through the mist he could see a wide horseshoe of rushing water descending into a dark hole. This close to the falls, the earth trembled with the roar of the water.

Turning, he found Jorad staring back down the path.

Corvan joined him. "Is something wrong?"

"Something is moving down by the stuffed man. There, behind the wall on the tier below."

Corvan squinted at the place Jorad pointed out. Someone was walking toward the stairs where they'd passed the scarecrow. The top of his red hood bobbed above the high wall.

"Let's get inside the tunnel." Jorad bent down and picked up the litter. "If he is following us, he won't know which entry we took."

Corvan's skin prickled. Jorad's plan wouldn't work if it were someone who did not need to see them to be able to follow.

They hurried through the entrance and up a steep incline. The air was moist and smelled like a barn long overdue for a cleaning. Luminescent purple moss hung in thick swatches from the roof, providing enough light for them to avoid tripping on the uneven floor.

After a short distance, the tunnel leveled out and ran straight ahead for what seemed like miles. Jorad urged him on but Corvan could tell by the tugs on the poles that the priest was constantly looking over his shoulder.

The passage twisted and turned, and they fell back into a steady, plodding pace. Corvan's arms ached. How much longer could he keep going? They traveled in silence around many corners before Jorad spoke. "I am grateful for your offer to help me rescue Tyreth. I don't think I can do it alone." They turned another corner. "As soon as we get your Kate to the healer, we must make haste to go to Tyreth. I did not see it clearly at first but now I am certain that her fate is intertwined with the future of the Cor. Her blood has permeated the seeds from the mother plant." Jorad's pace faltered. "If she dies, the seeds die. We all die."

An enormous weight pressed down on Corvan. The fate of the Cor was resting on his shoulders but what could he offer? He had meant what he said, but right now he was so tired he could hardly think.

The tunnel began to descend. It twisted through a series of tight corners before they emerged into a low cavern. There were no lumiens, just a few fire sticks around the perimeter and a bright spot far off to the right.

Jorad slowed his pace. "All the soldiers will be out by the light guarding the workers. Take the path to the left and let's hope Jokten still lives in the same place."

They passed the entrances to cliff dwellings carved into the side wall of the cavern. Between the dark doorways, narrow steps climbed up to dwellings on higher levels. Some stairs were cut at impossible angles where the wall jutted outward to join the ceiling.

The poles were almost yanked from his hands, sending Corvan sprawling to the ground. Kate's head just missed a rock protruding from the floor. Corvan let the poles go, jumped to his feet, and glared at Jorad. "Why did you do that?"

The priest placed his end of the litter on the ground, turned Corvan around, and pointed down. A deep pit opened up at his feet. Far below, water flowed past jagged rocks.

"Sorry Jorad. I was too busy looking around." He pressed his hands to his head, trying to force his mind back to alertness. Then, muscles trembling with exhaustion, he leaned in to get a closer look. He had read about formations like these in *National Geographic*. An underground river would weaken the ceiling of its channel until it collapsed. This one had fallen in to form a low, rocky island surrounded by fast-flowing water.

"In my world these are called cenotes," he told Jorad. "Ancient people thought they were doors to the world of the gods, and they'd sacrifice young women by throwing them in."

Jorad nodded. "Then our worlds have something in common, for that is what is done at the Wasting, when the water threatens to rise and flood the city. Here we call them *karst*. The soldiers use this one to execute workers who try to escape or who eat food without permission. They are lowered in on that." He pointed to a crude metal cage suspended from a crane. "The rest gather around to watch them die."

"They drown them?"

"No, no. Look, there, by the largest rock."

At first Corvan saw only a dark shadow. It shifted and took shape. Two red eyes stared at him.

It was the monster from his nightmare. Its gaze invited him . . . pulled him. Corvan's knees shook. He took a step closer to the edge. Then another.

"Do not look into its eyes if you do not want to die." Jorad's hand came down over his face, blocking the sight of the smoldering orbs.

Blinking, Corvan backed away from the edge. His breath came in ragged gasps. "What is that thing?"

"I do not know. It was brought here when the Watchers came into power." He looked across the pit. "Lights are headed this way. We need to find the healer's dwelling."

This time Jorad took the lead. As they skirted the edge of the karst, Corvan was certain his every movement was being followed. He wanted to look back, but he forced himself to focus on Kate's face. She looked more at peace now, her hands clasped tightly around the medallion. But she lay too still for him to believe she was just resting. Was this the deep sleep Tsarek warned would come before she died?

Jorad guided them past an area where a section of the ceiling had collapsed onto the entrances of the cliff dwellings below. The few visible doorways were almost covered in rubble. High overhead Corvan could see the faint glow of a patch of Cor shield. They walked on through a forest of boulders into the far corner of the cavern where a few doorways remained intact. Jorad stopped. He appeared uncertain of where to go. Softly the priest whistled a stanza from the song Corvan's father used to sing.

A lump rose in Corvan's throat as his thoughts turned to home. With the Cor shield so close, surely there must be another portal nearby. Madam Toreg said that the healer's husband knew about the outer passages. He must know of some way to get back to the castle rock.

A quiet voice called to them from a dark doorway. Jorad pulled the litter up a broken stair and into a small entry room. He whispered urgently to a hunched form, who beckoned for them to follow. Pushing past a thick curtain, Jorad pulled them into a another darkened room. A light flared and a thin, twisted fire stick was inserted into a holder on the wall.

The feeble light revealed a woman so bent with age she had to twist her head sideways and peer up at him through a swatch of thin white hair. Her skin hung on her body in wrinkled folds. She looked like she was living on the edge of death, but her eyes shone with vitality.

"I do apologize for the lack of light. The palace has forbidden the use of fire sticks unless they are only twigs smaller than a person's thumb." She held up her right hand. Only the four fingers remained. "They make sure you do not forget."

She nodded to the other side of the room. "Put her down and let me have a look at her."

Jorad and Corvan lowered Kate onto a short stone table that had been carved out of the cave wall. The old woman ran her gnarled fingers over the still body, clucking and muttering. When she came to Kate's hands, she gently caressed the ugly red welts from the black band. "Ah, the young. So easily tempted by empty promises."

She lifted Kate's hands, held them in her own, then pried them apart to pluck out the medallion. She held it close to her eyes, the green glow lighting up her wrinkled face. "So you have finally been found, have you?"

Kate moved restlessly, her hands grasping at the air.

The old woman twisted her body around and looked up at Corvan. "It would be better if I had the counterpart to this."

He glanced at Jorad, who gave a quick nod. Corvan slipped the hammer from the holster and held it out to her. She took it from him as if it were made of glass, then hugged it to her chest. The strong blue light flowed over her face, swirling together with the green from the medallion and turning pure white. She breathed in the light and straightened to her full height. Her eyes came level with Corvan's, a huge smile across her face. "Only our Cor-Van could have these in his possession. With your return I have hope for our people once more."

Before Corvan could say a word, she bent down to Kate and held the hammer and medallion on either side of the girl's head. A jolt of white light arced around the pale face. Her arms and legs stiffened and her body convulsed.

"Stop! You're hurting her." Corvan leaped forward, but Jorad pulled him back.

Kate's eyes flew open, her hands pushing the light away. The old woman allowed Kate's hands to wrap around her own. The lightning ceased. The woman released the medallion into Kate's grasping fingers and sat on the end of the table.

Kate's eyes opened, searched the room, and focused on Corvan. She smiled thinly. "I want to go home, Corvan. I'm sorry I took . . ." Her eyes glazed over and closed.

The old woman stood to face him. "So it is true. The Cor-Van has finally come to us."

He shook his head. "I'm not your Cor-Van. Its just a name my grandfather gave me. I can't stay here; I have to take her home."

The old woman looked at him long and hard before she held the hammer out and released its dead weight into his hand. The blue glow faded as she exhaled a deep sigh and sank back down like a deflated balloon.

She turned to cover Kate with a coarse blanket from a basket at the foot of the table. "You are correct that you must take this girl back. Her mind is purged of the darkness she allowed to grow there, but she will not survive if she does not return to her own light. She does not belong here." She twisted to look at Corvan. "But that does not mean you are not the Cor-Van. You are part of us. You and I must talk."

"Is the girl able to travel?" Jorad asked.

"No. She is very weak. I need to get some nourishment in her. Perhaps Jokten will be able to find something for her to eat."

Jorad turned to Corvan. "There is very little food here in the settlements. You and I should go back to the city. There is plenty of food in the storage rooms of the priest's compound. While we are there, we can find out when the Wasting is to take place and plan a way to rescue Tyreth."

There was no doubt Kate needed to eat. Her cheeks were sunken. Her hands were gaunt and dry. But he didn't want to go with Jorad. It sounded dangerous. "Jorad, maybe I—"

Pebbles clattered outside the door. The old woman put a crooked finger to her lips, took the sputtering fire stick from its niche, and slipped out into the entry room. The tattered dark curtain fell behind her, casting shafts of light through its threadbare folds.

A man's tense voice penetrated the curtain. "I was right; they are trying to break through the Cor shield. This clearing of new tunnels to grow food is just a ruse. They have been seeking a weak spot in the shield, and today they found it."

"Are you certain?" the old woman asked.

"The soldiers brought the entire tunneling crew back early, all in chains. I crept close and listened. They have found a crack in the Cor shield wide enough for a person to walk through. A report is being sent to the palace at first light. It will take a long time to tunnel beyond the shield and reach the surface but with enough fire sticks, it can be done. This can only bode ill for both spheres. All our work will be for naught."

"There is always hope, my dear," the old woman said softly. "Come and see."

The curtain parted and an old man pushed into the room. His keen eyes fell on Corvan's face and he drew a sharp breath. He raised a calloused hand as if to touch him, then pulled it back. "What is your name, son?"

Corvan stared at him. Other than the white ring of thick hair around his balding head, this man could have easily passed for his father. "Kalian, sir," he stammered.

The old man frowned. "What settlement are you from?"

The old woman pushed around the man. "He came to us from the world above. He carries the hammer." She poked the man's ribs. "And the girl called him Cor-Van."

A huge smile spread across the man's wrinkled face, and his blue eyes sparkled. "We have been waiting a long time for you, son. With your help, we will stop the evil from breaking out on your world and bring healing back to the Cor." He placed his hands on Corvan's shoulders, his eyes brimming with tears. "I always believed you would make it back. You have arrived just in time."

Corvan opened his mouth to protest, but a shout from outside the dwelling broke the silence. "Jokten," an angry voice called out, "you are under arrest for treason against the palace. Come out and face your judgment."

Jorad pulled the black knife from under his cloak, but the old man motioned for him to stand down. "Stay here," he whispered. "Do not interfere, no matter what happens." He smiled at Corvan. "Now that the Cor-Van has returned, my purpose is fulfilled."

He turned back to the entry, his wife close behind him. As the curtain fell, a bright light entered the porch and the old curtain blazed with dusty color. It was a piece of tattered old tapestry flowing with angular symbols around a green tree.

"Jokten," a gruff voice rumbled, "you have been found guilty of unlawfully consuming food."

Jokten's voice was firm. "I have done nothing of the sort."

"Your fellow conspirators have testified against you. You and the entire tunneling crew are guilty. You will all be tested in the karst."

Jokten snorted. "Tested? Don't you mean executed?"

"You will be given a weapon to defend yourself. If you win against the beast, you shall be proclaimed innocent."

A shadow fell across the curtain, and another man spoke in a shrill voice. "Look here, Sergeant, another proof of his treason. This is a piece of tapestry from the priests."

"It is irrelevant. Old scrolls and the priest's legends are meaningless. The high priest is dying, and the Chief Watcher has announced that his daughter will face the Wasting at first light tomorrow. The priesthood is done."

A thin hand slipped past the curtain. "But who knows what else Jokten might have in here? Perhaps he has been storing food illegally. I have not eaten now for three segments."

"I understand your need, Corporal. It is mine as well. But I have been told that what we found today will bring us more food than we could ever imagine. The Watcher has promised that finding a way through the Cor shield will fulfill all our desires."

"But I'm hungry now." A booted foot pushed in through the bottom of the curtain.

A high, thin shriek filled the air. "Do not take my husband from me. How will I survive? Please spare us. We are old; we will not cause you any trouble."

At the sound of a loud slap, the hand and foot pulled back.

"Do not ever lay your grubby hands on a palace guard, old woman. Corporal, bring Jokten along. Let's get out of here."

As the sounds of the soldiers faded away, Corvan heard soft sobs from the entry room.

Jorad brushed the curtain aside and bent over the old woman, dabbing blood

THE HAMMER

away from her mouth. She pushed Jorad's hand aside and leveled an unwavering stare at Corvan. "You must rescue him."

Corvan lifted his hands helplessly. How could he possibly save Jokten from the soldiers?

"Not for my sake," the healer said, "but for hers." She pointed to where Kate lay in the other room. "My husband is the only one who can guide you through the secret door back to the surface." Her voice shook with frustration. "He would not tell me where it was . . . for my own safety." She clutched Jorad's shoulder and pulled herself toward Corvan. "If Jokten dies in the pit, you will be sealed in the Cor and the girl will die."

CHAPTER THIRTY

Fear and anger tangled together in Corvan's mind. Kate was going to die if he didn't find a way to get her home. How could she ask him to rescue Jokten? He hadn't told the old man to sacrifice himself.

Surely someone else must know where the secret passage was.

The selfishness of his thoughts stung him. Jorad had helped him bring Kate to the healer even though doing so risked Tyreth. Even the old woman had risked arrest or even death to keep the soldier from discovering him.

As if reading his mind, Jorad spoke. "You must save Jokten from the karst. I will help you."

Corvan clenched his jaw and blinked back tears. He wanted to do what was right, but what if he failed? In all his nightmares he had never escaped from the beast. What good would it do if he died in the pit? He closed his eyes. The image of the monster bearing down on him crowded his mind. He clenched his eyes tightly and forced it away.

Someone touched his hands, and a sense of peace flowed through his body. The red eyes faded into two white stars that multiplied into a night sky. Calmness came over him with a new realization: Death was not the worst thing that could happen. Far worse would be letting others suffer while he ran away.

He opened his eyes. The hammer was in his hands, which were cradled in the hands of the old woman. She studied his face. "Death comes to all, but before it does, we have many chances to choose life."

Corvan nodded. "I will try." He gripped the hammer and its blue glow filled the cave.

She smiled. "I believe you will succeed."

Outside the entry, a drum pounded a deep, monotonous beat. Jorad glanced out the entrance. "They are calling the workers in to witness the execution."

Corvan frowned. "They will come just to watch? I thought those oppressed by the palace would care for each another."

The old woman patted his hands. "Evil runs through all levels of mankind, rich or poor, slaves or free. You will always find those who take pleasure in the misfortunes of others."

Corvan clenched the hammer tighter and looked to Jorad. "What will they do to him?"

"They will lower the prisoners into the pit one at a time to fight the beast. None will win, for its hide cannot be pierced by the crude wooden weapons they are given. Most will not even try. The beast will immobilize and crush them."

"Can they escape into the water?"

"The beast cannot go in the water. That is how they keep it confined to the pit. But none of the prisoners have sought to drown. That form of death is unacceptable."

"Could the hammer be used against it?"

"No," the old woman said. "The hammer judges a soul; this is but a brute beast. It will not have any effect on it."

Corvan fought back the rising fear. "Then what can I do?"

Jorad took him by the shoulders. "The only thing we *can* do. Step out this door and try our best." He pulled off the black scabbard. "Here, take this. I have my own, and you have proven you can use the black blade."

Corvan reluctantly extended his arm, and Jorad lashed the knife into position.

As he turned to follow Jorad out the door, the old woman tugged on his sleeve. "Jokten says he is an old man and he is ready to die, but I love him dearly and want him to live. Thank you for helping us." She turned and shuffled into her dwelling.

A ring of fire sticks blazed ahead. The pounding of the massive drum shook the ground with each beat. Above the crowd, the crane chattered into position over the center of the pit. In the cage below, a man stood in readiness, a sharpened wooden spear in his hand.

The pulley groaned and the cage dropped a foot, then stopped with a jerk. The crowd roared its approval as the man in the cage staggered and fell against the steel slats.

"It's Jokten," Jorad hollered over his shoulder. "They are putting him in first." He elbowed his way through the crowd. Corvan pulled in tight behind him, but in the madness he quickly lost sight of the green cloak. Crouching low he forced himself through the tangle of bodies, emerging on the very edge of the pit.

Across the chasm, a row of shackled men stood on the crane platform, eyes downcast. In the midst of them, a young boy, his hair closely cropped, sat tugging at his leg irons, his bony shoulders shuddering with terrified sobs. He looked up through his tears at the ring of spectators and his eyes met Corvan's. He stared at Corvan a long moment, then mouthed two words. "Help me."

The cage dropped another foot and the crowd cheered, their faces eager with the anticipation of suffering and death. Corvan stared into the young boy's eyes, everything inside him pounding with anger. If he ruled the Cor . . .

A guttural roar from the confines of the karst silenced the crowd. The immense black beast paced back and forth below the swaying cage, its clawed feet crunching through bones and broken spears.

Up on the platform the sergeant strode into position next to the prisoners. "You are all here today to witness the testing of these workers—men who took food that belonged to the settlement." Mutters of anger rippled through the crowd. "They have eaten what was to be shared by all."

"That's not true," one of the shackled men cried out. "We were working and found—" A blow from the sergeant caught him on the side of the head, and he crumpled to the ground.

"For speaking against the rulers," the sergeant announced, "this man shall go next." The crowd roared their approval as the guards unlocked the chains and pulled the dazed man to the front of the platform. The beast roared up at them. Startled, the guards dropped the groaning victim and retreated. The dazed man tried to sit up but caught the edge and dropped with a splash into the water. The crowd fell silent as the body bobbed to the surface facedown and slowly slid around the island.

"In the name of the high priest, I ask you to stop," a familiar voice called out. Everyone turned to find Jorad standing at the far end of the platform, his hand pointing into the pit. "The gods are not pleased with this testing. By returning this man's body, they have given us a sign that these men are innocent of the charges." The audience shrank back from the edge of the pit.

"Since when does the priesthood have jurisdiction in matters of treason?" The sergeant strutted to the front of the stage. "And why should I obey a priest who enjoys the comforts of the priest's quarters and all the food he desires?"

An angry murmur ran through the crowd.

The sergeant grabbed the underside of the crane with one hand and leaned out over the pit.

The audience gasped.

"And why should you listen to a priest? When was the last time you saw a green cloak out working in the fields?"

Shouts rang out.

The sergeant pushed himself back from the crane and pointed at Jorad. "Why are you even here? Did you not hear that all the priests have been commanded to attend the trial of the high priest and his daughter?" He spread his arms wide to the audience. "Why should these people, who work all the segments in the fields, listen to a priest who refuses to follow the orders of the palace?"

Jorad stepped forward to respond, but the shouts of the crowd drowned him out.

The sergeant grabbed the crane again. As the crowd hushed, he called out. "Since this renegade priest speaks on behalf of the gods, perhaps we should see if his god will proclaim him innocent in the pit."

The crowd loudly agreed, and the arrogant sergeant nodded to his men. Before Jorad could pull out his knife, the guards shackled him into the place formerly held by the drowned man and tied a gag over his mouth.

Corvan looked down the row of men. The young boy was on his feet, still staring across at him with desperation in his eyes. Corvan glanced into the pit. The black creature was hunched down at the bottom of the island, staring out over the water where the dead body had disappeared.

The pulley creaked as the cage descended. Jokten braced himself against the iron slats. The beast lazily turned its head. An archer guarding the crane loosed an arrow, and the point stuck in the monster's scaly hide. It leaped up, bellowing at the archers. Pulling the arrow out with its teeth, it stalked toward the cage.

Fresh cheers from the crowd drowned out the bellows of the furious beast as it arrived below the swaying cage. To help Jokten fight the creature he had to get down there—and fast. He leaned over the edge. Could he dive into the water? No. At this place, the rocky island was directly below the lip of the karst.

Corvan lost his footing and almost toppled in. Someone pulled him back and hollered in his ear, "It will get enough to eat today without you climbing in."

Corvan nodded to himself. Pulling the krypin from his belt loop, he sent the disk over the side. Taking a deep breath, he stepped off the edge. The rope tightened, slowing his descent. He let go as he neared the bottom, tumbling up behind the high rocks that surrounded the killing circle.

The screech of metal was followed by an animal's howl of frustration. He peered over the top. The beast's back was toward him. It had hooked one claw into the cage and was yanking with all its might. The platform buckled and twisted. The archer fell screaming into the water. The beast pulled again and the sergeant lost his balance, leaping out to grab the rope attached to the cage. He tried to climb back up to the tip of the crane, but he slipped farther down until he was standing on top of the cage.

Corvan crept between the rocks and drew the black blade from it sheath. As he neared the creature, the sheer size of it filled his stomach with cold dread. Stretched out on its hind feet and yanking on the cage, it towered over him, easily twice his height.

The screech of tearing metal filled the air and the cage crashed to the ground, spilling Jokten out its broken door.

The sergeant shouted and pulled his feet onto the large metal hook that still dangled from the rope. In the dead silence that followed, the monster sat on its haunches and watched the pendulum swings of the sergeant.

Jokten struggled to his feet, the spear hanging limp at his side. The beast turned toward him, and the muscles in the creature's great back tensed for the kill.

Raising the knife over his shoulder, Corvan jumped forward and plunged it with all his strength into the creature's thick neck. With a deafening roar, it leaped to its feet, carrying Corvan astride its back, his hands firmly clutched around the knife handle. The animal twisted and bucked, its body like writhing bands of steel beneath him. Corvan spun through the air, slammed against a boulder with a bone-jarring thud, and tumbled to the ground behind two large rocks.

Dazed, he lay for a second, listening to the furious bellowing. Then he forced his limbs into motion and pulled himself up to peer out between the rocks. Jokten was nowhere to be seen. The creature leaned on the empty cage, blood pouring from its wound as it bawled up at the sergeant swinging above him on the hook.

The sergeant was hollering for his men on the platform to throw down their fire sticks. His garbled cries were finally understood, and sticks of all sizes fell around the broken cage and into the water. A small one landed by Corvan's knee. He brushed it aside and discovered his numb hand still clutched the black knife.

The beast stepped on a fire stick and howled in pain. It shook the cage and then limped away from the ring of fire sticks burning below the sergeant. The scent of seared flesh stung Corvan's nose.

As it sat down to lick its burnt paw, an eerie silence settled into the arena. Nothing moved except the sergeant struggling to stay balanced on the hook. He tried to climb but dropped back. He tried again, and his body swung wildly across the circle of fire sticks that hissed like petrified snakes on the rocky floor. He slipped, caught his legs in the hook like a trapeze artist, and arced even wider.

The beast grunted and stood. It watched him swing out and back, waited, then batted him off the hook. The sergeant rolled to his feet, scrambling to grab a fire stick. As he turned, the massive animal fell forward, crushing him onto the rocks.

Corvan shrank back as the black form rose from the ground and stood over the broken body, shattering the air with a victorious roar that reverberated off the walls of the karst. As the echoes faded, the beast stared past the broken cage. Corvan followed its gaze over the smoking fire sticks to where the point of a spear moved in slow circles behind a pile of rocks.

The huge creature crept around the scattered fire sticks, all the while keeping its eyes on the jerky movements of the spear tip. Corvan could see the fierce hatred burning in its eyes.

It passed close to Corvan's hiding place as it circled wide around the burning sticks. He watched it go by, its muscles rippling beneath its dark hide. How could he fight something so strong? He couldn't do it by himself.

The hammer. Madam Toreg said it could help fight injustice. He drew it out and looked at the blue words. The hammer seemed small and useless, but as he raised his eyes he found the monster looked less frightening.

He slipped out behind it, hammer in one hand, knife in the other, and tensed for another charge.

An arrow flew past his shoulder and dug into the calf of the beast. It bellowed and spun around to face him.

The angry red eyes locked onto his. Dark fear devoured his will to move. The hammer slipped from his grasp and the black knife hung limply at his side. The creature crouched low, ready to spring, but Corvan could not make his body get out of the way.

A fire stick splashed out of the water and slapped Corvan's shin. The sharp jab of pain pulled his eyes away from the creature's gaze. "Point it at the beast," someone shouted. Corvan swept up the fire stick, pointing its flaming end at the broad chest as the huge animal circled him. "Don't look at its eyes," the voice commanded.

The crowd cheered as Corvan backed away.

Over the beast's shoulder, Corvan caught sight of Jokten shouting and waving his spear. Corvan didn't understand what he was saying until the butt end of the fire stick bit into the rocks behind him.

The monster had cornered him against the high rocks. With a blast of its rancid breath it sprang. Blackness descended as the fire stick was ripped from Corvan's hand.

The creature's roar engulfed him in darkness until it seemed his head would burst. The weight of the massive beast was squeezing the life from his body.

Suddenly the creature pulled away. Corvan blinked past the pain, expecting to see sharp teeth ready to devour him. Instead he saw the animal clutching madly at a fire stick protruding from its chest. Roaring in agony, it swiveled around. The fire stick had gone clear through its body and was still burning out its back.

Corvan pulled himself up against the rocks and stumbled off to the side. The beast stopped twisting and faced him, its lips pulled back in a snarl. Corvan stepped back. His feet splashed in the water, and the cheers of the spectators above penetrated his deafened ears.

Another arrow rattled off the stones at his feet and he finally understood. The arrows were meant for him. The crowd was cheering for their monster.

The beast tipped back its head and roared up at the ring of eager faces, its energy renewed. Corvan turned to escape into the water. He slide the knife into its sheath to free his hand and . . . The hammer! He had dropped it up by the rocks.

He twisted around. Two more arrows whipped past him. The creature waited for him at the water's edge.

Behind its back, an old man rose from the rocks, a spear in his hand and a triumphant smile on his face. Jokten stepped off to one side, raised the spear's haft high over his head, and brought it swiftly down on the fire stick protruding from the creature's back.

A blast of air and chunks of burning flesh pounded Corvan backward. Cold water cut into him, clearing his head. Arrows fell around him as he dived down and swam under the edge, where the archers could not reach him.

More fire sticks fell into the water above him. His fingers scraped at the far wall, but the current grabbed him and dragged him away.

Breaking the surface, he saw the black roof of the cavern sweeping down on him. He swam desperately to beat the current but it was too strong and he was pushed past the lower tip of the island. The roof met the water and he was dragged along into an underground channel. Turning around he swam with the current until it began to slacken.

By the light of the fire sticks bubbling in the water, Corvan saw the tunnel widen. The roof pulled away and he followed it upward, his lungs crying out for air. He tried to pull himself along the roof, gouging his hands on the rough surface. Panic gave way to despair, and his breath escaped from his lips.

A fire stick shot toward him in a cloud of bubbles that pulled him up to a small silver moon.

Just when he was about to give in and let the water fill his lungs, Corvan's face broke through the silver circle into a pocket of air. He took a deep breath and gagged. The air was mostly smoke from the fire sticks that moved past him. He fought to breathe, but the trapped air gave little satisfaction to his lungs. He was still drowning even as he tried to breathe in fractured gasps.

"You have to go on," said a voice in his head. "There is not enough air here."

The current pulled him back under the water, his body twisting in the bubbling froth. The dark shadow of a rocky outcrop loomed ahead. He turned to avoid it. A flash of light filled his head and then darkness closed in around him.

A roar pummeled his ears. Corvan's eyes flew open, searching for the beast. Pain shot up his neck and down his left arm.

A dense curtain of mist rolled toward him from a patch of ghostly light. A shadow stepped in front of it. Corvan tried to sit up, but his body flatly refused his command.

In the swirling fog, the shadow took shape. It wasn't the beast. A lizard approached, a short sword clutched in its claws. The Chief Watcher loomed before him, but Corvan had no fight left. He let his head drop back to the ground. Let the black lizard do what it would. He had failed both Kate and Tyreth. He closed his eyes and hoped the end would come quickly.

CHAPTER THIRTY-ONE

"Oh, sir, I am so glad you have awakened, sir. I was beginning to think the death of cold had caught you."

"Tsarek?" Corvan opened his eyes and found his friend standing before him, a short unlit fire stick in his paw.

"Yes, sir, it is I."

"But how . . . The burak had you in its mouth, like a dead gopher."

Tsarek chuckled. "Yes, sir, it did. But buraks like to keep their prey alive until they get them back to their lair. If you allow yourself to go limp, they think you are too hurt to move. They are lazy creatures and like to sleep after a hunt." He lifted a claw. "One of them will never awaken again."

Corvan managed a small nod. That was why only one burak had attacked at the door. If he had known there was only one left, maybe he would've fought it and saved Tarran. No, that was not the truth. One or two would not have made a difference. He had simply been too afraid to help Tarran.

Tsarek moved closer. "Is your pain great? Your body is much bruised but your bones are not broken." He gently rearranged Corvan's cloak. "I am so glad you have this Rakash garment. Without it you would have died from the cold water." The lizard stepped back and gave him a disapproving look. "But why did you close the door on me, sir?"

"What door?"

"After the last burak killed your friend, I ran to help you, but you closed the door on me."

"I didn't know it was you. I was sure it was the other burak coming to get me."

The lizard looked at him with a wounded expression. "It took me a long time to find another way into the Cor. I had to swim under the cold water. At least the water in this stream is a little warmer."

"Then it was you who threw the fire stick at my leg?"

"Oh, yes. I could see you were captured by the eyes of the creature. I threw the stick and shouted because I did not want to see it kill you." Tsarek leaned in close and wrapped his short arms awkwardly around him. "I missed you, Kalian."

"I missed you, too, Tsarek." Corvan ran his hand down the lizard's spiny back. Tsarek snuggled in closer to his neck, rumbling in his throat like a contented cat.

Tsarek pulled back. "I have something you left behind." The lizard scampered to one side.

Relief flowed over Corvan. Tsarek must have retrieved the hammer.

The lizard returned with a neatly coiled rope over his arm, a huge smile on his face. Corvan's heart dropped. He was glad to get the krypin back, but without the hammer, how could he go on?

Corvan wearily clipped the rope back onto his belt loop under the cloak. "Thanks, Tsarek."

Tsarek touched his shoulder. "I am glad we found some air in the tunnel. I know it does not help much to breathe those fire stick bubbles, but it was the only way to keep you from drowning."

"Was that the silver circle I saw?"

"Oh, yes. The pockets of air look shiny from below. That is how you find places to breathe under the water. There were so many fire sticks in the water, it was hard to see them. That is also why I did not see the rock that hit your head. Does it hurt greatly?"

Corvan touched his head and felt a large bump above his right ear. He winced. "It's not too bad. I'm just glad to be alive."

"I am glad too. Is the counterpart also alive?"

"She is hidden at a settlement up by the pit. She needs to go back to our home as soon as she can walk."

Tsarek looked out into the mist. "That will be difficult. You have locked the only door to my portal, and since I have deserted my post, I cannot ask the Chief Watcher to open it."

The situation seemed impossible, but Tsarek's return gave him hope. "It's not over yet, Tsarek. Jokten knows a way out . . . if he's alive."

"Jokten?"

"The old man who helped me fight that monster." Corvan struggled to his feet, his head pounding. His legs crumpled and he collapsed back to the ground.

"I did not see that man after the fire stick exploded. I do not know if—"

An arrow struck the rock where Corvan's head had just been. It sparked and shattered into splinters of wood. Tsarek yanked him sideways, and he landed with a painful crunch in the gravel. "Don't move," he whispered and was gone, the light from the fire stick quickly extinguished.

Another arrow whistled through the darkness overhead. One more struck the rocks to his right. Out in the mist, muffled voices argued.

Corvan listened anxiously but thick mist muffled all noise like a woolen blanket. A minute went by, then two. . . . He leaned against the rock and slid the knife from its sheath.

A fire stick sparked to life in the mist. Corvan pushed his aching body up and sideways into a cleft between the rocks. The light approached, casting a myriad of shifting shadows in the fog. Corvan stepped stiffly forward, his blade extended. He heard a shriek, and the burning fire stick fell backward.

"Don't do that!" Tsarek's irritated voice hissed. "I am nervous enough in the mist."

"Sorry. I didn't know it was you. Are they gone?"

The lizard came close and held out the light. "My claws are locked again. Please assist to release them." He sounded grumpy.

Corvan crouched and petted Tsarek's back until the fire stick clattered to the ground.

The lizard picked it up. "They could see our light from the other side of the small water. It was the Sightless one and four soldiers."

"The leader of the Rakash?"

The lizard nodded.

"I thought he drowned in the river."

"Oh no. You cannot kill these by water. I do not think you can kill them by fire either. They feel no pain nor do they—"

"I get the picture, Tsarek. Does it still carry a white scarf?"

"Yes. It told the soldiers that Tarran was on the other side of the water and that they should cross over. The soldiers refused."

"Why didn't it cross alone?"

"The Rakash do not have the strength to fight. They can track people but others must help them to kill." Tsarek looked into the mist. "It has taken the soldiers along the shore. They are planning to circle over the water where it comes out of the cliff. But we will fool them. I will go up and see where they cross. When they come down to this side, we will wait until they are close, then cross the water and leave them behind while we go back to the settlement. It is a great plan, yes?"

The lizard was obviously pleased with himself, and though allowing the Rakash and the soldiers to get so close to them sounded risky, Corvan could not think of any other means of escape. Tsarek helped him down to the edge of the creek that joined the main river just before it plunged over the falls. Pushing the fire stick into the gravel, and with a final pat on Corvan's shoulder, Tsarek waded into the creek and disappeared into the darkness.

Alone in the pool of misty light, Corvan considered his options. He felt a sense of relief that the hammer was gone. It was no longer his responsibility. He had returned it to the Cor; his job was done. Now he needed to find Jokten, and together they could carry Kate to the surface.

But Jokten was too old to carry Kate that far. Would Jorad help? Even if he could find the priest, Jorad would want him to go to the city and rescue Tyreth. But he could not leave with Kate dying at the settlement. Besides, without the hammer they didn't have a chance. Surely Jorad would understand.

Could Tsarek help carry Kate? He shook his head. That wouldn't work. But it was sure good to have Tsarek around again. Jorad had been a great help, but there had been times when Corvan wondered if he could really trust him.

The fog had lifted and hung just above the fire stick in a bright sheet of rolling cotton. Corvan peered upstream to where Tsarek had disappeared. In the shifting shadows thrown by the fire stick, a dark form slowly spun around in a back eddy. Corvan clambered to his feet and looked closer. It was the body of a man floating facedown. It must be the first prisoner drowned at the karst.

Should he leave him there? Somehow, it didn't seem right. He should at least pull him out of the water.

A pair of black eyes watched him as he approached the water. Across the pool a rantel perched on the top of a pointed rock, its long forked tail spread out wide behind it, the gray wings folded up at its sides. Was it like a vulture waiting to tear at the flesh of the drowned man?

Corvan ignored the creature, stooped to check his shoe, and slipped a round stone into his hand. He stood back up, taking note of the rantel's position, then fired the stone at it. It smacked the front of the pointed rock and ricocheted into the belly of the rantel. The creature sprang from its perch and sliced through the air toward him, hissing and clicking in anger. Its forked tail whipped down below its body as if it would spear him with the points. Corvan dropped to the ground as it swooped over him and vanished into the fog.

Corvan scanned the air around him. The rantel did not return. Most likely that meant it was on its way to show the rebel leader what it had seen. That was all he needed. Now the rebels would be on his trail as well.

Corvan struggled to his feet and waded out into the shallow bay. He pulled on the body's stiff hand. The corpse rolled over, and he looked into the face of Jokten.

Corvan's chest clenched and a low cry escaped his lips. He dragged the body from the water and felt Jokten's wrist. The lifeless hand still clutched the shattered stub of a spear.

Tears streamed down Corvan's cheeks as he looked down at the old man. His face seemed peaceful, as if he were dreaming about something wonderful.

Corvan sat back in the wet gravel. He had done the right thing by trying to save Jokten, but the man died anyway. Jorad had told him to step out and the answers would come in their own time. Now there were no answers, no hammer, and no way out of this terrible place. Kate would die and be buried far from her home. Buried? They were in a dying world far underground. They were as good as dead already.

His tears gave way to sobs that shook his bruised body. What was the point of even trying to do good? Pain and death were all around him. He could not win.

The words of his father came to mind. "*Love and pain flow together. If you choose to love in this broken world, you will experience pain.*" He had chosen to love. He had fought the beast to save Jokten and Kate. Now he was left alone with the pain. Had it been worth it to do the right thing?

Jokten had thought so. He knew he would die in the pit but he went anyway. He had lived and died on his own terms. He looked into the old man's face. A wry smile was embedded in the corners of the old man's mouth, the same smile that he wore while swinging the spear at the fire stick. Jokten was a great man. Perhaps that was the point. In the end, loving through the pain changed you for the better.

A muted shout came down the slope through the fog. The soldiers and the Seeker would be here soon. There was no way he would let them take Jokten's body to the palace. The old man deserved a proper burial.

Corvan pulled the body farther away from the water. At some time in the past the stream had changed direction, leaving an island between the dry gravel creek bed and the rushing water. He pulled the body up onto the high spot and laid it out.

Prying the broken spear from Jokten's grasp, he set it aside and folded the bruised hand onto Jokten's chest. Reaching over the body, he pulled the other arm into position. The soggy sleeve of the robe slipped back.

Jokten's other hand was wrapped tightly around the hammer.

Corvan looked in amazement at the polished stone head. He placed his hand over it and the hammer slid easily from Jokten's grasp, as if the man were giving it to him. The blue letters sprang to life and shone on Jokten's face, highlighting the crinkles around his eyes and the happiness etched around his mouth.

Corvan stood and held the hammer in both hands. It felt good to have his hammer back again. His hammer? Could it be that he was the person chosen to bring the truth back to the Cor? How could that be? He wasn't even from the Cor in the first place.

Placing the hammer back into its holster, he gathered flat stones from the dry creek bed to pile around and over the dead man. The work was painful at first, but as he moved, his joints loosened up and his movements became easier. When he was done, he took the broken spear and stuck it upright in the cracks of the pile.

He stepped back to inspect the cairn and almost tripped over Tsarek.

"I did not want to interrupt you." Tsarek jumped off the rock he'd been sitting on. "I tried to tell you earlier that I did not think your past-father survived the blast."

"He is not my past-father, Tsarek. My grandfather died at the entry."

"I know, but Jokten was also one of your kindred people."

Corvan turned back to the cairn. No wonder Jokten looked so much like his father. Tears fell afresh. He'd been so close to discovering more about his family, and now this one too had died.

The lizard placed a soft cloth into his hand, and he wiped his eyes with it. It carried a tender scent that permeated his soul and soothed his sorrows.

"Did I do well, Kalian? Does it make you happy to have it back?"

Corvan opened his eyes to find the white scarf in his hands. "How did you get this?"

Tsarek chortled. "The Seeker was walking along the path in the fog with all the soldiers following, holding the white cloth out in front of him like a flag. I was very still. When he walked by I leaped across the path, snatched it from his hand, and fled before he could even move." The lizard grimaced and Corvan saw fear steal into its eyes. "I touched the Seeker's hand when I grabbed the cloth. It knows now that I am in the Cor and will report my presence. We must get Kate and look for another way out, for I too must leave the Cor forever."

Corvan pulled the scarf around his neck and looked up to the pale light from the cluster of lumiens high above him on the cavern roof. To leave the Cor now was to condemn it to death. Their only hope were the seeds tucked away in his cloak and if Jorad was correct, Tyreth's life was now connected to the life of the red seeds. If he chose to run away and abandon Tyreth, the darkness would slowly close in. Their food would run out and they would starve to death in the black void. He thought of Madam Toreg and the hope she had for her new city, of Rayu and his compassion, of Gavyn and his childlike innocence.

He finally understood what his teacher had been trying to say when she compared her glass vase to a bad habit. If he was to be a man of integrity he needed to make a choice. He had to put the needs of the Cor above his own safety, even above the life of his best friend.

"We need to move quickly," the lizard urged.

"No, Tsarek." Corvan turned toward the river. "I am going back to the city."

In his mind, Mrs. Thompson's vase fell and shattered into a thousand pieces.

CHAPTER THIRTY-TWO

Tsarek's eyes grew wide. "The city? But the palace is searching for you, and soon they will be looking for me as well. No, Kalian, we must not go to the city. It is a terrible place. They have done cruel things to my kind in the city."

It took a while for Corvan to fill Tsarek in on everything that had taken place and even longer to try to convince him that he should go along. Finally, Corvan pulled out the hammer. "Tsarek, I made a promise on this, but I need your help. I can't do it alone."

The lizard took a step back from the black object. "Why didn't you say so in the first place?"

Corvan studied the hammer in his hand, then stooped to place it on top of a flat boulder. He took two long steps away from it and turned to the lizard. "Do you think I should leave the hammer here?"

"Oh no. You will need it to rescue the girl. Please pick it up. I will try to be more brave."

Corvan smiled. "I just wanted to make sure I could still understand you even when I'm not holding it." Tsarek looked confused. "I just realized that something has changed between us. I didn't have the hammer, yet I still understood everything you said."

Tsarek let out a low hiss and looked between Corvan and the hammer. "I don't know how—" A wide smile spread across his face. "But I am very glad."

They stood looking at each other for a long moment, then Tsarek jumped down into the stream and dog paddled out into the middle. Corvan grabbed the hammer and waded in after him.

The water came up to his waist in the center, and the current threatened to sweep his feet off the slick rocks. The roar of the falls just beyond the bend sounded a constant warning in his ears. One misstep and he would be swept over the falls and into the abyss. The current was sweeping Tsarek farther downstream, but he was making good progress at getting across to the other side.

The bank rose steeply. Corvan stumbled and crawled out of the water. The fog was thinning and there was enough pale blue light from above to make his way along the creek. The roar of the falls grew louder, but Tsarek was nowhere to be seen.

"I could use some help," a voice called from below his feet. Tsarek stood chest deep in a rocky bay, a pile of small capped fire sticks gathered on the shore. "I found them swirling around in here. We will need these." He handed the sticks up to Corvan and then sprang up onto the bank. Pulling out some of the long grasses that grew in tufts along the stream, Tsarek tied the sticks together and slung the bundle over his back.

Tsarek led the way down to the main river. The high levee and river road ended abruptly in a jumble of rocks. Tsarek climbed up toward the road but Corvan soon passed him.

At the top, Tsarek grabbed the cuff of Corvan's jeans and hauled himself up onto the road. He grinned. "It is not a good idea to fall back onto a pile of fire sticks, even if they are small ones."

"So why do we need them?"

"I discovered something that no one else knows." Tsarek smiled proudly. "You can breathe the bubbles by pulling the air back through the stem."

"What?"

"I'll show you." Tsarek pulled a short stick from his bundle and carefully trimmed the bark away from one end, as if he were starting to sharpen a pencil. Uncapping it, he stuck the trimmed end into his mouth and walked along like a businessman with an expensive cigar. "They don't last as long this way but it works great for swimming under the water."

"Let me try it."

Tsarek's eyes twinkled. "I will make one for you." He picked through his bundle and trimmed up another stick. He held it out to Corvan. "Are you certain you want to try it?" He pulled it away again. "It tastes funny and hurts the lungs a bit. Maybe it would be too much for you."

Corvan plucked the stick from the lizard's paw and flicked off the cap. He'd smoked almost every kind of dried plant his mom's garden could produce. This couldn't be any worse. He pulled softly on the stick. Other than a mild bitter taste, he could breathe without difficulty. He pulled in a deep breath and swaggered along beside his friend.

A loud bang sounded with a flash before his eyes. He squinted to find the smoking bark of his cigar stick peeled back toward his face.

Tsarek made a hissing sound that Corvan was certain was a laugh. "I forgot to tell you. You cannot use ones that are not perfectly smooth."

Corvan tossed the ruined stick into the water rushing by. He was sure the lizard hadn't forgotten. "I thought you told me that you don't laugh."

Tsarek scratched the side of his head. "I cannot remember making that sound before. It must come with being free from the band. You don't have time to laugh when you are always angry."

They arrived at the sharp bend in the river road where the dam and gates had been used to force water into the irrigation system for the fields. Corvan looked out along the aqueduct but saw no sign of the Seeker.

Tsarek suddenly stopped and pulled Corvan in tight against the small stone building that stuck out over the dam. The lizard jammed his scaly face up to Corvan's ear. "Listen," he whispered.

Corvan listened but all he could hear was the water rolling over the dam on the other side of the building. He shook his head at Tsarek, who gestured for him to sit against the wall. "Stay here. I will be right back." Tsarek got down on all fours and slipped around the corner of the building.

Corvan leaned his head against the cool stone wall and closed his eyes. It seemed he was always tired in this dark world. Then again, he had no idea of how regularly he had been sleeping or how many days he had been gone so far. Tsarek had said the door in the castle rocks only opened every month. Surely they had not been gone that long.

Tipping his head back, he opened his eyes. An ugly gargoyle crouched above him on the corner of the roof. It looked like some sort of dragon. He was about to stand and get a better look when its head swiveled in his direction. The rantel! It was scanning the valley beyond the wall. Corvan held his breath until the creature unfurled its glossy wings and soared out over the fields in the direction of the settlement entrances.

Someone grabbed his arm, and Corvan jumped to one side. His yell died on his lips as he looked into the face of Tsarek.

"So sorry, sir. I do hope I did not scare you."

A smirk curved across the lizard's face. Corvan wasn't so sure he liked Tsarek's newfound sense of humor.

"I was waiting for the rantel to leave," Tsarek said. "I believe he is looking for you."

"The rantel?"

"Yes, but also a very angry man with a bandage over one eye." Tsarek cocked his head to one side. "You seem to have made a lot of enemies in the Cor since you locked me outside the door."

"Does he know I'm here?"

"No. His connection to his guide is not functioning because of his great pain. When did you learn to throw fire? I often heard your mother tell you not to play with it."

Corvan waved his question off. "Where is the man with the patch now? We need to keep moving on to the city."

Tsarek held out a paw and pulled Corvan to his feet. "He is on the other side of the river. I crossed over on top of the dam. He is going back to his lair in the highest crags to heal. He will not bother us now but he is sending out his best trackers to find you." He started walking the road toward the city. "He's offering a great reward for your capture. One even a lizard might enjoy." His eyes sparkled as he looked back over his shoulder.

Coming around the bend, they found the city of Kadir shrouded in a thick bank of fog. The statue rising above it looked like a man with his feet in a snowbank.

Tsarek pointed. "The palace must be making sure people stay indoors until the light. Perhaps they suspect there will be trouble from the rebels."

"What do you mean?"

"The palace controls the fog and the floods. They use the water to keep people afraid of what might happen if they don't obey the Chief Watcher. It's done with large machines in the underground river below the karst at the top of the palace courtyard. I saw them after you shut the gate on me and I had to follow the cold water down into the Cor. But there is hot water too, where they create the fog."

"I saw the fog come out of that round wall at the feet of the great statue."

Tsarek looked puzzled. "There is only a karst between its feet. That's where they drown people at the Wasting ceremony. There has never been a wall around it."

"It's new. I saw the workers constructing it when I came out the door."

"The one you shut on me?"

Corvan nodded. Was Tsarek going to remind him of his mistake forever?

Tsarek gestured toward the city. "The statue karst is much like the one you were just in, except there is no island in the middle and no great beast. A water creature, much greater than the one we fought in the labyrinth, dwells in an underwater cave. It lives behind a gate that is opened whenever they throw someone in." Tsarek looked up at him, his eyes full of pride. "The gate was shut, but its arms almost caught me. I frightened it away with my fire stick."

"And that's where they control the floods?"

"I have seen it done. They can send water running throughout the city. They have drowned many people to justify the Wasting."

Corvan looked over the river at the fog-shrouded city. At first light Tyreth would be thrown into the water as part of the Chief Watcher's evil plans. Somehow, he needed to stop him. He glanced down at Tsarek, the lizard's short legs working furiously to keep pace. Surely things would work out better now that he had both Tsarek and the hammer back.

As they approached the ruined bridge, Tsarek yanked Corvan down behind the cover of the stone walls. "Rakash," he hissed and pointed down to the fields.

Corvan peeked over the wall. Down below, across the narrow end of the fields, five people walked in a row along a high retaining wall. One of them carried a staff topped by a red globe.

"That's a palace staff," the lizard said. "One of the soldiers was carrying it when I took the cloth. The Rakash is returning with the soldiers to report Tarran's escape." Tsarek gripped Corvan's arm tighter. "And my trespass in the Cor."

Corvan glanced over the wall. The group was close enough that any movement along the river road would be detected. "The soldiers won't cross the broken bridge, will they?"

"No, they won't go near it. They are passing by to take the high river road so they can cross at the upper bridge."

Corvan checked again. The wall the soldiers were on ended at the edge of the fields then climbed a steep path to join the end of the river road. He crouched back down. "Do you think they'll reach the Wasting on time?"

"No. The high river trail is very narrow and climbs up and down the cliffs near the river. Few people choose to travel that way, as they are afraid they will fall into the river. It is much longer and they will be moving slowly."

"But they'll see us if we try to use the broken bridge."

Tsarek sat back against the wall. "Then we must find another cat to skin. The dark cycle will soon end, and the Wasting always takes place at the first segment of light."

Corvan's stomach knotted. He couldn't be late getting to the city. Crawling over to the river side of the road, he looked across to where the outlet from Madam Toreg's secret city flowed out under the bridge. "What if we jump into the river and use the fire sticks to go back through the water outlet into the hidden city? Madam Toreg will send her gray men to help me save Tyreth."

Tsarek shook his head. "I cannot let anyone see me. Those who serve the Watcher will kill me on sight, and those who fight the Watcher will kill me for being of his kind."

"I'll look after you. I won't let them hurt you."

The lizard laid his paw on Corvan's arm. "You don't understand, Corvan. If you are seen with me, they will most certainly kill you as well."

Corvan hadn't thought it through until this moment, but it was true. His best friend in this hostile underground world would be seen as his primary enemy.

He placed his hand on top of Tsarek's paw. "It will be better once we get back to my world."

"No, Corvan." Tsarek's dark eyes clouded over. "I have decided that I must stay here in the Cor. Your world is not my home. Your people will not accept me. I have been shot at a few times by that large boy who lives near the rock. You cannot protect me in your world any more than I can protect you in mine."

"What are you saying?"

Tsarek swallowed. "Our ways are parting, Kalian. You must go ask your friends for help. I will stay in the river, swim up to the karst, and hide under the edge where the palace guard cannot see me. If you get in trouble at the Wasting, you can jump into the water. I will have fire sticks for you, and you can swim away under the water."

"What about Tyreth?"

Tsarek rolled his eyes. "I will have enough fire sticks for her too."

"What about the water creature with the long arms?"

Tsarek grimaced. "I will do my best to keep it away." He pulled two smooth fire sticks from his bundle. "You will need these to make it through that water tunnel. It will be hard work, so if you find it difficult to breathe, use both of them together."

Tsarek slipped over the low wall and hung by his claws. Corvan leaned down to him. "Tsarek, you have not called me 'sir' very much since you came back."

The lizard cocked his head to one side. "I guess after all we have been through I am thinking of you as my friend—sir." He grinned. "Like the Lone Ranger and Tonto."

"What? Where did you hear that?"

The streaks on Tsarek's face flushed. "The Kate's mother watched it on her TV box and I would peek through her window."

Corvan grinned and gave him a quick wave. "See you soon, Tonto."

"If my claws were free, I would return the waving to you, for I too hope to see you soon—keemosabe." His eyes twinkled. "This time, don't shut the door on me." He pushed off the wall and dove down into the water. A trail of bubbles worked its way upstream.

Corvan looked down into the water and his heart beat faster. He'd never jumped from anything this high.

CHAPTER THIRTY-THREE

"Don't move!" A hoarse voice whispered in his ear, and a sharp point dug into his back. "Put both arms flat on the wall."

Corvan did as he was ordered. The point pushed in harder as the person leaned over him, pulled up his sleeve, and removed Morgon's black knife. "Turn around."

Corvan turned to face a man in a green robe, his hood pulled low over his eyes. The man unsheathed the black knife and pointed it at Corvan's heart.

"So now you are working for the Watchers." The voice was harsh and strained. "What did he promise you?"

"I'm not working for him." Corvan protested. "You don't understand. This one is not like the Chief Watcher. He is my friend."

The man snorted. "They don't have friends. They only use us. You have been deceived, Kalian."

"Jorad?"

The hood swept back, revealing Jorad's angry face. "I promised the high priest I would train you to be a Cor-Van. Instead you have used me to aid the Chief Watcher in his plans to wipe out all the priests . . . and kill Tyreth." He jabbed the knife against Corvan's chest, pressing him tight against the low stone wall.

"No. I'm on my way to save Tyreth. I promised Madam Toreg upon the hammer. That's the truth."

Jorad's lips curled back in a snarl. "The only truth I know is that I have taken an oath to protect Tyreth. I will do anything to save her from the Watchers . . . and from those working for them." The knife pushed harder.

"Jorad, I said I would help you. Let's go together and rescue Tyreth before it is too late."

Jorad's eyes narrowed. "I heard what your lizard friend said. He plans to wait for her under the water when you throw her in. Is that his reward for helping you? Does he get her body after she drowns?" His voice rose higher with every word. He pulled the knife back, preparing to plunge it into Corvan's heart.

Instinctively Corvan drew the hammer from its holster and held it up between them. In blind fury Jorad slashed at it, but a pulse of energy from the black stone twisted the knife from his hand and sent it skittering across the road.

Corvan lowered the hammer. "Jorad, you have to believe me. I'm going to save Tyreth, not kill her."

The priest's eyes narrowed. "It is the worst evil when a man betrays a friend to get what he wants for himself."

As Corvan opened his mouth to protest, the palace guards appeared on the slope at the end of the road. One raised his bow and drew back.

"Jorad, behind you!"

"No more tricks, Kalian. I am not—"

Corvan threw himself toward Jorad, spinning the man's body to the side. The arrow tore through the bunched-up hood behind the priest's neck and clattered onto the ground. As Jorad whirled around to find its source, two more soldiers drew their bows. Jorad dropped to the ground behind the wall.

Corvan jumped onto the other wall and dove into the river. He hit the water cleanly and turned toward the far side, swimming hard against the current to get around the pillars supporting the bridge. Breathless, he pulled himself out of the water in a rocky bay where the water from the new city gushed out.

The chains above him rattled as Jorad clutched the sides of the bridge and tried to work himself around the missing floor panels. Above Jorad's labored breathing, Corvan heard the soldiers shouting as they ran toward the trapped priest.

Jorad stopped moving and called down to Corvan, his voice strained and hoarse. "Do as you have promised and rescue Tyreth. But I swear, if you are lying to me, you will never get out of the Cor alive."

"I promise you Jorad, I . . ."

"Get out of sight!" Jorad rasped. "They're coming."

Corvan pulled the cap from one of his fire sticks, stuck it in his mouth, and waded into the water outlet. The current was stronger than he expected. Clamping the unlit fire stick into the opposite side of his mouth, he felt along the bottom for handholds to haul himself through the water. His lungs labored to pull enough air through the slender stick to fuel his efforts. Jamming his toes into the rocks, he flicked the cap off the other stick. His breathing came easier, in through the mouth and out through the nose, just as Tsarek had instructed.

The current slackened, and shafts of flickering light shot through the water from above. He stood and waded toward the half-finished wall of the pool. There were voices on the other side. He knew that tone and the words all too well. A group of bullies was teasing a child. Looking over the wall, Corvan saw a circle of boys gathered around a child huddled on the ground. One kicked the child—a small, bedraggled boy clutching a flute. Gavyn.

A rush of anger propelled Corvan up and onto the wall with a great splash. He towered over them, water pouring down his body, a smoking fire stick dangling from each corner of his mouth. The boys stared, their mouths gaping like dead fish.

Corvan tried to say, "Leave him alone," but the fire sticks blocked his words. The sticks twisted down like glowing fangs so what came out sounded like "Eat them bones."

High-pitched screams erupted as a twisting mass of bodies scrambled over one another to get away from the flesh-eating monster.

As their voices faded away over the stairs, Gavyn rose to his feet, triumphantly holding the pan flute he'd been protecting from the bullies. Corvan jumped down from the wall. Gavyn ran and hugged Corvan around his waist, then pulled back to stare at the water dripping from Corvan's cloak. His eyes followed the puddles that led to the wall. Reaching up, he grabbed the steaming stub of a fire stick out of Corvan's mouth and shoved it in his own. His sunken cheeks pulled in, and his eyes brightened with excitement. Before Corvan could move, the boy thrust the panpipes into his hand and leaped over the wall into the water.

Corvan rushed over as the boy broke the surface, like a fish after a bug, and arced back in with hardly a ripple. The water grew still and the bubbles stopped. Corvan was about to jump in when a smiling face floated up in the center of the pool. Gavyn swam on his back to Corvan and pulled himself out to sit on the wall. He gave the fire stick back, took up his flute, and out burbled a funny little tune.

The blast of a trumpet rent the air. Gavyn glanced fearfully toward the stairs, then jumped down and tugged at Corvan's sleeve, pulling him down behind the stack of stone blocks.

The horn blew again. Corvan shifted to the left and found a crack between the rocks that exposed a narrow strip of the stairs. A short, balding man with a horn and a carved staff appeared—the mayor Madam Toreg had met at the city gate. A noisy crowd gathered behind him. He hammered his staff for silence.

His sarcastic voice carried over the noise of the crowd. "Yes, I can see that something came from the pool. But none of us has ever seen a man-eating creature with smoking horns that swims in the water." Loud retorts came from the audience. The mayor changed his tone. "I agree. I have no reason to doubt any of your boys. If this monster is still in the city, we should work together and find it."

"Perhaps we should consult Madam Toreg," someone suggested.

The man bristled. "Madam Toreg stands accused of breaking faith with our people and bringing strangers into our city. Her staff is broken and her authority has been removed. It may even be her fault this creature has found a way inside."

"Then maybe she knows how to get rid of it," another voice interjected.

The mayor's face grew red. "Madam Toreg will remain under house arrest until she is tried by the elders. We will not waste time asking her advice." He gestured to one side. "Tewbel, you stand guard here in case the creature comes back." He faced the crowd. "The rest of you divide into search parties and scour the city. Blow a horn if you see anything." He pounded his staff, and the people filed out.

When the crowd was gone, a muscular man stepped to the top of the stairs. He looked like the strong man Corvan had seen at the circus, except this one carried a short barbed spike in his hand. The man took a step down to study the scene before him, his eyes shifting to the pool and then over to the pile of blocks.

Corvan's stomach dropped. He'd left a trail of footprints that led directly to his hiding place.

The man put his horn to his lips, then let it fall to his side. He lifted his weapon as he descended the stairs.

Corvan turned to tell Gavyn to run, but the boy was gone. He glanced back through the crack and saw Gavyn run up to Tewbel. The young boy held his hand up to his head as if horns were spouting from his hair. He loped about in circles, growling like a mad dog, then ran to the stairs and beckoned for Tewbel to follow. The man gave one last glance toward the stack of blocks and climbed up after him.

Corvan heard short blasts on the pan flute. Gavyn was making sure he knew they were leaving the area. Corvan crept out, climbed the stairs on all fours, and peeked over the edge. The tunnel was empty. Jumping to his feet, he trotted along the road toward the city gates. If he were attacked, he could always take to the water and escape.

The entry to the city drew near. The gates stood open, but just inside, a guard stood at attention. Corvan slowed his pace and hugged the low wall that separated the road from the deep ditch.

The sound of running feet caught him off guard, but before he could get completely over the wall, Gavyn came into sight. The boy motioned for Corvan to keep going, hopped the wall himself, and pulled Corvan down, putting a finger to his lips.

A moment later Corvan heard marching feet on the upper road. It grew louder, passed them, and faded away. He stole a glance over the wall just in time to see a squad of armed soldiers enter the city gates.

Corvan leaned back against the wall. Madam Toreg could not help him. Unless he could come up with a new plan, Tyreth would die at the Wasting.

Gavyn grabbed his sleeve and pointed up along the wall where the water rushed out of a small cave and swept down a ramp to the channel below. The boy nodded encouragement, crouched low, and took off along the inside of the wall.

It was all Corvan could do to keep up with the agile boy. Gavyn ran like a spider monkey, his knuckles almost dragging on the ground beside him. He moved in this manner right up into the cave and disappeared inside.

Following him in, Corvan understood why Gavyn adopted this strange manner of locomotion. There was no other way to make it though the tunnel. The water was not shallow enough to crawl in, and the roof was too low for them to stand.

Gavyn was already out of sight, but Corvan could hear him splashing up ahead. The tunnel grew darker and when the floor dropped off, there was no chance to catch himself. He slipped under the water.

Corvan surfaced, choking and gasping for air. Treading water, he cleared his lungs. There was a bit more light here. Enough to see that he was in yet another karst, much larger than the one at the settlement, with a high island rising out of the center.

A thin tendril grabbed his ankle and yanked him below the surface. Corvan kicked furiously, and the creature released him. Surfacing, he swam like mad toward the island, his heart pounding as he imagined the snakelike arms pursuing him.

Bright laughter filled the cavern as Corvan pulled himself out of the water and scrambled up the rocks. Gavyn swam toward him, his mouth bubbling the water as he mimicked Corvan's panicked flight. Relief flowed with embarrassment. Corvan wanted to throw a rock at the little imp.

Joining Corvan on the pile of stone blocks, Gavyn shook out his hair like a scrawny dog, cleared the water from his ears, and pointed upward. Corvan followed his gesture through the circle of the karst. Familiar painted faces watched him. They were back underneath the great library.

Gavyn poked him in the side. He was asking him for instructions, his bony shoulders held up in an exaggerated shrug.

"I need to get to the Wasting."

The boy's eyes widened as he vigorously shook his head. He made motions with his hands and fingers of things swimming and being captured. Corvan grabbed his hands and held them still. "I know about the monster in the water. I don't want to go down inside the water. I need to get to the top before they throw Tyreth in."

Gavyn nodded and gestured for Corvan to follow him. He clambered over a jumble of broken stone blocks, and dove back into the water. Wearily Corvan followed him.

Across the water, a set of broken stairs led steadily upward. At times, they were almost impassable, but someone had gone through a lot of trouble to remove enough debris to open a way through. Corvan's legs burned from all the climbing, and his lungs choked on the residual water, but he had to keep Gavyn in sight. Once, he shouted at Gavyn to wait, but the boy just put a finger to his lips and climbed on.

They were on their way to the wasting, but without Madam Toreg's gray men. How could he possibly take on the Watcher and the palace guard by himself? He had no plan, and even if he did, every plan he'd made so far had fallen apart.

Just take the next step, he thought. *Just keep moving forward.*

The stairs became narrow tunnels that were almost level. Soon the rough stone walls were replaced by smooth brick. Other passages joined in, and Corvan lost all sense of how many turns they'd taken. He was falling behind. If Gavyn lost him, he'd never find his way out.

The boy disappeared around another corner and Corvan ran forward. Around the bend, an empty corridor climbed a flight of steps and ended in a circle of pale light. Corvan crept forward, trying to keep his labored breathing as quiet as possible as he ascended the stairs.

Reaching the top, he stepped through the jagged hole and found himself back in the hall of the high priest.

CHAPTER THIRTY-FOUR

A pair of bare feet stuck out below the ruined tapestry. He gave the thick fabric a poke, and Gavyn's smiling face appeared in the hole.

"Gavyn," Corvan said, "I need your help to save Tyreth."

The young boy backed into the passage, fear etched across his innocent face.

"No, Gavyn, I'm not asking you to come. I need you to find Madam Toreg and ask her to send her gray men. You must tell her the Cor-Van needs help."

The boy pointed to his lips.

He was right. And even if Gavyn could get through to Madam Toreg and make her understand, she might not believe him . . . unless there could be no doubt it was the truth.

Corvan removed the holster from his belt. Gavyn eagerly reached for it and Corvan pulled it back. This might not be a good idea. What if the boy lost it? Gavyn wrapped his small hands around Corvan's and looked into his eyes. This was a boy who understood much more than a child his age should. Corvan had no doubt he could trust him with this task.

Gavyn's smile broadened, and he pulled the hammer to his chest.

A drumbeat rumbled through the floor. Gavyn pointed overhead to where soft light fell from the dirty skylights. As the drum settled into a steady rhythm, the boy touched his arm and was gone, the secret door closing behind him.

The priest's gate onto the courtyard hung wide, its great wooden bolt shattered to bits. The empty plaza echoed with the rolling drumbeats as Corvan sprinted up the stairs two at a time, the throbbing drum matching his heart beat for beat. He sailed up the last set of stairs toward a wide arch in the high, circular wall. Through the opening, he could see a white-robed man addressing a great crowd.

A guard stepped from inside the wall, barring his way. Corvan skidded to a halt as a scarred face with bloodshot eyes thrust into his hood, along with the rank smell of rotten teeth.

"Where've you been, boy?" The ugly face pulled back, and for a brief second Corvan was sure the man would strike him. Instead, he bent down and picked up a long-necked clay jar from beside the door. "Lucky for you I saw this back at the barracks. If that new stone gets stuck again, it'll be your fault." He thrust the neck of the jar into Corvan's hand and pushed him off to the side. "Get down to the priest's entry before that old windbag finishes talking."

The clay vessel smelled of well-used engine oil and was almost too hot to carry. Corvan juggled it from hand to hand as he worked his way along the high, curved wall. Up ahead, a dark doorway jutted out and a stairway led down inside. Beyond the door there was only a pile of scaffolding and the high plaza wall. This had to be the right place.

At the base of the stairs, the tunnel curved down and stopped before an open door. To the left another tunnel beckoned. Which way should he go? Corvan pulled the door wider and it creaked on dry hinges. A steep stairway ran up and disappeared into a dimly lit room. The speaker's voice seemed louder up there, but the cheers of the crowd were louder from the passage to the left.

Corvan was about to follow the noise of the crowd when heavy footsteps fell on the landing above the stairs. Two large boots hung over the top step, and a voice growled down from the darkness. "About time. Bring that up here first. The rest of it goes in them two holes in the floor. See 'em?"

Corvan stayed silent. Should he run away?

"Ya see 'em or not? We don't have much time."

Corvan bent to check out the holes recently bored into the floor near the walls on either side of the passage.

"They say it'll work this time, but if not, it won't be my fault. You'll take the fall for this one. Now get up here." The boots left and Corvan followed. He couldn't take the chance of being chased out into the crowd.

He entered a curved stone room lit only by a narrow slit along the far wall. A large man had squeezed his bulk into a complicated system of gears and levers. He reached a pudgy hand over his shoulder. "Give me that oil. The idiots never even greased the main shaft."

Corvan moved into the room. A door at the back was open and rippling reflections on the wall showed him he was near the water.

The man took the bottle from Corvan and pushed his mass even deeper into the machinery. "If you ask me," he grunted, "and of course they never do, this plan of using Tyreth as bait to catch Tarran is a waste of time. If he's the brains behind the plot to overthrow the palace, he'd have to see this is a trap." He poured out some oil, and the burnt smell was added to the overpowering aroma of metal and sweat. "She wouldn't even want him to try. Probably told him that when she sprung him out of the cell and killed Morgon." He grunted again. "There, that should do it."

The man shoved the bottle back. Corvan leaned in past two of the levers to grab it. Through the narrow window, over the heads of the crowd, the gatekeeper was flicking a red flag back and forth.

"What are you gawkin' at? Get going and dump the rest down them holes, equally mind you, and don't get in the way when it lifts. We should get the signal any minute."

Corvan ran from the room and back down the stairs. Ahead of him in the tunnel, he heard the speaker talking passionately about the Cor. The crowd applauded and the sound rumbled down the tunnel.

Corvan looked at the holes. He had no idea whether following the man's orders would help or hurt his attempt to rescue Tyreth, but he didn't want the huge man to come down here after him. Brushing the cones of stone chips away from the holes he poured the oil into each one, alternating back and forth to let it seep down to wherever it was going.

Setting the bottle on the stairs, he turned back to see a slab of stone rise in spasmodic jerks from the floor between the two holes. Up in the control room, energetic grunts matched each rise as the stone inched upward.

The passage was half closed before Corvan came to his senses and leaped over the thick stone into the passage beyond. He'd barely cleared it when the stone found the grease and slammed up into a notch in the ceiling. There was no turning back now.

The voice of the speaker grew louder as Corvan edged around a corner and looked out into a wide amphitheater. The first four tiers of seats were crammed with green-robed priests. Many wore dirty robes and had unshaven faces. Behind their backs, a thick, curved wall the height of a man separated the priests from the crowd listening to the speaker in rapt attention. Over the heads of the audience, a small green flag fluttered.

Corvan stepped to the left, staying hidden in the shadows of the tunnel, until he could clearly see the speaker. The white-robed man stood on the tip of a balcony that pointed sharply out from between the ankles of the huge stone statue.

"For generations we have suffered while the battles between the rebels and the priests tore our beloved city apart. Although the palace sought to bring harmony to the Cor, our leaders were thwarted by accusations from both sides. Lies have become the stock in trade of those who would usurp the palace and set themselves up to rule the Cor. We must find a way to judge what these people are telling us. We must find the truth, for only then can we be free."

The crowd applauded and the man gestured around the arena. "Look at this grand temple the Chief Watcher has built for our gods. Today he dedicates this temple in thanks to the gods for providing the answer to the deceit that has ruined our civilization."

The black curtains at the back of the stage opened, and the Chief Watcher strode forward to stand between two short stone pillars. A large lumien on either side of the stage was suddenly unveiled, brilliantly lighting the stage and glittering off the sliver bracers on his arms and off every scale of the lizard's meticulously polished hide. The crowd collectively caught their breath.

"People of the Cor!" The Chief Watcher extended his arms and then brought them to rest on the pillars. "Most of you remember when the water of the gods ran through the streets, killing your families and friends. Will it happen again? None of us doubt the prophecy that our world could be filled to the top," he gestured overhead, "with water."

Corvan felt fear settle over the crowd.

"Over the years we have kept the gods pleased by our Wasting ceremonies. But why should the innocent continue to suffer while the guilty go free?"

His arm swept in a grand gesture. "This new hall of justice will allow the gods to show us who we can trust. Instead of throwing our children into the water, we will put those who may be guilty in the place of judgment." He gestured to a narrow stone pier that stuck out over the karst.

The lizard took a step forward. "If they are innocent, the water will remain below them, but if they are guilty, the water shall rise and punish them for their lies."

He waited, arms outstretched, until the crowd gave a halfhearted cheer.

The black lizard walked out to the lip of the balcony. "You have all heard that the high priest, his son, Tarran, and his daughter, Tyreth, have been arrested on the charge of treason against the palace. But before we could hold the trial, Tarran murdered Morgon and escaped. Tarran is clearly guilty of murder and treason, but were his father and sister part of the plan? In these days of perpetual lies, only the gods know." He gestured toward the karst. "Today we call on them to judge the truth."

Corvan scanned the audience. The priests sat stiffly in their places. A few older ones shook their heads, but above them, many in the crowd nodded.

A narrow door opened on the far side of the karst, below the heel of the statue's left boot. The high priest shuffled out around the sinkhole. His mouth was gagged and his hands bound behind his back but he walked past the priests with his head held high. He stepped purposefully onto the stone pier and walked down the shallow steps until he was well below the lip of the karst. He turned to face the crowd.

"High priest," the lizard said as he took a step back and brought his thick arms to rest once more on the two stone pillars, "you stand accused of treason. You are silenced before the people so that instead of hearing your words we shall hear only the answer of the gods whom we call on today to judge between truth and lies."

The Chief Watcher raised his long claw and pointed high overhead to the face of the unfinished statue. Corvan resisted the urge to follow his gesture and kept his eyes on the lizard. As the lizard's right arm went up, he saw the creature lean firmly on the pillar to his left so it dipped ever so slightly.

A geyser of water shot up around the high priest, and he was momentarily lost in the spray. Some in the crowd cried out and stood ready to run. The tower of water fell back into the karst, and the surface began to bubble and rise.

"If the water takes the man, the gods have found him guilty. If it subsides, we shall know he is innocent."

All eyes were on the priest and the rapidly rising water. A fierce look of determination covered the high priest's face. He glanced down as the water rose to his ankles. He looked over his shoulder up at the lizard and then stepped back off the pier to slip below the surface of the water.

The crowd sat in stunned silence. In shock, the Chief Watcher pulled back on his pillars. The water rolled, then grew still. All eyes turned to the Chief Watcher. A smug expression crossed his dark face.

"The priest has declared his own guilt by offering himself in an attempt to buy favor with the gods. It was futile, for he remains in the water. If he were an honorable man, the gods would return him to us, but they have not."

Corvan knew there would be no returning, for in the froth he'd caught sight of tentacles much larger than those he and Tsarek had encountered in the labyrinth. His stomach knotted. Tsarek had failed to get rid of the water creature.

"Perhaps our high priest sacrificed himself in an attempt to save his daughter, but the gods have decreed that each person must be judged separately." He gestured toward the left side of the karst.

A figure in white emerged from the doorway across the pool. Corvan's eyes followed Tyreth as she moved gracefully around the perimeter of the karst, her long hair flowing in black waves with each measured step. Her face registered no fear.

A young priest stood to his feet. "This is not acceptable!" Two other priests, their faces covered by their cowls, pulled him back down to the stone seats.

As Tyreth rounded the pool, she looked into the tunnel where Corvan stood.

THE HAMMER

A tiny spark touched his mind, and he heard her words as clearly as if they were spoken. "Do not give in to fear."

Tyreth turned to descend the stone pier, and Corvan caught sight of the jagged scar across her right cheek. She walked to the end of the pier, wavered for a moment, recovered, and turned to face the audience. She did not look at Corvan, but he knew her thoughts were bent toward him. As she glanced down, her lower lip trembled. She caught it in her teeth, turned her head deliberately toward him, and slowly shook her head.

She was telling him to let her drown.

CHAPTER THIRTY-FIVE

The lizard spoke from his perch above the water. "The gods have found the father guilty. Now we shall see if the daughter shares his treason."

Corvan stared trancelike at the water. Tyreth did not want him to save her, but how could letting her drown be the right thing to do? If only he had the hammer to help him. No. He didn't need to hold the hammer to understand the truth. He'd promised to do whatever he could to save her, and there was no way he would let her die just to save his own life. She was the key to the future of the Cor, not him. He raised his eyes. Tyreth was slowly sliding her feet toward the back edge of the pier.

"No!" Corvan shouted. He ran out into the light. "Do not die to save me!"

He raced toward the pier. The two hooded priests jumped from their seats and ran toward him.

"It's a trap," Tyreth shouted. "Run!"

Corvan did not slacken his pace. He beat the fake priests to the pier and ran out to Tyreth. He stopped a step above her and looked into her eyes. "Don't jump, Tyreth. We can escape." He turned to face the two hooded figures that stood at the base of the pier, looking up at the Chief Watcher for instructions. Neither of the hooded men noticed the thin tentacles snake out of the water around their ankles. In the blink of an eye, both men disappeared into the water with hardly a ripple.

The lizard spoke into the electric air. "The gods have judged your two friends, Tarran. You may have believed you could save your sister from judgment, but now the two of you shall be judged together." The lizard lifted both arms over his head. "Show us, O gods. Let us know if these two are the source of the lies that have caused you such displeasure."

Corvan put his hands on Tyreth's shoulders. "We're going to fall together into the water, but you must not panic. Keep your mouth closed. Don't let the air out of your lungs."

Tyreth nodded, fear rising in her eyes. Reaching into his robe, Corvan pulled out the stub of a fire stick as a wall of spray exploded around them. Wrapping Tyreth tightly in his arms, he toppled them from the pier.

Clouds of bubbles rose around them as they plunged deeper into the pool. Corvan flicked the fire stick open and filled his lungs with air. Pulling Tyreth close he tried to push the bubbling stick into her mouth, but her lips were clamped shut. Her eyes squeezed tight. A thin stream of bubbles flowed from her nose. She had to have fresh air.

Corvan pulled another deep breath from the fire stick, placed his mouth firmly over hers, and forced air into her lungs. Tyreth's eyes opened wide, and more bubbles flowed from her nostrils. Again, Corvan pulled air into his lungs and put his mouth to hers. This time Tyreth relaxed and allowed the air to flow freely into her body. Her eyes locked on his, and for the briefest of moments, Corvan found himself soaring free in a blue prairie sky.

Their intertwined bodies didn't have a chance to fight the tentacles that wrapped around them. Corvan strained against the thick arms, but the tentacles squeezed tighter and swept them back into a black opening in the wall of the karst. His breath was gone; he had given it all to Tyreth. The stub of the fire stick lashed firmly to his side.

Softness came against his mouth and air flowed back into his body. The air stopped flowing, but Tyreth's lips remained on his as they shared one final breath.

The tentacles jerked, squeezed even tighter, then suddenly they were gone. Corvan released a burst of stale air, then pulled up the fire stick and filled his lungs. Tyreth watched, then took it from his hand and did the same. Her bubbles climbed away from them toward a large silvery moon. Pulling on Tyreth's hand, he kicked furiously, swimming upward.

They broke the surface in a small cavern lit by patches of phosphorus yellow slime that floated on top of the water. Ahead of them, a shaft of light shone on a broken stone stair that descended into the water. Corvan towed Tyreth toward it, and they crawled out of the water, collapsing on the steps.

As his breathing returned to normal, Corvan turned his head to see Tyreth looking at the water in amazement. "My father told me it was possible to survive the water. But I did not believe him." She turned to look at him. "I didn't believe him about you either."

She studied his face for a moment and Corvan found himself wondering how someone so strong could also be so beautiful. A smile pulled at the corners of her lips. "So, what happened to that frightened boy I met in the prison?"

Corvan returned her gaze. "He found someone worth fighting for."

Tyreth's smile spread into her eyes, and Corvan's cheeks grew warm. He had been referring to Kate but he was not unhappy that Tyreth understood he meant her as well.

"Thanks for coming back." Tyreth said. "I am thankful you did not let me drown." A mischievous sparkle touched her eyes. "Of course you may have to go back to prison for kissing the high priest's daughter without his permission."

Corvan's felt the warm flush travel up to his ears.

Tyreth laughed and punched his shoulder. "I'm just teasing you. My father would have . . ." her voice trailed off. She bit her lip and turned to look over the water.

"I'm sorry I couldn't save him," Corvan said. "I didn't think he would jump in."

She nodded. "He knew it was just a matter of time before the poison killed him. I admire him for exposing the Chief Watcher's lies, even with his death."

The water in the cave exploded as huge bubbles of air hit the surface, sending them both scrambling up the steps away from the rising water.

"The water creature," Tyreth shouted, climbing higher.

"No. It's the Chief Watcher. He intends to drown all the priests."

"How can he—"

The water churned and belched another explosion of air.

Corvan hollered over the rising noise. "He controls the level of the water from the pillars where he stands. The place where the priests are sitting has been sealed off. When the water rises into the priest's area, none will escape the water, or the creature below."

Tyreth ran up the stairs, with Corvan close behind her. Muted echoes of the Chief Watcher's voice reached them as they squeezed through a crack into a narrow corridor. The Chief Watcher's voice came from both directions.

Tyreth grabbed his shoulder, "I'm going left. You go right. If you find him, come back and get me." She pushed him to go but then pulled him back. "Don't do anything without me. I need you to stay alive."

Corvan nodded and turned to go, but Tyreth pulled him back again. "Do you have it with you?"

His heart sank and he shook his head.

Her face dropped "But I thought . . . Do you have a sword?"

Again no.

Her voice rose. "Anything at all?"

Corvan reached under his cloak and held out the krypin rope. She hesitated, then took it from his hand and ran up the tunnel. Corvan watched her disappear around the corner, then sprinted in the other direction. What good would a rope be against the black lizard?

The tunnel grew dark and jogged to the left, bumping Corvan off the wall and into something soft.

"Clumsy oaf," a voice hissed in his ear. "We aren't moving yet. Stay in your position."

A burst of light shot into the tunnel from a small window. Blinking, Corvan found himself at the end of a row of palace guards, all crammed into a short, wide passage.

"Where's your pike?" asked the man in front of him. He reached into the corner. "Take this. You'll need something to keep them from coming over the wall. The idiots made it too short just so the spectators could see better."

"Blue flag," someone whispered. "Let's move."

A door opened at the end of the hallway, and the red cloaks marched out. Corvan followed as they spread out along the wall behind the priests, leaving him standing outside a door directly beneath the toe of the statue's boot. Each of the guards carried a long pike topped with a cruelly barbed metal tip. Corvan's was only a long wooden pole with flaps of leather attached to the end.

"I have brought in my palace guard to protect you," The Chief Watcher announced. "If the priests are all in this conspiracy, they may try to break out and harm you. As we have seen with Tarran, what begins as lies and deceit often turns into murder."

The black curtains behind the lizard parted, and the leader of the Sightless slipped in behind him to whisper in his ear. The Chief Watcher nodded and the bony creature slipped away.

"People of the Cor, it has often been the self-proclaimed Cor-Vans who have been the source of our problems. Whether among the rebels, the Broken, or our priests, these charlatans have led good people to destruction. Even our high priest and his family have succumbed to the wiles of one of these masters of deception. But we have finally caught him—the priest, Jorad."

The curtain parted, and the four Rakash escorted Jorad out. A gag was stuffed in his mouth and he was bound with a long blue krypin rope. It was forked at the end, and the separate strands spiraled down each of his legs. The Rakash leader walked behind the priest, manipulating the krypin to make Jorad walk stiffly forward like a puppet on a string.

As the Rakash guided Jorad to the front lip of the platform, the Chief Watcher pointed at Jorad. "This deceiver planned to use Tarran to take control of the palace through his army of priests." His dark eyes turned to the green robes. "So let us first test the priests in this conspiracy. If they are guilty, then Jorad also stands judged."

Without a moment's hesitation the lizard lifted his arms. "Answer us, O gods. Cleanse your temple so we might worship in truth." As he dropped his arms back onto the pillars, a massive waterspout spiraled out of the pool and dropped back as the water level rose.

The priests cried and pushed back to the wall as the water overflowed the karst. Some in the crowd stood and chanted, "Death to the priests!"

The water rose to the first tier and stopped. The crowd was intently watching the water but Corvan looked to the Chief Watcher. He was pulling on his pillars and looking anxiously at the narrow slit cut into the left boot of the statue. Inside the boot Corvan could see the huge man floundering about the control room, frantically tugging on levers. The Chief Watcher's pillars moved of their own accord as the lizard struggled to keep his balance between them.

The Chief Watcher pulled back hard and finally regained control. The water rose. The lizard looked into the karst with the same bloodthirsty anticipation Corvan had seen when he devoured the lumien's heart.

Corvan felt someone's eyes on him. Beyond the Chief Watcher, Jorad was staring at him, his face seething with anger. Corvan lowered his head to hide behind his hood and looked into the karst.

The speed of the water was increasing and a deep whirlpool formed, sending waves of water toward the priests. A few tried to climb the wall behind them, but they were met by pointed barbs. One managed to get onto the wall, and a guard knocked him off into the swirling water. His terrified cries circled around with his body until he plunged into the center of the vortex and disappeared. The spectators watched in dumb amazement.

"They may call upon the gods," shouted the lizard, "but they will be answered with judgment, for the priests are guilty of blasphemy. They have corrupted the worship of our gods."

The water swirled higher and climbed over another step. One more rise and all the priests would be either drowned or impaled by the guards.

Corvan watched in utter hopelessness. Tyreth must have been captured. Once again his best intentions had failed.

Or had they? A pale green spider, trailing a long thin web, was moving swiftly around the feet of the Chief Watcher. Once, twice and then it climbed up and around the black lizard's pillars. Tyreth. It had to be her.

Corvan glanced at the guards jabbing at the defenseless priests. The guards would no doubt swarm up the tunnel to rescue their leader. He had to seal the door.

Uncapping the last piece of his fire stick, he jammed it into the latch. Molten rock flowed down, sealing it shut.

As he turned back to the karst, a hand appeared out of the door's small window and flipped his hood off his head. Corvan jerked back as a smiling face appeared in the opening. It was Gavyn.

"Where's Madam Toreg?"

The boy shrugged.

"Where's the gray men?"

The boy shook his head.

Panic rose in Corvan's chest. "Where's the hammer?"

Gavyn stuck a hand through the window and held the hammer out in plain view, its blue light throbbing like a lighthouse beacon. Corvan quickly pushed it back inside. Power surged through him. He was sure that every eye was now focused on his back. He turned. Only one pair of eyes bore down on him. The eyes of the Chief Watcher.

Corvan looked into those dark orbs and his blood ran cold. "Gavyn," he whispered hoarsely, "go up the tunnel. Find Tyreth. Now! Run!" He heard the boy leave.

Time slowed as if Corvan were in a trance. The whirlpool churned one full revolution in slow motion. The Chief Watcher rotated in counterpoint to command the tallest of the Rakash. Then his arm swung back in a measured beat, like the second hand of a clock, to point out Corvan.

Just as his long claw clicked onto Corvan's position, the green rope bulged, its coils tightened, lashing the black lizard firmly to the stone posts as the whirlpool raced on around its track.

"Treason," shouted the lizard, its muscles twisting as it strained at the rope. "The priests are all guilty and resort to trickery." The lizard pulled against his bonds and the water swirled even faster. All eyes were focused on the struggling reptile.

"Listen to me," shouted the lizard. "I speak the truth."

"Then you shall be judged by the truth," a woman called out.

Tyreth stepped through the black curtain, her white gown shimmering against its velvet blackness.

"Another deception," cried the lizard. "More lies!"

Tyreth strode toward him. "No one can lie when they are holding the truth." She lifted both hands over her head, the hammer clearly visible in her grasp. Blue light from the handle enveloped her as she towered over the Chief Watcher.

Nothing but the water moved. "You say you have told us the truth, Chief Watcher. So now you shall hold the truth, and the truth will be revealed." She lowered the hammer toward the claw lashed to the top of the post. The lizard writhed and tried to pull away, but he was held fast. As the handle touched the top of the pillar, the lizard's claw clamped involuntarily around it.

Even the sound of water fell away as every eye fixed on the hammer clutched in the black claw. The lizard dropped down between the posts, a grimace on its face. Its head fell forward onto its chest, releasing its breath in a long hiss.

The Rakash leader took a step toward the throne just as a thin smile spread across the Chief Watcher's face. His thick tail whipped toward Tyreth, ripping the control end of the krypin from her hand. The lizard drew up to his full height, the ropes stretching as his claw raised the hammer off the pedestal. "Old superstitions do not work in my world. This hammer will not harm me, for I am the Chief Watcher. I am the truth!" The lizard tipped his head back and let out a loud chortled hiss that filled the amphitheater with his evil pleasure.

A brilliant explosion of electricity wrapped itself around the creature, throwing Tyreth to the ground. Sparks shot out from around the base of the pillars as blue flames blazed through the loops of the krypin. Lightning arced about the thick black band on the lizard's neck as the Chief Watcher's head reared back in a silent scream. The light left his eyes, and he slumped forward against the blackened rope, leaving the hammer perfectly balanced on top of the pillar.

The Rakash leader leaped past Jorad, its hand reaching for the hammer. In its haste, it released the priest from the blue krypin and in an instant the black blade was in Jorad's hand, slicing through the air. The hand of the Rakash leader fell twitching to the floor, still holding the krypin rope. The Rakash lost its balance, slammed blindly into the pillar, knocking the hammer to the ground. The creature staggered off the balcony and disappeared into the whirlpool.

Jorad jumped forward to stand before Tyreth, his blade extended toward the three remaining Rakash who spread out across the front of the balcony, short yellow krypins in their hands. Each of the ropes ended in a sharp barb. The Rakash played the krypins like whips around Jorad's body so it seemed there were a dozen barbed heads seeking to get past his blade. Jorad slashed at one and sliced it almost in half, but another sank its barb into his forearm. The priest yanked it out and pulled back, but his hand shook and the knife faltered.

The three Rakash stepped back and waited. Jorad's hand slipped down to hang limply at his side. The knife clattered to the ground near Tyreth. The three fanned out wider, their whips closing in like venomous snakes. The yellow ropes slithered around his body, wrapping him tightly as their poisonous stingers hovered over his face. The three Rakash drew close in triumphant arrogance.

"Tyreth!" Corvan shouted. Her head spun to look at him. "The hammer!" He pointed to where it lay just out of reach behind her. Tyreth grabbed it and leaped to her feet from behind Jorad, the black blade in her other hand singing through the air and slashing the yellow ropes into pieces that fell twitching at Jorad's feet.

The Rakash reached out for her, but she lifted the hammer toward them. A pulse of fierce blue light pushed them back toward the edge. But they were not defeated. Slowly they spread out along the front of the stage, pushing incrementally in through the light.

Subtle movement at the edge of the stage caught Corvan's eye. On either side of the platform, one of Madam Toreg's gray men threaded a long thin fire stick into the stone floor. Simultaneously, each of them gave his stick a sharp twist. A muted *thump* shot a narrow fracture clean across the balcony, separating the three Rakash from Jorad and Tyreth. The huge slab tipped downward. The three gangly creatures stumbled backward to grab the lip of the stage, and two more gray forms rose from the floor, pulling Jorad and Tyreth back to safety.

With a *crack*, the two pillars snapped off, plunging the body of the Chief Watcher into the water. The Rakash clung to the front edge. For a moment, the slab hung by the sturdy metal rods that had connected the pillars to the control room. As the whirlpool slowed and fell away, thick tentacles shot from the water and wrapped around the three white creatures, stretching their already long bodies to an impossible length.

An eerie, terrifying sound filled the amphitheater as the Rakash cried out in pain. With two loud pops, the control rods came apart. The stone shuddered then fell into the pool with a colossal splash.

A towering wave slammed the priests against the wall and dropped them back into the stone tiers.

"Save those men," Jorad cried out.

The palace guard looked up in confusion. Some used their hooks to pull the priests to safety while people from the stands behind them jumped in to help.

As the priests were being lifted over the wall, Corvan looked down into the karst. Through the ripples, he could make out the broken remains of the balcony lying on the bottom of the pool. The only sign of the Rakash was a severed hand trailing a long blue krypin and pointing down at the tangled body of the Chief Watcher.

He looked again. The lizard's body was green. That was Tsarek!

CHAPTER THIRTY-SIX

Without a moment's thought, Corvan jammed his long pole behind the topmost tier and vaulted out over the steps into the water. Dropping in feet first, he turned and swam down. A tentacle rose to meet him, and he knocked it to one side. Far below, he could make out the remains of the water monster crushed beneath the stone slab.

Grabbing Tsarek's arm, Corvan pulled him toward the dark opening where the water creature had lived. The dead weight of Tsarek's body dragged behind him but he would not let go. His lungs were almost bursting as he surfaced in the small cave.

Pulling the limp form behind him, Corvan swam to the closest side and pulled Tsarek up onto a slab of rock that hung into the water. Water trickled from Tsarek's mouth, but his friend didn't cough or move. From the cuts and gashes on the lizard, Corvan had no doubt that Tsarek was the reason the water monster had released him and Tyreth. It must have been quite a battle for such a small creature.

Tears fell as Corvan sat beside the body and stroked the ridges at the back of its neck.

A pebble splashed in the water. He turned to find Jorad standing at the bottom of the narrow stairs, black knife in hand. "When I saw you dive in, I should have known it would be to try to save that evil creature's life."

"He helped me save Tyreth's life, Jorad. And the Chief Watcher is dead."

Jorad picked his way around the pool toward Corvan. "I saved Tyreth. You? You were helping the palace guard drown our priests." He drew near. "I don't understand what the Chief Watcher could have possibly offered you to help him destroy us. Surely you didn't hope he would give you Tyreth."

"I have never talked to the Chief Watcher," Corvan replied calmly. "Ask Tyreth. She'll tell you that I saved her life today."

Jorad planted his feet in front of Corvan. "I will ask her. But first I will make sure that creature is dead."

Corvan looked up at him. "I won't let you touch him. He is a good friend and has saved my life more than once."

"Then he has deceived you, for his kind only serves their own selfish purposes."

Corvan looked at Tsarek. "You told Madam Toreg not to judge too quickly, yet you do the same thing. This creature has a good heart. If the hammer were here, I would swear on it that he is not evil."

"What you swear makes no difference to me." Jorad's face twisted. "What you believe may feel true to you, but there are some things that do not change. The Watchers are all evil, and the only way to protect the Cor is to make sure they are all dead."

"This one already is." Even as he said the words, Corvan thought he felt Tsarek's spines tickle his palm.

Jorad's heavy boot pushed into Corvan's thigh. "I spare you now only in return for saving my life at the bridge. But I will not let you go until I know that lizard is dead."

Corvan stood to his feet and faced the young man. "When you choose to judge someone before you know all the facts, you act more like the Chief Watcher than the new high priest."

Anger flashed in Jorad's eyes. He grabbed the collar of Corvan's cloak and Corvan wrapped both hands around the wrist that held the knife. Locked together, they stood over Tsarek's body. Jorad shoved forward, his weight shifting the stone slab down into the water. The lizard's body slid down the rock and slipped beneath the dark surface.

"Jorad, are you down here?" Tyreth's words floated down the stairs. "Did you find him?"

Corvan pushed himself away from Jorad's blade.

"Don't let her see you," Jorad hissed. "She believes in you. It would destroy her faith to know you were helping the Chief Watcher."

"But I . . ."

"Hide behind the rocks until we leave. Do this for me and I will let you escape from here to see Kate again."

A shaft of blue light probed the shadows of the cave.

Corvan nodded and Jorad whirled around to make his way back to the stairs. Corvan pulled back into the darkness of the cave and crouched behind a jumble of rocks.

The blue glow filled the cave as Tyreth descended the stairs. She smiled at Jorad, who took her hand and helped her over the broken steps.

"He is not here."

She gazed out over the dark surface of the water. "He must have seen a priest fall in and jumped in to save him just as he saved me earlier." Her fingers brushed her lips. "I don't even know his real name. I. . . . didn't even get a chance to thank him."

Jorad touched her shoulder. "His name was Kalian."

"Kalian. . . precious one," Tyreth said softly. "That's a good name for him. I felt something for him I can't explain. It was like my connection with Tarran, but even stronger. I was sure I would see him again."

Jorad glanced in Corvan's direction. "He is gone, Tyreth. He was sent to bring the hammer back to us. That was his mission, and thankfully he completed it before he left us."

"Left us? I don't think he is dead. With Tarran I knew he was dead, but with Kalian . . ." Her voice trailed off as she searched the surface of the water. "My father believed Kalian would be our Cor-Van." She lifted the hammer and looked at its glowing words. Her face looked older in the blue light. "Now some are saying I should lead the people. I don't think I am ready."

"The burden of leadership is great, Tyreth, but I believe you will succeed. You are much stronger than you know."

"But am I wise enough? All my life I have been pulled in different directions as people have used me, used my position as the High Priests daughter, to their own advantage. Now that I have the hammer, the stakes are much higher, the deceit will be more subtle."

Jorad gently pushed her hand holding the hammer down to her side and then cupped her chin in his hand. "I can help you to know whom to trust. And I will be at your side supporting you. You know I would do anything for you."

Tyreth smiled as they gazed into each other's eyes for a long moment. Jorad leaned in closer as if he would kiss her.

A sharp tug on Corvan's hood almost made him cry out. He whipped around and looked into Gavyn's grinning face. The boy pulled on the sleeve of the gray cloak and motioned for Corvan to follow him. Corvan nodded, but as they moved into the shadows, he turned back for one last look at Tyreth.

There was nothing but blue ripples on the water.

The Hammer

CHAPTER THIRTY-SEVEN

Swallowing the lump in his throat, Corvan turned to find Gavyn's sad eyes watching him.

"Gavyn. I must get back to the pool at the new city right away. Can you take me there? I need to go back to Kate." Gavyn looked puzzled. "The girl on the litter that Jorad and I were carrying."

Gavyn nodded eagerly and scampered away to disappear beneath a large slab of rock propped against the cavern wall.

The crawl space turned into a low passage that wound deeper into the rock. New passages branched off in all directions. There seemed no end to the tunnels, but Gavyn knew where he was going. He forged far ahead of Corvan, the glow of his fire stick often the only sign of his presence.

Crawling after him through a low spot, Corvan found Gavyn's light stuck in the rocks, but Gavyn was nowhere in sight. Corvan lay back against the tunnel wall and closed his eyes. He had to rest, just for a moment. Sorrow swept over him as exhaustion drained his will to move another inch. His head slipped over against a large boulder.

Before he knew it Gavyn was back and tugging on his hand. The boy held out a cup of cool liquid that tasted like weak apple cider. Corvan drained the cup. "That tastes good. I could drink a gallon of that."

Gavyn nodded enthusiastically and pulled Corvan to his feet. Corvan stood swaying on unsteady legs, dizzy with weariness.

Gavyn walked backward holding Corvan's hands and guiding him around corners and over ledges. Corvan stumbled along after him.

The sound of a rushing waterfall pushed into his hazy thoughts, and a dense mist fell on his skin as if he were walking right through it. The sound faded behind him as they turned a corner and were welcomed by a bright light.

Corvan lifted his eyes. They had entered a huge round room with a high domed roof from which hundreds of lumiens hung. Vines ran up the walls, trailing rows of tiny globes like strings of Christmas lights. Lush green leaves covered most of the stone walls. Raised garden beds divided the room, each growing a different variety of tree, shrub, or flower. The room throbbed with life and color.

In the center, surrounded by a low stone wall, stood the largest tree Corvan had ever seen. Its trunk was bulbous and smooth as a baobab tree, the thick branches fanning out horizontally like a massive green table sitting on a stout pedestal.

Gavyn pulled him along the path toward the great tree. Passing through a wide gate, the young boy dragged him down onto his knees in the thick moss that surrounded the trunk. A spring bubbled up from between the gnarled roots and flowed into a stone catch basin. Gavyn filled a wooden cup, passed it to him, and scampered away. Corvan drank deeply, re-filled it from the basin, and drank again.

Gavyn had misunderstood his desire for more of the apple drink. This was not where he needed to be. Kate needed him to return with some food to strengthen her for the trip home. Maybe Gavyn could help him find some.

As he waited impatiently for Gavyn to return, he studied the cup in his hands. It was intricately carved with symbols similar to the ones on the hammer. Corvan set it down and found that the ledge by the pool was covered with many other carved objects. Some were of creatures he did not recognize, but in the middle of the carvings he saw a replica of the plaza statue in Kadir. The woman's head was in place but it was not the same as the broken statue. This one had long flowing hair and a smiling face.

Finally Gavyn ran through the gate and placed a basket of strange fruits at his feet. A grubby hand held up something dark blue about the size and shape of a lemon, encouraging him to eat it.

"Thanks, Gavyn, but I'll take this along to Kate. She's sick and needs it more than I do." He tried to pull his tired body to its feet but Gavyn pushed him firmly back onto the moss.

The little boy pointed at Corvan's chest and shoved the fruit up at him again. He would not be letting Corvan go until he ate something.

Corvan tried to bite it and almost broke a tooth on the tough skin.

Gavyn laughed, took it from him, and smacked its pointy end on a rock. It split into five equal sections. Poking his finger under a thick white membrane, the boy pulled out a squishy purple tube and dropped the cool bubble into Corvan's hand. Corvan went to nibble the end, but Gavyn stopped him, pulled out another of the tubes, and showed him to put it all in his mouth and bite down hard. Corvan followed his example, and sweetness exploded in his mouth as the nectar was released.

Corvan grinned with pleasure, and purple juice squirted out between his two front teeth. Gavyn laughed again and Corvan chuckled with him. A feeling of strength and energy surged through him. Eating was a good idea. He would be no help to Kate if he was too weak to walk. More juice trickled down his chin, sending the young boy into hysterics. It was amazing that someone who suffered so much could be so full of joy.

Gavyn's love of living things reminded Corvan painfully of his mother and her garden. She would be worried about him, and he had no way to tell her he was okay. He pushed the thoughts of home from his mind.

Refreshed from the fruit, Corvan reclined into the moss to rest for a moment. It was a long walk back to the settlement. He would never make it if he didn't take a short rest. "Gavyn, can you wake me up in twenty minutes?" The boy cocked his head and Corvan realized how little sense that would make to someone in the Cor. "I need a short sleep, but don't let me sleep long, okay? I've got to take some food to Kate."

Gavyn nodded and sat beside him with a dark piece of wood in his hand. Deftly he began to carve something, but it was slow going with his crude blade. Corvan dug into his pocket, pulled out his Swiss army knife, and tossed it to the boy. Gavyn whittled away as Corvan closed his eyes and let exhaustion take over.

When he awoke, the light was fading and Gavyn was nowhere to be seen. He'd slept too long. He scooped water into the cup and dragged himself up against the trunk of the tree, downing the sweet liquid and studying his surroundings for a sign of the little boy or a clue of which way he should go to get out of Gavyn's tree room.

It was hard to know. The room wasn't round; it had seven sides, just like the hammer. Each section was divided by slender buttresses that soared overhead to meet in the center of the ceiling, and three of the sections had doors. Which one had he come in? Corvan stood to get a better view and discovered that the paths in the room formed the same star shape he'd seen on Kate's medallion. There was no way he could figure out the correct door.

Gavyn suddenly appeared from behind the tree. He pantomimed eating things off a table, motioned for Corvan to follow, then disappeared behind the tree. A few urgent notes on the panpipe pulled Corvan around the tree to see the boy disappearing into yet another door on the far side of the room.

"This is like following the White Rabbit around Wonderland," Corvan muttered as he loped after him.

A short distance inside the doorway, the passage was blocked by fallen rock. A pebble bounced off Corvan's head. He looked up to see a rope slowly twisting in circles as Gavyn climbed it. Using a boulder for a stepping stool, Corvan grabbed the rope and followed. He was halfway up before he realized that for the first time in his life he was climbing a rope with ease.

At the top he found Gavyn standing on a crude wooden bench, peering through a small hole in the wall. The boy jumped down, pushed on a rocky knob and the wall swung open. He entered and Corvan had to sprint to avoid being left in the hall before it closed again.

It was a large pantry, chock full of food. Cloth bags hung from pegs driven into the walls and on hooks that stuck out of the low ceiling. Baskets were piled on the tables that ran down the center of the room, and a rack of pointed amphorae occupied the far wall. Gavyn ran about, popping things into his mouth from the baskets on the table.

"This is great, Gavyn. I'll take some to Kate."

Long loaves were piled in one of the baskets. Dumping them out onto the table, Corvan put one back in the basket. It smelled mildly of cinnamon and he took a small bite. It was hard to chew, but it was the best bread he could remember eating in a long time. "Do you know every secret passage in this place?" he asked between bites. "Is there a faster way to get back to Kate?"

A proud look on his face, Gavyn went to the far wall. He pushed up on three pegs in succession, and another small door swung open. Soft light fell on a tight spiral staircase. Gavyn put a finger to his lips and motioned for him to follow.

Corvan kept piling food into his basket, but Gavyn shook his head and waved him forward again.

"Okay, but we have to be quick." He set the basket down and climbed the stairs with a growing sense of déjà vu. Reaching the top he realized why. It was the small door to the ledge above the high priest's hall, where he had first met Jorad. At least from here, he could find his way back to Jokten's place in the settlements. He put his hand on the latch and Gavyn shook his head, covering his ears and wincing. He was reminding Corvan that this was a creaky door. But Corvan knew how to beat that. Leaning hard on the latch, he eased the door slowly and quietly open. A voice floated up from below. Gavyn backed down onto the stairs as Corvan crawled out onto the ledge.

A chandelier of small lamps now hung over the great table, where seven men sat; three in white cloaks, three in the green cloaks of the priests, and one in a hoodless black tunic. Their eyes were on the wall beneath the ledge.

"No doubt the Chief Watcher had it destroyed," said one of the priests. "We will never know the message it contained."

"It is for the best." Jorad's voice spoke from below the ledge. "We have wasted much time and energy searching for a Cor-Van to come help us. Instead we should use what resources we have to work together and bring peace and prosperity back to the Cor."

"Then you no longer believe the Cor-Van exists?" an older man in white asked.

"The scrolls all describe the Cor-Van as a great leader, someone who speaks the truth and rules with authority. I no longer believe they point to a specific person but rather to the office of the Cor-Van, a leader we can all follow. Tarran was such a leader. He was a great man."

"Who found for us the lost hammer," a thin man in a green robe interjected.

"And who saved Tyreth from the karst," added another priest, "paying for his brave deed with his life."

"All of these are examples of a Cor-van, a true leader." Jorad walked into view and leaned on the table. "That is the point of the scrolls. Our leaders are here among us, whether in the priests or among the people of the city. We have only to open our eyes and we will find the Cor-van we require. Tarran was one. Tyreth is another."

The oldest priest shook his head. "Our people will never follow the young daughter of a priest. With the rebels threatening to tear the Cor apart, the Sightless at large, and reports of groups of the Broken gathering in secret caverns, we need an older priest to bring us through these troubled times." The three men in white remained silent, staring at the table.

A young man in a white robe spoke up. "After today, there is not a person in the city who does not believe she is capable of leading us."

"It is not up to the people of the city," the old priest retorted. The men in the white robes sat up straighter. "It is up to this council to decide." Heads nodded. "I think Tyreth is too headstrong, just like her father. He put his foolish plans with Morgon and Tarran into action without the knowledge of this council. We lost good men from the priests and from the city because of his foolishness."

Jorad folded his arms across his chest. "That is in the past. After today's events, I believe that if we do not appoint Tyreth to the palace, the city will rise up against us. This would tear the Cor apart and leave us open to any attack from the rebels or the Broken or even from . . . him."

The old man in white pointed at Jorad. "If the Cor-Van is not a specific person, the ruler of all evil is likely a legend as well. Do not try to use superstition to frighten us into agreeing with you."

Jorad walked back under the ledge. His voice floated back into the room. "If I were to be appointed the new high priest and Tyreth were ruler, would a marriage between the two offices dispel your fears?"

The old priest grunted and pursed his lips. "Are you certain she will accept you?"

"Tyreth and I have been close since we were children. She has no one else in her life to consider. Everyone she loved is dead."

"Your plan has merit," the man in the black tunic said. Everyone around the table turned to look at him. Corvan recognized that voice. It was the captain they had met at the city of the dead. "Many are still suspicious of the priests, but everyone trusts Tyreth. Now that she possesses the hammer, she will embody the truth. With you to manage the political sides of leadership, we may create the stability we all require, including the soldiers." He stressed the final word as he leaned back in his chair and dropped his dusty black boots onto the polished table. There was a long moment of silence.

"Then let us proceed," declared the old priest. "Jorad shall be appointed high priest, and Tyreth will be ruler of the Cor. In a short time Tyreth will be of age and permitted to marry. As soon as an agreement can be reached between them, we shall celebrate the first marriage between government and religion."

The old man in white rubbed his hands together. "This may yet prove to be a prosperous time for us all."

The men pushed back from the table. The man in black spoke again. "There is one other matter we must discuss. That is what to do about the opening my men uncovered in the Cor shield. It has been reported to me that there is actually an open passage beyond the opening, leading upward."

"It must be destroyed," Jorad stated emphatically. "No doubt the Chief Watcher used these places to bring beings such as the Rakash into our world. We should not wait for more evil to enter; we must keep ourselves separated from whatever is out there."

There were nods of agreement around the table but not from the man in black. "Take some of the priests with you tonight," the old priest said to Jorad, "and destroy that cavern. Remove the lumiens and seal off the settlement. We shall pass a law banning anyone from going that way again. Now that we have the hammer back, our laws will be judged much more swiftly and severely."

The men all stood and made their way to the front door.

Corvan felt panic rise in his throat. They were going to seal off the crack! And it was a way out! He had to beat them back to the settlement and Kate.

"What should we do with the remains of the great tapestry?" Jorad asked.

The old priest swiveled around. "Burn it. Partial knowledge is more dangerous than you know."

As the seven men filed out, Jorad walked into the center of the room with a satisfied smile on his face.

Corvan slid back farther on the ledge, brushing the door. It let out a muted squeak. Jorad's head perked up. Corvan pushed himself all the way back out the door and quietly descended the stairs.

Gavyn was waiting for him in the storage room, nibbling his way around the table like a fussy mouse.

Corvan shut the door behind himself. "Gavyn," he whispered, "I need to get back to the Molakar settlement as soon as I can." Gavyn did not seem to understand where Molakar was, so Corvan drew out a map in the dust on the table and told him why he needed to get Kate home before she died. "The only way out is the crack in the wall. I have to get there before Jorad does."

Gavyn added some of his own markings to the map, drawing strange figures around the falls. A tear splashed into the dusty map. Gavyn pointed to himself, shook his head, and pointed to the places beyond the broken bridge. More tears welled up into his eyes.

"Are you saying you can't go with me past the bridge?"

The boy nodded.

"Why not?"

Gavyn looked down for a moment, unwilling or unable to tell him.

"I'm sorry, Gavyn, but I have to go. Kate needs me. Can you take me as far as the bridge?"

Gavyn nodded and his eyes brightened. He moved around the room, filling a small sack with his choice of the various items in the baskets on the table. Drawing the string tight, he handed it to Corvan and beckoned him to follow.

The journey through the city led through various tunnels and the broken foundations of buildings. Gavyn did not seem to be in any hurry to get to their destination, and Corvan kept urging him on.

He wondered how long it would take Jorad to get his men together. If they closed that crack before he could take Kate through, she was as good as dead. Even if he could find someone to open the other door, he could never guide her back through the labyrinth.

At times, they crossed the streets above ground. There was no fog, but the darkness was almost complete and he saw no one as they passed. Finally, they arrived at the ruin of a gatehouse near the lower bridge.

Corvan turned to the boy. "I wish we didn't have to say good-bye so soon. Are you sure you can't come with me?"

The boy pointed out over the river and firmly shook his head. Corvan knelt

T THE HAMMER

down. Gavyn threw his arms around his neck and cried silently on his shoulder.

"I will miss you, Gavyn," he whispered into his ear. "You're like a brother to me."

The young boy pulled back, a pleased smile on his tear stained face. Reaching into his tunic, he pulled out the star-studded holster and held it out to Corvan.

"No, Gavyn, you keep it. I want you to have it."

The boy pressed its familiar weight into Corvan's hand. The hammer was back in its place. How could this be? He snapped it open and pulled it out. Gavyn had whittled an exact replica from his block of dark wood. Corvan's eyes were moist. "It's beautiful, Gavyn. I will always carry it with me to remind me of you."

He buckled the holster back in place. The carved hammer would remind him of more than the funny, earnest little boy who'd given it to him; it would never let him forget the importance of telling the truth . . . of being true.

Corvan wished he had something to give Gavyn. Something meaningful, valuable . . . he *did* have a gift like that. He fished out the pouch with the red seeds. They belonged here, not in his world above ground, and nobody would appreciate their worth more than Gavyn. "I want you to have these, Gavyn, so you won't forget me."

The boy tugged at the cord, and a soft red glow lit the tracks his tears had traced down his dusty face. He looked at Corvan in awe. Pointing to the roof of the cavern, he traced a wide arc with his hand. He took only one of the pulsing red tears from the bag and clenched it tightly in his hand. Pulling the pouch gently closed, he handed it back to Corvan as if it contained all the wealth in the world.

As Corvan returned it to his pocket, his hand fell on the two pebbles from the mirror. He pulled them out and offered them to the young boy. A huge smile broke over Gavyn's face as he picked up the sparkling white pebble and touched it to his heart. He closed Corvan's hand around the black one and pushed it up to Corvan's chest.

"For us to remember each other?"

The boy nodded and then reached into his robe. He pulled a silver chain out and over his head. Tugging Corvan down to his knees, he pushed the chain under his hood and around Corvan's neck.

Corvan stood and held out the chain. Hanging from the end was a silver medallion. It was smaller than the one Kate carried, but it had the same seven-sided star on one side. It did not glow when he touched it, but something sparked in his mind, as if Gavyn was wishing him good luck. He looked up, but the boy was gone. A mournful tune floated over the broken city.

Corvan turned and walked onto the bridge, surprised to find the metal plates replaced and tightly bolted down. The lumiens were getting lighter. The thought of Jorad rousing his men quickened Corvan's pace, and he jogged toward the great bend in the river road. Crossing the fields, he looked back along the river. There was no one in sight. He slowed his steps a little to conserve energy and began the long hike up the terraces to the settlement entrances.

At each corner of the trail, Corvan looked back to the city. He had to get back to Kate, but found it hard to leave Kadir behind. He was saying good-bye to people who were now a part of him: Rayu, Madam Toreg, Gavyn, and Tyreth. He had not felt this lonely since his journey began. His father was right. To love was to embrace pain, at times enough to break your heart.

Climbing a set of stairs, he passed the scarecrow with its painted eyes and thought of the Sightless. They could not drown. Were they still on his trail? He turned and looked back over the valley. Nothing moved on the ground, but high overhead a shadowy form on dark wings swooped past the blue lumien moon.

He pushed the thought away. One thing he'd learned on this journey was that he didn't need to fear what might be around the next bend. He just needed to take the next step. He looked at his feet and moved one in front of the other. "Okay, Corvan, that's one. How about another?" He moved his other foot forward. "Good enough. Let's keep going."

Where was he going? He was going to take Kate home. How would he get there? Right now, that didn't matter. All that mattered was the next step. His heart lifted and his head came up. He was not going to give in to fear. Stepping past the scarecrow, he whistled his father's tune.

Someone else whistled it with him.

He was not alone. A tall gray man walked beside him.

THE HAMMER

Chapter Thirty-Eight

The settlement was in darkness as Corvan walked in the glow of the purple moss. The leader of the gray men had departed as silently as he'd come, but Corvan sensed he still watched over him.

Corvan walked up to the karst and looked over the edge. The dark hole held no power over him. He had climbed down that rope and had faced his fears. Corvan looked across at the broken platform that hung sloppily over the mirror of black water below, a row of empty shackles dangling from its edge. The young boy with the crewcut hair must have escaped. He ran a hand over his head. His own hair had grown considerably longer during his time in the Cor. Now he was a member of the adult community. He turned away from the karst. If being an adult meant saving innocent lives then he was willing to embrace that responsibility.

The ring of cliff dwellings were all dark and Jokten's dwelling was as lifeless as the rest. Corvan crept quietly into the entry and set the sack of food on the floor. There was a cough from the inner chamber. A small fire stick sputtered, and the tree in the old tapestry came to life. Viewed from this side it was covered in pale blue blossoms. At the top left corner was a man dressed in a green cloak. On the other side, facing him, was a woman in a white dress. Between them were the hammer, the medallion, and a staff with a red globe.

The scene split in two and light fell across his face.

The old woman gave him a halfhearted smile. "I was hoping you would return soon." She held the curtain open. "Her strength is almost gone." She motioned for him to follow.

Corvan was shocked by the sight of Kate's white face on the stone table. Had it not been for the old woman's words, he would've been certain she was dead.

"She has been deep into darkness, Cor-Van. I thought the medallion might bring her back, but she continues to slip away."

He squeezed Kate's limp hand. "There has to be something we can do for her."

The old woman caressed the girl's forehead. "It is hard to know what to do when the good of many people is weighed against our love for one. It is possible to cut the centers from a few larger lumiens and squeeze their life into her mouth, but I do not know if that would be enough, and in the end the Cor would be a darker place."

She turned away from Kate. Corvan grabbed her shoulder. "What about these?" Pulling the pouch from his pocket, he lifted one of her hands and dropped the last two seeds into it. Instantly the room was infused with warmth and light.

"Where did you . . . It can't be. How is this possible?" She stared at the bright gems in disbelief.

"Can they help Kate?"

The old woman's fingers closed around the seeds. The pulsing red glow shone through her skin and outlined her bony fingers. A shaft of light twinkled at the gap where her thumb would have been. She twisted her head to look into his eyes. "These represent new life for the Cor. Would you deny an entire world their salvation to save one person?"

Corvan wanted to say yes, but the word stuck in his throat.

Seeing his hesitation, she shook her head. "We do not even know if it would work. If we allowed her to eat one of these, it would be more than her tired body could handle. Just touching them, I can feel the power flow through my hand."

Corvan wrestled inside. Gavyn had one seed, the healer could keep one, and the other could save Kate. But what if all three were needed to bring light back to the Cor? He looked at Kate's pale face. Could he let all these people die to save her?

"Could we at least let her touch them and see if that helps?" There was no answer. Corvan turned to find a dumbfound look of amazement on the wrinkled face. "Would touching them help her?" he asked again.

Ever so slowly, she lifted her hand before him and opened it wide. The seeds sparkled merrily on her smooth palm as she pushed her hand closer. "Look, Cor-Van. My hand!"

Corvan looked closely at her hand. It looked like a teenager's hand attached to a gaunt old arm. "Does this mean it can help Kate?"

"Corvan." She said his name the way his mother did when he wasn't listening. "My thumb is back."

Like a salamander could regrow its tail, the seed's power had regrown the old woman's thumb. But he did not have time to wonder about it, for the old woman pushed past him to the table. Gently she pulled Kate's hands down to her sides with the palms facing up. "Hold this for her," she said, handing him the medallion. "It is very powerful, but it cannot stop death."

Stooping lower, the woman dropped one of the seeds into Kate's right hand. Nothing happened. "Should we put one in the other hand?" Corvan asked.

"Do not be so hasty. A darkened soul is very different from a severed thumb. This may take some time."

"But she doesn't have much time."

"Look."

He turned back to find Kate's hand closing over the red gem. The light crept past the tightly clenched fist and up her arm. Color returned to her face. The healthy glow moved down her left arm then stopped at the welts around her wrist. The pale hand clenched, and the glow receded away from the welts.

"She needs the other one in this hand," Corvan urged.

"No," the old woman said firmly. "There is enough power in the one; she must make the choice to accept it. She must let go of the hate and accept the love she has been given."

Corvan squeezed Kate's forearm. The warmth was being pushed back by a deathly cold. He put his face over hers. "Please don't give in, Kate." He clenched her arm tighter and the cold stopped. "Your mom misses you. She loves you." He leaned in closer. "I do too."

A surge of warmth pushed under his hand. The welts around her wrist turned black and crumbled off like old scabs. Tears of relief slipped from Corvan's cheek and splashed on Kate's forehead. He wiped them away and she took a long slow breath, her face reflecting a deep calm.

The old woman inspected the seed in Kate's open hand. A pink glow flickered across its surface. "She has absorbed much of its life." She picked it up, and Kate's hands clutched frantically at the air. "Let her hold the medallion instead. It will comfort her."

Corvan placed the disk in Kate's palm, and her fingers wrapped tightly around it. "Is the seed still alive?"

"Yes, but I will need to plant it very soon." She held out her hand. "May I have the bag to keep them both safe?"

Corvan handed her the empty bag. Dropping both seeds inside, she tucked it away in her tunic and sat wearily on the bench.

"Do you think she'll be able to walk on her own?" Corvan asked. "I need to get her to where they found that crack in the Cor wall."

"The seed has done wonders for her, but I do not think she can walk." Her face brightened. "But when Jokten returns he can help you carry her."

Corvan looked into her hopeful face. What should he tell her? Painful though it might be, he knew in his heart that she deserved to hear the truth. He sat beside her on the bench and told her of the fight in the pit, how bravely Jokten had faced the monster, and how he slew it.

Tears rolled down her cheeks as he told her he'd buried her husband. "I wanted to put a sign there to tell everyone that beneath those rocks was Jokten, slayer of the great beast."

She brushed the tears from her cheeks. "You did right by him. You will be a great leader."

Corvan's shoulders sagged. "I don't think I can be a good leader; I fail more than I succeed."

She took his hand in both of hers—one frail and wizened, the other pink and warm with renewed life. "If you keep doing what is right, are merciful, and live with honor, you will become a great Cor-Van." She looked at Kate. "A now that the girl is well, you can stay here and help us drive the evil from our world."

"But she can't live under the light of your lumiens."

She pursed her lips. "I'm not so sure. That seed was powerful, it may have. . ."

"I can't stay." Corvan interjected. "I promised I'd bring her home."

The old woman patted his leg. "Get some rest. I would offer you food, but the soldiers will not give me a share because I could not work the fields." She held up her healed hand. "Jokten always regretted asking me to find him more fire sticks to explore the passages. I wish he was here to see this."

Corvan stood and retrieved the cloth bag from the entry. He placed it on the bench and untied the top. She gasped as he pulled out the different foods. After they shared an enjoyable meal together, Corvan replaced half the food back into the bag and pushed the rest toward her on the bench. She tried to put some back in his bag but he pulled the drawstring tight and held it high over his head where she could not reach it. She laughed out loud as tears flowed down her face.

Kate groaned and moved. The old woman hurried over and felt her pulse as Corvan hovered over her. "She's coming around. Her body is growing stronger."

"Good. I don't think we have much time before Jorad and his men get here to seal off this settlement." Corvan picked up the bag of food and flipped his hood back over his head.

She peered up at him through her white hair. "Why would they do that?"

"They want to make sure no one can enter or leave through that crack. That's why I had to come back so quickly. It's the only way to get Kate out of here."

Panic rose in her eyes. "You can't leave. There are many things you should know about your family's history in the Cor—who they were and who you are."

"My family was from the Cor?"

She threw her hands in the air. "Not just from it. Your family ruled the Cor before the rise of the Watchers."

Corvan put the bag down on the bench. "How can I be from the Cor, yet live up above?"

Kate rolled onto her side. The old woman sat and put a hand on Kate's shoulder. "I can tell you about that and many other things. There is much you need to know before you go through the Cor shield."

Jorad's voice spoke from beyond the curtain. "You shall not be allowed to pass through."

THE HAMMER

288

CHAPTER THIRTY-NINE

Jorad pushed through the curtain, the black knife drawn before him, grim determination on his face. "Give me the counterpart to the hammer. It belongs in the Cor. You do not and never will."

"Those are strong words." The old woman stood to her feet. "How do you come by this knowledge?"

Jorad glared at Corvan. "I have learned once again that things are not as they seem. Even the innocence of youth is false. I have decided to take matters into my own hands."

The old woman looked closely into his face. "And what do you intend to do with the counterpart?"

He leaned away from her. "As the new high priest it is my job to ensure that there is a balance of power between the palace and the priests. The counterpart will give me the leverage I require to ensure that the palace cooperates."

Corvan threw his hood back and frowned at the young man. "You mean Tyreth, don't you?" He shook his head in disgust. "You don't even trust the woman you are going to marry."

Jorad pushed the tip of the knife toward him. "I don't know where you heard that rumor, but I do know you understand nothing of how to handle power. That is why you will never be a leader."

Corvan did not pull back from the blade. "I don't want to be your kind of leader. The hammer is about truth, not power. I don't want to control people; I want my friends to know that I truly care about them."

Jorad lifted the point of the knife to Corvan's throat. "Then give what is around your neck. In return I will let you and Kate leave through the Cor shield before we seal off this settlement."

Corvan looked at the blade then to Jorad's face. "How do I know you are telling the truth?"

"Because I am a priest of the . . ." Jorad's voice trailed off. He stood blinking in the silence.

Corvan pulled Gavyn's medallion out of his cloak. For a moment, he regretted that this was not the real one. The real one might be able to heal the pain that filled Jorad's heart.

Keeping his knife extended, Jorad yanked the silver disk from Corvan's neck. Dark greed shone in his eyes as he tucked it away. "My men will arrive any minute with enough fire sticks to seal off the tunnel to this settlement. If you wish to leave through the crack, you must go immediately. I cannot allow them to see you."

Corvan leaned down to Kate and gently shook her shoulders. "Wake up, Kate. It's time to go."

Her eyes fluttered and focused on his face. "Where are we going?"

"Home. Your mother will be looking for you."

Kate nodded and Corvan helped her to her feet.

"Why is it so dark out?"

"It's nighttime."

"Where are all the stars?"

"They're covered up right now, but we'll see them soon."

Jorad stepped back and held the curtain aside. "Quickly now. We have no time to waste."

Corvan led Kate out of the dwelling and into the main cavern. Jorad followed them, holding the fire stick aloft to light their way.

From the entry a thin voice called out, "Farewell, Cor-Van. May you walk in truth until we meet again."

Corvan released Kate's hand and ran back to hug the hunched-over shoulders. "How can I say good-bye? I don't even know your name."

"My name is Saray." She kissed his cheek. "And when you come back to us, you must be sure to come and find me. I can help you become a great Cor-Van." She reached into his cloak and unclipped Gavyn's hammer. She turned it over in her hands, fumbled with the holster and then clipped it back into place. "You must keep this as your pledge to return to us. Unless you return it to the Cor, our people will all perish."

"But you don't understand, the real hammer is with Tyreth."

Saray nodded and patted his arm. "I understand and someday you will too."

"They're coming." Jorad pointed at a glow near the cavern's entrance.

The old woman pushed him toward Kate. "Until we meet again, Cor-Van." She gave him a tearful smile and turned back to her dwelling.

Corvan took Kate's hand and Jorad fell in behind them, urging them forward.

"Do not think you were sent to be our Cor-Van," Jorad said. "A Cor-Van must know how to wield power and shape the world in which he lives. You have been used by others to accomplish their goals. That is not the destiny of a Cor-Van."

Corvan did not respond. There was no point arguing with Jorad. He tightened his grip on Kate's hand and pulled her faster down the path.

Turning a corner, they entered a cavern full of debris and great boulders. A clear pathway ran straight ahead between crude stone pillars cut out of the solid rock. Ahead, at the end of the row of ragged columns, a patch of the Cor shield lay exposed in the cavern wall. A jagged crack ran up the center of the glossy rock. It was tall and easily wide enough for a man to walk through.

"Do not touch the walls," Jorad said. "Legend says the cracks will close on any who touch the walls. No one knows if this is true, but no one is willing to test it."

Just before the crack, Kate left Corvan's side and kissed Jorad on the cheek. "Thank you for helping us." She stepped back and stood by Corvan.

The lines on Jorad's face softened. "I am sorry it turned out this way. I want to believe that you were deceived by the Watchers, that you did not know better." He swallowed. "You do not know what evil they brought on us. Many good men were deceived by them—even my. . . my brother, Morgon. He betrayed our family . . . murdered my wife and child. He took them to the palace and . . ." His forearm bulged as his fist clenched tight around the hilt of the black knife at his side.

"I'm sorry Jorad, but I promise you, I did not betray—"

Jorad's eyes flashed. "No one who has been in the company of those evil ones can be trusted again." He gestured toward the crack with the blade. "You must leave the Cor and never return."

Corvan looked into his eyes. "I understand how much you must hate the Watchers. I only hope it does not blind you to the truth."

Jorad sheathed the knife. "I no longer believe that the truth even exists."

"It does," Corvan said. "I have held it, and it changed me for the better."

"Then you are more fortunate than most." Jorad held out the fire stick. "You may need this on the other side. Here come my men with plenty more." He pointed up to where the light of many fire sticks lit the front of the cavern. "Go quickly. I will stall them as long as I can."

Corvan took the fire stick from him and stuck out his hand to shake Jorad's.

Jorad looked at Corvan's hand, then back to his face. His jaw tensed. Then he turned abruptly and strode into the darkness between the pillars.

As soon as Jorad was past the closest column, a shadow stepped out. Corvan's heart thumped in his chest. What was that? Rakash? One of the gray men?

A tiny fire stick, like a lone candle, sprang to life in the darkness. In its glow, Corvan saw a small creature. It was Tsarek and he was waving good-bye. Corvan waved back and his eyes brimmed with tears. He blinked them away and the light was gone.

CHAPTER FORTY

With a heavy heart, Corvan turned to guide Kate into the crack. Though wide enough for the two of them to walk side by side at first, it soon narrowed. Walking through without touching the walls would be difficult—or impossible. He shuddered at the thought of being entombed in the Cor shield, like a fly petrified in amber.

Kate stopped. "I can't breathe. The walls are coming closer."

Kate was pretty tough, but she hated enclosed spaces. Her breath came in shallow gasps as her hand waved frantically in front of her face. "There's no air in here." She turned back, but Corvan pulled her close against his chest.

"Look into my eyes." Her brown eyes focused on his. "It's okay. Take a breath." He felt her take a shallow breath, but her heart beat madly against him. "There's enough air in here for both of us." He took a deep breath to show her it was okay and pulled in the faint scent of lilacs.

She nodded. Her face relaxed but her arms wrapped tighter around his back.

A shout in the cavern jerked Corvan's head up. Lights were coming toward them between the stone columns. Kate looked back and her eyes darted wildly about the narrow crack.

Tugging Tyreth's scarf from under his cloak he held it out to her. "Look at this." She turned toward him. "Remember how we used to play Blind Man's Bluff? I'm going to put this over your eyes, but I'll hold your hand until we reach the other side. Is that okay?"

She nodded. "I trust you, Corvan."

He tied the scarf behind her head and took her hand. "Keep your other hand tight around your medallion."

The fire sticks drew closer and Corvan caught site of the captain from the council leading the group. Black cloaked soldiers were mixed in with the green of the priests. He pulled Kate deeper into the crack. It was narrower than he'd thought. The wall slanted inward inches from his face, but the outer edge of the crack, and safety, beckoned only an arm's length away. The voices out in the cavern echoed louder. Closer.

A clink sounded by his feet, and Kate suddenly twisted her hand free of his.

"I dropped my medallion."

Corvan looked back in horror to see Kate pull the scarf up and drop to her knees, following the medallion as it bumped along the floor back toward the cavern and the approaching soldiers.

The captain's voice cried out, "Something is trying to enter the Cor! Shoot it!"

Corvan dropped to the ground as an arrow whistled overhead through the crack. Grabbing Kate's ankle he dragged her back toward himself with renewed desperation. She screeched and tried to hit his hand away.

"It's going to attack!" a man shouted, and more arrows clattered off the cavern walls. "Aim for the light!"

Tossing the fire stick behind him, Corvan grabbed a hold of the rocky floor and pulled backward, tumbling them both out into the darkness on the far side of the crack.

They lay in a heap, listening to the fire stick hissing somewhere behind them in the rocks. The noise from the soldiers ceased.

"Where's my medall—"

Corvan put a hand over Kate's mouth and whispered in her ear. "We must stay quiet, Kate. We have to play hide and seek for a few minutes. Don't move or talk and I will look for your medallion."

She nodded under his hand. He released her, pulled the scarf back down over her eyes, and crept closer to the crack. Corvan reached out his hand to the Cor shield. With one touch he could seal the crack. He peered into the gloom. The lights on the other side had been extinguished but in the soft glow of the Cor shield he could see someone crawling toward him.

Corvan moved his hand closer. He had to stop them. If they made it through to his world, there was no telling what they might do. The man in the crack coughed and inched closer. Corvan's hand faltered. Was it right for him to seal the man in the crack? He shook his head, he couldn't do that. The soldier was just obeying orders.

The man looked up. A tight grin spread across the wrinkled face of Rayu. He crawled up closer to Corvan but stayed within the crack, looking in awe at the dark tunnel beyond the Cor shield.

He turned to Corvan. "The soldiers are afraid so I told him I would make sure the monster was gone," he whispered, eyes twinkling. "Because I wanted to give this back to you." He opened his hand and the green glow from the medallion lit up his kind face. "It will be better for the Cor if you keep it until you return." He handed the medallion to Corvan, its light flowing around him. Rayu smiled and gestured to where Kate sat on the ground. "I see you finally caught up to your counterpart. That is good for you and the Cor. She is strong and you will need her beside you when you return to restore the Cor to its glory."

Corvan pushed the medallion back at the old man. "No, Rayu. Tyreth has the hammer. She will lead the Cor now. Take the medallion to her instead."

The old man replied, but shouts from the other end of the crack drowned him out. Fire sticks blazed to life. Men screamed in terror, "Rakash! Rakash!"

Panic rose in Corvan's chest. The seekers were still after the cloak. It was drawing them to him.

Rayu reached out a hand and patted Corvan's forearm. "Do not be afraid, Cor-Van. They shall not follow you." He pulled his hand back and held it up to the Cor shield. "Good-bye, Cor-Van. May your love always be guided by the truth."

Before Corvan could respond, Rayu winked at him, then slapped the exposed edge of the shield wall. A soft hiss escaped, like a pop bottle being opened, and then Corvan was looking at a perfectly smooth wall. He sat in the dead silence for a long moment, staring at the glassy rock.

Kate broke the silence. "Did you find my medallion?"

He placed it in her outstretched hand and she wrapped her fingers wrapped tightly around it. "Can we go home now, Corvan?"

"Yes Kate. Now we can go home." He hoped that once they got back the Kate he used to know would come back. He didn't mind so much that she was more dependent on him; it felt good to be the one taking care of her, but he missed her feisty attitude.

He located the fire stick and led Kate up the slope of the tunnel. Home must be up there somewhere.

"Can you see the stars?" Kate asked.

"We'll find them. But first, we have to go for a long walk. You should keep the scarf on for a while. I'll lead you."

The corridor before them was shaped like a squashed tube with a smooth rippled floor as if an ancient river had slowly carved its way through the rock. No water flowed in the channel now, and Corvan was keenly aware that they had none with them. He hoped he had kept enough food. For a moment he chided himself for leaving as much as he did with Saray, then he brought himself up short. He'd done the right thing by her. Now it was time to take the next step and keep moving forward.

THE HAMMER

Although the tunnel was smooth, at times it was extremely steep. Kate didn't have much strength so they stopped often to rest.

When the fire stick eventually died, they walked on in the light of Kate's medallion. Corvan had no doubt that the journey out would take as long as the days it took to first reach the Cor. It would be best to let Kate rest whenever she was tired.

Leaning against the cavern wall, he watched her sleep beside him. The medallion had slipped from her hand, and he picked it up. Tsarek was right; it did give a sense of calm, a feeling of hope for the future. Its light grew stronger as he studied the markings, turning the words around and around, flowing them from truth to mercy to justice and back to truth. It made sense that the medallion would belong to a Cor-Van. To be a good leader you had to hold all three in tension. If any of them were missing you would make a mess of things.

He wondered what would happen to the Cor with only the hammer as their guide. Perhaps it had been a mistake to let Jorad take Gavyn's medallion instead of leaving the real one behind.

Kate groaned in her sleep. She lay curled into a ball beneath her white cloak. Taking off his own, he spread its warmth over her. He brushed her long bangs away from her eyes, and a faint smile fluttered across her face. It warmed his heart despite the cold from the stone behind him creeping into his back. He shivered. It wouldn't do to get sick himself and not be able to help Kate. Putting the medallion in his pocket, he pulled up the edge of the gray cloak, and lay down a few inches behind her. In moments, he was drifting off to sleep.

When he awoke, the faint sent of lilacs hung in the cool night air and for a moment Corvan thought he was stretched out on the front porch swing at home, his mother's tabby cat curled up against him. A tickle of hair touched his cheek. He brushed it away to find Kate cuddled up against him, her head resting on his forearm.

Kate stirred, then rolled over toward him and snuggled into his chest. He lay perfectly still and waited as she relaxed and her breathing fell into a steady rhythm. One thing he knew for certain was that he would never again be bothered by the boys teasing him that he liked Kate. He was not afraid to admit it. He liked her a lot.

A cramp suddenly gripped his right calf, and he carefully eased his arm out from under Kate's head and struggled to his feet. Massaging his leg vigorously, he moved about the tunnel floor until the pain eased. His mother had warned him about getting cramps when he did not drink enough water.

"Is that you, Corvan?" Kate's tense voice echoed in the rocky confines of the tunnel.

"Yes, I'm getting our light going. Just a minute."

"I'm thirsty."

He pulled out the medallion, and Kate's sleepy eyes focused on him. "Let's go for a walk and see if we can find some water."

When they first left the Cor shield, they had come across small pools of water in deep pockets at the edges of the old watercourse, but lately there were none to be found. The last one had been more than six rests ago, and the effects of dehydration were setting in. The supplies in the bag were running low, but without any water, neither of them wanted to try to choke down the dried-out bread that remained.

Fear began to seep into his soul with the darkness that pressed in around them. He found it comforting to breath in the scent of Tyreth's scarf and hear her say, "Be brave, it will be all right." Holding Kate's hand, he felt somewhat guilty for taking comfort in Tyreth's scarf, so he offered it to Kate to keep her warm. She gave it back to him.

"I don't like the way it smells." Kate whispered past cracked lips. She looked up the dark tunnel. "Is it much farther, Corvan? This night is too long."

"We are getting closer, I think. How about we count out a thousand steps and see where that takes us."

Kate nodded and he began to count. It helped to give them a goal and to keep the fears at bay. At first it was a thousand steps and a rest, but as time wore on it fell to one hundred and then to twenty. Finally, Kate collapsed.

"It's okay." Corvan hardly had enough moisture in his mouth to get the words out. "Rest. I'll go find water." He waited until her eyes closed and her rasping breaths became regular. He didn't want to leave her alone in the dark but he needed the light of the medallion to explore up ahead.

Just around a bend, the cave climbed steeply over stairlike ridges. He tried to climb it but his strength gave out and he fell to his knees. Had they come all this way just to die of thirst? How was that fair? His father's words replied from the recesses of his weary mind. *Don't be looking for this world to be fair to you. Fair is what you do for others, not what you expect to receive.*

"You're right, Dad, I just need to be fair to Kate, I just need to take another step." He crawled forward. "Come on, Corvan, you can do it." But he couldn't. His remaining energy fled from his body, and he sank against the rock in utter exhaustion.

A green glow wavered before his eyes. The medallion slipped from his hand and landed with a soft metallic ring on the stone. It rolled away, and he heard it move down the stairs like a small bell fading into the distance. It ended with a soft plop.

It took a long time for the last sound to register in his brain. It had to do with wishing or praying or something like that. His mind slowly turned it over. He could remember having a handful of medallions, no, they were coins—and he was dropping them one at a time into a round hole; plop, plop, plop. He remembered wishing that one day he would grow up to be a great hero.

Corvan raised his head. A wishing well. The medallion must have dropped into water. He squinted down the slope, where green light danced off the ripples of a small pool.

He crawled back to find a tiny spring flowing into a shallow depression. Corvan lay on his stomach and drank deeply, then stumbled back to kneel beside Kate.

"I found water."

Kate's head rolled to one side but her eyes did not open.

Corvan pulled her toward his chest. He didn't have the strength to lift her. But if she helped . . . He shook her gently. "Put your arms around my neck. I'll carry you."

Her eyes remained shut, but her head dipped slightly. He pulled her up, and she clasped her hands behind his head. Summoning all his energy, he pushed to his feet and staggered toward the flickering green pool.

They rested by the water for a long time. Kate revived as she drank and finished off the last of the bread. Corvan let her eat her fill before nibbling on the last small pieces.

He let Kate doze one last time, then woke her, planning to go another five thousand steps. Kate said she was willing to try, but before long she was stumbling over the uneven floor, hardly able to lift her feet. Tripping over a rocky lip, she fell and pulled him down with her to the ground, his knees smacking painfully against the rocks.

"I'm sorry, Corvan, I can't make it." She leaned into him, her shoulders convulsing with dry sobs.

Fear swept down over him with a cool breeze that blew in from around the corner. He pushed it away with fierce determination. They weren't beat yet. "I'm not going to leave you." He reached down for the hand that held the medallion. Light flowed around their fingers. He took her other hand and pulled her to her feet. "We're not quitting." He took a step back. "Just keep looking in my eyes and follow me. We can do this one step at a time." He crept backward up the slope, his eyes on Kate's.

The wind grew steadily stronger. Kate eyes widened and she tried to speak, but the wind whipped her words down the tunnel. She pulled on his hands and he leaned back and forced her to keep coming. If they quit now they might never get up again.

Corvan took another step back. His foot found nothing but air. Kate yanked on his hands, eyes wide with terror. Together they toppled over the edge of a rocky bluff. Icy water cut through the gray cloak as the current tore Kate from his grasp.

The green glow of the medallion slipped away with her on the black surface of the water.

Corvan kicked and swam after her. The ceiling swept lower. The glow drew closer. His hand brushed Kate's face, then in a roar of foam, she disappeared as he tumbled over a waterfall.

Coughing, Corvan surfaced to the side of the falls in a shallow pool. He stood on the rocky bottom. "Kate! Where are you?" He saw nothing. He splashed to one side, his hands outstretched. He met a rock wall and heard his finger snap. Pain shot up his arm.

"Kate!" he screamed, his throat rasping with the panic that drove her name from his lungs.

He heard a low moan. He listened over the sound of the water. "Kate?"

He scrambled around the rock, and his hand fell on soft cloth. Falling to his knees in the shallow water, he pushed the cloth aside and uncovered Kate's medallion. He lifted the light to her face. Her eyes were closed. Her head resting in a shallow pool among the rocks. A gash on her head and a cut on her face were turning the water a deep red. "Are you okay? Say something."

Kate didn't open her eyes but a tiny smile touched her lips. "I can see the stars, Corvan. We're home."

THE HAMMER

Chapter Forty-One

Corvan stood at the window watching the remnants of a prairie sunset fade over the western hills. He was glad the day was over. The harsh sunlight glaring off the stark white walls of his hospital room was almost unbearable.

Footsteps approached the door and then retreated to answer the jangle of the nursing station phone. He hoped it was a long call. The nurses would not be happy to find him back in Kate's room again.

The lights were coming on over the empty parking lot below the window. His parents would be returning at any time with his clothes so he could go home, but he didn't want to leave Kate alone. Her mother would certainly not be coming to see her any time soon. Just a week after Kate had disappeared she had taken off with the man she had met at the diner. The police were trying to find Mrs. Poley to let her know that Kate had been found, but Corvan wondered if she would even come to see her daughter.

Turning away from the darkening sky, he looked to the clunky metal bed where Kate slept beneath a fuzzy white blanket. She looked somewhat comical with her hair sticking up in swatches through the bandage that had been wrapped around her head. He studied her for any sign of movement. He had heard the whispers of brain damage from the nurses—how Kate might never wake up again. He refused to believe that would happen.

The steady drip of Kate's IV had done its work, and her face was no longer drawn and thin. The cut in her cheek had been carefully stitched back together and was healing fast. She wouldn't have much of a scar, nothing like the one that Tyreth would have for the rest of her life in the Cor.

Corvan turned back to the window. Up here, with the vast sky overhead, Tyreth seemed like a figment of his imagination and the Cor as far away as another planet.

He gazed out over the trees to where a few stars struggled to outshine the parking lot lights. That was one of the things he disliked most about the city; it was hard to see the stars past all the artificial light. He needed the stars to remind him the universe was much larger than his problems. Maybe that was one reason why, when his adventures in the Cor had taken him further and further from their light, he'd felt so hopeless. He felt a sudden surge of pity for the people in the Cor. It was like they had been locked in a dark prison, paying eternally for some ancient crime.

"The stars are so beautiful."

Corvan whirled around.

Kate smiled faintly, then winced as the stitches tightened on her cheek. "What happened to me?" She tried to sit up but Corvan crossed over and put a hand on her shoulder.

"You need to lie still and rest. You fell and hurt your head. Don't you remember?"

She stared blankly at him. "I think so. Did I get hurt bad?"

"You've got a cut on your head and cheek. You'll be okay after you rest up a few days."

"I guess I shouldn't have been climbing on the castle rocks in the dark."

"What?'

"The last thing I remember was going out to the rock and falling down. I don't remember what I was doing out there." Her eyes crinkled in a teasing smile. "Maybe I was trying to catch your imaginary lizard so Bill wouldn't pick on you."

Corvan nodded, his heart aching for the things they had shared which she might never remember. "Don't worry about the lizard. He won't be back."

"That's good." Her eyes drooped. "I'm so tired."

"You should rest. I'll sit with you until my parents come to pick me up."

She nodded and Corvan sat down in the chair at the side of her bed.

Kate pulled a hand out from under the covers and opened it to expose what the doctor referred to as "that mysterious burn" in the center of the palm. A small, seven-sided star where the red seed had sent its power though her body. Corvan reached out and held her hand in his own.

A peaceful smile settled over Kate's face. She gave his hand a weak squeeze as she drifted off.

He looked at their clasped hands. What his mother said was true. Kate's skin was darker now, almost as dark as his own, like she had spent the last three weeks under a summer sun instead of wandering about in the dark.

The door opened a crack, and his mother stepped into the room. Her eyebrows rose slightly, and then she gestured for him to follow her out. Corvan eased his hand from Kate's and joined her out in the hall.

"How is Kate doing?" she asked.

"She woke up and talked a bit."

"That's great. I didn't think a bump in the head could slow our Kate down for long." She frowned. "Did she ask for her mother?"

"No. She seems a bit confused about what happened."

"She's not the only one." His mother shot him a questioning glance as she turned down the hall. "I've already checked you out."

Corvan looked at Kate's door. It didn't feel right to leave her behind. "Can you bring me back first thing tomorrow morning? I don't want her to be alone with her mom gone and all."

His mother nodded, a funny little smile on her face.

"Where's Dad?"

"He was called back to the mine. Tomorrow is the day they seal it off, and he's the only one who knows the location of all the charges. He'll be there most of the night I'm sure. They want him to make sure you two were the only ones to find a way into the mine. You're lucky those workers discovered you. Nobody can figure out how you and Kate ever got past the locks and down to the bottom of the mine." It was more of a question than a statement, but Corvan let it slide. His father had asked him not to say anything to her until they could talk about it in private as a family.

As they walked out the front doors of the hospital, Corvan stopped. The sky had seemed large from the window but outside it seemed to be pulling him right out of his tennis shoes. He breathed in the scents of autumn, the dying leaves, the crisp air. "I'm so glad to be back."

"The way you're behaving, you'd think you been underground in the mine for weeks."

He glanced at her and she gave him a knowing look. Corvan stepped down the stairs and headed for their truck.

As they left the city, the sky above them brightened into a star-encrusted canopy. It seemed the stars had multiplied since he had left. Resting his forehead against the cold glass, he stared up at them in wonder. Under their sparkling light, he felt both small and infinitely important at the same time.

The rough bumps of the railroad tracks banged his head against the window, and he sat back as they drove through town. He watched the empty schoolyard slide past his window and was surprised to find himself free of any fear of what might happen in the future. He was ready to grow up. In fact, he felt like he had already walked through that door and come out the other side.

The gravel crunched as they turned into their driveway. A smile crept over his face that would not subside.

Stepping from the truck he turned for the side of the house. "I'm going out to the rock for a few minutes."

"Don't be too long. The doctor said you need to get lots of rest for at least a week." As Corvan passed by her, she grabbed him and pulled him into an embrace. "I'm glad you're home."

He hugged her back. "Me too."

As he walked toward the dark mound a sense of loneliness grew. He missed Tsarek. His friend should be here with him to help him make sense of all that had happened.

Thin moonlight etched the castle rocks in silver. The door beckoned from the center of the stone circle. Corvan stood by the door a moment and then stooped to touch the edge. Nothing moved except for a beetle crawling around the keyhole. Without the hammer, he would never be able to open the door again.

He left the castle rocks behind and walked out onto the western slope.

He was glad he no longer had the hammer. Tyreth would need it to lead the Cor. It would help her to know when Jorad was telling her the truth.

Truth. His parents had drummed the need for honesty into him the past few years. Now he understood how important it was. Everyone suffered when lies and deceit grew unchecked.

The crescent moon cast a web of thin shadows through the stubble of their field. Corvan lay back on the rock and breathed in the soft scent of a prairie evening. A falling star arced across the sky and disappeared. Corvan smiled. For the past few years, all that the guys in school talked about was the dawn of space travel. Some had great plans of becoming astronauts and traveling to the moon. Others dreamed of winning a space suit and being picked up by aliens in their back yards. Space was the new frontier, where fantastic adventures would happen—new worlds explored and strange creatures discovered.

He placed his good hand flat against the cool rock beneath him. If only they knew what was going on beneath their very feet.

A faint tremor shivered through the tips of his fingers, as if a great stone door had opened somewhere down below.